HOLY GROUND

EVAN CURRIE

ALSO BY EVAN CURRIE

Atlantis Rising Series

Knighthood

The Demon City

Odyssey One Series

Into the Black

The Heart of Matter

Homeworld

Out of the Black

Odysseus One : Warrior King

Odysseus Awakening

Odysseus Ascendant

Archangel Series (Odyssey Universe)

Archangel One

Archangel Rising

Odyssey One: Star Rogue Series

King of Thieves

Heirs of Empire

Heirs of Empire
An Empire Asunder

Warrior's Wings Series
On Silver Wings
Valkyrie Rising
Valkyrie Burning
The Valhalla Call
By Other Means
De Oppresso Liber
Open Arms
Border Wars

Other Works
SEAL Team 13
Steam Legion
Thermals
The Infinity Affliction
I Was Legion

Copyright Info

This is a work of fiction. Names, characters, organizations, places, events, and incidents are either products of the author's imagination or are used fictitiously.

Text copyright © 2016 Evan Currie

All rights reserved.

No part of this book may be reproduced, or stored in a retrieval system, or transmitted in any form or by any means, electronic, mechanical, photocopying, recording, or otherwise, without express written permission of the publisher.

Chapter One

Kitakyushu, Japan 2078

Jonathan 'Mad Jack' Hadrian took a deep pull from the bottle of ji-biru in his hand, savoring the taste of the high proof local beer as he looked over the beach and waters of the bay, and the Sea of Japan beyond. It had been a lovely day, the sun beating down on the city as he relaxed as best he could while keeping watch on his little cadre of baby Marines who were availing themselves of the local hospitality.

For his sins he'd been promoted, and now was the Gunny to a bunch of wet behind the ears recruits. It could be worse he supposed, though for the life of him he doubted the difference could be that bad. At least his service hadn't been considered 'superfluous to the needs of the Corps', like many others had been in recent times.

Years of overspending, incredible waste, and a national debt topping one hundred trillion, had finally made the government start thinking about cuts. As usual, the Corps were the first on the chopping block.

Jack didn't have any real complaints, though. He'd had a good run in the Corps, raised a little hell, and put a lot of it down for the count. He'd probably voluntarily retire in a little while, get his DD-214 and call it a career. He wasn't a young man anymore, and roping young dumb Marines was a job for younger and dumber men than he.

He just hoped that he'd managed to talk some sense in his kid the last time he'd been home.

His bright-eyed little boy had told him that he wanted to enlist when he grew up. It had been one of the best, and worst moments of his life.

Jack loved his Corps, but there was no future in it for a young man, not anymore.

The Corps, and the military in general, were in their declining years. It happened to every Empire, eventually - it was just the way of things. The money wasn't there anymore to keep growing the services. Hell, it wasn't there to just maintain them properly. They did what they could with what they had, but it was telling just how many pieces of gear he had back at base, half torn down to provide parts that kept the rest running.

Bah, enough of this melancholy bullshit, Jack thought as he hammered down the last of the beer and got to his feet.

The warm sun was now dropping in the west, casting the island of Tsushima in silhouette. Heat haze from the water made it all shimmer in the distance, dancing in place as he made his way down the walk to where his baby Marines were lounging on the beach.

Thankfully, they'd not tried to play too much grab-ass with the locals this time around. He didn't need that level of bullshit once they got back to base, but at the same time the hairs on the back of his neck went up every time this bunch behaved themselves.

Thankfully, it was almost time for the final roundup of the day, and tomorrow he'd just have to worry about keeping them in line while they were doing their duties.

"Hey Gunny," One of the babies grinned at him from the beach as he walked by. "Having a good time?"

Jack snorted, "Charleson, watching over you bunch is like having hemorrhoids. It's not always painful, but it ain't *ever* a good time."

He kept walking as the private sputtered and snorted in his wake, the sand of the beach squeaking under his boots. He needed to stretch the stiffness out of his legs before they got back on the bus to run back to base.

Lights were starting to show out on the water he noted, though the sun was still high enough to wash most things out. He paused, lifting his hand to cover the sun as he peered into the distance.

Jack knew that South Korea was out there, just over the horizon, and the straight between them was one of the most heavily trafficked waterways on the planet, with thousands of ships and boats out there at any given time. He didn't think most of them would have running lights as bright as he was seeing though.

A flash in the distance briefly washed out the sun itself, leaving him blinking and automatically counting off the seconds in his head as he waited for the thunderclap to hit. Lightning wasn't unusual in these parts, of course, and that had been over the horizon he was pretty sure, so he didn't think too much of it despite the automatic response.

After ten seconds he stopped counting, the storm was far enough away that it wasn't going to have any effect on his day.

Time to roundup the babies, Jack decided, turning away from the water, and starting back up the beach.

"Alright you Leathernecks, grab your socks and clear the rocks from your skulls, time to head back to paradise."

The men groaned, complaining automatically, but were already moving even as they did so.

"Come on, Gunny, give us a few more minutes…"

"Jerry, if I gave you a few more days you'd still wind up begging me for just a little more, get you ass in gear," Jack rolled his eyes as he walked up between the slowly moving men, coming to a stop in front of a Corporal who wasn't moving. "What the hell is wrong with you, Marine? Lose your balls in the sand? Get moving!"

Corporal Brian Meer had an odd look on his face, his gaze locked out over Jack's shoulder.

"Gunny," He said slowly, "Those don't look like fishing boats."

Jack felt a chill, one that had nothing to do with the temperature. The tone of the corporal's voice had triggered something he'd not felt in a long time, not since he last played in the sandbox. He slowly turned on his heel, bringing the water back into his view.

"What in the fuck…"

He breathed out, eyes refocusing on the bright lights that were *much* closer now. Closer than they had any business to be.

How fast are they moving?

They couldn't be boats. There wasn't a boat on the *planet* that could cross that distance in so short a time.

"Jesus Christ, Gunny… They're *flying*."

Jack didn't turn around to see which of his baby Marines had just spouted the obvious. He was more focused on the colors the unbelievable large and low flying aircraft were showing. The red flag painted on their sides, decorated by a circle of white stars.

Sweet Jesus, what the hell are the Bloc up to? They can't be this crazy.

He grabbed for the phone from his pocket, thumbing into the system and trying to call out only to find that he had no signal. That was something that didn't surprise him as much as it would have a few minutes earlier.

Gunny Jack spun on his heel, his posture changing as he stopped being the semi-relaxed figure from moments earlier and became a Marine Corps Gunny in every facet save his actual uniform.

"Move your asses, Marines!" He bellowed as he flipped his phone over to radio transmission mode, "Triple time it to the bus, and I'll have the hide of anyone damn fool enough to have the audacity to miss a step!"

His Marines didn't talk back this time. They were all in motion before he finished bellowing.

"This is Gunnery Sergeant Hadrian," He said into the phone, "I'm transmitting in the open, any points copying this get your ass back to base and report for duty. I don't care if you just started a month-long leave, it's *canceled.* Say again, report to your duty station or the closest base for assignment."

He was in motion then, chasing his Marines up the beach toward the short bus they'd used to get to Kyushu from Iwakuni. He didn't know if anyone had gotten his call, cell jamming wouldn't do much to the radio in his phone, but if the Bloc had bothered to jam one then they'd probably gotten everything.

Wide spectrum jamming was tough to pull off, though. He was all too aware of that and, with some luck, a few would have gotten the signal.

He just hoped it made a difference.

*****

Marine Corps Air Station Iwakuni

Major Wolfe hit the tarmac running, alarms shaking the air of the base from every direction. He didn't know what the fuck was going on, but he hoped the hell it wasn't some demented drill. Because if it was, he was going to find whichever idiot paper pusher thought it up and express his… *displeasure…* in person.

He reached his F35 in seconds, halfway up the ladder to the cockpit before the flight crew even noticed him.

"Sir!"

Wolfe dropped into the ACES-VI seat and was reaching for the straps as he looked back out, "Tell me we're ready to fly, Kimmy."

Gunny Kimberly Jenson nodded instantly, "Hot to trot, Major. You're running an Air Intercept package, so keep that in mind. Turbines are good. Tanks are full."

"Good work, Gunny," he said, pulling his helmet on and plugging the oxygen mask into the aircraft's air-pump outlet. "You get any info on what's going on?"

"Not a thing." she shook her head. "Alarms just started screaming and the only order I've got is to get you in the air ASAP."

"Well let's not keep them waiting," Wolfe said, waving her back. "Get clear."

"You got it, Major. Good hunting."

He just nodded as the canopy descended around him, snapping his mask into place as he reached over to flip on the radio.

"Green Knights ready response squadron," he called. "Green Knight Actual, Lycan speaking. Chime in."

"Knight three, Hoover here."

"Knight Five, Eagle up."

"Knight Two, Paladin fires hot."

"Knight Four, Silver Bullet Ready."

"Knight Six, Dragon burning. Let's do this."

"Roger that, Knights," Wolfe said as he felt his turbine whining to life. "Tower, this is Green Knight Actual. Requesting taxi directions."

"Negative on Taxi directions, Major. You are cleared for immediate VTOL."

Wolfe blinked, momentarily shocked by that. VTOL was rarely authorized when they had a nice long runway available. Among other things, it was a lot harder on fuel than a normal takeoff, not to mention somewhat riskier. Since it was also a lot more fun, however, he wasn't about to complain.

"Roger that, Tower. Green Knights ready squadron lifting off, VTOL." He said, flipping to the squadron frequency. "You heard them, boys and girls. Let's get these pigs in the air."

He reached forward, pulling the controls that vectored the thrust of the F35 all the way back, and felt the vibrations through the seat as the big exhaust vectoring system was twisted into place. The squadron checked in and were doing the same as he applied power to the system and the shaking intensified around him for a moment before the F35 released itself from the ground and Green Knight Actual began to creep above the roofs of the nearby buildings.

Around him, the Green Knights were matching him, the ready squadron lifting uncertainly into the air as they stood on the narrow plume of exhaust and seemed barely managing to balance. A few dozen feet over the tarmac, Wolfe began pushing the lever forward again, lifting the nose as he kept the fighter balanced on the exhaust like a demented ballet dancer on tiptoes.

Slowly, the F35 began to move forward, climbing inch by inch as full power exploded out the rear and he finished the transition from lift off to flight.

Roaring out over Hiroshima bay Wolfe checked the computer and finally started to get some information on what the hell was going down.

Contacts from the West. Alright, let's get oriented first, then find out exactly what the hell is happening.

He looped around Kabuto island, still gaining altitude, and brought the squadron back around to the West. They cut across land, south of the city, pouring on the power and breaking Mach just before crossing the Gantoku Line.

Wolfe barely noticed. He was too busy talking.

"Command, Lycan. Give me the sitrep."

"Lycan, Command. Contacts crossing the Sea as of Seventeen Hundred local time. Wide spectrum jamming, all stations. Air contacts are presumed hostile, having refused all attempts to identify or redirect. Mission priority is to confirm identities of the bogey contacts, turn them back from mainland Japan. Secondary mission, should first mission prove untenable, provide cover for local JSDF and US forces as they wind up response."

"Understood," Wolfe said. "Green Knights moving on station, intercept contacts in… three."

"Roger that, Lycan. Good luck, good hunting."

****

Kitakyushu

Jack Hadrian flinched down as the shadow passed over him, flickering along so fast he'd almost missed it.

The boom hit a moment later, shaking him and everything around him.

He looked up, watching the aircraft scream away, frowning as he was unable to recognize the configuration. It definitely wasn't one of the Bloc's normal front-line aircraft: he knew those profiles like he knew his own hands.

"All points, Gunnery Sergeant Hadrian," He said into his phone, broadcasting still in the open, hoping someone was getting it. "What looks like combat aircraft with Bloc livery is in control of the air over Kyushu. Unknown profile. Say again, unknown profile. These are *not* standard Bloc aircraft."

He hoped someone was getting the signal, but it didn't matter to what he had to do. Reaching the bus, he pocketed his phone and threw the side door open, standing there and slapping his Marines on the back as they piled in. Jack made sure he had the headcount right before he climbed in himself and nodded to the driver.

"Get us back to base," He said curtly.

"You got it, Gunny," The corporal said, pulling the door shut and stepping on the accelerator.

The electric bus whirred away from the curb, only making the officially authorized vehicle noise for a Marine transport in a civilian area.

Jack held on to the vertical bar by the driver's seat, looking back over the Marines.

"Alright guys," He said, "Don't know what's going on yet, but it's safe to assume it's not a good thing. We're going to high tail it back to the base so we can get our orders. Oorah?"

"Oorah!"

He nodded, satisfied, turning back around to lean into the driver.

"Get us out of the city as fast as you can and keep an eye on the skies."

"Oorah, Gunny."

Traffic was a snarl, more so than usual, which didn't surprise Jack in the slightest. Chaos was beginning to erupt as the local civilians started to get an idea that something was amiss. Most probably didn't have any idea what, but they were stopping and staring, or trying to run off to somewhere or another, and generally just getting in each other's… and his… way.

He pointed, "Cut over the sidewalk there."

"You got it, Gunny," The Corporal grinned, laying on the horn as he turned the wheel.

They bumped over the sidewalk, cutting off a sedan, and got onto the on ramp for the highway.

He just hoped to hell it got better once they were clear of the city.

*****

FL-25 Over Yamaguchi Prefecture

The Green Knights were quickly joined by Japanese Self-Defense Force F35s and F-22s, along with US Air Force squadrons sortieing out of Yokota.

Wolfe plugged his squadron into the joint formation, linking up to the battle network, and generally just got ready for whatever was coming their way. The forward RADAR sweeps were showing fast-moving contacts all up and down the coast, a lot where they might be expected, but he was seeing a *lot* right down on the deck moving fast for the coastline.

"Is everyone seeing these fast movers down low," he asked over the command frequency. "Anyone have any idea what we're looking at there? They can't be ships, can they?"

"Negative, Lycan," an Air Force Captain, call sign Squealer, a name Wolfe both did and did *not* want to know how he'd gotten, responded. "We're showing them making three hundred and fifty knots plus. No surface contact makes that kind of speed. Not at that size."

"They are very low for aircraft, however," A JSDF Major interjected. "We have no reliable contact on the ground that can see them. This jamming is very aggravating."

"You're not wrong there," Wolfe agreed. "Do we have *no* contact with coastal spotters?"

"Nothing solid," Squealer confirmed. "There are intermittent broadcasts from different units, but the jamming seems to be adaptive. They get cut off again every time they manage to break through."

"Great. Well, nothing to it," Wolfe said, "We're loaded for the air contacts. Green Knights will provide cover to anyone who'd like to get a closer look at those skimmer contacts, especially if you're loaded for bear and can ruin their day."

"Roger that, Green Knights," Squealer said, "Panthers, I see you're packing some ground support ordnance. You want to take a look at those contacts?"

"You got it, Squealer," Captain Gordon 'High Rise' Decker said. "Happy to serve."

"Lycan, take your Knights and cover the Panthers," Squealer said. "We're going to see about making these skies friendly."

"Oorah, Squealer. You heard the man, Knights," Wolfe said, "On me."

The Knights pealed out of formation, dropping in a roll as they turned to provide CAP and cover for the Panthers as the air force unit dropped and made for the coast.

*****

Chapter Two

Kitakyushu

Hadrian hung on as the bus swerved, lane splitting a couple of slow-moving cars that didn't seem to know exactly what the hell they were doing. They swerved away from the bus, laying angrily on the horns, but he just patted the corporal's shoulder and nodded in approval.

"Just don't kill anyone if you can help it," he said.

"You got it, Gunny."

Jack Hadrian still didn't know what the hell was going on. But with the near constant sound of sonic booms rattling the bus, he didn't see how it could in any way be a good thing. Unfortunately, for the moment, the only thing he could do was focus on getting his Marines back to base so they could find out exactly what they were needed to be doing.

Even if he had any idea of what else to do, they were all running around naked as the day they were born as far as he was concerned. Civvies were no value in anything more than a bar fight.

He stepped down toward the door, reaching over to open the folding mechanism, and leaned out so he could look up into the sky. Overhead he could see the enemy fighter craft wheeling in the distance, clearly maintaining a CAP over the coast, he assumed they were covering the other craft they'd seen coming in from the Sea of Japan.

What the hell are those things, and why weren't we briefed that the Bloc was ready to field them?

Ever since the Eastern Bloc had been formed, at first through an unlikely alliance of China and India, intel on the ground had been getting spottier out of the region. However, he'd believed that they still had pretty solid intercepts and a good overview of what the Bloc's military was capable of.

Someone had apparently dropped the ball on this one, however, because what he was seeing was like nothing in any of the intel packets he'd seen and he paid attention to what the Bloc's Air Force was fielding, it was part of his damned job.

Something else flitted by over his head, making him duck a bit before he recognized the distinctive roar and following boom.

F35s, Jack thought, eyes tracking the squadrons. *Looks like Chair Force and the Ready Response out of Iwakuni too. God speed you crazy bastards, and give them hell.*

*****

Green Knights

Wolfe led the Knights in, staying above the Air Force squadron as the Panthers headed for the coast.

They had hot RADAR tracking up ahead, and *lots* of contacts on their screens as they approached the coast. As he watched, a set of signals peeled off from the main group, heading their way.

"Heads up, Panthers." He called, "Enemy contacts inbound."

"We see them, Lycan. Keep them off us, we'll see about those surface contacts," High Rise responded.

"You've got it," Wolfe said, arming his weapons. "Knights, we have what looks to be what we call a target-rich environment. Let's thin that herd."

"Hoorah, Sir!"

Wolfe grinned to himself as he picked one of the targets, lighting it up in his HUD and waiting for the tone to settle.

"Knight Actual… Fox Three."

He pressed the button and felt the fighter jump slightly as he put an AIM-120G AMRAAM into the air. The missile's rocket motor screamed into action, lancing the weapon away from his fighter, spewing white smoke in its wake.

He heard his squadron call out similar reports, AMRAAMs filled the sky.

*****

The AIM-120G was a RADAR guided air to air missile, capable of breaking Hypersonic with a top speed of Mach 6.5 at FL-35. At that speed, the birds made 5 thousand miles per hour when they topped out, fast enough to track any aircraft on the planet, run it down, and destroy it before the average person could do more than blink.

Six AMRAAMs lead the way as the Green Knights fired into the Bloc's advance line, hitting their top-end in seconds, and crossing the dozens of kilometers in just seconds more as they twisted in on their targets.

The unknown profile of the fighters they were targeting were closing with the incoming missiles, shortening the intercept time even more.

In the few seconds between launch and contact, however, the Bloc fighters suddenly accelerated.

Closing on the approaching missiles, the fighters suddenly went hypersonic themselves, climbing at blinding rates, evading the AMRAAMs in the blink of an eye, before arcing overhead and lancing back in toward the F-35s.

*****

"Fuck me sideways!"

Wolfe wasn't sure who said it, might even have been him. He was too busy working the stick and throttle while his brain was playing catchup to the goddamned *impossible* maneuvering the enemy fighters had just pulled out of their asses.

"Split S!" He ordered, "Evade, evade, evade! High Rise, we're in trouble here! Get your ass out of the hot zone!"

The Bloc fighters were in the midst of their formation before he was finished speaking, and Knight Two vanished in a blaze of fire and smoke as Wolfe threw his fighter over hard while abruptly pulling the thrust vectoring controls hard back in ways they were *never* intended to be used.

His fighter screamed in protest, the turbines threatening to tear the whole airframe apart around him as the thrust was put out perpendicular to the intended stress forces, throwing the F35 clear of an enemy fighter as its missiles chewed up the air he'd just inhabited.

"All points, Lycan. Enemy fighters, unknown configuration," he called out as he maneuvered, hoping someone was recording what he was saying, just in case the telemetry wasn't getting out. "Unprecedented acceleration! They must be drones, no pilot could have survived that! Speed is hypersonic, easily. They outran our missiles, outmaneuvered our fighters!"

"Roger Lycan," The calm voice of an air force Combat Controller broke in. "Pull back from the fighting if you can, continue to transmit any and all observation."

"No way we can withdraw… Fuck! They got another of my squadron!" He swore, bringing his fighter around to he could get the GAU-22/C gun-pod into play, but the enemy fighters were moving so fast he couldn't quite manage it. "Jesus, they maneuver like they're on rails! Gee forces have to be off the charts!"

He flinched as Knight Six vanished from his screens.

He'd lost half his ready response team in just a handful of seconds, and they'd not been able to extract anything from the enemy in turn.

"We're in trouble down here," High Rise was calling out urgently. "Need support! Right now!"

"Get on the deck and into the mountain valleys," Wolfe ordered, "Lose them in the damn trees if you have to! We'll give you what cover we can! Move, move, move!"

The Panthers broke from their course, dropping fast.

Wolf followed them, hoping that the enemy would have to slow down that close to the ground.

"Panthers," The Combat Controller calmly slipped in. "Get low, stay fast. Green Knights, provide cover as you follow. I'm directing anti-air forces to intercept, but you'll need to lead them into the kill zone."

"Fine by me," Wolfe growled.

"You should see a valley coming up on your right, tracing the highway. Follow the road."

"Roger that Control," High Rise acknowledged. "Panthers complying."

"Green Knights are all in, Controller." Wolfe said, "Show us the way to payback."

"Just stay with me, Lycan. High Rise, I've got you in my control path and all hell is waiting at the end of the road."

*****

Route 33 North, Kitakyushu

The traffic had thinned out drastically as they got out of the city, but Hadrian wasn't paying much attention to that as they sped along the highway, heading North to the Route 33 on-ramp that lay just a couple kilometers ahead.

He'd seen missiles fly on past overhead, but a depressing lack of explosions in the sky behind them… and a much more depressing number of them in the sky up ahead.

If he was reading it right, the good guys had just gotten a new hole ripped right up between their cheeks. He hoped he was wrong, but he was scanning the skies for chutes because he was pretty damned sure he wasn't.

"Hey Gunny… do you know what's going on?"

Hadrian glanced back, about to retort with a caustic remark until he saw the expressions of the men looking his way. His guys were good, but they were all new and, honestly, he didn't think any Marine had seen this for longer than he'd been in.

"At a guess?" He said as calmly as he could. "I'd say that the Bloc finally decided they can take us and made their move. I'm only surprised that it's here and not in Taiwan."

Assuming they're not hitting Taiwan even as we speak, He thought without speaking it aloud.

Hadrian expected they were.

In fact, now that he was thinking about it, he doubted that had been lightning he'd seen over the horizon earlier.

North Korea probably coordinated with the Bloc… assuming they haven't been fully subsumed already.

He doubted Seoul was still there, not if those flashes were what he thought anyway.

It's a bad day for a lot of good people.

"They're wrong, though, right Gunny?"

Hadrian blinked, looking back up, fighting to keep a confused expression from his face.

"What's that, private?" He asked.

"They're wrong. You said they think they can take us, but they're wrong, right?"

"Yeah, sure." He said, though he wasn't so sure of it.

The Bloc, hell the Chinese really, had been looking for this moment for a long damn time. The only thing that kept them out of Taiwan through the latter half of the twentieth and the twenty-first century so far was the fact that they *knew* they couldn't take the US Navy.

Invading China would be suicide for the West, everyone knew that, but no matter how many people the Bloc had, it just wasn't possible to move enough around fast enough to counter the force projection of the US Navy if they moved beyond their borders, saying nothing about American allies.

That had been changing over the last few decades, however. The old force projection capacity of the US forces was such that in their prime, Hadrian knew that American forces could fight off two full wars and still put down a major brushfire somewhere. That wasn't in the cards any longer.

They only had one carrier task group in the Pacific at the moment, and he wasn't even sure where it was, but he'd bet good money that the Bloc wasn't as in the dark as he was on that. If they were willing to move, they really thought they could do the job.

And he, for one, couldn't quite swear that they were wrong, no matter what he told his men.

*****

Green Knights

With the Panthers on the deck, screaming up the valley along the highway at better than Mach Two, Wolfe kept the rest of his squad above them in an attempt to give the defenseless fighters with their air to ground ordnance a chance.

The enemy were coming around, though, and he could *feel* them light his fighter up a moment before the computer started screaming at him that someone had a lock on his ass. Missiles were in the air a moment later, causing him to twist in his ACES ejection seat to get eyes on.

Those are standard missiles, no earth-shattering changes there, thank god.

The Chicom missile was reading as a Thunderbolt Thirty-Three to his computer, something he knew how to deal with.

He waited a moment after arming the jammers and flares, then launched a full set of angel's wings into the air behind him, throwing the enemy missiles off as they broke the lock. He kept an eye on them just the same, though, until the confused birds slammed into the mountains they were flying through.

"Enemy missiles are standard, expected ordnance," he radioed. "Nice to know they didn't hide something like that from us too."

"That's great news," High Rise growled. "But that doesn't mean I'm not going to strangle some intel weenie if I get out of this one."

"You and me both, pal."

The enemy fighters were flitting around, far too fast for him to track, and while he was confident in being able to spoof the missiles, it was goddamned hard to fool a bullet and he figured they had to have guns on those sleds.

"Keep moving, Panthers, we can only hold them off for so long." He called as he looked over his shoulder, rocking his fighter back and forth to confuse the enemy.

"Roger that, Lycan. Thanks for the cover."

"We said we'd give you a CAP, High Rise. We keep our word."

Wolfe just wasn't sure how long they'd be able to keep that up. The battle had turned into a rout so quickly he was still in shock.

He wasn't supposed to be running from the enemy, he was a goddamned US Marine. The initial engagement had been so one-sided he didn't even really know what had happened, aside from the fact that his squadron had gotten new assholes ripped hey diddle diddle, right up the middle.

The order to disengage had come so quickly Wolfe wasn't even sure where it had come from.

A glance at his board showed that the JSDF boys had gotten the shit kicked out of them as bad or worse than his own boys. There were maybe half the lights showing than when they started, and only that if he were being generous.

At that rate, if we'd pressed, they'd have wiped us out in seconds... long before any of the bases could even wind up.

That explained the disengage orders, at least. If they'd been able to put up a fight, even a losing one, he'd have been willing to press the engagement as long as he knew help was coming. If they were all going to go down in flames before the cavalry could even mount up?

Fuck that.

He was just surprised that someone put it together that fast and realized what a fucking disaster they were dealing with.

*****

Okumagura

Master Sergeant Kiran Jiang knelt at the edge of a small copse of trees that were growing along the ridgeline he'd been dropped off on with his gear just barely ahead of the ready response.

The Air Force had barely gotten any warning of the Bloc movement. They'd just suddenly appeared on RADAR and Satellite as they'd appeared from literal thin air.

That alone would have been workable, except that the heavy-lift units the enemy had fielded were a lot faster than anyone figured when they were first spotted. They'd crossed the Sea of Japan in minutes instead of hours, and landed in Taiwan barely fifteen minutes after they'd been first spotted.

Someone has been planning this one for a long time, Kiran thought grimly as he checked his gear.

"Panthers, Knights," The Air Force Air Combat Controller said calmly. "I've got you on my screens, bringing you right to me. How are you holding out?"

"These guys are fast, friend. Hope you've got a nice welcome ready."

That was Major Wolfe, Kiran noted, the leader of the Green Knights, call sign 'Lycan'.

"JSDF anti-air is all wound up and ready to roll out a good old fashioned Japanese welcome, Lycan. You just stay focused on getting here ahead of them and in one piece, you hear me?"

"Roger that."

Kiran left the fighters on an open receiver channel but killed transmission as he swapped over to the JSDF frequencies and began speaking Japanese.

"We have inbound hostile contacts chasing friendly squadrons," He said, "Confirm readiness to intercept."

"We are ready," The JSDF Major replied. "All units ready to launch."

"Thank you, stand by," Kiran said, again flipping back to the fighter's channel as he kept an eye on the skies.

The enemy fighters were visible in the distance now, and he quickly brought up an imager with good optics to grab some photos. He uploaded those to the overhead satellite while he spoke, "When you fly over, keep on the hammer. The sky is going to be *thick* with seekers, and in that mess, mistakes can happen boys."

He listened to the chatter between the Knights and the Panthers in response to that while he filled out an identification chart for the unknown fighter profile. His photos weren't great, but they were better than anyone else seemed to have, so he tagged them in it and added the speculated capabilities he'd gotten from Lycan's reports, crediting the Marine for it before he updated the file and sent it along to PACAFCOM.

That done, Kiran glanced back just as the Panthers screamed by overhead.

In Japanese, he spoke to the JSDF forces that were parked along the local highway wherever they'd been able to set up in a hurry.

"They are coming," He told the Major. "Friendly IFFs are in your system."

"We have them," The Major responded. "Friendly avoidance is entered. All batteries are preparing to fire."

Kiran nodded, speaking in English, "Light those bastards up."

"With pleasure," The Major told him, also switching to English as flashes of light erupted from the shadows of the valleys around him, missiles reaching up into the skies.

"Watch your asses, boys," Kiran said over the fighters' channel. "The sky just got a *lot* less friendly."

*****

"Holy shit."

Wolfe didn't reprimand Knight Three for swearing on an open channel, but only because he was too busy thinking pretty much the same thing to notice.

The hills of the prefecture below were sprouting more missiles than trees, or so it seemed, as the JSDF let loose with everything they had. He didn't know how they'd gotten it all out there so fast, but the Japanese had always taken the threat of the Chinese forces more seriously than the US had in his experience.

He just slammed the throttle forward, lighting the afterburner, and prayed that the IFF system didn't fail.

"Pour it on, Knights, don't look back."

With the enemy hot on their turbines, the Green Knights followed the Panthers through a killing field.

*****

Chapter Three

JSDF anti-air capacities were widely varied, from man-portable rockets to vehicle-mounted heavy missiles, and self-propelled guns aplenty. Since the Second World War, Japanese forces had been restricted, by treaty, to how powerful a military force they could field. Even when those treaties had been fully in effect, however, the Japanese people gamed them to the best of their abilities.

The Self Defense Force was constitutionally prohibited from being utilized in the pursuit of war, a remnant of the treaty enforced on them after the end of World War Two, but despite that Japan had one of the best-funded and most powerful militaries in the world. Fourth largest, and third best-funded, according to most reports by the year 2075.

In the waning years of the twentieth century, Japan vowed to become an unsinkable aircraft carrier in the pacific… a vow that any would be hard pressed to claim they did not keep.

There was a story that a Japanese Admiral had once said that invading the United States mainland would be the height of suicidal foolishness because any invaders would face a rifle behind every blade of grass. In Japan, rifles were not so common, but self-propelled artillery *did* lurk in near on to every shadow.

A significant proportion of which now opened up on the formerly peaceful skies, unleashing hell with a vengeance.

Twin thirty-millimeter Orlikons mounted on Type 87 tracked chassis turned the skies into shrapnel as HAWK, Stinger, and Types 81, 91, 93, 03, and 11 rockets filled the gaps.

All of which hit nothing but air.

*****

Green Knights

Wolfe twisted in his ACES seat, turning to look out behind him as the sky turned to a vision of hellfire the likes of which he'd never seen in the past. It should have been an exultant moment, but instead all he could manage was a gaping stare.

"Where the *fuck* did they go?"

And, more importantly, how the hell did they do it so damn fast?

The Bloc fighters were rewriting the playbook for air warfare, and he was starting to get an itching feeling along his spine that they were just playing with their prey. He was a God DAMN US Marine, and being anyone's prey just wasn't going to fly, however.

"Enemy fighters, temporary designation 'Mantis' type, went vertical while accelerating into hypersonic," The Air Force combat controller answered his question. "Currently circling at FL 85, lining up for a run. Advise all ground units to take cover."

There's a bastard with ice water running in his veins, Wolfe thought with grim amusement, knowing that combat controllers didn't just sit back in a tower somewhere. He was almost certainly perched on a hilltop somewhere below. "Roger that, Control, Green Knights will provide cover."

"Negative Lycan. There's nothing you can do up there," The controller said. "I've tracked their top speed in excess of Mach five, with acceleration beyond anything that should be survivable. Hell, I'm surprised their *airframes* survived some of those maneuvers. There's no way those things have pilots on board. Get out of here while you can."

Wolfe grimaced, but couldn't exactly contradict anything the Air Force man had to say.

He wasn't quite ready to tuck his tail between his legs, however.

"Yeah, sorry Control, but fuck that." Wolfe twisted the F35 around, working the pedals and stick to bring the fighters into a tight, flat turn. "We might be getting our ass kicked out here, but I'm not leaving this fight without drawing at least a little blood."

*****

Kiran just rolled his eyes as he watched the Marine Corps F35s come back around. The Panthers were already out of the immediate theater, having gotten their orders straight through their own chain, but the Marines Squadron Leader was still the top Devil Dog in this particular fight, and that dumb jarhead was too stubborn to get the hell out like he should.

Kiran himself wished them luck but was in the middle of packing up his gear as quickly as he could because he needed to be damn near anywhere other than ground zero for a heavy bombing run, especially not standing around in the open with his dick flapping in the wind.

Most of his gear was pretty lightweight, thankfully, and designed to pack in a rush.

He left his satellite interface tablet out, one hand gripping the rubberized shell of the mini-computer as he shrugged the pack on over his shoulders and started heading for his own exfil point.

"Suit yourself, Lycan," he said, eyes checking the display in his hand. "You've got some very pissed off Chicoms coming your way, though. Now at FL70 and dropping like rocket propelled stones."

"Roger that, control."

"I've got orders to exfil, but I'll keep you up to date while I can Jarheads," he said, "Locals on the ground are bugging out. Don't get your ass shot down, word on the net is that you're flying over soon to be hostile territory."

"Yeah, we got that."

"Ok, enemy is at FL55, descent easing. Coming in on your position from the North, North West."

"North, North West, confirmed. Green Knight Actual, Lycan, Going Guns."

Kiran reached the edge of the clearing he'd been aiming for. A low hovering UH-72 was waiting on him. The Air Force wanted combat controllers out of the theater until they had a better handle on what the hell it was the enemy was fielding, though Kiran thought that was likely a mistake.

He could probably do more good getting embedded with the locals. The odds that the JSDF was going to just roll over and let the Bloc roll in on them like this were right up there with winning the lotto… when you didn't buy a ticket.

The JSDF had been planning for this since before World War Two ended, and he really didn't think that the Bloc was going to much enjoy any fruits of victory here, but that wasn't here nor there.

He had his orders, so it was time to get out.

Reaching the chopper, Kiran flung his pack in and threw himself up on the floor of the utility bird, feet dangling out over the edge.

"Alright, get us going," He called to the pilot as he kept working. "Heads up, Lycan, they're at FL40 and leveling out, coming right down your throat. They have to see you!"

"They better, I'm through hiding."

*****

Green Knights

Wolfe glanced out his left, then to his right, the remaining three F35s of the Green Knights settled in beside him as he checked his ECM and made sure everything was squealing to plan.

"You guys should head back to base," He said, flipping a couple switches and opening his fighter's weapons' bay.

"No offense, boss," Eagle told him from Knight Five, "but get fucked."

Wolfe smiled lightly but didn't bother saying anything about the comment. In the moment, he wasn't going to be a stickler for radio regs, and if they lived... well, odds were good that no one was going to make much of a fuss over it even in debrief.

"Alright," he said instead, "Let them come. I want ECMs running hot as hell and twice as bright. Blind those fuckers, they aren't packing anything new in missile tech that we've seen, so I'm betting that their detection gear isn't much better than Intel reports say."

"Those flight platforms might seem to be disagreeing with you, Lycan," Hoover told him, a little nervous but tone steady.

"Yeah, they snuck those past our boys," Wolfe agreed. "But that doesn't mean they got lucky *every* time, Marines. Drinks in the O-Club say they can't see jack through our ECM."

"Screw you," Eagle laughed. "If you lose, we're all dead and you can't pay up."

"Why do you think I'm willing to make the bet?" Wolfe asked, laughing himself, "I've seen how much you assholes drink."

The levity didn't last long. They were professionals no matter how it sounded, and the situation at hand wasn't going to wait for them to have their moment, unfortunately.

"Alright, ECM up," Wolfe ordered. "Burn out your systems if you have to. I want them to get exactly two things over their scanners while we're sitting here. Jack and Shit. Watch for ARAD launches, though. Let's not make it easy for them."

The squadron nodded, while Wolfe tapped the side of his helmet, the aging Gen V HMD was still pretty damn good, but like everything else in the fighter he had strapped on, it was feeling its age. In fact, it was 8 years past retirement, and still flying, they all were.

The F35s should have been cycled out in 2070, replaced by the now canceled F-43 project that had been dropped when it went over budget in 2055. The new F-41A was due to take over in the 2080s, but until then, the F35 was the man on the wall it seemed.

It seemed to Wolfe that the man on the wall had just been introduced to a Main Battle Tank.

*Well, the tanks may roll over the wall, but a man **in the right, at the right**, can throw spanner in even those armored treads. Come and get your spanner, you bastards.*

"Blinded, they're going to come into knife range," He said, spinning up his GAU-22 Equalizer. "K-bars out Marines."

"Roger that, Lycan."

The four Marine F35s flew in loose formation as twenty lights became visible against the darkening sky, moving against the background with unreal speed.

"Here they come," Wolfe said, "Don't fire until you see the whites of their nosecones."

*****

Air Force Helo

"Hold position!"

"Sir, we're sitting ducks out here!" The pilot snarled over his shoulder. "I've got orders to get your dumb ass back to the base for evac!"

"Fuck the orders!" Kiran snapped right back, pulling out his satellite uplink and getting it connected to his tablet. "Those Marines need every bit of intel they can get, and SO. DO. WE."

The pilot swore but kept the Helo orbiting close enough for him to watch the fight. Kiran made sure that he was uploading everything in real time, using the military's LEO satellite constellation to do so.

"Lycan, you've got an entire Bloc combat squadron coming down on your ass," He said. "I've got a bird's eye view with vectors and a supercomputer crunching the math back in Virginia. Feed is yours, do what you can."

"Roger that, Controller. Thanks for the feed," Lycan said in clipped tones. "Any sign of missile launches?"

"Negative. They're inside the range too," Kiran said, frowning.

"They're blind. These birds are one trick ponies," Lycan responded. "We're hitting them with every bit of ECM we've got, they can't get a positive lock. They're going to come into knife range."

"They may be one trick ponies, Lycan, but they're *fast* one trick ponies. You sure you want to tangle with them that close?"

"You ever take on a Marine in a knife fight?"

Kiran rolled his eyes, "Never been that stupid."

"These boys are. Let's see how that ends for them… They're here. Green Knight Actual… Guns, Guns, Guns."

*****

The Bloc J-192 airframes were swept wing designs, with smaller overall lifting area than would seem wise, even considering the speed they were capable of. Running near hypersonic speeds on their approach, yet none of them showed the heat sign that one might expect at those speeds.

At Mach Four they crossed into knife range, just over three kilometers out from the handful of Marine F35s standing in their way.

The Bloc craft didn't have their own autocannons, the designers having elected to leave the weapon out as superfluous when considered in line with the missiles and laser projector each carried. However, with their systems being blinded by the American ECM systems, neither their missiles nor lasers would properly lock on.

Orders were requested, but in the *seconds* they had before contact, there was absolutely no chance for those to be responded to in time.

Falling back on the doctrine they'd learned, developed from studying every American combat manual and classic encounter over the last century, the pilots prepared to go to hypersonic to evade the American missiles when they fired.

The J-192s could do that all day, until the Americans fired their last bird, picking off the slower fighters at their leisure.

Oddly, however, there was no tone of missile lock being established and no sign that the Americans had opened fire.

At Mach Four, the squadron of J-192s ran headlong into a wall of steel coming the other way at Mach Three.

*****

Green Knights

Someone cheered, he thought, though Wolfe wasn't certain if it was a cheer or a scream as he flinched away from Knight Five's F-35 as it erupted in flames and dropped out of the formation.

Three of the Mantis birds were dropping in burning pieces as well, though, he saw with some satisfaction as he pumped the pedals and put his fighter into a flat spin to track the craft as they swept past him.

He leaned on the GAU firing controls, tracking the fast-moving targets as they went past until he realized that the damn things were flying *faster* than his cannon rounds and there wasn't much point any longer.

They'd proven something important, however.

You bastards are not invincible.

"Nice work, Marine, but you'd better get the hell out of dodge now," The Combat Controller advised him. "Radio traffic just spiked, and I think I'm seeing three additional squadrons looking your way. Get out there!"

"Roger that," Wolfe muttered. He'd done what he intended, "Green Knights, RTB."

The remaining fighters acknowledged the order and banked off, getting low and fast as they tried to get under the enemy RADAR to make their escape.

Wolfe did the same, it was time to get the hell out of this fight. He would be back, he knew, hopefully packing better intel and a plan, but either way, this war was just getting started.

*****

Air Force Helo

"Get us out of here," Kiran said, satisfied.

He'd gotten a lot of key intel, and it was already back with PACAFCOM being crunched by experts.

The Bloc had caught them with their pants down, no question about that. Those airframes he'd dubbed the Mantis, they were something else.

Someone has to know something about them, how they got something like that into significant production without dropping a major dossier on every intel desk on the planet, I'll never know. Hope we can figure out a counter... one that doesn't involve sending Marines to challenge them to a knife fight every time.

"Might want to hang on, Sir. I think we overstayed our welcome."

Kiran looked up, concerned as the pilot dropped them hard for the deck, twisting the helo around to make a run North up the valley. He took a few seconds to spot what the helo pilot had already seen. While they'd been paying attention to the new Mantis platforms it looked like a group of Chinese attack helos had been coming in using the same hills for cover they had.

Shit.

He started packing his gear back up, calmly making sure everything was in the protected cases once he ensured that the encryption locks were in place. He'd rather not burn it out if he didn't have to, but he was prepared to ensure that none of his gear was taken by the enemy no matter what the outcome.

The pilot was low and fast, using trees and hills for cover as they ran for it, but the Bloc attack helos were already on them. The UH was good, but Kiran knew its limits. He primed the charges on his gear, leaving them on a timer just in case he couldn't set them off in what was coming.

"Hot missile in the air! Hold on!"

Kiran threw himself into the jump seat, grabbing for the straps as the helo pitched and wove. The sound of countermeasures launching could be heard over the beat of the blades as he locked the straps down around himself and his kit.

This is going to suck.

The helo was struck as if by a hammer, slamming Kiran into the straps. The reinforced canvas bit into his side, then everything began to spin.

"We're going down! Hang on, hang on!"

The pilot worked the pedals, trying to control the spin as the hills and trees spun around them in a blur.

There was a rush of air, then a massive crunch, and everything went black.

*****

Green Knights

Wolfe swore as he heard the mayday call from the Air Force Helo and twisted in place so he could check out the side. In the distance, he could see smoke already rising.

"Shit."

He hesitated, knowing there wasn't anything he could do really, but ultimately it didn't matter.

"Keep going," He told the other Knights. "I'm going to fly over and see if it looks like anyone survived. Para-jumpers could use the intel."

"We'll stick with…"

"No, this is an *order*," He told his remaining squad. "Get back to base. I'll be right with you. Now go!"

The remaining Knights reluctantly continued on while Wolfe turned back while checking his load out.

Missiles may not be much threat to those new bastards, but I don't think these attack helos are going to be dodging quite so easily.

*****

Route 33, East

Gunny Hadrian winced as he watched the smoke crawl up from just over the hill.

They'd watched the Air Force bird try to outrun the Bloc attack helos and knew that it was only going to end one way once the full squad turned up on their tail. He wasn't sure what he could do about it, however, since anyone approaching that crash site was going to be under those guns and his men weren't armed.

He was about to order his driver to move on when a familiar shape screamed through the valley along the highway, chasing its own missiles as it just *unloaded* a full payload on the Bloc attack choppers.

Predators turned into prey in an instant, the F35 turning the Bloc helos into burning scrap.

Hadrian let his Marines whoop it up, while he only threw a salute to the fighter he recognized. The emblem on the stabilizer was one he knew intimately, having worked on that fighter more than he cared to remember.

Good hunting, Major, and godspeed.

"Alright," he said aloud. "The Green Knights just took care of our helo problem, so while we have a chance, what's say we go see if any Air Force pukes need a lift?"

"Oorah Gunny!"

*****

Chapter Four

Green Knight Actual

Wolfe waggled the wings of his F35 as he flew over the wreck of the chopper. He could see someone crawling out of the hulk, and hoped more survived, but he was out of time. The enemy Mantis fighters were coming back around, and he was pretty sure they were looking for some payback.

The figure below waved at him as he flew past, and that was all Wolfe had time for. He angled his fighter down the valley, pushing the throttle forward and let the fighter strapped to him push him back into the ACES ejection seat as his instrumentation screamed warnings at him from all directions.

He turned in his seat, looking over his shoulder, and easily spotted a couple of the fighters chasing after him. He was unsurprised to find that they were flying slower than they normally would, as they tried to keep an eye on him flying nap of the Earth.

"Come on, boys, let's play a game," he grinned darkly, banking into a sharp turn as he cut down a branching valley between two rolling hills, trees flashing past on either side. Behind him the Bloc fighters screamed after him while others flew over, keeping him in sight and directing their fellows.

*****

Kiran reset the destruct charge on his kit, not disabling it but giving himself more time to decide. The Helo had taken a hell of a hit when it went in, and the flight crew hadn't survived the front heavy impact, but the airframe had done the job it was designed to do in keeping the passenger compartment as safe as possible.

The Marine F35's turbine roar was fading into the distance as he took stock of his situation.

He wasn't quite fucked, but it wasn't too far from that either.

Kiran had been able to avail himself of the latest intel on the invasion before the attack choppers shot him down, and he knew it didn't look good for Japan at the moment.

The Bloc had managed to build some serious air power without anyone realizing what exactly they were putting together. Worse, perhaps, was that they'd managed to apply that same bit of stealth to troop transports. Heavy low flying ekranoplans, at least that was what people were thinking they were, had ferried *hundreds* of thousands of troops across the Sea of Japan in the time that an aircraft would have made the trip.

No one was ready for that level of an invasion force.

That meant he was in the very middle of a currently hotly disputed territory that was shortly to become hostile ground.

Kiran swung his pack up over his shoulder and started walking, wondering if he should be looking to go native, or keep trying to get back to base. There were advantages to either, of course, both for himself and for the service.

In the absence of orders to the contrary, he'd keep making for the base until it was clear he couldn't manage it. Then it would be time to embed with the locals, find some JSDF people and get into the resistance.

Interesting times, Kiran thought.

Tires crunching on gravel caught his attention, and he half turned to see a short bus slide up a few hundred meters down the hill on the side of the highway he'd come down near to.

"Hey, anyone else make it out?" An American voice asked, a big guy dropping to the ground from the door.

Kiran shook his head, "Just me."

"Fuck." The man said, "Name's Gunny Hadrian. You need a lift?"

*****

Green Knight Actual

Warnings screamed in his ears, getting so mixed up with one another that they almost merged into one incomprehensible morass of sound. They certainly would have, if not for the hundreds and thousands of hours of training he had to ensure that precise thing would not happen.

Wolfe fired flares and ECM jammers again, spoofing the missiles tracking him, and pulled back hard on the stick to send his fighter hard vertical. Standing on its turbine, the F35 obeyed even as its airframe howled around him. He stepped into the pedals, putting the fighter into a flat spin that brought his guns around to bear on the pursuers.

They weren't about to give him another shot like that, though, and the Mantis fighter he was bearing on hopped suddenly out of his gun's sights in a move like nothing he'd ever seen.

Damn. The fucking things must have thrusters mounted under the airframe to pull that off, he thought while fighting to complete the spin and put his fighter back on course. Nose down, picking up speed again, he banked into a ravine to buy a little distance before the Bloc fighters could pull another shot off.

Hitting the afterburners again, and generally just ignoring every Marine Corps regulation there was for the operation of the F35B as his computer informed him that he was over the duration limit for using the damn thing, Wolfe broke Mach a little over a hundred feet off the deck and tore the hell out of the valley around him with a sonic boom as he headed for the East Coast.

*****

Marines' Short Bus, Route 33 East

"Not that I'm ungrateful, but where the hell did you guys come from?" Kiran asked from where he was slumped into the front seat of the bus as they sped along the highway, headed East.

He was moderately surprised that this group of Marines was headed in the sane direction. But then again, he supposed that had more to do with the fact that they were all unarmed than it did with their relative brain power.

"We were on leave, enjoying the beach for a day, when we saw the landers come in," the man beside him, a private named Charleson, told him in a midwestern drawl. "Gunny packed us up and we've been driving ever since, heading for Iwakuni."

"You're with the Air Station?"

Charleson nodded, "Usually spend time making sure whirlybirds and fighters *aren't* falling out of the skies, but I guess picking people out of the wrecks is a nice change of pace."

Kiran shot the man an annoyed look, but just got a grin in return.

"Hey," the man who'd introduced himself as Gunny Hadrian said from where he was standing beside the driver. "You linked to an FOB with any of that gear?"

"Yeah," Kiran confirmed. "And before you ask, it's not looking good. Landers came in all up and down the coast, real blitzkrieg stuff. Bypassed a lot of the planned defenses like they were the Maginot Line, and our boys are fighting under a *very* unfriendly sky."

"Well, shit," Hadrian muttered. "I was hoping it wasn't as bad as it looked from down here."

"If anything, it's worse. Green Knights out of Iwakuni managed to down a few of the Bloc Mantis type fighters," Kiran said, "Better than most have managed, and they only managed it by going gun to gun with their Equalizers."

"Missiles won't lock on?"

"They lock on fine. The Mantis fighters just sneer at them and leave the missiles sucking air in their wake. I've got them moving faster than almost anything in our inventory," Kiran said, shaking his head. "Doesn't make any sense. Those things should have burned up at the speeds they were going, and crushed any pilots dumb enough to pull those maneuvers."

"Drones?" A corporal offered from a couple seats back.

"That's what we thought, until Lycan splashed one. I saw a chute," Kiran said. "They're manned."

Hadrian grunted but didn't have anything to say about that.

Kiran might have hoped otherwise, of course, but he wasn't surprised either. The puzzle of the fighters was something he knew was giving migraines to some of the best analysts the US had. No one knew what the hell was going on, and every time they got new information it just made the situation even worse.

For the moment, however, he was out of the fight.

All he could do was catch the lift with the Marines and hope they all got to Iwakuni before something else got to them.

*****

Green Knight Actual

Warning tones brought Wolfe's attention to a set of signals dead ahead and he swore as he recognized them as enemy contacts.

The Bloc fighters were fast.

Alright, it seemed stupid to think that after everything else that had happened, but they were fast enough to get ahead of him, whether they intended it or not. He checked his fuel status, making fast calculations in his head.

He still had enough to detour around the signals, but if he guessed wrong or they got ahead of him again, he'd be bingo for fuel.

Alternatively, he could try to blow through.

He didn't much like his odds on that, now with his opposition being capable of hypersonic speeds and reaction maneuvering that looked like something out of a movie or video game. A slim chance in hell was still better than his odds of negotiating with gravity once his fuel ran out, however.

Banking left, he cut down another valley in the rolling hills of the central island, green blurring past on either side and a little above him as he flew, snaking his way toward the coast and the Air Station that was his goal.

Another tone caused him to glance down, then up over his right shoulder, before he started swearing.

Goddamn it. These bastards just don't give up.

Two Mantis fighters were coming in from his Seven O'Clock high, and they didn't seem like they were looking to play nice.

Here we go again.

It was like a demented game of chicken, played partially in reverse. He kept up his speed while watching the approaching fighters. They were closing on him easily, of course, but weren't trying for a high-speed pass either. Wolfe figured that they didn't want to miss their engagement window by blowing past him and be forced to circle around, potentially losing him in the hills before they could line up again.

That gave him a chance, though not as good of one as he might normally have expected or wished for. Wolfe's hands gripped the controls tighter, knuckles white as he kept looking between his instruments and over his shoulder while trying to keep from plowing into the local landscape.

"Come on, you bastards, don't keep me waiting…"

As they got within three kilometers the tension ratcheted up. Every meter closer shortened the reaction time he would have to anything they opted to do. They knew it too, otherwise they'd have locked on and fired missiles from a lot farther out, but the Bloc pilots had obviously worked out that he could spoof and evade those.

They couldn't nail him easily, and conversely, he couldn't nail them either. Not with the standard go-to weapons of air combat for the last century, at least. It was a standoff that that favored the faster and more maneuverable Bloc fighters, but it did mean that they had to bring the fight into him.

They were going to make this personal, and that was just fine by Wolfe.

At two kilometers and closing, Wolfe moved first.

The afterburner coughed out, his F35 shuddering as it dropped below Mach, and he put the nose up into a steep climb. Standing the fighter on the turkey feathers, he worked the pedals to put the bird into a flat spin while he was nearly vertical.

The enemy fighters got a lot closer, a lot faster than they'd expected, as he slowed abruptly but they saw the move coming and adjusted. Looking up through the bubble canopy he could see them lining up for their shot while he was a sitting duck, all by the playbook.

Let's see how you handle going off book.

He grabbed the VTOL controls, redirecting thrust in ways that were *definitely* not approved by the Corps, Pratt and Whitney, or Lockheed Martin. He was wrenched around as his fighter *barrel rolled* in place, the maneuver turning into a spiral that quickly became something else as he worked the pedals furiously.

There was an inhuman sound of metal shearing off and Wolfe winced as he glanced back to see the duct cover for the center thrust module just simply *gone*, but didn't have time to worry about it. Not like he needed stealth cowling at the moment anyway, as long as it didn't take any control surfaces with it when it tore off, he was golden.

"God created man, the Wright brothers gave us flight, but tonight? General Dynamics makes us equal." Wolfe snarled as his finger tightened on the trigger of the GAU-22 Equalizer, and the 35mm rotary cannon spun up and chattered out the last burst of ammo in his magazine, sending ninety odd rounds downrange.

He walked the burst across the two fighters, praising their tight formation in his head as he saw fire and smoke erupt across their fuselage from only a couple hundred meters away.

Wolfe held his aircraft in a controlled hover as the flaming wreckage split his position on either side, crashing to the ground past him, then worked the pedals again to spin in place before putting more power to the turbines.

He checked his fuel status and grimaced.

So much for trying an end run. Alright, I'll have to bull through and take my chances.

"Iwakuni Control, Lycan." He said wearily, "Am BINGO on fuel and Winchester on ammo. Heading for home. Any support running the line would be appreciated."

There was a pause before anyone got back, longer than he wanted to be hearing.

"We're sorry, Lycan, everything we have is assigned, loaded on ship… or gone."

He nodded, unsurprised. "Well then, wish me luck. One way or another looks like I'm coming home tonight."

"Good luck, Lycan."

"Thanks, Iwakuni."

He closed the channel, letting out a long breath, and glanced down at his map to get an idea where he was. He was mapping out a route in his head when a flash of light in the sky to his left caught his attention.

A flare? What the…

Curiosity overrode sense, and he shifted his course slightly to overshoot the area the flare had been launched from. It wasn't far off his intended path anyway.

Wolfe's confusion turned to consternation when he found the source, a group of JSDF uniforms from the looks of it, waving at him from the ground. He couldn't imagine what the hell they wanted, he was out of ammo and damn near out of fuel. There wasn't a damn thing he could do for…

He paused, blinking furiously as they pointed to the side of a mountain that was slowly *opening*.

Is that a hangar in the side of the mountain? What. The. Fuck.

*****

Iwakuni

The highways were mostly clear. Surprisingly, the Japanese government had issued alerts to everyone asking them to stay home so that military traffic could have priority on the roads and tracks. Shockingly enough, at least to Hadrian, people seemed to have actually listened.

Wouldn't want to see the mess back home if that happened.

For them it meant that they'd been able to make good time, ignoring posted limits and pushing the bus as fast as it would go. The few times they were flagged down, he just showed his military ID and told them where they were going, and they were sent on without any further fuss.

They made Marine Corps Air Station Iwakuni before midnight and were hurried through the gates by the sergeant on duty.

Hadrian was struck both by how busy and…how empty the streets were.

There was a lot going on, no doubt, with trucks mostly moving near constantly, but a lot of the usual traffic he'd come to expect even in times of emergency was just clearly gone.

"Hey Gunny," Charleson said softly, looking over at one of the docks they were passing. "They moved all the Tenders."

"Yeah, I see it."

"Where are they?"

"Put to sea," Hadrian said. "They're not going to risk having them sunk in the harbour."

"Gunny, but what about…"

"Can it," Hadrian said as the bus rolled to a stop. "We've got work to do. Get to your bunks and into unies. Meet you at the shop in ten minutes, and God help you if you're late."

*****

Mountain Hangar

This is the sketchiest flying I've ever done, Wolfe thought as he eased the thrust on the fighter and slid it sideways into the hangar, a dozen feet off the ground with maybe that much clearance above.

The camouflaged hangar had clearly been built with *just* this sort of use in mind… *Well, perhaps not flying an aircraft in, that's just insane…* but with the intent of hiding military equipment from hostile invaders. It was massive, and hidden right in the mountain, with real trees and brush growing on the door.

How long have they been working on these things?

He knew that the Japanese had built massive hidden facilities toward the last days of World War Two, specifically to provide their forces with fallback positions from which to strike American invaders in the event of a landed invasion. That hadn't panned out, of course, with the advent of the nuclear bomb, but they had built quite a few.

He'd even toured one that was open to the public once, but he'd never heard a whisper that they had maintained any of them for military purposes, let alone built new ones.

Cutting thrust, he landed the fighter on the concrete inside the door, having had to do that because directly outside was covered in shrubbery and low trees.

JSDF flight crews rushed up, swarming him as he popped the cockpit and pulled himself out.

"I need a secure comm," he said to the first man, his Japanese rough but serviceable. "Line back to Iwakuni."

"Of course, Major," The crewman told him in barely accented English, pointing. "Base commander has instructed us that you are invited to use our fiber link."

"Thanks."

"Thank you, Sir," The man told him. "We observed you shooting down two of the invaders, and the cover you provided allowed many others to make it to their base locations."

"Good," Wolfe nodded, sighing as he pushed his sweat-slicked hair back. "Thank god for small victories, I suppose."

*****

Across the island chain, however, there were more losses than victories, even small ones.

The Bloc offensive, despite meeting heavy resistance, had unloaded over eight hundred thousand ground force infantry troops by nightfall, with more crossing the sea in heavy transports every hour. Tanks rolled out of the big low flying craft in smaller, but still significant, numbers, and by midnight, the western seaboard was under Bloc occupation.

Fighting intensified in the hills, and the Bloc weren't getting a free pass as they pressed on, but fighting under a friendly sky made the final outcome inevitable.

American forces received the orders to withdraw from the bases in the region at Oh One Thirty-Five that morning.

Japan had fallen.

Chapter Five

Alamagordo New Mexico

"Eastern Bloc forces successfully secured a beachhead on the Japanese archipelago, driving American and JSDF naval forces away from the island chain last night…"

A half empty beer can slammed into the digital assistant, knocking it off the table it rested on and sending it sprawling across the cement floor, the voice dying when the wire was knocked loose from the wall plug.

"Jesus, Bradley," Eric Stanton Weston snapped as he jumped in surprise from the noise. "I was listening to that!"

Bradley Cohen snorted, the older man adjusting the straw hat he wore as he spat at the ground. "Fucking Chicom bastards."

"Bloc," Eric corrected him wearily. "They've not been communists… well, since ever really, but not even pretend communists for at least fifteen years."

"Pfa," Bradley spit. "Same bullshit, different name. I'll call em what I want."

Eric shrugged, "There's truth there. Sounds like our boys had a rough night of it."

"Not just in Japan."

Nodding, Eric walked over to the middle of the hangar he and Bradley were working in. On a makeshift old bench a large piece of machinery rested, power cables running off to the mains.

"Yeah, heard about Taiwan too. You thinking what I am?" Eric asked, staring at the kit.

Bradley kicked at a piece of debris, sending it flying off across the hangar where it clattered out the large open doors to the old beat-up tarmac beyond.

"They got it figured out," He said, coming over to stand beside Eric.

"Yeah. I hoped we'd crack it first."

Bradley sighed. "Chicoms, or whatever the fuck you want to call them, they've got the money these days. Big labs, lots of well-educated people. Us? Well, it ain't the glory days anymore, is it?"

"No, no it ain't," Eric said. "Hasn't been for a long time."

"It's World War Two, buddy," Bradley sighed, "Only the Commies beat us to the bomb."

"Maybe," Eric said, even partially agreeing with his friend.

The economy was in the crapper, something that couldn't really be laid at the feet of the Bloc, he knew, but they certainly had a hand in triggering the crash. Not that Eric could really blame them. It wasn't like the West hadn't spent the previous half-century making it easy for them. Building debt like it was pretend money, hell it even was… right up until someone called in the markers.

The Bloc had waited on that, timing it just to perfection. China and India alone had accounted for a little over ten percent of US debt when the boom came down. The economy had been in a predictable boom and bust cycle for decades, all through the twenty-first century. No one really even bothered to fix it, even though every economist knew the cause, because a bust economy was a boon to people with real money.

It let them buy up property, assets, whatever they wanted at pennies on the dollar from those who hadn't been able to make their lives quite so secure.

A former President had said it best, actually, back when he was still a businessman. A recession? That was a good thing, it was when you could make real money.

No one counted on a coordinated short sell of US debt timed to coincide with the bust phase, though. The resulting economic spiral had been enough to flatten the economy of the States and did a pretty good job on every economy connected to them too. Which was pretty much every economy on the planet.

That was why no one expected it to happen. Who nukes their own economy?

Well, someone had seriously overestimated human sanity.

Fifteen years they'd been fighting their way out of this depression, well a little less than ten really, but even though technically out of it, it didn't feel much better than when they'd been wallowing in the middle of the worst of it.

And now? Now the Bloc had finally made their second move.

"I'm only surprised it took them this long," Bradley said, echoing Eric's thoughts as though he'd spoken them aloud.

"They wanted an ace," Eric nodded to the contraption in front of him. "We've taught them everything we know over the years, guess they wanted to make sure it wasn't everything *they* knew."

Bradley snorted, about to say something else when a stray bit of movement in the corner of his eye caused him to turn around and glare.

"Hey! Get the hell out of here!"

Eric sighed, seeing the subject of his friend's ire scrambling to leave, and lay a hand on his shoulder.

"Relax, he's just a kid."

"Damn fool brat needs to stop snooping around," Bradley sighed, shaking his head.

"He doesn't mean any harm."

"How old is he now? Twelve?"

Eric laughed, "Eighteen. Oh, I pity your daughters when they start dating."

"They'll be the safest girls on the continent."

"From everything except trauma," Eric shook his head. "You're going to owe a fortune in therapist bills."

Bradley shook his head, "Just get rid of the kid, will you?"

"Yeah, yeah," Eric sighed, "I'll be back."

Bradley waved him off and he made his way out of the old hangar, glancing around as he stepped out into the beating sun. It didn't take long to find the kid, and Eric waved him over. The teenager reluctantly approached, looking like he was about to get a beating.

"Come off it, Stephen, you know better than to be sneaking around here," Eric sighed. "You could get hurt screwing around the junk here, and that would completely fuck our insurance."

"Sorry Mr. Weston," Stephen Michaels told him.

"Why do you keep coming back around here, kid?"

"Come on, Mr. Weston, you guys are doing some of the coolest shit in this piece of crap town. I've seen you fly stuff that comes right out of the sci-fi films."

"And most of that is classified, or at least proprietary kid," Eric chastised him, sighing.

"Come on, I don't tell nobody what I see here."

Eric shook his head, though he knew the kid was being straight with him there. "I thought I told you to stay clear until you had your pilot's license and a hundred hours in a T-6?"

Stephen straightened up, "I got my hundred hours last month, Sir."

Eric blinked, "No shit?"

"No shit."

Eric looked him over, "Go home, kid."

Stephen looked down but nodded.

"Come back tomorrow. Bring your flight log."

****

"You get rid of him?" Bradley asked as Eric came back.

"Until tomorrow anyway," Eric said, shaking his head with an odd smile on his face.

Bradley looked over at him, "Why tomorrow?"

"Never mind, Brad, I'll deal with it." Eric looked back over the device on the table. "The question right now is whether or not we can figure out what they beat us to."

Bradley let out a breath, gesturing uncertainly. "Been at this for three years, since you got this tech out of Beijing and the government decided it wasn't worth their time. How long have they been working on it?"

"Probably twenty."

"No pressure, then."

"We're close," Eric said. "I can feel it. We just need to figure out the mass variable, this thing does something we haven't quite quantified yet."

"It makes physics roll over and tie itself in knots," Bradley snorted. "Turned the last airframe we put it in into some kind of modern art display. Could have done the same to you too, if you hadn't bailed as fast as you did."

Eric nodded absently as he ran a hand along the rig.

Bradley was right, of course. They'd completely destroyed the old F-16 airframe they'd last mounted the device in.

Hell, device. We still don't know what to properly call this thing.

It was some sort of mass altering technology, something Eric was able to get his head mostly around in concept, but there were aspects of the practical application that just weren't playing nicely with the theory, and that was what was giving him and Bradley kittens.

We're missing variables, Eric knew. The issue was determining what variables those were, because there were so very many at play.

The Bloc had been working on the tech for decades. It had been considered a boondoggle actually among western intel. Eric had a chance to pull their files during an op he'd run in country, but when he brought it back to stateside it had been laughed off.

His intel contact had told him it was the Chinese version of MKUltra and other time and money wasting projects. Just something that kept them pouring money down an endless hole, which was exactly where the Company wanted that money going.

Eric had never quite bought that idea, though, so he'd taken the file and found Bradley. Between them, they'd built the first prototype and while it didn't work it did... things. Things that no sane universe should allow, but things that were more than enough to feed their own obsession.

Eric had retired from the Marines, they'd pooled their savings, and this was their life for the last three years.

And now the Bloc had beat them to the punch.

*****

NAVPACCOM, San Francisco

"Gentlemen, how in the fuck did we miss this?"

The men in the room flinched, not so much due to the language of course. They were all sailors, though these days they all sailed desks rather than ships, and had heard a lot worse in their times.

Few were the times they'd heard such from the President, however.

"We're reviewing intelligence now, Mr. President," Admiral Baker responded, "Digging through that material is going to take time however…"

The President held up his hand on the screen, causing Baker to come to a halt.

"Don't blow smoke up my ass, not now, Baker. We just got well and truly fucked, right in front of the whole damned planet, so let's focus on getting this situation *unfucked*, shall we?"

The men again winced, the President making it clear to them that he was in no mood to be playing the usual games of political niceties, which was very much out of character for the man who'd been elected as a fresh breath of civil air when compared to the growing crassness of many of his predecessors.

In private, however, and given reason, he was more than capable of talking down to any level someone wanted to push him to. Especially if it made a point.

"So, gentlemen, stop blowing smoke and lay it out for me."

Benjamin Givens had been elected largely by an uninterested electorate, tired of each election being hyped as the most important of their lives, people who just wanted to be done with it all so they could go back about their lives. They didn't care about the world, many could barely care about other states, and Ben had taken the election largely on the promise that he wouldn't involve the US in foreign wars or other adventurism.

He supposed this was karma, though for his very soul he wasn't sure what he'd ever done to deserve quite this level of comeuppance.

"The seventh fleet is in retreat from Japan, Mr. President," Admiral Baker said tiredly. "Along with a considerable number of JSDF ships and a smattering of other allies, however they're being harried even as we speak. The Bloc air forces are…"

He trailed off, uncertain how to say it.

"Are overwhelming, Admiral, that much I can read from the reports," Givens growled. "Let's talk about that. How in the *hell* did happen, and why didn't we know about it?"

Baker squirmed under the glare from POTUS, "Well sir, that really isn't my field…"

"It's someone's field, and I want answers. What the hell are they using? Drones?" Givens demanded. "Can we drop a Treaty of Miami violation on them?"

"No sir, we have imagery from the fighting when a Marine F35 managed to shoot one down, there was a chute deployed."

The President look puzzled, glancing down at something in front of him.

"Really? My briefing indicates that they were managing maneuvers that should have severely injured any human pilots…"

"Ah, yes Sir. That is correct. We don't have an answer to that, as of yet."

Givens slumped. "Gentlemen, the people of this country are going to be asking us all these questions in a very short time. It behooves us to *have* answers to them, don't you think?"

"Yes sir."

"Then find out!"

"Yes sir!"

Givens shut off the connection from his side, the screen going blank as the men and women in the room got to work.

*****

NSA HQ, Maryland

The building was not normally one of the busiest places, despite a fairly constant level of work being conducted at all times of day or night. When the NSA headquarters building began buzzing, however, it was a fair bet that something rather serious had gone down somewhere on the planet.

When that something was a rout of US forces in a national ally as important as Japan, busy was apparently an understatement.

Simone Roarke had to push through the crowd in the outer office, ignoring the shouted demands for information she didn't have, letting herself into the inner section and forcing the door closed behind her with her entire body weight as she stared around with wide eyes.

"What the hell is going on out there?" She gasped, stunned by something she'd never seen in her entire career.

Peter Karrol, her supervisor, was looking harried and worn as he turned over to her.

"We have high level requests across the board from everyone from the White House to the Boy Scouts, and I'm only slightly exaggerating," He said. "The Bloc just pulled the rug out from under our feet and slapped us upside the head on our way to the ground. We need to find the intel failure that let them field those aircraft without warning, and we need to find it *now*."

"Easier said than done," Simone groaned. "We have decades of Intel stored on cloud sites across C2S, and at least ninety percent of it has never been properly analyzed. You know that."

"Yeah, and right now I'm guessing that something important slipped into that ninety percent. That's your job today," Peter told her. "Find it."

She stared dumbly.

"Really? Is that all? Maybe I should pull up the blueprints for their new fighter too while I'm at it?"

He looked at her seriously. "If you find that in there, and it was overlooked, someone will be shot over it. I'm not exaggerating this time."

She swallowed, hard, but nodded.

"Yes sir."

There was nothing else to say, really. Simone sat down and got to work.

The NSA was a central receiving source for all the electronic intelligence of the United States, which also tended to mean that they got copies of pretty much everything their allies had, particularly those with reciprocal agreements. Since the 1950s, the so called 'five eyes' had managed a worldwide intercept program that recorded effectively every conversation, transmission, you name it.

The NSA had all of it.

All. One hundred and twenty plus years. Of it.

There had always been more data than could be analyzed in any given year, even with computer aid. And, even as computers got better at crunching that data, so too did intelligence gathering and intercepts. More data, and even less time. Priorities had to be made, some intel declared to be more important than others, and inevitably that meant key pieces of intelligence were missed.

Nothing like this had ever happened, however.

She signed into her secure terminal, one of few in the entire country with straight line access to the raw data, and got to work.

Simone's job was primarily as a coder. She had worked in Silicon Valley after she graduated university, hired by one of the largest search engines in the world to ensure that the results on their system were more competitive than that of any of their competitors. That didn't always mean bring the most accurate, of course. Generally, in the commercial sphere the goal wasn't to deliver accuracy so much as to deliver what the user *wanted*. Often there was a fine line between the two, but sometimes it was quite blatant.

Here, however, she was tasked with writing code, often on the fly, to find scraps of relevant data from the largest repository of intelligence ever accumulated. Uncountable exabytes of information, almost all of it worthless, and her task was to filter it all until the few gems and gold were revealed.

All she needed was somewhere to start.

"Get me everything we have on the Bloc fighters," She demanded, "I need more information to narrow this search, damn it."

*****

Washington DC, White House Oval Office

Givens glared at the blank screen for a moment, then looked up balefully at the people who'd been listening in.

"What I said for them goes double for everyone in this room," He growled out.

They just nodded.

Finally he signed, "I need a written declaration of war. Silly, I suppose, but let's make it official in the paperwork sense of things, and someone start getting our allies on the line. I'll want as many of them signed on as possible."

"Yes Sir, I can get Germany, The United Kingdom, and Canada on the line…" The Secretary of State started, only to be interrupted by a strange cough.

Everyone turned to look at the Secretary of Defense who had an odd expression on his face.

"Something we should know, General?" Givens asked.

"Well Mr President, Canada actually declared war just before we started this meeting."

"Seriously?"

The former General sighed, looking a little embarrassed, "Damn canucks beat us to the punch in World War Two as well. Declared war on Japan almost a full day ahead of us."

"What."

The President waved his hand, "Never mind that. Just, get them on the line anyway. We should make a coordinated statement."

"Yes, Mr President."

*****

Alamogordo New Mexico

Eric listened to the news, having plugged his digital assistant back in after its unfortunate encounter with Brad's beer can, trying to piece together what he could from what the reports had to say about the Bloc's new fighter.

They haven't figured out yet that it's not just a new thrust system, He noted as he leaned over the table, looking through photographs from independent journalists in the regions under attack.

The internet was still active in many of them and would be very difficult for the likes of the Bloc to shut down since the ground stations and fiber were no longer the only portals the average person could use. Low Orbital Satellite Constellations provided fast, cheap access to anyone in the world now, and those connections were often directional and very difficult to either jam or track.

That was likely to play an important part in how things went over the long term, he had little doubt, but for the moment Eric was more concerned with the fact that it meant that a lot of photos and video of the fighting were already out and online. He quickly found a few sources that were aggregating the best of those and began pouring over them for himself.

The videos were stunning, the few that were through decent enough lenses not to be mere specs in the sky at least. He was looking at fighters that were capable of maneuvers that he was *certain* would turn human bones to jelly, a determination held up by the calculations others had already done in the forum posts.

What he found curious, though, were the close ups of the bottom of the aircraft.

Those look like... thrust vents. But if they're running an anti-gravity system like we think, why would they...

Eric paused, straightening up, "Bradley!"

He barely waited a second before yelling again, "Bradley!"

"Hold yer horses," The older Engineer grumbled as he made his way across the hangar, "what the hell are you screaming about?"

"Look at these photos and tell me if anything jumps out to you."

Bradley leaned over the tablet, frowning in annoyance. The frown quickly vanished, however, as he began to flip through the images over Eric's shoulder.

"What... why would they...?"

"I know, right?" Eric asked, "Maybe we got this wrong. Maybe it's not anti-gravity."

"I thought that's what the files called it," Bradley grumbled. "We checked the equations, hell we even farmed it out to experts. Everything says that this thing is supposed to be a gravity manipulation rig."

"Yeah, agreed, but if it's anti-grav, why put thrusters on it like that?" Eric wondered. "Shouldn't you be able to gain altitude just by throwing more power to the drive?"

"Should, sure. Maybe it's not fast enough? Chemical thrust puts out a hell of a high of a specific impulse, maybe the drive doesn't?"

"Yeah, maybe," Eric nodded.

It made sense, he knew, but something was nagging at him, He felt like he used to on a mission when something had changed but he couldn't quite figure out what it was but knew it was important.

"Goddamn it, that kid's back."

Eric looked up, "I'll handle it, Brad. I need to clear my head anyway."

*****

Chapter Six

Pacific Ocean, Two Hundred Nautical Miles South South East of Japan

USS Enterprise CVN-80

Admiral Bonet glowered as he stalked the deck of the big Aircraft Carrier. The Big E was to this day, even old as she was, one of the most powerful ships ever built and put to sea. That fact made the situation he was facing all that more frustrating.

Their fighter squadrons had been sortieing nonstop since the withdrawal from Japan almost two days earlier, covering the task group as they struggled to gather all the strays that had been scattered to the seas in the chaos of the order to pull forces out of Japan. He thought they had most of them now, though far too many had been sunk to enemy air cover.

Thus far, at least, they'd been able to keep the enemy ships at bay, for what that was worth. It made the fighting a long grind that was slowly wearing them down rather than a straight up rout, but the end result would be the same if they couldn't figure a way to counter the enemy's airpower.

No American has fought under anything worse than a neutral sky in so long, I worry we might have forgotten how.

He had no doubt that Americans would learn, the hard way if they needed to, but it would be a bloody lesson. Worse, he suspected that the job he and his men now held was not to be the sword and shield of their nation, but rather to just buy time with their lives that other men might learn the lessons needed.

It was a bitter pill to swallow.

"Inbound strike force! FL-35, approaching from three miles. Hypersonic."

Bonet grimaced but didn't say anything. The responses were already set. The Enterprise's destroyer shield was moving to intercept, AEGIS arrays coming online as they began to pour power downrange.

He counted off the time in his head, looking up just as the smoke plumes rose from the Lake Champlain and the Chesapeake Bay. He knew their response times down to the second, and didn't need to give the order.

The surface to air missiles quickly accelerated to Hypersonic themselves, ranging in on the hostile squadron, but the Bloc fighters just changed course so quickly that it left *him* with a headache just contemplating the forces involved, and proceeded to make a mockery of the weapons tracking them.

"Birds losing track, enemy squadron has broken through, still on approach."

The ready squadron was screaming off the deck, moving to provide backup for the CAP the Enterprise already had flying overhead. The Navy F35s were screaming off the deck while the CAP squadron was already in position.

He turned to watch the screens, practiced eyes turning the dots and lines and icons on the screen into a visual of what was happening.

The lead squadron, the Jolly Rogers, were adding their jamming to the mix already flooding the area from the ships and drones in the air. They'd learned from the events in Japan, particularly the engagement of the Green Knights. With the power of the task group at hand, they could take most enemy missiles out of the skies with little problem, but they still couldn't *hit* the damn things.

That largely took missiles out of play, which was better than one might expect since they'd been able to determine that the Bloc sleds had been built without guns.

Unfortunately, they *had* been mounted with what was likely intended to be anti-missile lasers, and those worked pretty well against fighters it seemed, though they had to suck up juice like no one's business since they didn't seem to have a lot of shots per engagement.

That meant that the enemy fighters couldn't be touched easily, but they could only pick off the task group's fighters in drips and dabs.

Cold comfort that was.

*****

Jolly Rogers Actual

Captain Grace 'Hela' Dearborn flipped the switch to open up her fighter's weapons bay. There was no point trying to hide at the moment, and she wanted everything she had ready to go. The Fighter shuddered a little as the bay in its belly opened up, exposing the missile hardpoints.

She was loaded for bear, however, with even the external hardpoints bristling with ordnance. Unfortunately, as had been proven out over Japan, nailing the Bloc fighters with a missile was a seriously non-trivial feat.

Grace would take her chances, though, as there was nothing left to lose.

"Here they come," She said, eyes on the scanners.

The Mantis fighters were coming in fast, moving at Mach Four, a speed her Jolly Roger squadron couldn't even hope to match, so they didn't bother even trying. Cruising at a comparatively sedate six hundred knots, the Jolly Rogers wheeled in formation to meet the approach.

"All points, Hela," she said as she switched over to her cannon. "Going guns."

Her squadron acknowledged, their own guns spinning up.

"Hold fire until they're in range," She ordered, "Don't get jumpy. We don't have nearly enough bullets to start wasting them now."

The enemy were a hundred klicks out now, closing fast. The fleet was beginning to respond, the anti-air lasers firing first. Invisible beams lancing out from the task group. She spotted the first flares of flame erupting in the distant sky, some of the Bloc fighters vanishing from her scopes.

They were fast, though, too fast. The hundred klicks dropped away in seconds, and abruptly Jolly Rogers Two screamed as his F35 went up in flames, the enemy lasers finding their mark. Jolly Rogers Four followed suit a moment later. She could hear swearing but held steady on the mark.

"Hold fire," She ordered, eyes on the instruments.

Ten klicks.

Five. Four.

Her finger was just tightening around the trigger, then the enemy fighters went vertical and hypersonic.

Grace screamed, almost firing into the air in frustration. "Get back here you fucking *COWARDS!*"

They were gone, however, having changed course before they slipped into the three-kilometer effective range of her GAU-22 Equalizer.

Fuckers learned from Japan too.

A quick check indicated that she'd lost three planes, though all the pilots had punched out successfully. Boats were already in the water, heading to pick them up, for which she was grateful, but Grace knew that they couldn't keep losing fighters like that.

At least the fleet got some of them.

*****

USS Enterprise

Bonet growled as he examined the data from the fight. The ship lasers were the only thing they had to keep the enemy fighters at bay. Sending his own air group out after them was just sending lambs to the slaughter, it seemed.

"Call them back," He ordered.

"Sir?"

"Bring in our fighters, all of them."

"Sir, protocol dictates we maintain a CAP at all times…"

"I know the book, Commander," Bonet snapped. "And I'm tossing it out. There's nothing they can do up there, not against those fighters. The gun gambit isn't going to work anymore. Bring them home."

"Aye Admiral."

Bonet planted his fists on the table as he looked at the disposition of his fleet. He knew that the planes were just harassing them, keeping them busy while the Bloc fleet moved into position. Normally he'd welcome a chance to exchange shots with the enemy, confident of his crews' capability to give more than a good accounting of themselves.

Now, however, he realized that the enemy was simply keeping him busy until they had enough forces in position to saturate his fleet's missile defense.

A Carrier task group was arguably the most powerful single force on the planet, but even a Ford class carrier and its escorts had limits. Limits he knew the enemy could easily surpass if he had to fight without the force projection capacity of his aircrews.

They had to withdraw, away from the Japanese territorial waters, out deeper into the open ocean. If they didn't, he was sure the enemy would shortly have them flanked.

Bonet plotted a course, trying to decide on his best action.

Satellites were scanning the ocean around his position in real-time, and they'd already located several elements of the Bloc fleet closing on their position from around the Northern and Southern points of the Japanese archipelago.

He traced his finger south, debating on whether it would be better to run for Australian waters, or perhaps loop around Iwo before making for Pearl through the deep blue of the Pacific.

Play it by ear, I think, He decided as he straightened.

"Signal the fleet," He said to the Commander. "We're making for Iwo."

"Iwo, Sir?" Commander Johnson sounded confused as he passed on the orders. "Why there?"

"Convenient marker, Commander, nothing else," Bonet said.

There was little or nothing at Iwo that would matter to anyone at the moment, aside from a few supply stashes he supposed. Some bunker fuel, diesel, and gas as well. Probably anyway, since he knew there was a monument there and a small airfield. He doubted any of it would amount to anything of value to the fleet, but that was fine. He just needed some time to think, to plan, and it would take a day or two to get the fleet there.

They just needed to be moving.

Almost anywhere would do.

So Iwo it was.

*****

USS Miami SSN-898

"Roger that, Enterprise. Miami tasking to point on new course, heading to Iwo."

Captain William Burke closed the network connection and rubbed his face before he looked over to his XO. "You get that?"

"Iwo Jima, Aye Sir. Orders passed along." Commander Morgan Passer responded. "Seems like an odd destination, if you don't mind my saying, Sir."

"Go right ahead, Commander," Burke said with a tired smile.

There was a beat before Morgan rolled his eyes and sighed, "Seems like an odd destination, Sir."

"Yes, I suppose it does."

"Is there a reason?"

Burke shook his head. Probably just convenience. We have converging Bloc task groups moving toward us, we just need to be moving. Iwo happens to be along a course that is neatly away from both of them. Our job is simple enough, thankfully. Just need to keep sweeping these waters, make sure the Bloc doesn't sneak any fast attack boats upon us."

Morgan nodded.

The Enterprise Task Group had four fast-attack subs for that job, and they were going to earn their pay on this run.

"We're taking point then?"

Burke nodded. "The Los Angeles and the Dallas will be running deep and quiet, holding back in reserve, while the Detroit is going to cover the rear position."

"So, if there's a trap, we get to trip it. Lovely."

"Welcome to the Navy, son, you new here?" Burke asked, cracking a smile.

"Not new enough to find that joke funny, Sir."

"Everyone's a critic. Come on, Commander, let's get our game faces on."

*****

EBAN HuangLung

Admiral Chien stood quietly in the center of the surprisingly spacious command deck of the submersible, eyes on the satellite feed they were receiving through their towed array.

The American fleet was moving south, likely heading out of the territorial waters under his protection, but he would make certain that they left with no question as to the power of the Eastern Bloc's Navy.

His mission was to make certain that the Americans learned that lesson, but not to push them beyond the point of which they lost whatever generally counted as their senses. That could be a fine line when dealing with the Americans, but he would at least refrain from engaging civilian targets as that was one of the touchier points that their media loved to scream about.

Military targets within the territorial claims of the Eastern Bloc, however, were most certainly fair game.

"Admiral, we have the information you requested."

"Yes, and?"

"It is the Enterprise, Sir."

Chien nodded slowly, unsurprised though he had not been certain. The Enterprise was one of the Americans' favorite ships if he recalled. Within their military circles, it was widely known as... He frowned, thinking for a moment before his expression cleared.

Ah yes, the Big E. Arrogant, but fitting.

Adding a carrier kill to the glories won thus far would seal the supremacy of the Eastern Bloc in the minds of both their own citizens and place a shard of fear in that of the West.

"Very good," He said finally. "Inform navigation to prepare the drive. We have much to accomplish."

"Yes, Admiral."

The aide left quickly to pass on his orders, leaving Chien to begin calculating the course that would best allow him to make his strategy into reality.

The American Task Group would be eliminated, and he would ensure that the world saw the supremacy of the Eastern Bloc's new military might.

It was destiny.

*****

Beijing Head Offices, Eastern Bloc Alliance

"Chairman," The man on the screen nodded.

"Mr. Minister," The elderly man seated in the large conference room returned the gesture. "It is pleasant to speak with you again."

"And you, of course," The Indian man on the screen said with a genial smile. "I trust all is going well?"

"Very much so. Our operations continue apace, but thus far we have met every objective in the plan."

"Excellent. We as well have taken our objectives with speed, such that they had no chance to properly resist."

"The traitors have reaped as they sowed," The Chairman said with satisfaction. "Are you able to continue with the next phase?"

"We are. Our allies have been alerted, and we will eliminate the American sources of oil in the East by tomorrow night."

"Excellent. It has been a good day."

*****

The Enterprise Carrier Strike Group, augmented by as many strays they'd been able to pick up in the withdrawal from Japan, came around in the deep blue waters and turned their prows to the South. Miles of churning water, faintly glowing with bioluminescence lay in their wake, the heaving seas ahead.

Behind them, two Bloc Strike groups continued their pursuit, each containing three dozen surface ships and four fast-attack subs.

Communication bounced back and both between them and the Bloc's orbiting Satellite constellation, decisions being made quickly. In the end, the groups increased their speed, intending to push the Americans out of the Bloc's newly claimed territorial waters.

For too long the Americans had ruled over their empire of trade like the uncouth tyrants each and every one of them was. The Bloc Navy would ensure that no such action was tolerated into the future, and with just a little luck they would even get to extract a little revenge for previous slights.

Everything thus far had gone within the parameters of the grand strategy of the Bloc's ruling council.

A new day was dawning, and with it a new era for the world.

The Pax Asiatica would shortly replace the failing Pax Americana and the world would fall in line, or just fall.

It was written in the stars.

Chapter Seven

USS Miami SSN 898

They'd been underway for the better part of the day, Iwo was nearly another day out. Normally, they'd make the island in just a few more hours, but the fleet was being held back by some of the ships they'd taken in after the withdrawal and it was showing.

Morgan had taken the watch, and the Captain was sleeping off two back-to-back watches of his own. The life of a submariner was even more boredom and tension-filled than most members of the military, but for Morgan, there had always been a sense of quiet relaxation in the slow rush he could feel more than hear of the water over the hull of the Houston Class Fast Attack Sub.

He quietly walked across to the SONAR station, nodding in greeting to the sailor sitting watch.

"Sir," Lieutenant Mitchel said.

"Lieutenant," Morgan returned. "Anything interesting?"

"A few biologicals moving around, a pod of whales hunting giant squid about a klick out to the west," Mitchel said. "No signs of enemy submersibles, though, and while I can occasionally pick up heavy blades in the water, I don't think they're close. Echoes, maybe hundreds of miles out."

"Good," Morgan said, patting the lieutenant's shoulder. "Let me know if anything changes."

"Yes Sir."

The Miami continued on through the dark sea, carving through the water ahead of the task group.

*****

EBAN HuangLung

"They are approaching, Admiral."

"Good," Chien said softly, though the hull of the HuangLung was well insulated against sound. "Ensure all systems are silent. Where are their submarines?"

"One is leading, the other is in the rear, Sir."

"Only the two?"

"Yes, Admiral."

Chien nodded thoughtfully, considering that. The Americans did not publish the movements of their submarines, of course, but Bloc Intelligence had pegged several more being dispatched to the Pacific and South China Sea Theaters in recent days. However, there were many places the others could be. In fact, he would have been surprised if at least one or two were not circling quietly around Taiwan.

Two with this group was within what he had expected, though the paranoia that served him in his career thus far told him that when he saw what he expected, he was seeing what his enemy wanted him to see.

Hesitation would avail him nothing, however.

If there are others, we will deal with them as they come, Chien decided.

"Put the location of all current contacts on the screens," He ordered. "I wish to see our foes."

"Yes, Admiral."

The large screens flickered to life, showing an interpretation of their SONAR readings.

The American strike group was moving slowly by their standards, a little under thirty knots. He assumed that some of the ships they'd picked up from Japan were to blame, but it mattered little. The HuangLung was more than capable of running circles around even the fastest of the American vessels above.

As they ruled the skies, so too would the Americans soon learn that the Eastern Bloc Alliance also ruled the seas.

The submarine in the lead was one of the newer American Fast Attack ships from what he could tell. He couldn't be bothered remembering the name of the class, but their specifications came quickly to his mind.

"Allow the lead submarine to pass over us," He ordered. "I wish the Enterprise in our range before we reveal ourselves."

"Yes, Admiral."

Chien wondered what it would have been like, not that long ago, to be in a submerged position such as they held. Could they hear the screws of the enemy vessels pass overhead? He liked to think so, imagining the romantic notions of the old films. Men dueling with ships as they once had with swords or pistols.

Such days are dead, more is the pity.

They couldn't hear the screws of the American ship as it passed overhead, but the HuangLung's SONAR had no such issues.

The submarine moved on past, and the rest of the strike group approached right as planned.

Excellent.

"Stand ready," He ordered.

*****

USS Enterprise

Bonet was tired. He'd been up far too long and he knew it, but there always seemed to be something else that needed doing. His crews were in the same shape, and he knew that too. They'd had to do repairs while under sail, not so much for the E, but certainly for many of her escorts that had taken damage in the withdrawal.

That was only part of the story, however. He had taken time for rest, but sleep wouldn't come. No matter what he did, Bonet inevitably found himself walking the halls of the big carrier, finding himself right back where he was. On his bridge.

He didn't bother the officers on duty, leaving them to their tasks, but quietly he logged into the computers and got their systems echoed to him so he could keep an eye on things. It was an old habit, one that some might argue to be a bad one, but it had saved his life a time or two in the past, so he wasn't going to question the urge.

There wasn't much of anything out there to see, though, so he just let the sound and feel of the sea lull him into a quiet near-sleep.

Until he heard an officer mumble from across the deck.

"That doesn't look right."

Bonet's eyes snapped open and he turned to look at the source of the voice, ears perking up.

There were few phrases guaranteed to get his attention faster than a confused voice saying something like that. Quietly, Bonet accessed the officers' instrument cluster on his repeater so he could see what the young man was looking at.

It was the MAD, or Magnetic Anomaly Detection, system and Bonet could see instantly what had drawn the attention. There was a bulge in the local magnetic field, one that could be the result of natural fluctuations, but he wasn't going to leave that to chance at the moment.

Bonet climbed to his feet.

"General Quarters, if you please," He ordered. "Fleet wide."

Alarms began wailing, boots pounding the deck and men rousing themselves as everyone got ready for... whatever.

Bonet walked over to the MAD system, nodding over the young officer's shoulder, "Refine it if you can. We need a location."

"Aye, Aye, Admiral."

The MAD detection was sensitive to submarine threats, but it could be a little overly so, which made it difficult to pin things down to a specific area.

"SONAR, if there's something out there, find it." Bonet ordered. "But give our subs a heads-up first."

"Aye, Aye!"

He looked out over the deck of the carrier that was buzzing just meters from the command deck on the Island, men working furiously to prepare for something no one was certain was actually there. There had been a time, long ago, when he had done those jobs, hating every single time it turned out to be nothing.

Now, he was praying it was just some natural fluctuation.

Funny how things change.

*****

USS Miami

"ELF contact, Commander, from the Enterprise."

"I've got it," Morgan said, walking over to the Extremely Low Frequency transceiver.

The message was short and to the point, and just enough to set a fire under his ass.

"Sound general quarters," He ordered, "And standby to go full active on SONAR."

"Aye, Commander. General quarters!"

He grabbed a crewman, nodding to the young man, "Go wake up the Skipper."

"Yes sir."

Morgan took up position in the center of the boat's command center, eyes on the activity around him. He didn't know how they could have missed anything, they were on full alert, but the Admiral wanted the entire region examined down to the molecular level if that was possible, and what the Admiral wanted, the Admiral got.

"Commander, I've got heavy SONAR picking up behind us."

"Come about, hard to port! SONAR, go full active!"

"Aye Commander, full active!"

Morgan reached up a hand to keep himself steady as the boat tilted a little under the power of the turn. If there was anything out there, they were about to stir up all hells' worth of it.

*****

EBAN HuangLung

"Heavy activity, Admiral. They are looking for us."

"So, I see," Chien nodded.

He wondered idly what had tipped the Americans off, though he expected it was likely the magnetic presence of the HuangLung. That was particularly difficult to mask, though they had managed to lower the signal it presented considerably.

The American ships were scanning the sea heavily with their SONAR, but he expected that they had a little time before any positive detection was made. The HuangLong's hull was coated with sound-absorbing material, rendering it not quite invisible to the likes of SONAR, but certainly a much smaller profile than it should present.

"Prepare to surface," He ordered. "Are the weapons ready?"

"Yes, Admiral. Firing solutions have been calculated, we await only the order to launch."

Chien nodded casually, rising from his seat to walk to the middle of the deck where he could observe every station as well as the main displays for all primary systems.

"Consider the order given. Launch."

Slowly rising through the deeps, the HuangLung's torpedo and missile tubes flooded and the doors opened.

*****

USS Miami

"Someone just flooded their tubes, Commander!"

Morgan snapped around. "Localize that sound! Find them! Now!"

"Tube doors open!"

"Flood our tubes, open the doors!"

"Tubes flooding, Aye!"

The Captain strode onto the deck, bouncing off one wall as the boat tilted into their turn.

"Sitrep," He ordered.

"Orders from the E, Sir, look for target in the water," Morgan said in clipped tones. "Shortly after beginning the sweep, we picked up the sound of someone flooding their tubes and opening torpedo or missile hatches. We flooded and opened ours in response."

Burke nodded, "Got it. Do we have a target?"

"Not yet, Skipper."

"Keep looking."

"Aye, Aye, skipper…"

The Miami was coming around hard, forward SONAR array sweeping the water intently as they looked for their target.

"Fish in the water! We have cavitating contacts, moving fast! Calculating course..." The SONAR man paused, then turned with wide eyes, "They're heading for the Enterprise, Skipper!"

*****

USS Enterprise

"Torpedoes in the water! Signal collision alert!"

The Enterprise went to full power, turning hard to starboard as the tracks for the torpedoes were plotted. The massive ship leaned over, sending anything loose skittering across the deck as men hung to whatever they could while they made sure that everything possible was secured.

The deck shuddered under his feet and Bonet held on to the console in front of him, eyes on the SONAR. The torpedoes were still deep, but they were coming up fast and loud.

Too fast.

And it was still accelerating. Well past the seventy to eighty knots a standard ADCAP Mark Eight would top out at.

It's super cavitating.

The Enterprise had no chance of dodging.

Depth charges were deployed, anti-torpedo torpedoes lanced into the water from the Enterprise and its destroyer screen. The water was filled with cavitating props, churning the sea into a white-blue mess.

The first explosions went off, plumes of water leaping high from the surface as the Lake Champlain interposed itself between the contacts and the Enterprise, still firing everything it had.

It was a good effort, and he appreciated it, but Bonet knew that the contacts were still too deep in the water. They sped along under the keel of the Destroyer, entering terminal guidance as they locked onto the Enterprise.

Three torpedoes survived the massed fire arrayed against them, slamming into the side of the Carrier and sending shockwaves, flames, and smoke erupting everywhere.

"Affected sections are sealing off, we've got teams pulling men from the damaged compartments as fast as they can, but water is rushing in."

Bonet nodded. "Leave that to the DCS teams, they know their job. Just find that son of a bitch."

"Aye Admiral."

The Enterprise was one of the last Gerald Ford class carriers ever built. She could take a few torpedoes without significantly losing fighting capacity. What they couldn't take was an unknown enemy striking at them from so close without being detected.

*****

EBAN HuangLung

Admiral Chien was moderately impressed with the American defenses, if he were to say so himself. They'd absolutely saturated the sea with their defensive fire, destroying the majority of his first salvo before they could reach the target.

That would not save them, however, as even then the HuangLung was firing the second of many more to come.

"Admiral, one of the American fast attack submarines is coming around, they're seeking us."

Chien glanced at the screens, acknowledging the report.

"I see them. They are no threat, as of yet. Continue to monitor, but I want the Carrier first. This is a message we are sending," He said. "The rest we can pick off at our leisure."

"Yes, Admiral."

He had confidence in the HuanLong's acoustic absorbing hull to keep them hidden for a while longer. Long enough to finish the primary job, at the very least.

*****

USS Lake Champlain

"Fish in the water! Hot and fast, bearing on the E, Skipper!"

Captain Jerimiah Horner scowled but didn't say anything. He could see them.

"Keep us interposed between the E and those fish," He ordered the helm, despite knowing it wasn't going to do much good. The torpedoes were too deep, and wouldn't go terminal until they had a direct line on the Flagship. The bow thrusters whirred, keeping the ship in position as the sound of anti-submarine weapons firing filled the air and sent vibrations through the dock.

"And someone FIND ME that damned submerged contact!"

The Destroyer's SONAR was in definitive seek and destroy mode, and the beats of chopper blades announced the lift-off of her Anti-Submarine Warfare assets.

Other ships were in motion as well, the sky now filled with choppers that were dropping sonobuoys as the entire group sought out the sub that was attacking the Enterprise.

Concussion blasts from their torpedoes took out a pair of the attacking fish, another being jarred off course by the blast but still in motion. Captain and crew watched helplessly as another two slipped the net and hammered into the side of the Carrier they were trying to protect.

*****

Chapter Eight

Alamagordo New Mexico

Eric dropped from the cockpit of the Tutor Jet. The model he had was a two-seat trainer he'd purchased from Canada when he had a contract for training pilots in jet aircraft. Stephen had hopped out practically as soon as the aircraft had stopped and was hopping around like he'd just consumed a metric crap-ton of some illicit substance.

Eric held back the smile. He remembered that feeling.

"You did well," He announced. "Some mistakes we'll need to work on, but they're expected things. Not bad kid."

"I can come back?" Stephen asked, practically vibrating as he asked the question.

Eric chuckled softly, rolling his eyes. "Tell you what, you want to hang around, sure. But you're going to work…"

"Deal! I'll do anything!"

Eric held up a hand. "Wait for it, kid. First lesson. Don't *ever* volunteer. Trust me on this."

"He ain't bullshitting you kid."

Eric turned at the sound of the voice coming up behind him, surprised to see a pair of people in dark suits approaching. One of them he recognized, however, and he winced ruefully.

"Dear God in heaven," Eric said. "What sin could I possibly have committed to bring you to my door?"

"Well hello to you too, Eric, or should I have said 'Chaser'?" The other man asked, smiling wide with a full mouth of gleaming white teeth.

Eric rolled his eyes, "I'd say it's good to see you, Murph, but…"

"Yeah, yeah," Maximillian 'Max' Murphy gestured idly. "Sorry about that by the way. You were a handy distraction."

"Fuck you too," Eric said evenly, his expression neutral for a moment before a grin broke out.

The pair laughed, clasping hands briefly before they separated.

"What brings you to my humble abode, Max?" Eric asked, glancing at the other person beside his old friend.

"First, this is Sue Biggs," Max told him, "She's with No Such Agency."

"Not a lawyer, is she?"

'Sue' grimaced. "Get it out of your system, I've heard them all before, but no. I'm with the research division, usually attached to DARPA."

Eric lost his smile, nodding absently. "You're faster than I expected. Came to the same conclusion we did, I'm figuring."

"Haven't come to any conclusions yet," Sue corrected. "But your project turned up on a targeted search we ran through our database. I'm here to evaluate."

Eric nodded, turning to Stephen, "Get the plane post-flight checked and put away. After that you may as well go home, won't be anything for you to do here today. I'll see you tomorrow."

Stephen looked like he wanted to object, but a glance at the pair he didn't know was enough for him to nod silently and walk away.

Max watched him go, waiting until he was out of sight before speaking, "Smart kid."

"He's not bad," Eric said before gesturing to the main hangar, "Come on, it's in here."

*****

"Doesn't look like much."

Bradley looked up, irritated by the presence of a voice he didn't recognize, but any objections were cut off when he saw Eric escorting them.

"Neither does a nuke if you don't know what you're looking at, Max," Eric said, patting the device. "We've confirmed that it *does* have an effect, the issue we're having is controlling it. We've been trying to get it to lift even its own weight, but we just can't seem to cross that last line in the sand."

"But it does reduce its weight?" The woman asked.

"Effectively, sure." Eric nodded over to Bradley. "Power her up."

Brad raised an eyebrow but nodded and hit the lever to close the mains. The system began to humm immediately, a feeling like ants crawling along his skin passing through him and the others almost as quick. Eric ignored it and walked up, grasping the device by protruding handles and lifting it off the table with relative ease.

After he set it back down, Brad killed the power and Eric gestured to it.

"Have a try if you want."

The man did, straining to pop a blood vessel for a brief moment before giving it up.

"Ok, I'm convinced," Biggs said. "What do you need?"

Eric blinked, "What?"

"This is the most likely project we've found that can explain the Bloc fighters," She said calmly. "What do you need to make it work? Or at least figure out what the hell we're up against and how to fight it?"

It didn't take long for Eric to compose an answer to that.

"Other than more help? Physicists, Engineers, and the like?" He asked rhetorically, "Airframes."

That caught her aback, and Biggs went from nodding along agreeably to looking confused.

"What?"

"Airframes," Eric said again. "We need airframes to test on. We managed to destroy our last one, an F-16 we bought out of a junkyard a couple years ago. Twisted the frame all the hell, it probably had weak points we missed when looking over it."

"We can do that," Max said. "Anything you'd prefer?"

Eric shook his head. "No. We don't have time to design something bespoke to the system, so it doesn't matter. Just solid airframes that aren't pitted and twisted from decades in a junkyard."

"Done. We'll also get some experts down here to help," Sue said before she paused, then looked at him evenly. "You do know that this project just became a matter of national security, of course?"

"Bradley and I both still hold our clearances," Eric said.

"What about the kid?" Max asked.

Bradley blinked, "The kid? Michaels? What about him?"

"I'll talk to him," Eric said. "But he's with us."

"He is? Since when?" Bradley was lost at sea.

"Since today," Eric said firmly. "I told him he could work for us, and I'm going to hold to it."

Sue started to say something, but Max held up a hand to stop her.

"Don't bother, I've seen him like this," He said. "You're not going to budge him."

He looked back to Eric, "We'll run checks on the kid. He clears, we can talk, he doesn't... then he's gone."

Eric nodded slowly, "Fair."

"Alright, good luck with that thing," Max said. "We'll be back."

Eric and Bradley watched the pair leave until they were out of the hangar. Only then did Bradley turn to Eric, looking peeved.

"Since when is the kid with us?"

"Since today, checked him out on the Tutor," Eric said, "He's good, really good. I've not seen better in a long damn time, just don't tell him that. He'll work out as a gopher while he's training up."

Bradley sighed, "Oh save me from your damn complex."

Eric just laughed at him for a moment before looking back over the device.

"Alright, we've got work to do if we're going to get prepped. I had an idea," He said. "I think I know what we have here, and it's not anti-gravity."

"You sure? We crunched those numbers, had specialists double-check even..." Bradley looked uncertain.

"Sure? No, but I've got an idea, and we'll get more specialists now," Eric said, "I suspect that we're about to be swarmed by them."

Bradley looked out of the large hangar door, where the pair of government types had vanished.

"Yeah, I think you're right about that. Hey," He said. "You think we might be able to get a direct feed on the fighting?"

"To see the enemy fighters in action? Probably," Eric said.

"Nah, I just want to know how bad it really is."

*****

"Really?" Sue asked as they drove. "You want to run a security check on a kid?"

Maximillian chuckled, "You've never worked with Eric, Sue. Trust me, it's easier to just bend the rules a little than fight that stone wall. We could probably win. Eric knows how important this could be, but if we bend on this first it'll earn us points with the man, and we might need those later."

"Weston's a pilot," Sue said, exasperated, "We don't need him. We could pull his research tonight."

"Yeah, but then we'd lose Eric's experience, and his partner," Max said. "Didn't you read their files?"

"Of course, I did," She rolled her eyes. "What about it?"

"Eric is a man who doesn't bend easily, and never breaks," Max said. "And he's not just a pilot. He got out of the Marines and got a degree in aviation engineering, then went on to study in Beijing at their top universities."

"I know, I read the files," She said. "So?"

"So, he wasn't actually studying… or, I should say, he wasn't *only* studying. It's not in the file, probably classified all to hell, I haven't checked," Max said. "But I was his handler during those years."

She snapped her head over to look at him, "*HIM*? He was an agent?"

"No, but your reaction is exactly why he was so damn good," Max chuckled. "No one who's ever met him believes Eric could be anything but blunt and right in your face. I was the agent. He was my asset. Between us, we pulled a *lot* of data out of Beijing before the wall came down… including the gizmo on the bench in there, well the plans anyway."

"How did *that* slip through the cracks?"

Max shrugged as he drove. "Honestly no clue. In the files, it's listed as a failed project, a Bloc boondoggle, just a money sink that they should be encouraged to piss their budget off on. I guess Eric saw something different."

"I'm thinking we should look into how that file got classified that way," Sue said darkly. "His qualifications aside, if he saw the potential and managed to convince even a few other people to follow him along on that path, someone in government should have seen it too."

"Maybe someone did," Max said, sighing. "We didn't exactly have a monopoly on agents, Sue. Plenty of Bloc Counter Intel people are still in the country, and we don't know where all of them are."

"You think someone misfiled the project?"

He nodded seriously, "Yup. And that will be my job in the coming weeks, seeing if I can find out who pulled it off. Might be able to flip him or her, might not, but we can't leave someone like that embedded as deep as they'd have to be… maybe deeper now."

"So I get to bootstrap a project we might need to save this country, and you're going spy hunting?"

"Refreshing, ain't it?"

"Smartass."

*****

Washington, DC

White House

This is an unadulterated nightmare.

Benjamin Givens, President of the United States, found himself looking over the books with something he identified as a feeling of near despair. The only thing keeping that at bay, frankly, was the downright furious rage that had been keeping him going since the attack on Japan and Taiwan had been announced.

The Bloc forces had swept their targets, redrawing the map in the East in a single day.

He still had two fleets out there in hostile territory, being picked away by dribbles and dabs, which was almost a relief considering how quickly US forces had been pushed out of Japan and how ineffective the attempt to provide support to Taiwan was.

It's a damned **relief** *to only be losing a few fighters every few hours, or a ship here and there. Goddamn it, what the hell has become of me?*

He knew that they needed to get a handle on things shortly, or the US would lose the Far East and, it appeared, the Middle East entirely within days.

While there were many who would consider that to be far from a negative thing, Givens was not among them. Most isolationists didn't realize just how much of the American economy was tied up in foreign military bases and the 'gifts' the American people gave in the form of foreign aid.

All of that investment in other countries was no gift, however it was presented in official documents. It was an investment in America's economic trade. The bases ensured that no matter what job someone had, if they gave it to an American company, anywhere in the world, it got done.

Over the last few decades, the Chinese had been building their own version of that trade empire. They had begun in Africa, then extended their influence into South and Central America where they still had great sway in Nicaragua. They made similar moves into Europe and Australia, but had mostly been rebuffed there, a process that would almost certainly be completed after this move, but he doubted the Bloc now cared.

Going to have to do something about Nicaragua, though. The Bloc control over the Nicaragua Canal there has been a pain in our ass for too long, and they've been underbidding Panama for so long that I'm not even sure they don't own that as well now.

He closed the books in front of him tiredly and checked the time.

Givens winced.

He'd been up for two days, unable to sleep, and still had too much work to do to even think about a nap.

It was going to be a long week.

Hell, who am I kidding? If I get any sleep for the next couple years, I'd bet good money on it being only from exhaustion.

*****

Across the nation, it was only beginning to properly sink in that they were effectively at war with the largest military force in the world, and despite the feeling of confidence that had largely existed within the nation, it seemed like they were losing.

Reports from Japan were growing grimmer and grimmer as the fighting dug in and turned into a mile by mile of hill-to-hill combat in the country, while the cities were under the martial law of the Bloc military.

Taiwan was even worse, with thousands reported dead in the initial bombing, and a brutal occupation apparently in its opening hours.

The Bloc forces in the region were predominantly Chinese, and they had deep national grudges with both countries that were now set loose.

The harder the fighting got, the worse the reports seemed to become. But despite all attempts by the Bloc forces, it seemed that it was impossible to stop those same reports from filtering out. Ground to satellite internet connections were unblockable and with the transceivers already in place being linked to companies who weren't headquartered in Bloc countries, there was no way to stop the signal.

The world watched, getting an entirely unfiltered view of unrestricted warfare for the first time in, possibly history.

Slowly, dawning horror was giving way to another emotion.

*****

Chapter Eight

USS Enterprise

Admiral Bonet gritted his teeth as the SONAR system warned them of another fan of torpedoes in the water.

The warning had come in conjunction, this time, with AEGIS systems picking up another sortie against them from the air. He had destroyers already in motion, preparing to cover the group with their anti-missile lasers, but that left them out of position to protect the Enterprise from the torpedoes.

Exactly as intended, no doubt.

Thus far the damage to the big ship had been relatively small. A ship their size could take a hell of a lot of damage, but it was still enough to be noticed. The Enterprise was limping slightly, one screw damaged by a hit to the aft, and the drag by damaged compartments causing her to favor her port side.

With another salvo in the water, the collision alarms went up again, a familiar sound to everyone on board but the enemy had a new twist for them this time.

"Birds in the air, coming hot!"

"Get the destroyers on it," He ordered. "Shoot them down."

"Not from the air assault, Skipper, from the other side. We're wide open!"

Bonet swore, lunging over to check the readings himself. Sure enough, the young officer had been right. They had cruise missiles approaching fast, low on the deck, from a section of the water with no sign of contacts.

Submarine-launched, no doubt.

"We'll have to handle it ourselves," He said. "Point defense up. Take those out of my sky."

"Aye, sir!"

*****

The Point defensive armaments of the Enterprise were composed of short-range surface to air rockets, SeaWiz RADAR guided rotary cannons, and anti-air laser emplacements. All of them were already in motion on automatic when the Admiral ordered them into play and the safeties came off.

The lasers fired first, tracking inbound missiles and hitting them with megawatts of heat, turning four into falling pillars of flame in just moments. Rockets roared from their tubes next, lancing out in a blink of the eye and exploding ahead of several more, detonating them early.

Finally, the SEA Wiz systems spun into action, throwing up a final wall of steel for the missiles to cross before they could touch their target. This system was only effective at *very* close ranges, and men were screaming and running for cover by the time the first SEA Wiz rotary cannon opened fire.

Three more were intercepted just short of the Enterprise, waves of fire from their warheads washing close enough that men on the open deck felt the heat change in the air.

That still left two more to slam into the big ship, exploding as they tore up the flight deck and carved gaping holes in the steel hull above the waterline this time.

*****

JS Haguru

"Captain! More cruise missile launches detected!"

Shimoda Urusa nodded grimly at that but was otherwise unmoved. He had ordered his Maya class destroyer, the Haguru, to break formation and come around after the launch of the first wave of such missiles.

"Track their launch point," He ordered. "And plot the approach."

"Yes, Captain!"

Urusa already knew where they were going, of course. The Enterprise was the target the enemy wanted, a feather in their cap worth risking a lot even if only for the bragging rights. Anyone who took out an American Carrier would be infamous, for good or ill, as he wasn't certain when the last time that happened was.

Likely in World War Two, by a Japanese attack, He thought with some irony given what he was about to commit his vessel to.

"Interpose us between the missiles and the Enterprise," He ordered. "But find me that launch point!"

His crew didn't hesitate. The Haguru was already in motion before he finished his second order, the bow thrusters bringing them around to show broadsides to the attack. Their laser defense system was already firing, burning missiles out of the air, but that wasn't his focus.

"Launch point, Captain! On your console!"

Yes! Urusa bared his teeth, checking the math quickly, then nodded and shot it over to missile control. "I want torpedoes in the water at this point, no safety fuse."

They looked at him sharply at that, but no one questioned the order, and in moments the Type 09 Anti-Submarine rockets exploded from the vertical launch bays, arcing away from the ship as the survive cruise missiles from the second wave screamed past overhead and around the Haguru.

More exploded as the Enterprise took over with their point defense, but even as he watched another three slammed into the Carrier, sending fire washing across the decks.

*****

USS Miami

Morgan and Burke were leaning over the SONAR station, eyes on the data as they tried to determine just where their target was.

They'd had whispers of a submerged contact a few times, but it was nebulous, obviously using some sort of sound dampening and one of the new Bloc nuclear piles that could be powered down to allow the entire boat to run on batteries, which brought it to new levels of silence.

A series of rushing sounds could be heard, causing the SONAR officer to quietly speak up.

"Missile launches, from one of the JSDF ships I think."

Neither Morgan nor Burke could hope to tell that with any accuracy, but they weren't going to second guess the expert either.

It only took a moment longer before he nodded, "Anti-submarine rockets, their Type 09s I expect. They just landed."

"Where?" Burke asked, leaning in closer.

The SONAR operator checked, double-checked, and only then read off the coordinates as Burke and Morgan straightened up.

"New course!" Burke called. "Come about to heading Two One Eight, even bubble! All ahead Flank."

The Miami slowly heeled over as it came around sharply to the new course, screws spinning up to full power as the boat surged forward through the waters of the Pacific.

*****

EBAN HuangLong

"Admiral, we have contact change. The American submarine is turning this direction."

Chien grimaced, irritated by the news. They were already dealing with the active torpedoes in the water above them, and hardly needed yet another distraction from the task at hand.

"Power levels?" He asked.

"Battery cells register Sixty-eight percent, Admiral."

"More than sufficient," He decided, "Ahead one third, do not cavitate."

The order given and put into action, the HuangLong set into motion.

The big submersible, one of the biggest ever built, in fact, did not accelerate quickly even under full power, but it did move and with purpose.

The passive SONAR was monitoring the actions of the torpedoes above them while Admiral Chien examined the deployment of the surface vessels through the satellite relay link they had through a shallow towed array.

The Americans and Japanese were defending well, but that had been expected. Taking down an American carrier was not a feat that could be accomplished in a single salvo, no matter how powerful your weapons. It would be the death of a thousand cuts to make it happen, but Chien was confident in the combined armed approach the Bloc forces had fielded.

With their carefully guarded ace cards, they had negated the American's traditional strengths, forcing them to fight under hostile skies and deal with threats from the sea that could not be easily overcome.

He was enjoying the turning of the tables, deeply so in fact.

"Tubes are loaded for the next salvo, Admiral."

"Very well, slow to firing speeds and launch."

*****

USS Miami

The young officer at the SONAR station, Lieutenant Mitchel, stiffened suddenly and sat straight up from his previously hunched position.

"Skipper!"

Burke immediately walked over, "What is it, Lieutenant?"

"Contact in the water, it's shallow... I think it's missile pods rising through the thermocline, Sir."

Burke grunted, "They're deeper than we expected then. Good catch, Lieutenant."

The Captain of the Miami turned to the Helm, "Make our heading... two degrees port, one degree down bubble."

"Aye Skipper! Two degrees to port, one degree down bubble!"

The deck of the fast attack submarine shifted so that Burke reached out to catch the corner of a console to steady himself as the whole boat dipped its nose and they began their descent.

The ocean thermocline in this part of the ocean was resting around a hundred and twenty meters and was probably a dozen meters or so wide, an area of the ocean where the temperature changed rapidly from one layer to the next.

That change in temperature meant that the transmission of sound through the thermocline was markedly different than the layer above. If the enemy submarine was below the thermocline, that could explain why they'd evaded contact with the Miami and Surface vessels, however the two boats on bottom duty should have spotted them, Burke expected, so there was more to the story than just that.

"Coming up on the thermocline," Mitchel said, "Entering it… now. We'll be through in seconds, Skipper."

"Ears open, Lieutenant," Burke ordered. "Find me that bastard."

"Aye, aye, Skipper."

*****

Crossing the thermocline, the USS Miami leveled out to zero bubble with everyone onboard practically holding their breath as the forward SONAR array listened for *anything* out of the ordinary ahead of their course. The forward array, listening passively, could detect impressively small sounds from dozens or even hundreds of miles, but it did have its limits.

One such limit was that sound had to exist, either sourcing from or bouncing off a target.

In the deep of the Pacific, natural noises normally were prevalent and anything mechanical would stand out by contrast alone. At the moment, however, there were a *lot* of unnatural sounds flooding the sea from above, making it a mess for the system to differentiate anything of value.

At the SONAR station of the Miami, Mitchel listened intently as the sub pushed forward through the cold water of the deep sea, adjusting different levels, and playing back anything that seemed off, but through all that he could find nothing.

"I don't know, Sir. It's out there, I know it is, but I can't find it," He said, frustrated.

"Understood, Lieutenant," Burke said with a measured tone. "Why don't we give you a hand? Standby to go full active."

Mitchel twisted, surprised by that order. "Sir, they'll know right where we are."

"Who says they don't already?" Burke asked absently. "They're focused on the Enterprise. Let's give them something else to worry about."

The Lieutenant nodded nervously, turning back, "Aye, aye skipper, ready to go full active on your command."

"Seek and destroy, Lieutenant."

"Yes sir."

*****

EBAN HuangLung

The sudden sharp tone of a ping echoed through the sound-insulated command deck, broadcast from the ship's SONAR station after being picked up from the external arrays.

"Report," Chien ordered curtly.

"The American submarine has descended and is looking for us directly," His SONAR officer said warily. "That was a very tightly aimed tone, Sir."

"Did they detect us?" Chien asked intently.

"Uncertain," The SONAR officer responded. "We've calculated the return signal and it will be close to their detection threshold... according to our Intelligence, I believe we are safe. They are closing, however, Admiral."

Chien nodded, "Very well. Helm. Stand by the come about. Course bearing..."

*****

USS Miami

Mitchel frowned, cocking his head to one side.

"What is it, Lieutenant?" Burke asked softly, eyes on the instrument panels.

"I'm... not sure," Mitchel said slowly. "There's something out there, though, that I'm sure of."

"Range?"

"No way to know, sir. The return was too faint, distorted. Like..." Mitchel nodded slowly. "Like they're using baffles. Sir, that means they're closer than they seem."

"What's your best guess, Lieutenant?"

"Two-thirds of a mile, Sir. No more."

Burke nearly swore. They were right on top of the contact then, far closer than he wanted to be with an unknown and *highly* stealthy contact. He leaned over, "Morgan, are our tubes still flooded?"

"Yes sir, doors open too."

"Lieutenant, send bearing to contact to Weps."

"Aye Skipper."

"Weps," Burke said softly, "give me a spread along that bearing. Shoot from the hip."

"Aye, aye, skipper," The weapons control officer said, putting the code into the system. "One shot from the hip coming right up."

"Fire when ready."

*****

EBAN HuangLung

"Torpedoes in the water!"

Chien hissed, frustrated by the fact that the enemy had, indeed, apparently detected them. *Should have known better than to trust Intelligence to get it right.*

"Are they tracking?" He asked.

"Uncertain, Admiral. They are coming this direction…" The SONAR officer frowned.

"What's uncertain then?"

"I… I don't know."

"Then they're tracking," Chien decided, irritated. "Adjust course and dive, prepare to withdraw from the combat zone temporarily."

"Yes, Admiral!"

The HuanLung turned languidly in the cold waters of the pacific, screws slowly turning up to speed as the big vessel dipped its nose and went deeper as above them the torpedoes passed by without incident.

*****

USS Miami

"I didn't hear any earth-shattering kaboom, Weps," Burke said dryly as the ADCAPs whirred out into the depths.

"Sorry Sir," The weapons control officer said softly.

"It's alright," Burke patted him on the shoulder. "It was a long shot anyway."

The Captain of the boat walked back to the rear of the command deck, stepping up beside his XO.

"Do you think there was anything out there when we fired?" He asked softly, keeping his voice low.

Morgan considered it for a moment before he nodded, "We both saw the return. It was faint, but it was there."

"Not there now," Burke said tiredly.

"Nope."

Burke nodded slowly, "Best get to looking then."

"Yup."

*****

Chapter Nine

USS Enterprise

Admiral Bonet watched the repair work as the men feverishly went about setting the ship to rights as much as they could outside of a drydock. It was grim work, especially under the threat of continued attack at any time.

The enemy submersible had withdrawn from action some hours ago or at least gone quiet as there had been no further attacks. The enemy airstrikes had also abated, but he doubted very much that they were done with his little task group just yet.

The Enterprise and other vessels were still only a few hundred miles from the coast of Japan, and well within Japanese territorial waters. Since the Bloc seemed determined to claim that entire region as their own, he expected that the attacks would resume as soon as the surface group caught up to the submerged threat.

It was what he would do, at least.

The Enterprise was now running lame, and it wasn't the only ship in the group that had limited speed in the open ocean. They were days from any friendly port, weeks from home, and the closest land of note was Iwo Jima, which was little more than a tourist spot though there would be some supplies they could scavenge there if needs must.

Orders from PACCOM were simple, in theory. Get his ships back to Pearl by the most direct route possible. No reinforcements were forthcoming. The only other fleet in the area had been in the South China Sea and they weren't doing any better than he was.

The Dory was leading its little group South, hoping to lose the enemy in the islands of the Philippines before making a run for friendly shores in Australia, primarily because they didn't want to risk a transit East through the shark tank the Enterprise was sailing through, and because West lay the Middle East and Africa, both of which had powerful Bloc presence deeply entrenched.

This war could have been avoided. So many bad decisions built a foundation for it that I suspect hundreds of historians will make their life's work of mapping them all out.

That was for others to worry about, however. His job was the here and now.

*****

EBAN HuangLung

The big vessel was rocking gently in the surface waves as Admiral Chien stood out on the open deck, thinking about the previous engagement.

He had perhaps been too cautious, but that was the side he would prefer to err on at the moment. There was time to deal with Americans, and he had the forces to make certain that it was the message he and the Bloc leadership wanted to be sent to the US.

These waters belonged to the Eastern Bloc, and the peoples therein would no longer tolerate foreign interference from those who had only their own interests in mind.

Chien had little real hatred for Westerners or even Americans in particular. They tended to be brash and brazen, but they were a young people, with only centuries of culture behind them. Thousands of years of cultural learning and development made a difference, of course.

What he did hate was their incessant interference in matters that were none of their business.

Flagging the emotions of the rebellious province, making them think they were not a part of China, that would only bring generations of pain to the people of the Island. There was no reason for that, no point in it. Just American arrogance and divisive obstinance.

Fools that cannot even unite themselves, and they think they can bring freedom to the world? Arrogance.

He and the HuangLung were waiting for the rest of the fleet. It was a wait that was almost over. Once the last of the ships were with them, they would end this as it needed to be ended and send a message once and for all.

Chien smiled thinly.

The leadership Council were driving themselves quite mad, trying to shut down the satellite internet services that were broadcasting to western devices within the captured territory. They had spent a decade hunting down any within the mainland territories, as those devices were not only nearly impervious means of sending intelligence out, but also feeds for propaganda.

They were right, of course, to remove them in the long term.

In the short term, however, Chien felt that they were missing the true value of the devices.

Let them broadcast our victories. Let the world see our power. A hundred years ago, an emergent Superpower rewrote the world... now, it is our turn.

*****

USS Enterprise

"That's them, Sir."

Bonet quickly looked over the display, nodding his understanding. The task group they were looking at was not something to be underestimated. He'd love dearly to know where the Chinese or Bloc had amassed that kind of sea power, but for the moment it was a problem to be dealt with rather than a mystery to be solved.

"This, I assume is our mystery sub?" He asked, pointing to a semi-submerged contact resting in the center of the group.

"We believe so, Sir, yes."

"That's a big mother," Bonet grumbled.

"Three hundred meters, bow to stern, almost the size of the Enterprise itself, sir."

"Damn."

That was a *big* sub. Hell, it was a big *SHIP* of any type. For a Submarine, that was insanity.

It brought to mind a serious question, however. If that was indeed the sub they'd tangled with earlier, how the *hell* did they not detect it? Something that size should have had a significant return on SONAR. Instead, the first hint they'd encountered was something on the MAD gear, and even that was well below the threshold a boat like that should have put out.

The enemy aircraft isn't the only new thing they're bringing to the table. They've been prepping this for a long time.

"PACCOM is telling us that they expect the group to move to intercept within the hour, analysts have been monitoring transmissions from the area," his aide told him. "Fleet Commander is an Admiral by the name of Chien. He's got a file."

Bonet snorted.

"If a Bloc admiral doesn't have a file then our Intelligence failure has been far more complete than we'd best hope," He said unequivocally. "I'm not familiar with the name, at least not tied to an Admiralty rank. Anything of interest?"

"Mostly suppression assignments," his Aide said, "Putting down minor revolts within Bloc territory. A lot of brown water experience, but a lot less blue water time than you'd expect."

"The bloc has been holding back their navy for a long time," Bonet said grimly. "I think we now know why. They were waiting until they figured they could take us clean."

That was the key that most worried him, though he wouldn't say it alive. The Bloc Council, like the Chicom Party before them, were not the sort to make a move unless they felt they had the win in the bag. This open warfare was the culmination of *decades* of preparation at a minimum. That was how they thought, decades and even centuries into the future.

He honestly would not have been surprised if the foundation for the plan they were following had been laid down by Mao himself.

Playing the long game was an art that the West had lost a long time ago. The economic system the US championed had advantages, including a powerful multiplier in terms of technical development as corporations competed to push forward, but the focus on profit also brought built-in obsolescence and more worry about the next quarter rather than the next quarter-century.

He didn't know for certain that their calculations were right, but Bonet *was* certain that the Bloc trusted them.

"Thank you," He said aloud. "I'll have some time if you please."

"Aye, sir."

The aide left Bonet to his thoughts as he overlooked the repairs that were underway.

Ultimately, he had to believe that the Bloc had miscalculated, but he doubted it was a miscalculation that would play out quickly.

Bonet turned his focus back to the screen with the satellite imagery of the Bloc task group, noting that they were indeed maneuvering about and looked to be getting underway.

"You wanted this war," He said softly to the screen. "And so you'll have it. I may not live to see it, but I think you'll find you'll come to regret awakening the ire of this giant. We may not be long-term planners like you, but when it comes to fighting from behind? You don't have a chance."

*****

On two separate fleets, under two separate commands, very similar actions were being undertaken. The sea was a harsh mistress, such that she demanded respect and knowledge in similar effect no matter what ideology you claimed as your own.

Men cleared their ships, made certain they were ready to fight, going over weapons and drives even as the officers charted their courses and prepared the tactics for what was to come.

On the Bloc warships, there was a palpable eagerness. Men who had trained for this very moment, much of their young lives, and now saw it approaching could feel the moment of history being made about them.

For those in the American and Japanese vessels, the feeling was different. Several days of demoralizing defeat and withdrawal was now weighing on them. They could feel that the tide had shifted, and it was not in the favor.

Still, they were professionals to the person and none of them even considered shirking their duties. Oppressive atmosphere be damned - there was work to be done.

Two fleets, one inevitable collision, and the history of the world would never be the same again.

*****

EBAN HuangLung

"Admiral, we are ready to move out."

Chien nodded, determination welling within him. He had gone over all the data from the previous engagements and knew he could finish this now, deliver an unforgettable message to the Americans once and for all.

"Signal the fleet, to move out according to orders," He ordered. "and prepare to submerge the ship."

"Yes, Admiral!"

Alarms sounded about the HuangLung, men quickly heading for the hatches that would let them below decks. Chien himself took his time, casually making his way and even waving other men along ahead of him. He didn't mind the chill of the night air as it cooled, and it would not do for the men to think he was worried about being above deck.

It wasn't like the HuanLung was diving without him anyway.

Chien smiled at the idea, the very lunacy of it pleasing him.

Finally, he stepped into the hatch, walking down the spiraled staircase as the last man hit the command to seal the ship up.

The Yellow Dragon was on the hunt once more.

This time, she would have her prey.

*****

USS Enterprise

"That's it, Sir. Here they come."

Bonet nodded grimly, "That they do, Commander. How go the repairs?"

Command Hiller grimaced, "The port screw is, well, screwed sir. Pardon the language. We had to cut it loose, it was dragging that badly."

Bonet winced but nodded in understanding. "Without it?"

"Another three knots, Sir."

"Well good work on that."

He didn't like losing the screw, of course, but if it were dragging them back then it had to go. The Enterprise was going to need a drydock for repairs anyway, assuming they made it back with damages that were even considered repairable.

"Hull damage?"

"Better news there, we've got all the leaks sealed up below decks," Hiller answered. "A few holes still open to the air, but…"

Bonet nodded, waving him on. The priority went to damage below the waterline, of course, that was just the facts of the situation.

"Thank you, Commander," He said, "Good work."

"Sir."

The Commander saluted, stepping back as Bonet turned to his XO.

"How are we looking for munitions?"

"We've finished UNREP from the supply ships," He confirmed. "We're as ready as we're going to get, Sir."

"Alright. Let the men know, round two is about to kick off."

"Aye, aye, Sir."

*****

Chapter 10

Washington DC, Whitehouse War Room

President Givens sat at the table in the secure communications room, eyes on the screens that made up the entire far wall. Satellite surveillance of the Bloc task group in the Pacific was the focus of the moment, showing the task group gaining on the slower moving American and Japanese forces as they continued south out of Japanese waters.

"What do they hope to gain?" The SecDef asked, looking mystified. "Our forces are withdrawing. Why are they chasing them down?"

Givens shook his head, "They want a Carrier group under their belt, George. It's bragging rights. When was the last time we lost a Carrier?"

"1945, assuming you mean in battle," Admiral James Macavoy answered. "To the best of my recollection, at least. The, hum... Bismark Sea, sunk not four hundred miles from where the Enterprise is right this moment."

General Graves grunted, "Off Iwo, in fact."

Givens nodded wearily, gesturing idly, "That is what they hope to gain, George. They want a Carrier. They want an American Carrier."

That brought silence to the room, the very concept anathema to the military people in the room, while the civilians had more mixed reactions.

Normally the response would be a mix of incredulity and anger. The idea that they even had a chance of such a goal would be ludicrous. But a few days earlier, the idea of the Bloc just steamrolling Japan and Taiwan, well that was unthinkable too.

No one wanted to voice it, but everyone in the room was wondering whether the enemy task group might not get exactly what they wanted.

*****

Alamogordo New Mexico

It was late, either really late or possibly really early. Eric glanced out to the East, and he could see the false dawn showing over the horizon.

He'd been at the hangar all night, making changes to the device, hoping he was right about it. Sometime after three he'd fallen asleep in the ratty old sofa chair they kept in the corner, until a coyote howling woke up. He felt like crap, but that was nothing new to him, he'd worked through worse in the past and likely would again in the future from the looks of things.

Bradley had gone home to his bed. The older man wouldn't recover quickly if he tried to match Eric's hours. His body wouldn't be able to deal with either the rough sleeping conditions, or the beating his wife would lay on him if he tried.

So, Eric was alone, staring at what might be the most important piece of tech in the country, wondering if they would be able to get it working or if maybe they were barking up the wrong tree entirely.

He didn't think they were, at least. What he knew of the device seemed to fit, but there was always the chance that he was wasting everyone's time.

Why is it that uncertainty always starts eating at you after everyone sane is gone to sleep?

Eric snorted, walking through the darkened Hangar. He didn't bother turning on lights. The moon was bright and his eyes well adjusted. It wasn't daylight by any means but he could see well enough.

He stopped as the sound of glass breaking startled him, starting to turn and call out automatically before his training clamped down on his civilian instincts. Slowly turning, Eric looked back into the hangar before stepping to one side so he wouldn't be silhouetted in the open hangar door.

Probably just a rat or something.

He didn't move from his position, though. His body was tingling, he could feel the Adrenaline ramping up. It had been a few years, but it was an old friend come home at that moment.

Eric cocked his head when he heard something else, the scuff of a shoe on the cement that lay around the hangar, a whispered word that he couldn't quite make out but recognized the language from the rhythm of it. *Mandarin.*

There was a local Chinese community actually, not far away, but he doubted strongly that any of them had decided to drop in for a visit, and that was only marginally less unlikely than some of them deciding to rob him.

Eric pressed himself to the hangar wall behind him, edging up against the door as he listened.

The night sounds were almost gone, local animals had fled. That should have tipped him off earlier, Eric chastised himself. Silence was unusual, even in the desert. A slight crunch of a stray bit of gravel was his warning just before he saw a dark shape protrude through the door.

He snapped his hands out, grabbing the gun and the arm it was attached to, pulling as hard as he could.

The man hit the door frame hard. There was a crunch of a bone-breaking, but impressively the man didn't do much more than grunt in pain. Eric levered his arm up and smashed the bridge of his nose with the rifle, then again, and a third time before the man slumped and relinquished the weapon.

Eric flipped it over, pleased to note that it was an AR model carbine. Civilian version, but that was ok since the military extras were less than worthless if you didn't have a well-trained squad backing you up, and were willing to waste a hell of a lot more ammo than he had on him. After over a century in production, the basic frame of the sporting rifle was still the most popular rifle in the country by a good margin. That was probably why the intruder had picked it. It was effectively untraceable if you took some care in its acquisition, and it was very easy to acquire, The upshot for Eric was that he wouldn't be fiddling with any controls, since he had drilled with the AR for countless hours, and didn't need his eyes to run a quick check on the weapon. Eric dipped his thumb into the breach as he half pulled the bolt back, confirming that a round was loaded before he did the same to the magazine and felt the cool brass through the witness hole in the bottom of the composite box.

Full mag, one in the chamber.

He shifted the weapon to his right hand, settling the buttstock in the crook of his arm as he dropped to one knee, keeping the weapon at the ready while quickly patting the body down. He found an extra mag but didn't want to turn the body over to look for more so decided one was enough.

It went into his belt, jammed against his back and pinching every time he moved, but that too was fine.

It's been a long time.

When he'd been in, Eric had been a Marine aviator, not one of the trigger pullers. That didn't mean he didn't know how. All Marines are infantry first, whatever else they trained for second. That was the theory, at least. In practice, he was a lot deadlier with a stick in his hand than he was with a gun.

Every sound around him was an intruder now, though, and he had to focus on keeping his heart rate down as he tried to filter out the false positives from the real threats.

Man at the door. Won't be alone, someone else will be close. Did they see me take out their guy?

He risked a peek out, eyes sweeping the tarmac in the moonlight.

Nothing.

He ducked back in just before the side of the door where his head had been exploded, showering him with debris and shrapnel. Eric dove for the ground, warmth trickling down his cheek as he scrambled away from the door as quickly as he could crawl.

Vaguely he heard the boom of the rifle shot roll through.

Concealment is not cover!

The walls of the hangar wouldn't provide cover from a .22, let alone whatever beast that sniper was using. Eric elected to not hang around any longer as he heard voices now, apparently the intruders having given up on stealth.

"Shit. Shit. Shit." He swore as he crawled, looking around, trying to remember where the hell he'd left his cell phone.

Feet scuffing behind him caused him to flop over onto his back, half sitting up with the rifle snugged to his shoulder.

Three rounds, fast as he could squeeze them off, barked sharply as the rifle thudded into his shoulder.

The figure silhouetted in the door shuddered slightly, but that was all before it dropped right in place where they'd stood. It wasn't like the movies, Eric knew, though sometimes a body could do some crazy stuff as muscles twitched and jerked in an attempt to get away from the pain of a bullet. Mostly, however, if you were on target, they just dropped.

He froze for a moment, listening intently, then covered his face as an explosion of rounds went off, riddling the hangar walls.

Eric had a flash of calm then and almost laughed as he came to a realization.

Apparently, we're on the right track with this thing.

He wasn't so concerned about wasting time and money with the device now, if someone wanted to kill him to stop the proj-

Eric froze, blood running cold.

Bradley!

"Fuck," He hissed under his breath, rolling over and getting his legs under him to come up to a kneeling position as the fire died down.

He had to get out of here.

Eric scrambled over behind the old engine out of the Ford he was rebuilding, crouching behind the cast iron mass, thinking furiously.

Two down. How many would they have come with? Strike team can't be large, even in these parts someone would notice a caravan of vehicles. Two, maybe three SUVs max. Room for gear... four people per?

That made twelve. Two on overwatch, including the bastard with the sniper rifle. Ten, then, for the strike team. Eight left, plus the sniper and his spotter.

He had a forty-five in his desk, and a lever-action .45-70 for dealing with coyotes and any other pests that became too much trouble, but they weren't in reach and he was pretty certain he'd be mowed down before he got halfway to either.

Same was true for the dead man's rifle there by the door.

Shit.

Knowing that there was nothing to be gained in hiding until they broke in and shot him, Eric pushed off the ground and bolted for the office.

Gunfire erupted in his wake, which only egged him on to run faster. Searing pain in his back was the impetus he needed to dive for the door, landing on the floor heavily as he slid into the office and out of sight.

The mantra *concealment is not cover* repeated over and over in his mind as Eric rolled out of the line of sight of the door and under the heavy desk that had served him and Bradley both for a while. He planted his shoulders on the ground, ignoring the pain from them, and kicked up, flipping the desk over on its side, with the top now facing the rest of the hangar.

Breathing hard, he rested a moment, cursing the loss of conditioning in the years since he'd been out of the Corps. He was going to have to start working out again.

I bet Stephen could use a workout too, Eric thought idly as he leaned out along the side, leading with the carbine, firing two rounds into the man who tried to rush the office. The body hit the ground, sliding into the desk with a soft thump. *Pretty sure I remember enough from Basic to make a decent run of it. Not sure I can take that kind of workout anymore, but it'll be good to find out.*

There was yelling from outside, several voices he didn't recognize. More shots, but none of them seemed to be coming through the office. Eric waited for a while longer, hesitantly wondering if he should make another move. He was just starting to look around for a tablet or his phone when a voice he *did* know called out.

"Eric! Eric, you ok!?"

"Max?" Eric asked, eyes dancing from side to side.

"Hey, I'm coming in, don't shoot me ok?"

"Keep your hands where I can see them!"

He heard feet shuffling at the door, shadows dancing against the wall, and risked a peek out from behind the desk. Max was standing in the door with a powerful light shining on him from the side.

"You hurt?" Max asked as Eric showed himself.

"Don't know, think I picked up an extra asshole in my back, but nature doesn't seem to be telling me to slow down," He said, looking around cautiously. "What happened?"

"Bloc strike team," Max replied, "I'm happy I put a team watching you… but happier that I had a team watching *them*."

"You had people watching me? Where were they when this kicked off?"

"Dead. Strike team took them out first," Max said tiredly, "but we had a remote unit on them, so the alarm went up. I got the call ten minutes ago."

Eric blinked, "Where the hell are you staying? Town is fifteen minutes away."

"Tractor-trailer unit on BLM land up a ways," Max gestured. "All the amenities of home. You sure you're ok?"

"No," Eric said warily, keeping his carbine at the half heady as he made his way out to the door.

Max stepped aside and Eric glanced out, noting the men with flashlights standing over bodies. Everyone was in black tactical gear and looked to be carrying government-issue weapons rather than the old AR carbines he'd seen on the first team.

"Ok, I'm figuring that you're probably on the level," Eric said after a moment.

Max snorted, "Seriously? Are you still holding a grudge over Beijing?"

"You almost got me killed!" Eric grumbled, "And worse, you left me with that fucking reporter. Crazy bitch."

Max laughed at him, "Turn around you dumb jarhead, let me see your back."

"Someone needs to check on Bradley," Eric said, doing as he'd been bade.

"I'll call it in," Max nodded soberly as he looked over his friend's back. "Well, you're still a luckier son of a bitch than anyone deserves to be. Looks like a graze. Bet this is gonna sting when you come down."

Eric grunted, clenching and unclenching his fist as he let out a shuddering breath.

"Yeah," He agreed.

"Well, we know one thing now," Max said, patting him on the shoulder across from the damage.

Eric nodded, "Yup. Pretty sure this isn't a boondoggle after all. No one sends a strike team to take out a project that's just wasting the enemy's money."

"You might, chess playing prick that you are," Max rolled his eyes, "but the odds of a double fake seem pretty low, yeah."

"I need to check on the device."

"You need a hospital before that shit gets infected. We'll secure the area. You can check in daylight."

Eric grumbled, but allowed himself to be pried out of the old hangar and led to a black SUV.

A hospital did sound good.

His hand started shaking, the adrenal response falling off.

This is going to suck.

*****

Chapter Eleven

USS Enterprise

"Enemy air assets on the screens, Admiral."

Bonet nodded. "Shift the destroyer screen to cover their approach but stay with the plan."

"Aye, sir."

The Task Group was still moving south as quickly as they could manage, but the raids were coming fast and constant now. The fighters they could hold off, anti-air lasers mounted to the destroyer screen was enough to make even hypersonic fighters think twice, though it was only a delaying tactic.

"Sir! Missiles tracking!"

Bonet twisted to lay eyes on the task group's RADAR tracking system, and they widened as he spotted the contacts. Swarms of missiles were showing up now, fired from over the horizon, presumably by the enemy task group. The fast, low flying cruise missiles were coming in quick, and he could hear the alarm go up across the Carrier, echoed across the waves by the closest destroyers in their escort group.

"God damn it," He swore.

"Anti-missile defenses online, target sweeps beginning."

The group's powerful Aegis RADAR arrays swept across the sea, pouring power down range in order to spot and track every airborne target. On the screen, positive contacts began to multiply.

"Twenty missiles, Sir… No, make it thirty… Jesus, thirty-five… still counting."

"Brace for impact," Bonet ordered, knowing that there was no way they could intercept every one of the inbound missiles, which was of course the Bloc's intent.

In fact, with the task group's defenses saturated, it was worse than just the missiles. The Destroyers wouldn't be able to use their laser defense systems to hold off the fighters.

That left only one option.

"Scramble the ready response squadrons," He ordered. "Get those birds in the air."

*****

Jolly Rogers Squadron, *Hela*

"Enterprise Control, Jolly Rogers Actual Hela Speaking."

"Go for Control, Hela."

"Jolly Rogers are ready to fly, Control. Let us loose."

"Roger that, Hela. You are clear for launch. Control has been remanded to the Aircraft handling officer."

"Roger Control."

A glance outside the bubble of her cockpit showed her the yellow vest of the aircraft control officer approaching. She and her wingman were first on the cat, already lined up with their engines running in high readiness. They would overheat quickly in that mode, without the cooling systems running at full efficiency as they would in flight, but she knew they wouldn't be on the deck for very long.

The Air Boss waved her the signal and she put power to the engines as he took a knee and signaled the cat officer to put power to the electromagnetic rail. She was slammed back into her seat as the F35 hammered forward, boosting off the deck, her guts leaping up into her throat briefly as the fighter dropped until the engines took up the slack.

Putting the fighter into a power climb, Hela glanced out and back to ensure that her wingman was holding with her.

"Right with you, Hela," Commander 'Hurricane' Longworth said, having either guessed she was checking or spotted her motion from where he was following in close formation.

"Just checking, Hurricane," She said with an easy tone that belied the feeling in the pit of her guts. "Looks like we're going to get another crack at these bastards."

"It does indeed. Looking forward to it, boss lady."

She didn't doubt that actually, though she knew that Longworth was at least as twisted up over this as she was. The enemy fighters were too fast and could hit from too far out for conventional tactics to work, and there were limits to what they could do unconventionally when they were out in the middle of the Pacific Ocean.

Whatever. Not going to stop us from doing our jobs, she thought, putting the grim feeling down firmly as she circled her fighter about, waiting for the rest of the Jolly Rogers to join her and Longworth.

It didn't take long, not with the Enterprise's catapults running full tilt to get every fighter possible into the sky before the cruise missiles could prevent them from taking off.

"Alright, boys, let's go to work."

*****

EBAN HuangLung

The HuangLung was running shallow, allowing Admiral Chien to monitor the developing battle using satellite observation, as they circled the American formation while the rest of the Bloc task group maintained their direct intercept course.

The American response was, thus far, largely by the book though they had taken longer than expected to put their aircraft into the skies. That wasn't particularly surprising, of course, given the threat of the Bloc's Type JF198 fighters. The Americans had not had time to develop any sort of standard response, so some variation in their playbook was to be expected.

Chien was hoping to saturate the air defenses of the American and Japanese vessels with the cruise missile attack, which would largely leave them open to the air assault from the hypersonic 198s. The Americans' own aircraft were not a significant factor, their aging F35s had proven to be somewhat more formidable in the right hands than expected, but only using tactics that were easily countered once known.

It was the surprises that he was concerned with, however.

The Americans were known for having little care for their own rules in the face of a challenge. They even had been known to joke that it was impossible for an enemy to learn about them by reading their playbooks, as so few of them bothered to read the books themselves.

He doubted there was much actual truth to that. Most of it was just American self-aggrandizement. His own experience with them tended more to show them as officious rule lawyers who enjoyed twisting the system until it broke.

The fact that they considered that a good trait was all the more evidence of the sheer degradation of culture that existed in the West.

"Admiral, our first missile salvo is entering the American's air defense line."

Chien nodded soberly.

It began.

*****

Chinese built DF-19A cruise missiles were hypersonic capable weapons with 1500- kilogram warheads. Moving at speeds in excess of Mach 4 they were all but invulnerable to conventional anti-air defenses. Only ship and aircraft-mounted lasers were considered effective against the fast-moving delivery vehicles, both of which were heavily in demand on the American ships.

Nevertheless, the laser blisters on the outer line destroyers hummed into action first, tracking and firing as the missiles entered their engagement envelop. It took several seconds of consistent heat to burn each missile out of the skies, and in that time the rest had moved several kilometers closer.

Alarms wailed across the task group, anti-air missiles firing, while above them the Enterprise's fighters roared into the fight to meet the incoming Chinese fighters that were looking to take advantage of the current state of the group's air defenses.

The skies were rent with explosions, beams of unfathomable energy invisibly crossing the air, and screaming missiles flying in both directions as the battle was met.

*****

Jolly Rogers Squadron

Hela thumbed the safety off her weapons, opening up the bays and laying her fighter bare to the world as she pushed for as much speed as she could coax out of the aging bird. Her computer was dividing targets up among the rest of the squadron even as the others from the Enterprise were launching behind them.

She had surface targets in the distance, and this time around her fighter was loaded to make their day hopefully as miserable as they'd managed to make hers, but her real concern was with the Bloc fighters.

For them, though, the Jolly Rogers had a little surprise.

"Alright boys and girls," She said evenly. "Leave the missiles to the destroyers. We're looking for a little payback with those fighters."

The Mantis class fighters were approaching fast, just behind the missiles in fact, and keeping pace. Hela targeted the lead fighter, while the rest of her squadron picked out their own in turn, and waited while they got the shots locked in. They wouldn't get many chances at this, and she knew that they needed to make this one count.

A glance at the network showed that everyone was linked up and had their targets haloed, so Hela let out a breath.

It was time.

"Jolly Rogers Actual… Special Load… Out."

She triggered the weapon as her squadron repeated her words, and the Jolly Rogers filled the sky with megawatts of energy.

*****

The Lockheed Martin X-12 Chemical Laser Pod was a rarely used system that could attach to the F35's mounting racks, allowing the fighter to deliver a one point two-megawatt beam on a target, almost effectively within line of sight. Unlike the range of the cannons, which were limited to a little under four kilometers, lasers just kept ongoing.

The only real limit on them in terms of range was atmospheric diffusion, which was not an issue at the mere dozens of nautical miles the engagement was currently working at.

At the speed of light, several Mantis fighters erupted into flame.

Unfortunately, the Bloc fighters had their own laser mounts and the invisible flames were returned just as quickly.

*****

Hela twisted the stick, evading fire as best she could with something she couldn't see until her fighter was aflame. The first engagement had favored the black flags of the Jolly Rogers, but only marginally and they'd had the advantage of a surprise strike.

The enemy now knew they were packing laser modules as well, and could target them, and the best data they had indicated that the Bloc lasers, while limited, did carry more shots per load. The Lockheed Martin modules on the F35s were chemical boosted lasers that would only get about five good burns before they needed to be pulled and refurbished.

There was a reason they were rarely used.

We need better laser modules, a lot better if we're going to close this gap, Hela thought grimly as she flew.

The money had not been there for research, not for decades, but somehow, she had a feeling that was about to change.

*****

USS Enterprise

Bonet stood out on the overwatch platform attached to the carrier's command Island, watching the exchange through powerful binoculars.

The Jolly Rogers had lost three more fighters. All the pilots had been able to punch out, however. Small boats were already in the water, rushing to pick them up. The Sidewinders were in the air now, backing them up, while the deck crews rushed to move the next squadron into launch positions.

He wanted every fighter in the air. Despite how little effect they might have, it would be better to have some effect than none at all if they were destroyed on the deck.

Sweeping his glasses to examine the sea, he could see flashes of light that signified cruise missiles being destroyed, and in the distance, he could hear the SeaWiz guns screaming as they defied the surviving missiles.

"Admiral, we need to get you to cover."

Bonet looked aside at his aide, sighing, "Yes, you're right."

The aide breathed a sigh of relief, opening the door and ushering him in. The alarms were sounding inside as they had out in the open. The missiles were only moments out, at most, and while he knew they would give a good accounting of themselves, Bonet was also quite certain of the final outcome.

A few more would slip through the saturated defenses.

A death of a thousand cuts.

The enemy ships were holding off just over the horizon, likely using that submarine or another one, as a spotter to guide their missiles in. His ships had returned fire with their own cruise missiles, of course, and likely they'd sink a few Bloc ships, but there were a lot more of them where those came from.

The deck under his feet vibrated as more aircraft screamed along the catapult, being thrown into the skies.

"Hold on!" someone called. He didn't know who but didn't question it either and grabbed a rail as the Enterprise was suddenly slammed as if by a giant hammer.

Bonet was thrown to the ground, falling the last few steps, but other than a few bruises, was in good enough shape as he picked himself up and stumbled into the command deck.

"Damage report," He croaked out, eyes sliding to the shattered windows and the smoke that was curling in.

"Still waiting on it, Sir. We got hit hard, though, at least three got through… maybe more."

"Incoming! Second wave!"

Goddamn it. Bonet grimaced, holding on tightly to the console in front of him.

The deck suddenly heaved under him and he was thrown forward, head smashing into the console before everything went black.

*****

USS Makin Island LHDN-19

Being a Marine in the middle of a naval battle sucked, Hadrian decided as he tried to throw himself into his job. The Marine F-35 he was working on didn't need much, but he didn't have much else to do for the moment and didn't want to be in the way of anyone who actually had a useful duty at the moment.

"They hit the E! They hit the E!"

Hadrian twisted from where he was working, his heart dropping as his guts clenched. He got up, pushing his way through the Marines who were watching the monitors that were showing the outside.

"Don't you lot have anything better to do?" He snarled. "And before you answer that, I'll remind you that I can *find* things for you to do if you want me to."

That broke up most of them, Hadrian ignoring the rest as he looked over to the screen and grimaced.

The Enterprise was ablaze, clearly having taken several more direct strikes. He didn't know how much more the big ship could take.

Major Liam Gibb, the CO of the Makin Island, was on the speakers, giving orders to get boats in the water and pull as many men from the Enterprise as they could.

Hadrian swallowed.

He didn't have enough curse words in his vocabulary.

*****

The Enterprise was blazing, black smoke pouring from a hole in the deck as Hela swept back over the scene and winced.

One of the missiles, at least one, had struck a magazine as best she could tell. The flight deck was just gone. There was no chance of landing her fighter back on that, even if they got the fires out. She couldn't tell what sort of damage the ship had below the waterline, but for the moment it seemed stable in the water... mostly.

How long that would last, she didn't know.

For the moment they had a lull in the fighting, but again there was no telling how long that was going to last.

"Jolly Rogers Actual, Makin Island Control."

"Go for Rogers Actual, Makin Island."

"Air Control duties have been handed off to us, need a sitrep on your fuel and weapon status."

"Roger that," She said, reading off the numbers, wondering what they were going to do.

The Makin Island was a Marine Corps amphibious assault ship. She wasn't actually sure if she could land a Navy fighter on its deck but figured it was just remotely possible. What she was sure of, however, was that they didn't have *room* onboard for all of the Enterprise birds still in the air.

It took a few moments before Makin Island control got back to her.

"Alright, you're good on fuel for the moment. Move BINGO up by twelve percent," Makin Island Control ordered.

"Roger that, Makin Island," She said while making the adjustment. "Reason for change?"

"We're considering Iwo Jima as an alternate landing zone," came the reply. "The Island has fuel and a strategic munitions depot."

She blinked. "It does?"

Hela had never heard of that before.

That did bring up something else rather important, however.

"What's the chain of command, Makin Island? Is the Admiral ok?"

"Don't worry about it, Hela," Makin Island control told her. "The Major has that covered."

Well.

What the fuck does that mean?

*****

USS Enterprise

"Doors jammed!"

"Break it down!"

The sound of steel on steel reverberated, coming from every direction as the smoke-filled the interior of the ship's Island.

Admiral Bonet groaned and coughed as the world swam back amid flames and fury. His head swam almost as much as it hurt, his lungs screaming for air. The sound of steel being wrenched in ways it was never intended to twist, filled the room next and then a rush of feet on the deck surrounded him, arms clad in thick material pulling him out of the room.

"The… others," He coughed out.

"We're getting them, Sir."

He let the fire crew pull him out, the smoke clearing as they got out of the island, but things didn't get any better. He was dismayed to see the deck on fire, black smoke just *pouring* from a breach in the deck about where he knew one of the munitions magazines was located below.

"How bad?" He asked between coughs.

"Still getting that intel, Sir, but it's pretty damn bad." The fire crewman said. "Reports from below decks say we've got water filling a couple compartments where the missiles struck low. Lost a magazine entirely, destroyed the deck. That's just what I know now."

Bonet nodded grimly, levering himself to his feet. "Thank you, sailor. Who's coordinating?"

"Commander Jinta, Sir."

"Thank you again."

Bonet shook off the helping hands and started walking unsteadily to where he could see a temporary command setup. Commander Marrianne Jinta was indeed coordinating the damage control teams when he arrived.

"Admiral!" She said upon his arrival.

"As you were," He cut off the salute before she could even start it. "Just give me the sitrep and don't let me get in the way."

"Yes sir. One of the missiles hit our primary magazine, punched through three decks and the armor to do it, somehow," She said. "We don't know what yield that one was packing, but it had the punch to it."

She paused, turning away as a report came in. Admiral Bonet waited for her to get the men moving in the right direction before she turned back to him.

"We think we took five or six direct hits, maybe one or two more," She said. "The Deck is a lost cause, Sir, and we've handed flight control operations over to the Makin Island."

"Understood. What about propulsion and hull integrity?"

She shook her head. "Honestly, we don't know Sir. Lost contact with the reactor crew, still working on re-establishing it."

A chill ran down his spine, but Bonet forced himself to only react with a nod.

The Enterprise was a nuclear vessel, of course, and the last thing you wanted to hear when dealing with nuclear power of any sort was that you'd lost contact with the reactor crew.

"I've got a team running a hardline down there, but they're having to fight through a lot of fires on the way," She told him.

"That's good work, Commander," He told her. "You keep at it, let me know the second we have contact."

"Aye Admiral."

He nodded wearily and limped over to where someone had set up a folding chair on the deck.

I really need to sit down.

*****

Chapter 12

USS Makin Island

Major Liam Liam glared at the screens in front of him hard enough that half the people around him were expecting them to burst into flames. The Carrier burning just a few hundred meters over his shoulder didn't do anything to soften the image, either.

"We've finished contacting all the airborne assets, Sir," Colonel Uru said. "All report within the required limits to make Iwo."

"Good," Liam said, using a digital pen to draw out a series of course calculations on the computer in front of him. "We're going to need to start moving them off soon. Do we have any contact with the Enterprise yet?"

"Yes sir. They found the Admiral, Major," The Colonel told him. "Shaken up, bloodied, but alive and awake."

"That's excellent news," Liam said. "Inform the Enterprise that the Makin Island stands ready to receive him if it is required to move the flag."

"Hoorah, Major."

With the Colonel off communicating to that effect with the current command chain of the Enterprise, Liam returned his focus to the work at hand. With the Admiral up, his plan might not be implemented, but he would make sure it was ready just in case it was needed all the same.

He'd done work with the JSDF in the past and knew that there was in fact a military depot on Iwo. It wasn't huge and, fortunately, or unfortunately depending on how you looked at it, no longer housed Special Munitions. But it would have jet fuel for the fighters, munitions, and such stock for a small army.

The Japanese had wanted it there as a strategic fallback, precisely in case of what had happened. The US Government hadn't thought it necessary, but since the Japanese were picking up the tab, they'd been willing to sell the weapons. He had been a Colonel at the time, advising on proper storage preparation.

He'd not thought it would come to this, though.

They're going to keep picking us off, one by one, and with those damned fighters making the skies friendly for the enemy, they'll succeed too. Sixty-five hundred kilometers to Hawaii. We'll never make it with them on our ass the whole way.

The only thing he wasn't sure of was whether the Bloc would actually keep up with them the whole way.

Invading mainland America was insane.

While Yamamoto never actually said the infamous quote often attributed to him, there was truth in it. Invading the mainland of North America was all but impossible. You might not be facing a rifle behind every blade of grass as the facetious and possibly imaginary quote claimed, but trying to take the country would require more logistical support than even the Bloc could conjure.

However, he'd have said the same thing not long ago about Japan.

The bloc had taken actions that left the Major strongly doubting the sanity of their leadership, which meant that he had to consider just what might happen if the Bloc Council truly had lost what little remained of their sanity.

On the screen, Liam reached out and circled a spot in the middle of nowhere with his pen.

Iwo Jima.

*****

USS Enterprise

This is going to be one hell of a way to make history, Bonet thought grimly as he winced at the pain that knifed through his skull. *First American commander to lose a Carrier in over a century. Fucking hell.*

He didn't know if the damage to the Enterprise was enough to actually sink her, but he was pretty damned certain that it was more than enough to cripple her. They still didn't have a list of the dead, but the tally for the injured was growing by the minute.

"We've got a line to the reactor crew, Admiral."

"Thank God, I'll take it, Commander," Bonet said, getting up, ignoring the pain in his head. He grabbed the old handset that was wired directly to the reactor via cable the DCS teams had run over the last few minutes. "This is Admiral Bonet. I need a sitrep on the reactor."

He listened for a moment, nodding unconsciously, "I understand. How much power can you get out of her?"

Another moment, another answer.

It wasn't what he wanted, but it was enough.

"Alright, I need you to do something for me," Admiral Bonet ordered. "And then you get your team out of there. There's a boat waiting to take you to the Makin Island."

*****

USS Makin Island

"Orders from the E, Major. The Flag is transferring," Commander Uru said. "Admiral will be coming over with the last boat."

Liam nodded, "Understood. Prepare an office for him, did he send ahead any orders?"

"Just that you have tactical command until he is aboard, Sir."

"Very well, we'll go with Plan Iwo until further notice," Liam said. "What's the status on the Enterprise?"

"She's not going to make it, Major."

Liam grimaced but didn't say anything. Hell, what was there that could be said? He knew the ramifications as well as anyone, but if the Carrier couldn't keep up and couldn't land aircraft, it wasn't a carrier anymore.

"Get the group moving as soon as the last of the boats is on board."

"Aye, aye, Major."

Liam looked out over the stretch of sea that separated the Makin Island from the Big E, and wondered what else could go wrong?

He didn't voice it aloud, however, because while he wasn't superstitious as a rule, neither was he stupid.

*****

Admiral Bonet forced himself to stay on his feet as the last of the men were loaded into the Admiral's gig.

Only then did he allow himself to be helped on, waving the coxswain on as he was seated. The powerful little boat was pushed off the Enterprise, engine surging to life as they started to cut across to the Makin Island. He didn't look back, didn't have to. Bonet knew what his Command was now, and what it was to become.

The crossing took only minutes, and he was shortly being helped off the gig as the boat was lifted and locked into place.

"Welcome aboard the Makin Island, Admiral," An ensign saluted him. "Major Gibb extends his regards and invites you to the bridge at your pleasure, Sir."

"Thank you, Ensign," Bonet said, returning the salute as the men unloaded behind him. "Run along and inform the Major I will be there in short order."

"Aye, Admiral."

Now Bonet turned to look back on the burning hulk of the Carrier he'd called his own. The Enterprise was falling behind them, the deck surge under his feet told him that they were in motion, the rest of the fleet with them.

He hoped they'd gotten everyone off but knew that the odds were they'd missed someone.

Lord, forgive me.

Lights in the distance showed that the enemy fleet was closing in, chasing them off. The enemy commander would have his feather, a rare pretty one indeed for his cap. There was nothing Bonet could do about that now, he knew.

*****

EBAN HuangLung

There were sights of rare beauty in the world, things that mortal men could only dream of for the most part. For Chien, however, none of them quite compared to what he was seeing through the periscope of his great ship. The great American carrier had long been a sign of the invulnerable power of the US Navy, and its ability to project power anywhere on the planet.

While much of that was, certainly, just American propaganda, it was an image that remained just the same.

"Ensure that the Council and our Media Propagation Unit has all the video from this," He ordered without turning from the sight.

"Yes, Admiral. Live feeds are already being broadcast to both."

"Excellent. The world needs to see this," Chien said calmly. "This is the end of the Pax Americana."

"Yes, Admiral."

*****

The Enterprise drifted, aimless in the current without power to her screws, the fires still burning but mostly just black smoke pouring out of the shattered holes in her hull. The Bloc fleet approached cautiously, ships moving close enough to get a better look at the floating wreck.

Ideally, the Admiral wanted the hull towed back to Beijing, though that was considered to be a long shot given the damage that has been dealt out to the big ship.

A pair of destroyers moved in close, men in protective gear carefully reading devices out on their decks.

Radiation in the area was normal, which was encouraging.

They'd half been worried about a meltdown, either accidental from the attack or intentionally left behind to poison the prize. The best of their gear, including thermal examination of the carrier, indicated that the reactor had been properly locked down, however.

More ships closed in, orders dispatched, while others continued on to push the Americans ahead of them according to the original plan.

A groaning sound from the big ship could be heard for a thousand meters across the sea, and the men on four destroyers and two cruisers turned just as a flash turned the world white.

The shockwave slammed sidelong into the Bloc vessels, shattering thick glass that could take the storms of any ocean on the planet, and pushing them over almost ninety degrees, dunking the ships into the Pacific for several moments before they surged back upright.

*****

USS Makin Island

"Admiral, welcome on board the Makin Island," Major Gibb said, frowning as he noticed the Admiral seemed distracted.

"What? Yes, sorry Major," Bonet said, looking a little lost. "Thank you for the welcome."

"Do you have orders, Sir?"

"Huh? No," Bonet shook his head. "You seem to have things well in hand. I'll review the situation first and…"

A flash in the distance caused them all to turn before automatically taking cover.

During the cold war, in the early days, schools had been shown videos on how to survive a nuclear explosion. Among those lessons were the instructions to immediately take any cover possible, primarily by crawling under the wooden desks they were likely to be sitting at if they were in class.

In the decades that followed those videos were much maligned as jokes, instructions by a government that didn't really care about people too stupid to question the intelligence of hiding under a wooden desk to save oneself from a nuclear fireball.

The criticism of those videos was imbecilic.

If you were that close to a nuclear explosion, you were dead. The true danger was not in the fireball, it was in the difference between the speed of light and the speed of sound.

Any explosion would send out a great flash, that in turn would propagate outward at the speed of light. Three hundred thousand kilometers per second, roughly. The shockwave, however, would only travel at the speed of sound, a mere three hundred and fifty *meters* per second. Again, roughly.

At distance, it meant that you would see the flash of any particularly large explosion and have just enough reaction time to walk over to the nearest window before the shockwave blew the glass in, right into your face.

Hiding under your desk from flying glass *was* actually a survival tip that made a lot of sense.

The explosion on the Enterprise wasn't nuclear, but it was about as large as it got without an atomic chain reaction. The remaining munitions, including a few MOAB explosives going off were enough to shake, though not shatter, the armored glass on the Makin Island as the shock wave rolled over them, but the men on board were taking no chances.

After it passed, people slowly got back to their feet and Major Gibb turned back to the Admiral.

"Sir, did you rig… Sir?" Liam shifted, head tilting as he looked at Bonet.

The Admiral was gazing out at the sea, motionless despite the heaving of the deck underfoot. Liam waited a moment, first curious, and with growing alarm as he saw the Admiral's eyes roll up in his head.

The Major barely caught the Admiral as he fell, screaming as he lowered the man to the deck.

"Corpsman! Corpsman!"

*****

EBAN HuangLung

Chien gritted his teeth, frustrated though not particularly shocked.

The Enterprise would have been an invaluable prize but, of course, the Americans knew that too. It was a pity. The explosion had damaged several ships and killed many, but he had known the risk when he sent them in.

He had not really expected the Americans to trap the ship in such a manner, though. Scuttle it? That was a high probability, of course.

Despite everything, they had still held back, however.

He was aware that the Enterprise carried special munitions, American talk for nuclear bombs. The explosion, while large, had not been nuclear.

Holding back was foolish, but it was very American.

So violent, yet so oddly weak.

Chien had often found the study of American psychology an amusing pastime. They were a violent, barbaric sort. Slaves to their emotions, and unable to force themselves to take a breath and *think* about the problem in front of them.

Every problem to them was a nail, as the Americanism went, because Americans only had hammers with which to solve them.

If they had the inner cultural wisdom of an older civilization, they would be truly formidable.

*****

USS Makin Island

In the medical center of the Makin Island, Liam was waiting when the doctor stepped out.

"Doctor, is he going to be alright?"

"Admiral Bonet is dead."

Liam blinked, "What? How? He was fine, talking and walking. I didn't see any injuries…"

"Subdural hematoma," The Doctor said tiredly. "From the bleeding in his skull, Major, I have no idea how the hell he was still walking, let alone talking. He should have been dead hours ago."

Liam didn't know what the hell had just happened if he were being honest. Subdural hematoma? How the damn man was still living long enough to make it to the Makin Island he didn't know, but it didn't matter at the moment.

"Thank you, Doctor."

"Major."

Liam looked back, "Yes?"

"I've already got people asking me what happened," The Doctor said. "What can I tell them?"

Liam didn't have to think about that.

"Tell them the Admiral died on the Enterprise, but his body kept going long enough to see his last order out to the end."

*****

Chapter Thirteen

Alamagordo New Mexico

Eric stood on the street looking at the fire that had engulfed the place Bradley called home. The police had reported on it before Max got his people there, and Eric had shaken off the well-meaning help from the government people and gotten in his car without a thought. His injury would wait.

"Sheriff," He called, climbing out of the classic 2015 Challenger.

"Eric," Sheriff Jim Snow looked over and nodded to him. "Bad piece of business this."

"Tell me they weren't at home," Eric begged.

Snow looked down and shook his head, "I'm sorry, Eric."

Eric looked out over the suburban home, taking a halting step toward the fire until Snow reached out to stop him.

"Don't. There's nothing you can do," Snow said before he lifted his hand and twisted it around, frowning as he saw blood on it. "Eric, what the fuck... what happened?"

"Some intruders decided they wanted to scuttle the project Bradley and I have been working on," Eric said dully.

The Sheriff looked back to the burning building before he focused on Eric again. "Jesus, Eric, are you saying..."

"I'm saying, check the bodies," Eric said tiredly. "Look for bullet holes."

With that, he turned around and started to stagger back to his car. He got around halfway there as three military transports whirred up behind it, coming to a silent stop. Max hopped out of one, already swearing at him.

"Jesus Christ, Eric, you can't run off like this. We'd have given you a drive, goddamnit," Max snapped at him. "You need medical attention."

"Bradley's *family* was in there, Max!" Eric snapped, pointing. "His wife. His *daughters*!"

"And I'm fucking sorry about that, but you running off and getting killed won't bring any of them back!"

Eric glared but was face to face with a glare in equal portion coming right back at him. Finally, it was Max who broke the standoff.

"Give me your key fob, Eric, and get in the damn transport. You need medical attention, and we need to get to work."

Eric slumped. "Bradley's dead, Max."

"And we're at war. A lot of people are going to die tonight, and more tomorrow. Your project might help cut that number down," Max said, sternly. "Do your duty, Captain. Semper Fi."

Eric let himself be guided to the transport. Those words caught in his head.

Do your duty.

Semper Fi.

*****

"Well, it's good to know that there's something about this project that was important enough to try and destroy it," Max said, looking over the old airfield and hangars Eric had been working at.

They had military security creating a perimeter, mobile buildings being put into place, and hooked up to utilities. It would probably be easier to move the project to somewhere like Groom Lake, but honestly, he doubted it would matter much and it could delay work by days, maybe weeks, while they did it.

Sue was standing beside him, far from convinced by his logic but he'd overruled her.

"We still haven't cracked it," She said. "And until we do, the Bloc forces get to enjoy an effectively uncontested friendly sky over every battlefield they choose to fight on."

"That's why we need to make this happen and do it as fast as possible," Max said. "Eric and Bradley have given us a head start. So now, let's not waste it alright?"

"I'm all for that. We have experts in the air already, they'll start arriving within six hours."

"And the supplies?"

"Tomorrow."

"Good." Max said firmly. "We can make this work. We *will* make this work."

"I hope you're right." Sue told him, "I really do."

They stood in silence for a while before she continued.

"Because if you aren't, we're all in a world of hurt."

*****

Washington DC

White House Situation Room

Givens rubbed his face, skin ashen as he looked over the reports and satellite feed.

They'd lost the Enterprise, an American Carrier, something that had not happened for over a century.

In some ways, it hit home harder than being forced to withdraw from Japan. The last time an American carrier had gone down in combat had been during a world war, and Givens was now quite certain that they were now in the middle of the next one.

World War Three. People have been expecting it for over a century. Maybe we just got lucky holding it off this long, I don't know, but it's here finally.

So many predictions about it had been made, all of them came and went without being realized, but now he was sitting in the hot seat when everyone got to find out what form it would really take.

At least the Bloc has held off on nukes so far, He thought, though whether that would hold if either side were hard-pressed remained to be seen.

ICBMs weren't the threat they used to be. Ground-based laser systems could pot an orbital vehicle during the boost phase easily, and without too much more problem even after they went ballistic. Stealth wasn't as effective against the Bloc forces as he might wish, either, since they used older style RADAR systems that were less precise in some ways but also less susceptible to the sort of spoofing that modern stealth technology used.

In many ways, the battlefield had been reset, with many of the standoff weapons of the past few decades being rendered largely inconsequential.

"Sir? Mr. President?"

"What is it?" Givens asked, looking up.

"You wanted to be alerted when the Pentagon people were here."

"Yes, of course. Thank you." He said, getting up.

He had a meeting concerning strategy, which would boil down largely to whether or not they would move on to Nicaragua in the next few days. With the powerful Bloc military stationed at the Canal the Eastern Alliance Block had carved across the country there to compete with Panama, there were concerns that put the Bloc too close to American soil for comfort.

They weren't wrong, of course, but no one seemed to know if taking the country was even possible despite the much shorter supply line. If the Bloc had enough of those new fighters, it would be a grueling series of battles under hostile skies.

Probably they could do it, but the country would not take well to that kind of fighting, that kind of dying, that close to home.

There were already people arguing that the US should never have had a base in Japan in the first place, saying that America First should be the credo. Isolationists were growing in strength, but the anger was there too, the rage at what had happened in Japan and Taiwan.

It remained to be seen, which would win, but Givens knew which he was going to side with.

America First just means we fall last. If the Bloc is going to take this world, I'd rather go down first and go down fighting, then sit around waiting for them to come.

*****

Alamogordo New Mexico

Stephen looked around with wide eyes as he approached the airfield, wondering what the hell was going on. There were people *everywhere*, and it looked like a fair number of them were carrying guns. All of the guns, apparently. All of the guns, everywhere.

He was stopped at the gate by a guy in desert fatigues. "Sorry sir, this area is off-limits."

"I was told to come in for the morning," Stephen objected. "Eric told me to show up."

"Eric?"

"Weston. He owns the Hangar or rents it or something."

The man shrugged and checked his tablet, "Well you can give me your name if you want, and I'll check and see if you're on the list, but I'll tell you right now, you're not on the list."

"I didn't give you my name yet," Stephen objected.

"Kid, no one is on the list."

"Look, just let Eric know I'm out here ok?" He tried, rolling his eyes.

"Don't know anyone named Eric."

"Well, someone has to know him, it's his hangar!"

"Look, kid, just go back to your video games or whatever, ok. This area is now a secure zone."

Stephen let out an exasperated breath, "Look man, what the hell is going on? I was *told* to show up, alright? I'm supposed to be here! I don't even know who the hell you are."

"What's going on?"

The pair half turned, seeing someone approaching from the other side of the fence.

"Kid here says someone named Eric asked him to show up today," The guard said. "You know any Eric, Sir?"

The man smiled, "Yeah I do. Let the kid through, I'll take him."

"Yes sir."

Stephen smirked at the guard as he walked through the gate, coming up to the other man.

"I know you," He said, looking the man over. "You were talking to Eric yesterday."

"I was. Name's Max, kid," Max told him. "And you are Stephen Wilson Michaels, eighteen, recently qualified for a private pilot permit, congratulations on that by the way, have a record of misdemeanors half the length of my arm but no felonies."

Stephen pulled away, eyeing the man with open concern now.

Max just smiled thinly at him. "Something tells me you owe the local sheriff for not listing a few of those as felonies, kid. If he had, I would have had you escorted off already."

"Who are you?"

"I'm the man in charge of security here now," Max said. "Eric may like you, but if I decide you go… you're gone."

"Look, I just want to talk to Eric…"

"You can't, he's at the hospital."

"What? What happened, is he ok?" Stephen stiffened, turning to Max again as he demanded answers.

"He's fine. You don't need to know what happened yet, and we need to have a little chat."

Stephen suddenly felt rather nervous as Max pinned him with the creepiest smile he'd ever seen in his life.

*****

Eric stretched slightly, feeling the skin stretch under the bandage, the stitches pulling slightly before he let up and gingerly got his shirt on.

His mind was still back at the burning home however, the shock now receded and being replaced by rage. Attacking him, even going after Bradley, that was understandable. He didn't like either, of course, but he and his friend had dealt themselves into the game by working on the device.

Bradley's family, though, that was just beyond the pale.

Eric shrugged on his jacket and opened the door of the hospital room, stepping out into the corridor. The nurse spotted him before he was a third of the way out of the ER unit.

"Sir! Sir! Mr. Weston, you've not been discharged yet."

"Sue me."

Eric kept walking, the exasperated nurse chasing after him, "Mr. Weston, the doctor hasn't gotten you your prescription yet."

"Just email it to me, you have my information. I'll pick the antibiotics up later, you already gave me enough to choke a horse anyway," Eric rolled his eyes. "I have work to do."

She stopped chasing him at the doors, where he stepped out into the open air, mildly amused to see the military transport waiting for him with a US Army private in fatigues standing beside it.

"Captain," The driver said.

"Former Captain, just Eric now, soldier," Eric said. "You my ride?"

"Looks that way, Sir," The soldier confirmed.

"Fine," Eric climbed in, pulling the door shut with a slam, "Get me back to the hangar."

"Yes Sir."

The soldier got in and they pulled away from the hospital, driving in silence. Eric was fine with that, he had a lot to think about... some of it he didn't want to think about, of course.

So, what else is new?

The device was the key, it was the reason the strike teams had hit them. He wasn't foolish enough to think that it was some coincidence that the government had shown up literally the same day that the strike team had hit either.

The Bloc has moles everywhere, Max is going to have his work cut out for him.

That meant that he couldn't trust the government to handle anything. Not the research, not the testing, and sure as hell not the security for the project.

I'm going to have to do this myself.

*****

Chapter Fourteen

USS Makin Island

"There she is," Major Gibb heard someone say as he turned around.

Sure enough, in the distance now they could see the Island of Iwo Jima.

The Bloc raids had continued, costing them a Destroyer and several more aircraft to fight them off. He had done the calculations, then checked and rechecked them. If they kept on running and the Bloc continued to press the assault, not a man would live to see Hawaii.

The general belief was that the fleet chasing them would back off once they were out of Japanese waters, but he didn't know where the fuck anyone was getting that idea. It seemed more like a wild ass hope than anything else to him.

If they didn't, then what? He was far from certain that Pearl could deal with fighting an enemy that could force project and establish air superiority at the moment. The Island was stripped down, a quarter of the power it had held at its peak. If the Bloc pressed the attack there, thousands would die.

And if they did leave off, what was the outcome then? The whole world watching the US running for home with its tail tucked between its legs?

That was propaganda coups many would have cheerfully died for in the past, and he didn't want to see it handed over to the bastard butchers of Taiwan and Tokyo.

That was a secondary concern, though. For Liam, it was the fact that he didn't see any reason why they would not continue to press the attack. They'd gotten their carrier kill, but why not the entire task force? If they were looking for a propaganda coup - and he knew that they were - that was the big one... and it wasn't as if people were going to any more pissed off than they were going to be anyway.

Still... if we try to fight...

He shook his head, there wasn't any real good answer. His orders were clear - they'd pick up the pilots from the Enterprise on Iwo, grab what supplies they could, and make for Pearl.

*****

The Makin Island cut through the surging seas, destroyers on all sides, and fighters flying top cover. In normal circumstances, it would be an inspiring sight, one of power and strength. The smoke pouring from several of the ships gave truth to that lie, however, if one somehow missed the fleet of ships following in the distance.

The Bloc Fleet had joined up with a second force, nearly doubling its numbers, now boasting three carriers and a division's worth of destroyers, cruisers, and support vessels.

They seemed happy to continue picking at the American fleet, keeping them pressed and running, denying them time to rest. They were hounds running the fox into the ground before the hunters, waiting for the beast to tire so it would be easy to take.

Patience in all things.

*****

EBAN HuangLung

Admiral Chien looked over the reports with satisfaction. The plan had continued apace while he was working on his small part of things which had been a source of slight envy for him earlier, though he had fought that emotion down for the good of the Eastern Alliance Bloc. He had originally wanted to be assigned to one of the occupation forces, where a great deal of glory was to be had.

Chasing down fleeing enemy ships had felt like an insult slipped in to mock him when it was first presented.

Being the first Commander in over a century to sink an American Carrier, however, had gone a long way to smooth over those concerns.

Still, the eighth fleet had finished its duty to the south and was moving North now to join up with his forces.

Guam was now under Bloc control. All remaining American forces on the Island were burning on the beaches. The Pacific would be the damascene of the Eastern Alliance, a vital buffer between the United States, their Allies, and the easternmost domain of the Bloc. To the west, that barrier would be Africa and the Middle East.

The Eastern Alliance Bloc was now the preeminent power on Earth, and there was nothing the West could do. The Americans had frivolously cast their wealth about, allowing it to be stolen rather than used as it was intended because to their governments the money they played with was someone else's.

All things within the Bloc belonged to the council, and those who worked within the government were not merely stewards of the nations' wealth, but also it's owners.

That was the difference that would tell.

*****

USS Makin Island

A fighting withdrawal was one of the most difficult maneuvers in military operations, no matter what level you engaged in. Maybe of the issues that gave the most trouble at a squad level were considerably easier to deal with when you were commanding a small flotilla, however, at that scale logistical problems began to swamp even the most prepared command structure.

For Major Gibb, rather than it being a matter of combat, the entire maneuver quickly became one of ensuring that all of his forces had the fuel needed to make it to the next objective and that no one got left accidentally out of the cover of the defensive fire zone such that they might be more easily taken out by the enemy fighters.

"Sir, call for you from PACOM."

Liam managed not to swear, but it was close thing. He did *not* need the Pentagon sticking their noses into this at the moment, and it was a fair bet that PACOM would be relaying orders from them.

"I've got it," He said, turning in his seat and opening up the appropriate app on his console. "Liam."

"Major, we've been monitoring your situation," An Admiral told him seriously over the video call, his eyes appearing to look right into Liam's lower chest.

"Sir," Liam said, looking right into the camera as he spoke. "We've moved as many people from the Enterprise as we could before moving on, unfortunately, the Admiral…"

The man on the screen held up a hand, the motion stopping Liam. "We know about Bonet. This isn't about that. They hit Guam, Liam. Last sighting of the fleet that did it, they were sailing North."

That did manage to make Liam swear, for two reasons. If the Bloc had actually taken a US Territory, that was a strong signal that they didn't intend to stop with Japan and Taiwan, not that he'd expected them to. Guam was not merely a place where Americans were stationed, it was American territory. For them to take that meant that they were willing to engage in total war with the US.

And, secondly, Guam was almost due south of his ship's current position.

"So, they're coming up after us," He said, eyes on the camera. "Sir I cannot guarantee that any of my command will reach Hawaii. Support…"

"Is not available, Major, as much as I hate to say this, you're on your own. The closest task group is in the South China Sea, but they've been driven South, through the Philippines and are going to group with the Aussies and try to hold the line there. Nothing else is close enough to get to you in time."

Liam nodded slowly.

He'd known that, of course, but thought it was remotely possible that there might be some sort of air support the brass might be able to commit within range. Of course, if they had anything that could take on the bloc fighters that would be news to him so, as he'd thought, a remote possibility.

"Do you have orders for me, Sir?"

"I wish I did. Officially, you're to get your ships and your people back home by any means available to you," The Admiral said. "Unofficially…"

The last word just dragged out.

"Just do what you have to, Major."

Liam gave a single curt nod, "We will give a good accounting of ourselves, Admiral. Of that, you have my word."

The Admiral looked pained when he said that, and like he wanted to say something, anything else, but finally he just nodded in turn.

"Godspeed, Major."

"Semper Fi, Admiral."

The screen went dark, leaving Liam thinking furiously.

The situation was evolving extremely rapidly, leaving him with fewer palatable options and even less in terms of resources with which to make those choices work.

He quickly logged into the SIPRNET through the satellite network and pulled the data on the Bloc fleet to the South.

They didn't have a current location, but their projections made it clear that the fleet was moving to cut off their withdrawal to the East. If he turned to make the Trans-Pacific crossing as he'd been intending, they'd have him between a hammer and anvil.

An unpalatable option indeed.

What else is on the board, though?

He could turn southwest, head for Australia as well. That would be the better of the two options, it appeared, except that the moment he did they'd move to hammer his flotilla before they could get close.

Damned if we do, damned if we don't.

Liam found himself eying the little Island on the map, the digital circle he'd drawn around it earlier still present.

Iwo Jima.

*****

Iwi Jima

Jolly Rogers Squadron, Hela

The island was a rock in the middle of the deep blue sea, barely more than a mile across in any direction, and as completely alone as any place she'd ever seen. Hela shook that from her thoughts, however, and brought her F35 around to line up with the runway.

Iwo didn't have a full-time air traffic control, but they'd gotten someone to the field to get things ready, not that she thought there was much hope of that happening. There just wasn't any way the little Island could be ready for what was about to hit it.

"Iwo Control, Jolly Rogers Actual."

"Roger Jolly Roger, this is Iwo Jima," A fairly badly accented voice responded. "We have cleared the runway for you."

Well, that might be about as good as I'm going to get, she thought, glancing at her fuel status. The JSDF had once run a military base off the Island, but that had been shut down years, perhaps decades for all she knew, ago and it seemed that the facilities weren't quite up to protocol any longer.

She wasn't on fumes, but it was close enough that she didn't have a lot of options either way, so she just acknowledged the call.

"Roger Iwo, we're coming in." She said before switching off to her squadron. "Alright, by the books on this one. Call out your fuel numbers. I want the lightest down first in case anything untoward happens on the ground or in the air to delay operations."

*****

One by one, the F35s of the USS Enterprise began their approach to the Iwo Jima landing strip. The runway had been built and maintained by the JSDF after they took the Island back over in 1968 and had run it as a base for several decades before it was decommissioned. The facilities had been kept up, however, partially paid for by the US Government to allow for yearly memorials to continue.

The runway was over two and a half kilometers long, more than sufficient for the F35Cs off the Enterprise as they began putting wheels down as quickly as they could with minimal traffic control.

Behind them, still hours from the Island, the US and JSDF ships continued their path toward the Island.

*****

USS Makin Island

Gunny Hadrian looked out over the deck to the heaving seas, the island was now clear in the distance and getting closer by the moment.

"That's Iwo Jima, huh?" Meer said from over his shoulder. "Don't look like much."

"It's five thousand acres of hell, corporal, soaked in the blood of Marines and Japanese soldiers, and left the ferment for over a century," Hadrian told him sharply. "And not one of them, on either side, gives a damn whether you think it looks like much."

Meer flinched back, looking down from Hadrian's sharp look. "Sorry, Gunny."

Hadrian sighed, figuring he'd probably overdone it a little.

"Don't worry about it, corporal. Ignorance is forgivable, willful ignorance is not," The Gunny said. "But I've got a feeling that you won't be ignorant of this for much longer."

Meer frowned, "Gunny?"

"Look around," Hadrian said, nodding back to the ship. "Notice what they're prepping?"

His squad were aircraft mechanics, and good ones, but there wasn't much work to be done for the F35Bs currently resting in the hangars of the Makin Island. There was, however, a lot of work going on in other sections.

The Corps had officially divested of Main Battle Tanks in the 2020s, so they didn't have any of the big Abrams being prepped, but the landing vehicles were being loaded up with striker vehicles and mobile rocket launchers.

There weren't too many reasons to be putting those on landers, not as far as Hadrian could tell.

Only one came to mind.

The boss was intending to fortify Iwo.

Meer looked pale, having obviously put two and two together himself.

"That's crazy."

"Crazy is running while they pick us off one by one," Hadrian said, looking out over the heaving seas. "This? This is just desperate."

"That's not any better!"

He looked at the young man sharply, "Are you or are you not in the Marines, corporal?"

"Oorah, Sir."

The response was automatic, Meer didn't even think about his response. Hadrian nodded in satisfaction.

"Then suck it up, and start thinking back to basic," He told the mechanic. "Because unless I very much miss my bet, you'll have a rifle in your hands very soon."

*****

Liam watched the island approach through the armored glass of the *Island's* well, Island. The control tower mounted to one side of her flight deck offered the best view of the area around the ship, and it was a breathtaking one in actuality.

The sea was breaking on the reefs around Iwo, the Flotilla aiming for the beach where they could land as much gear as possible. The ships were now overloaded, with more men than they could comfortably carry thanks to pulling men off the Enterprise and other lost ships, but they had a few Marine Corps ships in the group with enough amphibious gear to land what they had in a relatively short period.

Fortifying Iwo was probably not possible if he were being honest with himself, and he was. Like the Japanese commander during the Second World War, Liam was aware that he had no real chance of actually holding the Island, and exactly like that man he was hoping instead that he could *bleed* the enemy as much as possible before he fell.

That was something he couldn't properly do with more than half his firepower and fighting men stowed below decks, unable to give a response, as they would be at sea.

As he watched, the first of the amphibious landers were already launching from the Makin Island and other Marine ships.

Physically, in terms of a proper location to defend, the Island left much to be desired.

Liam had to admit, however, there was something… *poetic*… about the situation.

He looked back over the sea, out to where he knew the enemy ships were lurking.

Now, I just need to convince them to face us here, rather than just destroy our ships and leave everyone to starve after they sail off.

"Oorah," He said softly, reaching for the radio.

*****

Chapter Fifteen

EBAN HuangLung

"They're doing *what*?"

Chien wasn't certain he believed his ears, and he felt the need to have it repeated just in case he'd just completely invented something out of the air.

"It appears that the Americans are landing forces on Iwo Jima, Admiral."

That was oddly what he'd thought the man had said.

"Are they mentally deficient?" He asked without thinking before sighing. "Of course they are, they're American."

Granted, he could appreciate that the commander of the little flotilla didn't have many, or any, attractive options. However, he had to realize that the Island was indefensible, and had a paucity of any sort of resources that could be utilized even were that untrue.

Chien finally decided that he needed to see this entirely for himself, getting up from his office desk, "Very well, I'm coming down to the Command Deck."

"Yes, Admiral!"

He arrived on the deck a few minutes later, walking directly to the Intelligence section. "Show me."

"Satellite imagery, Admiral."

Chien frowned, leaning in to look closer.

He could see fighters lined up along the airfield, some clearly in the dirt and on grass covered areas, which made sense. Fighters from the Enterprise, he would presume. He'd expected them to make use of the Island to recover their pilots before they moved on.

The amphibious landers that were lined up on the beach?

Those made much less sense.

They're actually landing on the Island. This is... I don't even know what this is.

He knew that the Americans had some nostalgia for the hunk of rock, the location where they fought one of the battles of the Second World War. It hardly seemed like an important one, however, when one looked at the history.

At the time, however, the Island had some strategic value at least.

Now, it was just a chunk of rock sticking out of the ocean, so far from anything resembling value that even the Japanese had abandoned it long ago.

"Admiral..."

The man at the communications station sounded... puzzled. Chien looked over, frowning.

"What is it, Lieutenant?" He asked, mildly irritated at being interrupted.

"The Americans, Sir... they're transmitting."

"So? I expect they're in communication with their mainland."

"No Admiral, I mean in the open, unencrypted."

"To who? Us?"

"Yes Sir... but more than that, it's going out over several frequencies in addition to ours and..." The man blinked, tapping in commands. "And over the internet as well. It's worldwide, Admiral."

"Play it for me."

*****

USS Makin Island

"Is it ready?" Liam asked, glancing over at his communications officer.

"Yes sir," The young woman nodded. "You'll be going out unencrypted on multiple frequencies, including several major ones in use by the Bloc, and we're live feeding it to several social media sites through the US Marines account… Sir, are you sure about this?"

Liam snorted, "If I were, I'd expect you to have me committed. Hell, no I'm not sure, but we need to do something. If we can get them focused on us, that's *three* less fleets attacking US assets for the near future… We'll never make Pearl anyway if we run. I say we fight."

"Oorah, Major," The young woman nodded. "With you."

"Never a doubt, Lieutenant," Liam smiled thinly, picking up the mic. He glanced once more at her and got a nod back, then thumbed down the transmission button.

"Bloc Naval Forces, this is Major Gibb, US Marines Corps, Commanding Officer, USS Makin Island. I hope you've enjoyed the chase, because this is the end of the line." He said firmly. "We're done running."

He paused, letting his words settle.

*****

EBAN HuangLung

"Is he serious?"

Chien snapped his hand up, silencing whoever it was who'd spoken.

"Be silent," He snapped. "This is important."

The American had paused, letting his statement have the fullest impact it could. Chien knew it would play well with the American public, but he honestly did not particularly care. He was more concerned with what impact it would have on the immediate future of his war plan.

Do I split off the fleet to other targets? I won't need more than one task group to handle them if they're pinning themselves down like this.

"You might not know what this Island is. To most people, it's just a rock in the middle of the ocean, if they even know it exists in the first place… but this is where six thousand US Marines and damn near twenty thousand Japanese soldiers left this world. It's holy ground, and if you want us off it, you're going to have to come drive us off."

Chien looked around at the other officers around him, not quite believing what they were hearing.

"He's insane," A commander said, "Blow their ships from the sea and leave them on that rock until they starve. What do we care?"

There was truth in that, Chien had to admit. The Bloc didn't give a damn about some tiny rock in the middle of the Pacific, not for any strategic reason at least. However, the American was right about one thing… symbolically, the Island meant something to his country.

It was suicide to try and hold it, however, so Chien honestly couldn't imagine what the American was thinking.

It made no sense.

*****

The words of Major Gibb went viral, almost as he spoke them. Almost two hundred nations on Earth, and not a single one wasn't playing the words on *some* channel, whether it be official or illicit.

In the United States and the nations allied with them, people stopped what they were doing as it played and slowly gravitated to the source of the broadcast. In Eastern Bloc nations, where the broadcast was run on pirate stations, those listening were confused, many not knowing what the American was talking about but knowing that it was something of importance even as the National Council quickly put out their own version to ensure the spin they wanted was made.

For a brief moment in time, however, the attention of nearly the entire planet was focused on a single island in the pacific of barely more than 5000 acres and with no population on record.

Iwo Jima had just become the most important location in the world.

*****

EBAN HuangLung

Chien narrowed his eyes as he listened to the Marine as he continued talking… taunting, actually, *daring* him to take his forces against that tiny insignificant spec of rock, as if it were an actual fortress that could be defended.

It was lunacy, nothing else could explain it.

He'd always known the Americans were mentally fragile, but he hadn't expected their military to crack quite this easily.

"He doesn't truly expect us to bother assaulting that island, does he?"

That was exactly what Chien was wondering, and what he didn't have any answer to that made any sense. Because everything he was hearing told him that was precisely what the Americans were expecting, but he couldn't imagine that even they could believe in something that insane.

"Admiral, we should simply disable their vessels and leave them to starve on that rock," A commander said.

Chien was having a hard time disagreeing with that assessment.

"There may be an issue with that, Commander," The lieutenant at the communications system said cautiously.

"What do you mean, Lieutenant?" Chien asked, looking sharply at him.

"The broadcast has gone viral, worldwide… and has been rebroadcast within the borders of the Alliance, Sir."

Chien closed his eyes, masking a groan.

That was… not good.

"How is the Council reacting?" He asked, uncertain if he wanted to know.

"They've already assured everyone that the Island will belong to the Bloc forces by this time tomorrow, Sir."

The Admiral didn't swear. He was more disciplined than that, but it was a closer moment than he'd had in a long time.

"Signal the fleet," He said, "I want them prepared for an assault before the Americans can entrench their positions."

"But Admiral…" The Commander tried to object, but Chien cut him off with a gesture.

"Go," He ordered. "Prepare. I need to contact the Council."

"Yes, Admiral."

*****

USS Makin Island

"Major," The Lieutenant at the communications center softly, eyes on the screens in front of her, said. "I think you should see this."

Liam set the microphone down, crossing the short distance to her. "What is it?"

"We're monitoring the response to your statements, particularly in the Bloc," She said, "The official mouthpiece for the Council has made a statement."

Liam felt his pulse speed up. This is what he was counting on.

"And?"

"They've promised that the island of Iwo Jima will be in Bloc control within twenty-four hours."

Liam settled back on his heels, a satisfied expression taking over his face.

"Excellent."

"Really, Sir?"

He lost the look as he turned back to her, his expression now neutral. "Lieutenant, they were going to pick us off slowly, one by one, without incurring many losses if we tried to run. That was option one. Option two was for them to blow our ships out from under us and leave us here to starve until someone got around to attempting a rescue, which I'm betting would take a while. We needed a third option."

She looked skeptical, causing him to sigh slightly as he looked out on the Island through the armored glass of the Makin Island's tower.

"Do you know the history of the island, Lieutenant?" He asked.

"Of course, Sir, one of the major battles of the second world war, and Marine Corps legend among other things."

He nodded, "That's correct. Now, what do you know about the Commander of the Japanese forces here?"

She blinked, thinking back, but finally gave up, "Not much, Sir."

"Pity. Tadamichi Kuribayashi," He said. "Was a Lieutenant General in the Japanese army. When he was assigned the defense of Iwo, he knew he couldn't win. It was an impossible task, however. Survival really wasn't a mission requirement. What he set out to do was *bleed* the US forces as much as he could, in the hopes that we wouldn't be able to mount as effective an invasion of his homeland as we might otherwise have done."

Liam paused soberly. "As it turned out, it was a pointless sacrifice on both his side and ours, nuclear weapons made the entire exercise one of futility."

He pursed his lips, looking discomforted at having said that, but then his expression cleared. "BUT, neither he nor any of the men involved had any idea of that at the time. They fought with what they knew, and it was the *only* battle of the war in which US Marines had a higher casualty count than the enemy. Twenty-five thousand dead and injured on our side, twenty thousand on theirs... almost all of the Japanese fought to the death."

He looked around, noting that everyone on the command deck was now listening.

"They did that. They fought that *hard* because they knew that every man they stopped *here*, on this island right out there, was one less rifle that could be pointed at their country later."

Liam turned, nodding back out to sea to the North, then waved roughly to the south as well.

"There are *three* fleets out there, gunning for us. That's Three less fleets that are not hunting down other targets or securing the Canals at Nicaragua and Panama. Three less fleets that aren't preparing to land on Hawaii or, God forbid, the West Coast." Liam doubted the Bloc was actually crazy enough to land forces on the mainland, of course, though he'd have sworn they weren't crazy enough to invade Japan a few days earlier, so he wasn't taking that chance either. "Three fleets that we can pin down here if we play this just right."

"Oorah, Major!"

The response had come so fast and in unison that he'd almost been surprised.

Almost.

"Hoorah, Marines. Let's get to work."

*****

Chapter Sixteen

Alamagordo New Mexico

Eric eyed the radio in the transport, not quite believing what he'd just heard, though he supposed he shouldn't be nearly so surprised.

"Did that guy really just call out the entire Bloc Navy over a rock in the middle of the ocean?" The driver asked, unbelieving.

"It's not a rock," Eric said instantly. "That's Marines Corps holy ground, and yes he did."

"I always knew that Marines were out of their gourds, but this? This takes the cake."

Eric wasn't about to argue that Marines weren't nuts. He'd been a Marine. He knew too well just how crazy it could get. He wasn't sure that this, in particular, was insanity however, nor was he entirely sure it wasn't.

The military transport hummed through the old chain-link gate that blocked off access to the runway and hangar he was renting, leaving Eric to look around and see just what was going on since he'd left.

Max had moved in military police to run security from what he could tell, Air Force from the badges. He just hoped they were all vetted properly. He'd had his fill of gunfire already.

They pulled to a stop and Eric dropped out of the transport, boots crunching on sand and gravel as he started walking into the hangar. Inside he could see people gathered around the large TV he and Bradley had been using as an organizer for the project, and as a TV of course.

"What's going on?" He asked, leaning over to check what was on the screen. It looked like a war film.

"The forces on Iwo are live-streaming their preparations," Max said.

Eric blinked. "You're shitting me."

"I... honestly, I don't get it myself," Max admitted. "Though they are being careful not to show too much from what I can tell. It's hard to figure exactly where on the Island they are, and I'm not sure how much is real and how much is decoy work, but yeah they're actually streaming defense preparations."

Stephen scoffed, "You think that's crazy? The Bloc has started streaming their preparations for the assault."

Max and Eric both turned to where the kid was sitting behind a laptop.

"They're *what*?" the pair asked in unison.

"I know," Stephen shrugged. "It's nuts."

Eric strode over, leaning in to check the screen. Sure enough, he found himself looking at what appeared to be a hangar deck of some sort, though it was cramped by the standards of a US Carrier. The new fighters were instantly recognizable, though, so there was that.

This was the first time he'd gotten good imagery of them while they were sitting on a deck. Most of the pictures he had were a little blurry due to how fast the damn things were moving. Eric memorized the features as best he could, noting the minimal wings and sweeping design with interest.

"So, we've got a bunch of American Marines and sailors..."

"Don't forget the JSDF people," Eric said absently.

"Right, and JSDF forces," Max amended. "All getting ready to re-enact the Alamo... live on worldwide streaming, no less, while Santa-anna's forces, who will be played today by the Bloc, are *also* running the whole thing live for the whole world to see? Have they both lost their goddamned minds?"

"It's propaganda," Eric growled. "The Bloc expects a rollover curb stomp. They want the world to see the remains of the Seventh get turned into paste."

"Yeah well, they're going to get what they want," Max sighed. "I called the office. They've got three fleets converging on Iwo. Even with proper forces, there's no way they hold that Island."

"They're not planning on holding the Island, Max," Eric said softly. "They're planning on dying on it."

*****

Washington DC

White House Situation Room

"Who authorized the Marines to stream the preparations like that?" the Vice President asked, more curious than anything.

"No one, Sir," The SecDef responded. "I believe they're currently operating more on a beg forgiveness than ask permission basis."

The VP snorted, but only rolled his eyes as they continued to watch the streaming feeds while the Generals and Admiral present argued over what could, or more accurately could *not*, be done.

"There have to be some forces we can direct to them," Givens said dully, not believing what he was hearing.

"No sir. The closest fleet is the Fifth, and they're several days away… and they're harassed by the Bloc forces themselves," Admiral Corrigan said, his tone angry even as he managed to keep his face from showing much expression at all. "Nothing from Pearl could get there in anything resembling a timely manner."

General Jannis, the Air Force Rep, was having less luck hiding his anger. "We could get air support on-site, but we've got nothing that could take the Block fighters. They own the skies, Sir."

Givens grimaced. *That* was a bitter pill to take. US Forces had owned the skies for more than a century, always fighting under friendly… or, at worst, neutral skies during that time. The fact that they'd been leapfrogged so effectively *and* been blindsided by it at the same time?

Infuriating.

"You're all telling me," He said slowly, looking around, "That those men and women are on their own?"

The men and women at the table looked at each other uncomfortably, each hoping someone else would answer the question.

"Yes sir," Brigadier General Kitts cut in. "Most of them are my Marines. So believe me when I tell you, we don't have a damn thing we can cut loose for them."

Givens slumped in his seat, looking like he'd aged twenty years in the last few days.

Kitts sighed, "I'll call Major Gibb and get him to at least cut off the streaming…"

"No."

Everyone looked at the President, shocked.

"Sir…"

"I said no." Givens straightened up. "If they're going to die on that Godforsaken Island, we're going to watch. We're *all* going to watch."

He looked around the room.

"Get angry, ladies and gentlemen. Get very goddamned *angry*," Givens told them all. "Because this war is just getting started."

*****

Alamogordo New Mexico

Max glanced up from the screen where he was watching the Marines and JSDF digging into some part of the Island, putting trenches and tunnels down. He didn't know if it would help much, but it was keeping them busy he supposed. He noticed, however, that Eric wasn't watching anymore. Instead, he was laying on a garage creeper and clanking away from under the device that took up the center of the hangar.

Max made his way over, frowning, "Eric?"

"What?"

"What are you up to?"

"I think I've cracked it," Eric said. "You get your experts here yet?"

"Some," Max nodded.

"Good. I need an Engineer."

Max started to say something but thought better of it as he turned.

"Hey! If you've got a PHD get your ass over here!"

Wheels scraped on cement as Eric pushed himself out far enough to look up at him as he turned back.

"Really?" Eric asked, eyebrow cocked as men and woman started filtering over. "That's your way of calling them?"

"It works."

Eric rolled his eyes and slipped back under, going back to work.

Max laughed, turning around to the group that had circled him. He pointed to Eric's feet. "You all work for him now. Don't fuck up."

Then he pushed through them and headed back to the screen.

*****

Eric groaned when he heard Max's enjoinder to the group of doctorates. The last thing he needed or wanted was to ride herd on a bunch of eccentric doctors, but screw it, he needed help.

He pushed out from under the device, looking at the faces staring back at him.

"Aeronautical Engineering?" He asked hopefully.

A woman and a man raised their hands.

"Good, get down here. I need some advice," He said. "The rest of you, have you done the reading?"

The expressions were enough to answer that. "Go to it then. We don't have time to dick around and I'm going to need you all up to speed on what we're starting with." He said before looking to the two engineers, "You'll have to get caught up on the reading as you can, but in the meantime, you get to hit the ground running."

The two nodded.

"Eric Weston," He said, grabbing a wipe to clean off his hand before extending it to shake. "I was the assistant on this project until recently, in addition to being the chief test pilot."

"The assistant?" The woman asked, taking his hand. "Who is in charge? Is he or she available? Oh, I'm Diane Garrow, by the way."

Eric's expression darkened, "No, I'm afraid he won't be available."

"Brian Cooke," The man said, kneeling and looking under the device. "What seems to be the issue you need a hand with?"

"Last time we plugged this into an airframe it turned it into modern art," Eric said, nodding. "Fighting Falcon out back, if you want to check the stressors."

"Without a doubt," Brian said. "So it works, then? anti-gravity?"

"I don't think that's what it is," Eric shook his head. "I think… I think it does something with mass."

Brian blinked, "Wouldn't that be anti-gravity?"

"Not if I'm right. It manipulates gravity certainly, if only indirectly…" Eric said thoughtfully. "But anti-gravity implies a reflective component, something that repels gravity. This doesn't do that."

"Huh. I'll have to read what you have then," He said. "Ok, I'm going to survey the airframe and take pictures and notes. Did you mark where this thing was mounted?"

Diane nodded. "I'll go with him."

"Mounting points are sprayed in red paint," Eric nodded. "thanks, and good luck."

*****

Stephen looked around uncomfortably, feeling rather out of place in the hangar he'd been hanging out in for quite some time. There were new faces everywhere, and a lot of them were armed. He had been engrossed by the news, of course, as had everyone. But for now, there wasn't a lot to watch coming out of the streams and he was starting to wonder if he really should be there.

He knew a lot about planes. He'd always wanted to fly since he was a kid, and he'd learned a lot from local pilots and mechanics over the years, including a lot from Eric after he moved into the area a few years earlier.

He couldn't hope to keep up with the talk that was surrounding him at the moment, however. Men and women talking about quantum entangled particles and propagation of gravity fields and stuff he couldn't even understand enough to remember the words properly. It was a long way from the discussions with Eric about aerodynamics and mechanical engineering.

Hell, even Bradley had helped him a lot with the sciences…

Stephen felt the discomfort intensify as he remembered what happened to Bradley. He shuffled his feet before slowly making his way over to where Eric was working, dropping down to a crouch.

"Hey."

Eric glanced at him before returning to what he was doing. "Hey kid. You ok?"

"I don't know," Stephen said honestly. "Everything… It just seems to be changing, all at once."

"Yeah," Eric said. "The world will do that to you once in a while. It's never pleasant."

"How do you deal with it?"

"You suck it up, if you can, and just slog forward. As long as you keep moving, you'll get through it eventually."

"And if you can't?"

Eric sighed. "Then you swallow your pride, and you ask for help… you asking?"

Stephen had to think about that for a moment, "No. I think I can keep moving."

"Good man. Come on, give me a hand here."

*****

Within hours of going live, the streams coming from both the island of Iwo Jima and the Bloc fleet had exploded across the internet, going viral in the way few things ever managed.

Tens of thousands were watching in minutes. Hundreds of thousands within the first hour, and before three hours had passed no one was entirely sure how many were watching because so many millions were live on dozens of different sites.

Hundreds of millions were the conservative numbers. All of them, at that moment, watching men dig into a small island in the Pacific… or prepare aircraft to assault said island.

Nothing much was happening, but no one was turning off the feeds.

Bars across the world ran them instead of sports. People just stopped what they were doing to watch.

Everyone had the dawning understanding that they were watching something that, one day, they'd be asked "where were you when this happened? What were you doing?"

They all wanted to have an answer when the day came.

*****

Chapter Seventeen

EBAN HuangLong

"Admiral, crews report ready for the assault."

Chien nodded, licking at his lips slightly, "Very well."

He'd checked with the Council and his chain of command, and his orders were quite clear. The defiance of the Americans and their JSDF lackeys had to be punished, and publicly, no less.

It put him in an annoying position, but with the forces at hand it should merely add to the glory he'd accumulated thus far. The sinking of the Enterprise would still be the ultimate trophy for his wall of honor, of course, but in many ways Chien expected the conquest of Iwo Jima to be even more spoken of.

The Americans had opted to make it public, likely as part of their ploy to ensure he had to do exactly what he was now ordered to.

Well, congratulations were due to them, Chien supposed, as it had worked.

His two fleets were preparing to make the strike, which would likely take all of the following day and night if the Americans were as dogged as he expected them to be. The destroyers that screened the Island would be able to keep his airpower from completely overwhelming the Island in minutes, their anti-air lasers being effective against the new fighters.

That meant he would need to bring the fight in close, ship to ship.

It would eat up hours, and incur some inevitable losses, but Chien was confident that he could take the enemy ships. After that, with the new aircraft providing cover and softening up enemy positions, landing on the Island and securing it would be a matter of straightforward combat.

Irritating, but it would make for good public relations material the bloc could use to confirm their power to those nations who had yet to come down on a side.

"Initiate the plan," He ordered finally.

"Yes Admiral. All ships confirm, we are underway. Aircraft is launching from our bays. We will immediately dive when they have gone, and the hangar bays are sealed."

*****

USS Makin Island

"Contacts in the air, Major! Moving fast."

"Alright, this is it!" Liam snapped. "General quarters across the fleet! Alert the Island, tell them to get hunkered down."

"Yes sir, General quarters sounding!"

The alarm beat out across the Island as the Marine's F35Bs roared into the air. From the corner of his eye, Liam saw the first of the Navy fighters roaring off the runway on Iwo as well. They'd gotten missiles and cannon rounds into them, and there had been plenty of jet fuel already on the Island, thanks to the JSDF not entirely abandoning Iwo when they officially shut down the base.

"Keep the fighters inside our air defense envelop," He ordered, not wanting any useless sacrifices if he could avoid them. "Make those bastards come to us."

"Yes sir!"

*****

Alarms sounding, the destroyers of the Seventh and the JSDF brought their anti-aircraft lasers to full power as they got ready for the assault.

With the enemy still tucked down just over the horizon, and no spotters to speak of, they couldn't launch cruise missiles yet, but those vertical launch cells were prepared just as the ones with Anti-submarine warfare loads were as well.

Aegis RADAR poured downrange, painting the aircraft in the distance, and getting positive locks on each.

They did not fire, however, because the enemy aircraft were still at a range at which the atmospheric interference would warp the laser's beams and render them largely ineffective. While they were within missile range, anti-air missiles were barely capable of hypersonic flight and since the enemy aircraft could easily outrun them, firing those would be a waste.

The task group wound up… and waited.

It was the enemy's move.

*****

USS Miami

Morgan Passer, Commander and XO of the boat, leaned over the SONAR station intently watching the data that was scrolling past, hoping that an extra set of eyes would luck into something that the SONAR operator might miss.

They knew the Bloc boat was out there, somewhere. It was running quiet and muffled, as it had been before making a run on the Enterprise, but it wasn't impossible to detect either.

Like the other boats in the task group, the Miami was running on definitive search and destroy. Any Bloc ships that they could take out now was less for the task group to deal with, and a lot less for those on Iwo to handle. However, they also had eyes and ears out for the enemy boat.

All four crews wanted that trophy hung on their proverbial wall.

"Screws in the water, shallow… enemy fleet is coming this way." The SONAR operator told him.

"Good. Get firing solutions for each of them and send it over to Weps," Passer ordered, pushing off the console.

"You got it, Commander."

He made his way over to the weapons and tactical control station, "When SONAR gets solutions to you, coordinate with the other boats. Let's not double up our efforts."

"Yes sir."

Captain Burke appeared from the rear of the deck, making his way to the command area, so Passer moved over to meet him.

"Sitrep."

"We've moved to General Quarters, along with the rest of the fleet, Sir," Passer said. "Enemy fleet is moving in, fast and loud. Weps and SONAR are picking out targets and sharing info with the others."

"Good work," Burke confirmed. "Any sign of the enemy Boat?"

"No sir. We're listening, real hard, but they're running quiet."

"Understood. Keep an ear out."

"Aye, sir."

*****

Jolly Rogers Squadron

Hela checked the formation, thumbing the squawk to confirm the orders as she did.

"You heard the Makin, boys," She said simply. "Stay tight, don't get ahead of yourselves. Let them come to us, and then mess them up."

She let her squadmates talk back a bit, refocusing on the task.

The Aegis units on the cruisers and destroyers below them had turned the skies for *miles* around into energy, their multi-megawatt RADAR systems pouring power in all directions and painting targets for the entire battle group.

The Bloc fighters would be tough. They'd learned that the hard way, but first they'd have to come into laser range, and that would not be as easy as she knew the Bloc would want it to be. Ship mounted lasers were more powerful and had higher ranges than the ones carried on her own F35B or, as best they could determine, the similar pods the enemy fighters had.

Even the ship mounted units had limited engagement capabilities, however, and could easily be saturated.

"Watch for cruise missiles," She said. "They'll try to take out the destroyers and cruisers, or at least thin the numbers down before they bring the fighters in."

It was going to get… loud… in short order.

*****

EBAN HuangLung

"The Americans are keeping their forces close to the Island," The XO of the ship said carefully.

Chien nodded, "They hope to prevent our fighters from ruling the skies. They will use their anti-aircraft lasers to defend the Island, with an eye to bleeding off our fighter complement. They have no idea how limited they are, but they know that we cannot easily replace them at the moment."

The XO nodded unhappily, "That is how I read it as well. This will cost us more than it should, Admiral."

"I am aware," Chien said, refusing to allow any hint of his frustration to show either on his face or in his voice.

The orders from the Council tied his hands, however. The Americans, whether brilliantly or utterly stupidly, had managed to force this.

"Do you feel we cannot take the Island?" Chien asked mildly, looking over at his executive officer.

The man's eyes widened, "Of course not, Admiral. They have no chance, that is obvious. It would, however, be far less costly to handle this in a different manner."

There was truth in that, Chien knew, at least in terms of material costs.

"The Americans have turned this into a matter of pride," He sighed, smiling slightly. "No, Commander, the cost would be quite high if we left them alive on that rock, in terms of public perception at least."

Slowly the Commander nodded, "I see."

"Instruct all ships to initiate the final actions," Chien said, leaning over the screens. "Fire."

*****

As one, the dozens of ships that made up the first fleet under Admiral Chien's command launched cruise missiles. Vertical plumes of smoke erupted in all directions, obscuring the ships that fired them, as the missiles climbed rapidly to several hundred feet before leveling out and accelerating toward the Island in the distance.

Above, the Bloc fighters accelerated to match, intending to force the American ships to decide between the fighters and the missiles while they cleared the F35s from the sky above.

With control of the skies, the operation would become far simpler, after all.

*****

Jolly Rogers Squadron

"Here they come," Hela said, flipping the safeties off her weapons and opening the fighter's internal storage. "You know what to do. Hela, Fox Three."

She fired, feeling her fighters lurch a little as the weapon dropped loose, its rocket motors firing. The advanced air to air AMRAAM-260B screamed away from her fighter as she hot keyed another target and fired again.

Around her, the other members of the Jolly Rogers were following suit, as were the Marine F35Bs and the other squadrons from the Enterprise, as well as the cruisers and destroyers as they flushed their vertical launch tubes of their anti-air ordnance.

From the North, the Bloc line of cruise missiles were tearing in fast, barely a hundred or so feet off the deck, and from the South, the American and JSDF response roared defiance. Hundreds of missiles filled the air over the ocean, along with dozens of aircraft as the battle officially kicked off.

The Bloc fighters reacted to the missile launches, climbing fast to outrun the weapons, but the missiles didn't give chase. They'd been aimed at the cruise missiles, not the fighters.

The two lines of weapons interpenetrated somewhat closer to the American and JSDF ships than the aggressors, explosions filling the Pacific skies as the radar-guided missiles sought out their targets and took them out of the sky.

Not all were hit, however, and from the wall of smoke, a few Chinese cruise missiles exploded forth, continuing on target.

Close in SeaWiz roared into action, throwing up a wall of steel as the ships enacted their final defensive fire option, blowing a few more from the skies, but after all of it… some made it through.

*****

USS Makin Island

"The Mikuma's hit! Looks bad."

"I see it," Liam growled. "Get boats in the water, I want men off that ship before she takes them down with her."

"Rescue teams are moving."

Liam nodded, sweeping the fleet with his binocs.

The fight was progressing well so far, the Bloc had obviously expected them to split their attention, maybe even focus their fire on the, admittedly, more dangerous fighters. However, that would have been wasteful, so he'd ordered them to take out as many of the incoming missiles as possible.

Their AMRAAMs weren't as effective against missiles as they were against larger aircraft, unfortunately, but they had done a decently admirable job all the same.

Some got through, that was inevitable. He could see a couple more Tin Cans smoking, but they looked to be still in the fight unlike the Mikuma, who took a hit amidships, near the waterline, causing sympathetic explosions from her magazines.

The air defense lasers were firing constantly or had been up until the Mantis class fighters had climbed out of range. From the smoke trails he could see in the sky, they'd scored some hits, but Liam really didn't know how effective they'd been.

We blunted their cruise missile assault, maybe scorched a couple fighters, but in turn we lost a Tin Can and took hits across another five ships.

"They're pressing forward, Sir. Enemy destroyer screen is in range."

"Check fire, all points," He ordered. "I want their cruisers."

"Yes sir."

The enemy destroyers were small enough that they wouldn't be the same level threat to the forces onshore. They could shell the island, but the cruisers would be able to deliver a hell of a lot more firepower. Cutting them down was his primary goal in the opening engagement.

"Tell the cannon crews that the enemy tin cans belong to them," He ordered. "Save our missiles for the cruisers."

*****

USS Miami

"It's noisy as all fuck up there, Commander," The SONAR operator said softly. "Someone opened a whole can of whup-ass, hard to hear anything else."

"I know," Morgan said, leaning in. "Just keep at it. The enemy boat is out there, and I want that one painted on our hull."

The man smiled, "Aye, aye, sir."

Morgan pushed off the station and carefully made his way back to where the Captain was standing. The Miami was fairly well insulated against transmitting sound to the sea, but any sound was too much in the current situation.

"Getting noisy upstairs, Sir," Morgan said.

Burke nodded, "No surprise. I've spoken to the other skippers. We're going to take a shot at the enemy. See if we can't draw the Bloc boat out, they'll be holding back."

"We're bait, Sir?" Morgan winced.

"Yup," Burke said, popping the 'p'. "So, go get on the hook and wriggle."

Morgan shot him an irritated look, but nodded, "Aye, aye, skipper. Have any preference?"

Burke shook his head, "Just start sending them down to Davy Jones. Dealer's choice, XO."

"Yes, Sir," Morgan said, turning around. "Weps, do we have a firing solution for the lead destroyer?"

"Yes sir."

"Load a pair of ADCAPS and send them along with the Miami's best."

The young officer at the weapons station smiled, "Yes sir."

*****

EBAN HuangLung

"Torpedoes in the water."

Chien looked up at the announcement, "Location?"

"Tracking fifteen degrees south by southwest, distance… four-point two kilometers, Admiral."

Chien nodded, walking over to examine the track.

"Targeting the lead destroyer," He said softly. "Are the surface ships reacting?"

"Deploying anti-submarine warfare as we speak."

"Good. Stay the course," Chien ordered.

"Yes, Admiral."

He didn't want to get the HuangLung involved in some petty shootout with the American submarines. They were of no particular import in this battle as long as the surface ships could keep them busy.

"They've fired again… Destroyer screen is launching anti-submarine missiles."

Chien listened to the reports but kept his focus on the target. The Americans had another carrier in play, though they didn't call it such. He'd had to reference his files to determine the class of the ship.

The USS Makin Island, Marine Corps vessel. Nuclear powered Yellowjacket class amphibious assault vessel, He recalled the official designation.

It carried an impressive array of sea, air, and land combat tools from F35 fighters to light and medium armor. No heavy or Main Battle Tanks, however, since for various reasons the Americans had decided that their Marine Corps didn't need those and had officially retired them in 2024.

Easier for my men, I suppose.

It didn't make much sense to him, but then little that the Americans did made any sense to anyone… themselves included. It was somewhat disturbing how often that insanity seemed to work out for them.

He supposed it made sense at the time, given the sorts of wars the Americans seemed to prefer to fight, but chasing peasants in modified pickup trucks around the desert was a far cry from what they were about to face now.

And it is time to show them just how far.

"Flood the vertical tubes," He ordered.

"Vertical tubes flooding."

"Open the hatches."

*****

USS Miami

"Whoa!"

"What is it, Lieutenant?" Morgan demanded, walking over to the SONAR station. "Did they take the bait?"

"I don't know about that, Sir, but someone out there just flooded their tubes and opened the hatches."

Morgan shivered, a chill running down his back. "Can you get a vector?"

"Yes sir, on the board."

Morgan looked up, eyes on the threat board. The SONAR operator had put a nebulous icon to indicate the new contact there, running a little North-East of their position, behind them in fact.

"You yell the second you hear screws in the water," He ordered.

"Yes sir."

Morgan walked over to the Captain, who nodded.

"I heard. Talk to the other boats, see if they can help triangulate something more precise."

"Yes sir," Morgan said, eyes drifting back to the board.

"What are you thinking, Commander?"

"They're not aiming for us," Morgan said without thinking, causing him to stop and rethink what he'd just said.

"What makes you say that?"

Morgan thought about it, trying to work out what *did* make him say that. It hadn't been something concrete or fully formed, he'd just blurted it out. It took several moments for him to put together an argument to back it up.

"They're already between us and the task group. I don't think they did it to get behind us, Sir. They're going for the… the Makin Island, sir."

Burke was silent for a moment, nodding absently as he considered that.

"You're right." Burke said abruptly, straightening up. "Standby to come around."

"Aye skipper," Morgan said instantly, turning to the helm controls. "Standby to come around!"

"Helm standing by!"

"New course," Burke said, "One twenty degrees, even bubble."

"Make your course One Two Zero degrees," Morgan ordered the Helm. "Zero bubble."

"Course adjusting… One Two Zero degrees, Commander. Coming about."

The Miami tilted slightly as she turned, causing the men on board to catch onto whatever they could to keep upright as the nuclear fast attack boat went on the hunt.

*****

Chapter Eighteen

Iwo Jima

Hadrian grabbed a shovel and threw in beside his squad, digging a trench as the heavy equipment started piling berms.

"Backs into it, boys," He said cheerfully. "Nothing like a good sweat to get you ready for a fight."

His Marines were grumbling, as he'd expect of them, but the dirt was flying ferociously through the air as they worked.

"Remember to put a right angle turn in every ten meters or so," A man said from behind him, grabbing up another shovel and digging in.

"Right," Hadrian said, glancing back. "You with the JSDF?"

The man nodded, "Hirogawa Kiraso."

"John Hadrian," Hadrian said as he worked.

They had backhoes digging along with them, and loaders with buckets clearing and piling the dirt, but the line of men were probably moving more dirt than those machines just from sheer numbers. Hadrian could see Navy, Marines, and JSDF, as well as a smattering of other services and nationalities, packed shoulder to shoulder, flinging dirt, and found the scene somewhat surreal.

It was like he'd been thrown back in time into some bizarre combination of the first and second world war, with an alternate reality twist. Hadrian shook off the feeling, though, and just got back to work.

The trenches would be needed once the bombs started falling. Anything that shielded them from shrapnel and gave the shockwaves somewhere other to go than through his men was a good thing.

In the distance, he could already hear the explosions as the fleet went about their jobs.

Soon enough, it'll be our turn.

The good Lord knew, there would be enough of the Bloc to go around this time.

*****

Kiran Jiang knelt in front of the hole, eyeing it with some uncertainty before he sighed and got to work setting up his gear. He was almost to the top of Mount Suribachi, the volcanic mound that took up the southern tip of the island. It was the highest point on the Island, with the best vantage for the work he was trained to handle.

His comm gear was easy. There was a clear signal to the satellite constellation, and once he had that patched in he was back in contact with the USPACCOM network and had full access to the Air Defense network and the supercomputers the Air Force had wound up for this sort of job.

He patched into the AEGIS network as well, getting the feed from the ships piped into his Augmented Reality hardware.

The hard part wasn't going to be on the technical side, unfortunately. He knew his gear would eventually be picked up by the Bloc forces, and when that happened, he'd prefer to survive their attempts to take him out of play.

"I told you, the tunnels are still here, a few of them are even intact."

Kiran looked up, nodding to the JSDF Commander he'd teamed up with, "Not sure they'll hold up for long, but I guess we're going to find out."

A few of the Marines and JSDF people were of a historical bent, and Iwo Jima was a location of intensely avid interest for both groups. Those with knowledge of the Island, mostly from books but a couple of the JSDF people had been assigned here before the base was shut down, had stepped up to help the rest figure out the best places to dig in for what was sure to be an ugly fight.

"That we will," Commander Shiro said grimly, handing down a computer and battery pack to Kiran, who accepted it and slid the gear into the hole.

They would have to set up a solar array next, but Kiran would run a cable for that and put it a decent distance from the hole. It was designed to reflect a minimum of light, but if it were spotted, he did not doubt that the enemy would make taking his power out a priority.

"I believe you should hurry up," Shiro informed him, looking to the skies. "I believe that the air battle has begun."

"Shit."

*****

Jolly Rogers Squadron

Hela looked up through the bubble canopy, squinting through the glare of the sun. The enemy fighters were above them, descending fast, and that was bad news.

"Get your heads in the fight, boys," She said. "Here they come."

The destroyers and cruisers below were burning down the enemy fighters as fast as they could, their more powerful anti-air lasers tracking and hitting the aircraft with enough heat that the aluminum and titanium skin ignited under the intense radiation, causing some of the Bloc craft to blaze through the sky like meteors.

Keeping them tracked was tricky, however, and lasers took precious seconds to burn their targets down. If the beam wasn't kept on the same spot on the target long enough, in fact, the enemy fighter could escape with nothing more than scorch marks.

"Jolly Rogers, Master Sergeant Jiang."

"Go for the Rogers, Jiang."

"I've got an uplink to the Air Force combat controller network along with their supercomputers winding up to provide better tracking data. I'm on-site and dug in. If something happens to the Makin Island, I have you covered."

"Roger that, Master Sergeant. Good to have you with us."

She wasn't making that up either. An Air Force combat controller would be invaluable in the fight that was coming. Even if the Makin Island was somehow spared the fury that was coming, they didn't have the capability to run this many fighters at peak efficiency.

"Take care, Rogers," the Master Sergeant said. "The enemy have evaded the ships' lasers and are descending fast. Passing FL50, they're going to be gunning for you."

"That's mutual." She said grimly, while thinking, *we need better lasers. The ships should have been able to burn more of them out. Damn.*

Hela could only wish, however, and there were no genies in the air with her so wishes had as much value to her as a solid gold F35 would have just then.

Mind in the moment, she put the nose of her fighter up, lining up for the shot along with the rest of her squadron. Her system, patched into the Aegis network and getting data from the Air Force Combat Controller, quickly locked onto the descending enemy fighters and distributed the target selection across the available fighters.

With the targets spread out, she locked in on hers and shifted over to the laser pod underslung on her F35.

The lock-up tone rang in her ears as she flipped off the last safety, finger curling around the trigger.

"All Fighters, Hela. Special Munitions, Firing."

*****

Noses to the sky, the F-35's from the Enterprise unloaded dozens of beams from their underslung laser pods, energy landing up to burn the Bloc fighters from the sky.

Even as they fired, however, the Bloc Mantis class fires returned the favor with a fevered pitch. Beams of light in the megawatt range *instantly* interpenetrated the two ranks of fighters, igniting flames and throwing smoke into the skies over the small Japanese island.

Below them, on the ground, the troops paused in their digging, some diving for cover as fires ignited from nowhere around them, the Bloc lasers that missed cutting swaths of devastation across the land. Even a small island was a big place, however, compared to the beam diameter of the laser pods, and no one was struck directly.

*****

Iwo Jima

"Alright, quit your gawking and get back to work!" Hadrian growled, throwing his own back into the job.

The scorching of laser fire from the Bloc weapons pods hadn't come too close, but it was enough to remind him… remind them all… what they were digging for. Things just erupting in flames for no damn visible reason, though, that was creepy as fuck.

Even as he worked, though, he couldn't help but steal glances above, scanning the skies for fighters… but more importantly for any sign of chutes. He had no illusions about the eventual outcome, though he had every confidence that the Navy fliers would acquit themselves well, and the Marine Aviators weren't even a question, of course… but sometimes, you did everything you could, and it just wouldn't be enough.

That was just life.

Between the manpower and shovels, the backhoes, and the other heavy equipment, they'd managed to dig in some serious stretches of trenches into the Island already. He was standing at the bottom of a seven-foot-deep trench that stretched out for a couple dozen meters on either side before turning at right angles and continuing on.

He didn't know how much they had, but he'd bet it was *miles* of trench overlooking the beach and defending different points on the island.

"Gunny, delivery."

Hadrian looked up in time to catch the end of a box being handed down. He checked quickly and saw that it was a supply box with ammo and grenades.

"Thanks," He said. "How are we looking on supplies?"

"The Island unloaded everything she had, Gunny," The corporal said. "We've got enough for a small war."

"That's too bad," Hadrian said dryly. "Cause I'm not thinking this is going to be *small*."

The corporal nodded, "Probably right."

"Well go on, get back to work," Hadrian told him. "We'll be done with the hard stuff shortly, nothing but fighting left."

"Hoorah, Gunny."

*****

Jolly Rogers Squadron

Hela screamed as her wingman punched out, his fighter in flames.

She wasn't frightened, not anymore. She was just *pissed off*.

Her laser pod was dead, fired dry, but she still had her Equalizer and a full 180 rounds. The enemy was closing. They seemed to have given up on the idea of hit and run tactics.

Below, another wave of cruise missiles had slammed into the defenses of the small flotilla. Again, most had been shot down, but not all. The destroyers and cruisers were running out of munitions. They weren't dry yet, but it was only a matter of time. There were still pallets in the transports, and they would try to do a replenishment, but in the middle of a fight that was a dicey proposition, to say the least.

The Mantis fighters slashed past her position while she was thinking that, but Hela was already standing on the pedals and throwing the F-35 into a flat spin.

The fighter swung around *hard*, airframe screaming in protest, bringing the gun mount onto target. The Mantis fighters could normally outrun the munitions from her Equalizer, but at the moment they had to kill their speed in a hurry, or they'd be the ones plowing into the island or sea below.

She led one fighter just a bit as she called out a warning that she was firing.

The equalizer snarled, shaking the cockpit as a short burst of twenty rounds tore through the sky and chowdered the Mantis fighter as it was pulling out of its dive.

The fighter broke up, airframe unable to take the stress after being blown full of holes, the high speed and high-gee maneuver turning it to shards. She didn't see a chute or any sign of a bailout as the fighter exploded in fire a moment later.

Hela took a breath, looking around quickly as she got her fighter back level and put more power to the engines.

The skies were a slaughterhouse, with more smoke than air and shrapnel from destroyed aircraft falling like rain. She didn't know for sure how many fighters were still flying on either side, but both had taken heavy hits.

The Bloc were deadly serious now, no longer content to play at their previous tactics.

The enemy was going to win, she knew that, but they were going to *pay* for the victory.

It was the most she could have hoped for after the last couple days, and Hela was almost… almost, mind you, happy to take it.

*****

USS Makin Island

Liam reached out to steady himself as the ship bucked and shook. A missile had made it through the defenses and struck them towards the stern. The deck was destroyed, but he didn't think there was anyone left to land on it, so he supposed it didn't matter.

The Bloc had done what he'd goaded them into doing, pushed forward and engaged his forces with the intent on gaining a decisive victory in a single battle.

He'd already lost three destroyers and a cruiser, plus innumerable damage to the others, but they'd taken out almost ten enemy cruisers in exchange and now the Bloc destroyer screen was fully into gun range.

"Fire!"

The cruisers and destroyers remaining opened fire with their 5-inch guns, 25mm cannons, and torpedoes.

Liam had been hoarding those back, knowing they'd be of little use until the enemy was in close, and the cruise missiles would be far more effective for dealing with the enemy cruisers than any of the smaller ships' armaments. For the enemy tin cans, however, he expected they'd do just fine.

The withering fire tore into the Bloc formation, but the destroyers didn't falter as they immediately began to return fire and the seas became a killing field.

Torpedoes crossed paths, ADCAPS heading North, the Bloc's equivalent sailing south, explosions tearing through ships with increased fervor as the battle continued to pitch upward in a frenzy of destruction and death.

*****

Jolly Rogers Squadron

Hela swore as she twisted her F-35 about to evade the close-in fire from a passing Mantis Fighter. She'd lost all track of her squadron in the fighting, and the area was so plastered with ECM and other countermeasures that she didn't even know if any of them were still in the air.

At that moment, however, it didn't matter.

She violently brought the nose of the F35 around, grimacing through clenched teeth as the old airframe screamed its protest at the treatment, but she ignored it as she squeezed the trigger again.

A burst from the equalizer stitched a line across the sky, most missing short of the target, but the last few tearing into one wing. The Mantis fighter started smoking and breaking up, going down fast as it bled speed, but she was surprised to see that it wasn't torn up by the stresses the way others had been.

Hela eased her finger off the trigger, pacing the fighter down for a moment as the Bloc pilot struggled to get it back under control but only seemed able to barely affect its direction. She noted the course and keyed open her radio.

"Master Sergeant Jiang, Hela."

"Go for Jiang."

"Scored a hit on an enemy fighter and it's going down," She said, calling out the course. "Looks like it might make the Island. Maybe partially intact."

"Roger that Hela, thanks for the call out. I'll see that it gets checked."

"No problem, Jiang. Hela out," She said, pulling the stick over and banking away from the stricken fighter.

There were more kills to be had.

*****

USS Makin Island

"We just lost the Earhart!"

Liam swallowed the urge to rage at the air as that call went out. The USS Amelia Earhart was one of their transport and munitions ships. He lunged over to the port side and looked out in time to see a fiery blaze rolling up into the sky, turning into black smoke, just as the shock wave from the explosion rattled the glass.

That was easily ten percent of their remaining munitions, though thankfully they'd already offloaded everything the men and women on the Island could use. The loss of torpedoes and missiles, however, would be painful in short order, to say nothing of the crew.

He hoped they got off but doubted it from the looks of things. They'd been trying to cross load supplies to the Tico when she came under attack from the last wave of cruise missiles.

He didn't know if the Earhart had been targeted or if they just got unlucky, but either way it didn't matter now.

He wanted to be dramatic, give the order to keep firing or some such nonsense, but every ship was unloading everything they had, and no one was going to stop until their magazines were empty, the last shell on board was expended, and they'd literally fired their anti-air lasers so much that the ship was drifting from lack of fuel to power the generators.

Fighting spirit wasn't lacking in any corner, of that he was certain.

Unfortunately, the Bloc forces were plenty eager for a fight themselves. They'd sucked up losses that any sane force would have broken under already. Liam was certain that the crews of those ships were no happier than he and his were, but they were holding.

Disciplined. Equipped… and trained.

This war will not be decided here, but they'll damn well know they were in a fight.

*****

Chapter Nineteen

Washington DC, White House Situation Room

"Dear sweet lord."

Givens couldn't help but swear as he looked at the fighting, while little they could see through the smoke. Such was the burning and destruction that clouds of it were completely obscuring large warships on either side, making it difficult to maintain a count on which ships were still active as the fighting proceeded.

"How long has it been since the attack started?" He asked.

"Forty minutes, Sir."

Givens blinked, "What? Only that? I thought…"

"Combat is like that, Sir. Sometimes seconds feel like hours. Other times, hours pass by so fast you'd swear they were seconds." The Marine Brigadier said. "I promise you, Sir, for those men… it's felt even longer still."

Givens nodded reluctantly, "I just hate this. We should be able to *do* something… anything."

"Even if they didn't have those fighters, Sir… we couldn't get a force there before this would be over."

"How long?"

"Mr. President?"

"How long to get reinforcements to Iwo Jima, General?" The President asked firmly.

"If we moved everything right now, four days sir."

Four days.

Givens felt a knot in his gut twist.

Those men didn't have four hours.

"What about the Air Force," He looked over to the General representing that branch.

"We could have a response flight in the air in forty minutes, and over the site a few hours or so after that," The general said. "However, as long as those fighters control the airspace... our long-range bombers wouldn't get within five hundred miles before they were taken down."

"We send escorts then," Givens said.

"Fighters can refuel en-route," The General acknowledged. "And they've proven that they're not entirely helpless against the enemy fighters, but they have to get close. Really close, Sir. Sir, we have a wing of F-22s at Hickam. They're higher performance than the F-35 but it will be... touchy."

"I don't care for touchy, General. Make it happen."

"Yes sir," The Air Force man said unhappily, though not so much with either the President or his decision, mostly just with the situation. "I'll make the call."

*****

Alamogordo New Mexico

"Alright, good news and bad news."

Eric pushed himself out from under the device, head-turning to see Max approach.

"Bad news," He decided grumpily.

"Just got word, the Bloc moved into the Middle East as well, securing everything east of the Nile, excepting Israel. They're still holding, somehow." Max said.

"Jesus," Eric pushed his sweat-slicked hair back.

That was bad news, though not as bad as it could have been just a few decades earlier. The country was mostly powered by renewables and nuclear energy now. What little oil demands there were could easily be handled by American and Canadian sources. North America actually produced more oil than it needed by a decent amount, however it didn't *refine* as much as it used. Most of that work was still done by Eastern Bloc nations at this point for reasons that made about as much sense as anything did, he supposed.

Still, the Middle East wasn't as important as it once was, but it was still a strategic buffer between Europe and the Bloc.

A buffer that just got a lot thinner.

"What's the good news?" Eric asked, shaking his head as he got up.

"Delivery arrived for you."

Eric frowned at Max, then looked in the direction the other man had pointed. His eyes widened as he saw a big airframe being lifted off a truck and slowly lowered to the ground outside the open hangar door.

"Well holy hell, is that a Raptor?"

"The airframe anyway," Max said. "We found a couple hundred of them unused in Nevada, the Testing Grounds. They're all earmarked for you now, assuming this project works out. The first dozen are outside."

"Alright, I'll take em," Eric said, grabbing a cloth to wipe his hands off. "Get that thing on a set of rollers and bring it in here."

Max nodded, waving the men outside on before he turned back to his old… friend? Something like that anyway.

"I… have a suggestion," He said hesitantly.

Eric looked at him suspiciously. "Why does that worry me?"

"Because you know me?"

"Unfortunately." Eric told him sourly before sighing, "Alright, what is it?"

"There's an advanced interface program I know of. It's having trouble because of the physiological requirements," Max told him. "But I checked your file, and you fit the bill."

"What kind of interface?"

"Mind-Machine," Max said seriously, looking at the fighters. "No matter what else, we're not going to be able to match the Bloc number for number, not at first. I'm just thinking, maybe we should palm an Ace of our own."

Eric didn't much like the sound of that. He'd worked with mind-machine interfaces in the past, and they certainly had their place, but he'd never found any that truly could replace a hand on the stick and throttle.

"Look, Max, those things are fine when you *need* a workaround. I've seen great stuff for prosthetics, for example, but I'm not strapping on a fighter and trying to fly the damn thing by *thinking* at it."

"It's not intended for that. Look just let me get someone down to talk to you about it, ok?" Max said. "If you're not convinced, no harm no foul."

Eric shook his head, waving the man off. "Fine, but I'm not making promises, and I need to get to work."

Max nodded and left, leaving Eric to look at the big airframe that was slowly being rolled into his workspace. The F-22 Raptor had been a *beast* in its day, probably the most capable production fighter ever made, well until recently at least, but also one of the most expensive. The F-35s were a lot cheaper and little less capable, which worked out to more successful overall in the real world.

If he was right about the device, he probably would have preferred an F-35B airframe to work with, but he could work with this, Eric decided.

He grabbed a flashlight and started going over the airframe, trying to figure out where he was going to mount the device. Luckily, there was a *lot* of room.

This is a big boy.

*****

Stephen stared, wide-eyed, at the new airframe being rolled in. He'd read about the Raptor but knew there were many left in active service. He didn't know where Eric had gotten these from. They were all wrapped for storage in white plastic and he could tell that the powerplants weren't installed and guessed that neither were any of the avionics, but they were still beautiful.

The sleek lines of the fighter were even more impressive in person than he'd thought from seeing them in pictures or documentaries. There had been other, arguably more impressive, prototypes made in the intervening years… but nothing that had gone to production.

He snuck a little closer to one as it was rolled into place, running his hand along the underbelly. The metal and plastic wrap were hot to the touch, the sun-soaked material threatening to burn him, but he didn't drop his hand despite the heat.

Incredible.

Stephen decided right then, that there was no doubt.

He was going to fly one of these beasts. He didn't care what he had to do, it was going to happen.

*****

Hickam AFB, Hawaii

Captain Anthony Dawson waved to his aircrew as he climbed into the cockpit of the F-22 Raptor, sparing a moment's glance to watch the refueler as it roared down the runway and took off.

The bombers would be next, loaded for grizzly with enough ordnance to blow any five fleets out of the water. He and the others in the 19th had an interesting mission profile this time around. He wasn't sure, but he'd never heard of fighters running a bomber escort in the modern era. That was the sort of thing that you heard about from documentaries of world war two missions.

Over three thousand miles to the target, running sub-sonic the whole way, the mission was a four-to-five-hour turnaround with a hell of an exciting few minutes at the pivot he was guessing. Not that he or any of his pilots were complaining. They'd been watching the streams from Iwo for the last few hours, constantly calling up the chain and asking when they were shipping out.

The briefing on the Bloc fighters was lighter on details than he wanted, and certainly he wasn't too happy about tangling with anything that could manage hypersonic, but hell, the 35s had gotten a few kills. He was confident that he could pot a few more in a 22.

That didn't mean that either he, or any of his pilots, were under any illusions.

As he ran the checklist, Tony thought about the streams he'd watched, running the enemy's capability through his mind, thinking through his options and how he wanted to approach the fight.

They'd had better access to the fighting than civilians, getting direct feeds from the F-35s and units on the ground who'd been filming the fight through their onboard cameras. Footage that wouldn't be available to the public for, well probably years unless someone edited together some stuff for a quick recruiting vid or some other such thing.

He'd been riding with Lycan over the hills of Japan when the Marine had potted two over-confident enemy pilots with a short burst.

Balls of steel on that one, just stopping like that and letting them come to him, Dawson thought with admiration. He'd not admit in public anytime soon, lest a Marine overhear, but he also promised himself to buy a round in the man's name when he next got a chance.

The Navy fighters had not quite managed as well, but by the time they'd engaged both sides had learned lessons. Tony still couldn't believe that they'd actually lost a carrier, let alone the Enterprise.

That was just fucking sacrilege.

Tony flipped a switch and powered up the Raptor's avionics, letting everything settle before he lit the fires.

His Raptor rocked a little as the twin powerplants roared to life and, after checking the readouts, Tony flipped a switch to open his channel to the tower.

"Tower, Raptor Lead."

"Go for Tower Control."

Tony glanced to either side, checking on the rest of the wing before he continued.

"Raptor Squadron is fired up, ready to go."

"Roger Raptor Lead, you're cleared to queue on runway Twenty-Six Left. Say again, Two Six Ell. Confirm."

"Confirmed control, twenty-six left. Taxiing now."

He edged the throttle a little, rolling out of the hangar and easing the fighter into the path down to the causeway across the harbor to the assigned runway.

There was already a hell of a lineup. All the runways were jammed, and they'd put the commercial flights in and out of Inouye on hold as well, probably pissing off every civilian for miles. Not that he gave a damn.

There was a war on, and it was time for the 19th to take their shot at it.

*****

Chapter Twenty

DDH-181 Hyuga, JSDF Destroyer

Captain Ichiga held on as a missile slipped through the defense network and slammed into the bow of the Hyuga, tearing her armor up and leaving a gaping hole and twisted metal where her name had been painted just a moment earlier.

"Get teams up there to put that fire out," He ordered.

The Hyuga's cannon was firing fast, each shot blending into the next as they poured the five-inch rounds downrange into the advancing Bloc destroyer they were tangling with. He could see the rounds connecting, tearing up the ship in turn as the Hyuga continued to be the shield of the fleet as she had been designed to be.

"Captain, we're taking on water from the bow!"

"Run the pumps!"

"They're not going to be able to keep it out, we're pushing too deep into the waves!"

Ichiga swore, they couldn't stop now, there were too many holes in the defense net already. Those enemy destroyers had to go down, as many as possible. He gritted his teeth, checking the munitions supplies, and then their course before he made the call.

"All ahead flank."

"Captain! We'll drive her right under…"

"Then drive her under," He ordered. "Just empty the magazines before we go down."

His XO swallowed, but nodded, "Aye skipper. Ahead flank!"

The Hyuga surged forward, driving into the waves, and firing everything she had as the engines screamed. Water was pumped out by the thousands of gallons, but it was driven in by far more than that. The cannon never let up, however, and the last of the vertical launch magazines were flushed, putting everything they had into the air and water.

Nothing but cannon munitions and power for the laser were left, so that was what they kept on firing.

The alarms were screaming, damage from all quarters, such that he almost missed the warning of the next wave of cruise missiles.

Three slipped through this time, slamming into the Hyuga from fore to aft along the port side, rocking her over heavily and breaking the ship in half. Ichiga felt the deck heavy under him and start to slip under, the gun finally quieting.

In the distance he saw the Destroyer they'd been targeting on fire and settling lower in the water, going down fast, and he bared his teeth in a bloody grin.

The Hyuga had three kills to her name before they dragged her down.

*****

USS Makin Island

"The Hyuga is out! Men are hitting the water, sir."

"Get boats out to them," Liam ordered.

"We don't have any in that area. We've got them pulling men out of the water in sector three, Sir."

"Damn it."

The fighting was going about as well as could be expected, he supposed, but since he'd *expected* to die, that wasn't much of a good thing. The enemy might have leapfrogged them in the skies, and that was a bitch and a half to deal with, but on the sea, they weren't nearly so formidable.

The fighting had favored the American and JSDF forces in terms of kills, but the problem was that the IndoChina backed Bloc forces just had too much in the way of numbers. They had two full fleets to the partial one that Liam commanded, and he knew there was a third one out there somewhere on the way.

Their air cover was gone. He didn't even know when the last of the Navy fighters vanished from the sky, the fighting in the skies had been intense. Unfortunately, even with the lasers on the destroyers practically dedicated to keeping the Bloc fighters at bay, the weight of battle there had been heavily against his forces.

He didn't know how many enemy fighters had been downed, but if it was better than a four to one ratio in the Bloc's favor, Liam would be very much surprised. Honestly, he thought that was being optimistic.

It was just a matter of time now.

"Sir, we're out."

"Of?" Liam asked, half looking over.

"You name it, Sir. There's nothing left in the magazines."

Liam wanted to stare. That was something he'd *never* heard before and had never expected to.

"Understood, XO. New Course," He ordered.

"Aye Major."

"Bring us about, heading... one thirty-nine degrees."

"Sir... that..."

"I know."

"Aye Skipper."

He picked up the mic to the ship's caller, "All hands, brace for collision. Say again... all heads, brace for collision."

*****

Gunny Sergeant Hadrian heard a call of shock and looked up in time for his own eyes to widen as he focused on the smoking wreck of the Makin Island, somehow still under power, as it plowed right into the beach and ran itself aground.

The tearing sound of the ship scraping aground as it did, died out, and the big ship tilted dangerously for a moment before coming to a rest, and then ropes were thrown over the side as men began to abandon ship.

He shook himself, trying to clear the shock, quickly calling up the men around him.

"What the hell are you waiting for!?" He demanded. "Let's go get those poor bastards."

His Marines roared, and he led them over the top of the trench and down to the beach. There were hundreds still on the Makin Island, and he knew the major had to have ordered her beached rather than lose them to the sea, which was fine with him. Every Marine and Sailor on board could hold a rifle, and while they had rifles aplenty, hands were in short supply.

Some of the men had been chucked into the surf and were swimming or wading ashore as Hadrian and his men arrived, rushing in to pull them out. They all flinched as a six-inch shell exploded on the beach, showering them with sand and water, but Hadrian kept them working.

A glance to the sea showed that the Bloc cruisers and destroyers had punched through the last of the defenses and were now bringing their guns around. In a few moments he knew they'd be shelling the beach, but he couldn't leave the men on the Makin to die in that hulk either.

"Corporal!"

"Yes, Gunny!" Meer called back.

"Take a little jog back up the beach," Hadrian said. "And pick up one of those Javelins. I think our company needs a proper greeting."

"Oorah gunny!" Meer said, turning and belting it in full sprint back up the way they'd come.

Hadrian kept pulling people out of the surf and pointing them up the beach while keeping the hull of the Makin Island between them and the enemy as much as they could. A roar from the big ship startled him and he flinched back as it started to move again, engines screaming in protest as the rear end began to twist.

He realized that someone on board had the same idea he had, only they knew a better way to go about it, and the ship was bringing its aft end about to cover more of the beach with the hull so he and his men could work.

Hadrian hoped no one in the water was caught by the screws, but he wasn't going to look this particular gift horse in the mouth. In the shadow of the stricken vessel, Hadrian rallied his men and the men and women abandoning ship as explosions began to rain down on the beach of Iwo Jima.

*****

EBAN HuangLung

"The fleet has broken the resistance, Admiral."

Chien nodded, looking through the periscope as they cruised along parallel to the northern shore of the Island.

Several enemy destroyers were still fighting, but they were all smoking and clearly severely damaged, making it only a matter of minutes in all likelihood before the seas belonged to him as the skies already did. He could see more that were sinking, or sunk and resting aground in the shallows, and the rest had run themselves aground when they were unable to keep fighting.

Men were swimming for the beach or jumping off a grounded vessel. A few small boats were picking up the swimmers, but they were being picked off by his destroyers if they strayed about for too long.

The battle was done, with only the mop-up left to be accomplished.

The HuangLung was primarily directing the battle, but they'd spotted an enemy submarine a few times during the battle, and it seemed to be attempting to stalk them even as it was, in turn, stalked. For all that, however, he was not overly concerned. The Americans had once been the masters of sea and air, but that day was in the past.

The American sub would sink just as easily as the surface ships had.

That left the island itself.

"Signal the fleet," He ordered. "I require a landing force to be prepared."

"Yes, Admiral."

It would be best to take the Island quickly before the men on the ground could finish digging in.

The toll of the battle would not make his superiors happy, Chien knew. He hadn't seen the full list yet, but he knew that he'd lost most of his destroyer screen, and the cruisers had taken heavy hits as well.

No Matter, we will take this island to please the Council then link up with the reinforcements before continuing on to secure the former holdings of Japan.

First, the Island, however…

And this annoying submarine sailing about.

*****

USS Makin Island

Liam climbed out of the tower, dropping onto the tilted flight deck as he made his way forward, helping a person here and there to get their own balance as they moved to abandon the ship. He'd ordered everyone off, but some people were taking longer than others.

Beaching her had been a painful choice, but easy all the same. There was no reason for the Island to go down in the deep waters surrounding Iwo, especially not with the fighting only half over. He'd rather die with a rifle in his hand than in the deep blue, and he was confident that most of his men felt the same way.

Artillery explosions were blowing sand and water into the air, and the ship was shuddering from the occasional hit as well as he scrambled over the deck and found where someone had already tossed a rope ladder over the side.

Liam swung over, pausing only when he heard a familiar rushing sound that made him look about. He spotted the trail of a man-portable stinger as the missile roared out over the sea and slammed into a Destroyer that was shelling the beach.

The island was already repelling the invasion.

Liam slid down the rope, dropping into the water at the bottom, and found that he'd have to swim for it. Shore wasn't far, though, and the ship was keeping the waves from pummeling him as well as it was providing shelter from the ship's artillery.

He felt ground underfoot and started stumbling forward through the surf, quickly being caught by a pair of strong arms and helped the rest of the way.

"Thank you… Gunny," He said, checking the Marine's insignia. "I'll be fine."

"No problem," The Gunnery Sergeant said, glancing down before his eyes widened, "Major, Sir."

"As you were, Gunny," Liam laughed tiredly. "In fact, give me a moment to get my breath back and I'll be right with you to help. Get everyone off."

"Hoorah Major," The Gunny said, not hesitating before he ran back into the surf after someone else.

Liam took a couple breaths before he shucked his jacket and followed the Gunny right back into the sea.

*****

USS Miami

The Miami now had three Destroyer kills to her credit, but Morgan was still looking to add a submarine to that tally as was the rest of the crew.

They'd been stalking the elusive Bloc boat for the past couple hours, the deep waters around Iwo perfectly suited to this sort of hunt, but unfortunately the enemy seemed to know it as well.

They'd had her in their sights a couple times. It was hard to hide a boat with this much active sonar bouncing off everything and anything. However, that seemed to count double for them, as every time they thought they were going to get a shot it had faded on them, going deep or just disappearing into the surface turmoil long enough that they lost the track.

Good news, the 'surface turmoil' is rapidly dropping off, Morgan thought grimly, *bad news, it's dropping off because all the ships causing it are sunk or grounded... and they're ours.*

The Captain stepped quietly up behind him, "Anything yet, Commander?"

"No, they're quiet, skipper."

Burke nodded, dropping a hand on Morgan's shoulder.

"Patience, Commander. We'll find them," He said firmly.

"Yes sir."

Morgan took a couple of deep breaths, recognizing that he had been letting his frustrations get to him. That was not a good thing on a sub. There weren't many places one could go to flip out after all, and it was downright lethal in the midst of a mission.

The enemy sub didn't make any sense to him, however. It was big, what they'd managed to record of it made that clear, too big to have been built easily without *someone* taking notice. Yet there had been no reports come down the chain, no rumors, no *hints* of this thing out there.

The Bloc had gotten far too many things past them, between this beast and the fighters above them.

Morgan found himself worried deeply about just what other surprises there were coming down the pipeline from the Bloc in this war.

Hopefully, the bastards have blown their wad, He thought crudely, malice touching his thoughts. *Because if they've got too many more aces up their sleeves, this war might be over before it properly gets going.*

That, of course, was no doubt the plan the Bloc were working toward.

*****

The ships of the Eastern Alliance Bloc settled into a patrol off the shores of Iwo Jima, the men on board getting ready to put assault landers to sea while the Bloc Army officers got their soldiers in line and ready to move.

With the area secured, the supply ships and amphibious assault craft were brought in closer to the island, a thousand soldiers preparing to land.

With the orders in place, and video streaming from nearly as many cameras right back to the Eastern Bloc Council to be edited into a future propaganda film, the landers set off on schedule through the Pacific waters toward those awaiting on the island of Iwo Jima.

The assault landing had begun.

*****

Chapter Twenty-One

Iwo Jima

"Here they come!"

Liam didn't know who'd called that out, and didn't care. Stating the obvious wasn't terribly useful, but he supposed someone had to announce it.

"Give me a rifle," He said, reaching out to his left.

"Here you are, Major," A man said, passing him a Sig M-28 6.4mm assault rifle.

Liam cleared the rifle, then checked the breach and the mag before reseating the magazine and chambering a round. The amphibious landers he could see coming weren't any new big surprise, thankfully, but were the standard Chinese built models that he'd trained his men to deal with for years.

"Alright, men, settle in," He ordered, dropping low behind the berm he was using for cover while the rest of his men did the same.

The trenches and berms were the best they'd been able to get together in the few hours they'd had since the fighting began, but Liam was honestly shocked with how very *much* the men on the Island had dug out, and he was sure he hadn't seen any significant fraction of it.

Thankfully the facilities still maintained on the Island had included some earth moving gear. Most of it was practically antique, but it had worked and that was all he could ask for.

Distant flashes of light from the enemy ships made him hug the dirt tighter, knowing what was coming. Ahead of the landing force, the shelling started along the beach and up into the island, looking to soften up the landing zone for the troops.

All by the books thus far.

"Check fire," Liam ordered over his comm. "Everyone bunker down and weather it. Save your ammo."

That was all they could do, weather the steel storm that was raining down about them. Here and there a shell found its mark, landing in a trench or on top of a berm, the explosion and shrapnel tearing men apart even as dirt and blood were scattered across the island.

It had been more than a century, but the shores of Iwo were tasting blood again.

*****

Hadrian patted the private on the shoulder as the man hugged tight to the Three Oh Seven heavy machine gun, ignoring the explosions as they tore about around him.

The way he figured it, if one of them hit him he was dead. Short of that, he had work to do.

"Major says check fire, private, so you ease your finger off that trigger," He counseled softly. "Your time is coming."

"Oorah, Gunny." The private said, relaxing marginally. "Sorry, just never saw this coming."

"No worry, private. None of us did," Hadrian forced himself to be cheerful. "But hell, it don't get much better than this, does it?"

The Marines around him, and the JSDF people, all turned and looked at him with varying degrees of incredulity.

"Gunny?" The private asked incredulously, packing so much meaning into that one word.

Hadrian laughed, "Think on it, son. This is Holy Ground, is there anywhere better to be fighting an impossible battle against overwhelming odds?"

He gestured behind him, to the volcanic mount south of them, "From one side of this island to the next, the spirits of almost thirty thousand souls, Marines and Japanese Army, are standing and watching over us."

A Corporal a little distance away nodded slowly, "My great-granddad fought here, he made it out. Quite a few of his friends didn't."

One of the JSDF sailors looked sad, "My great grandfather died here. Almost all of the defenders died."

Murmurs of agreement traveled down the line, covered up quickly by the explosions around them. Shared stories, mostly myth Hadrian had no doubt, quickly began to be passed around. He heard men laughing, saw Marines and JSDF men grinning shoulder to shoulder, and couldn't help but wonder at the vagaries of fate.

Bitter enemies, once, the Japanese Imperial soldier and the US Marine could have fed that bitter hate for centuries. Hell, once in history they almost certainly would have. Instead, enemies had become allies, and all of that history led them here.

Hadrian grinned, teeth gleaming.

"Look alive boys, our guests are here."

*****

Amphibious landers hadn't really changed all that much since their first use. They still consisted of an armored shell with a ramp in the bow that men and vehicles could charge down. Unlike the earliest ones, of course, the newest generation had some weapons of their own and they had some cover to protect the soldiers within from above. Oh, and they were a lot larger.

The Chinese built landers pushed themselves up on the beach as the forward ramps came down, light armored vehicles leading the way as the mounted machine guns on the landers opened fire.

Treads dug into the sand as the armored vehicles rolled out, turrets sweeping the area and looking for targets, for long moments no sign of which was to be found.

Then the moment passed, and the air was filled with a long hissing sound as rockets struck out from behind the sand berms, slamming into the armored vehicles as an explosion of machine-gun fire erupted to fill the air.

The Bloc soldiers flooded out of the landers, firing as they hit the beach.

Bullets tore the air apart as the battle for Iwo Jima began in earnest.

*****

"Turn them back!" Liam screamed at the top of his lungs, calling on everything he had to be heard over the raging maelstrom of steel that whirled around him.

He was standing behind the berm, pacing behind the Marines and JSDF sailors and soldiers who were flat out on their bellies, firing prone, pausing only on occasion to fire off a round or two at a particularly interesting target.

It was more exposed to be doing things this way, but he'd learned to lead from the front and had no interest in burying himself in a command post deeper into the Island.

The guns from the ships had slowed, mostly hitting farther inland now that they were trying not to hit their own people on the beach, though not every shot was so conscientious. Every now and then one would explode over the beach, throwing shrapnel into the Bloc forces as well as his Marines, something that Liam expected balanced out in favor of the Bloc since he didn't have any reinforcements to call on.

He brought his Sig up to his shoulder again, firing a trio of high velocity 6.8mm rounds into the charging Bloc soldiers, dropping one hard and maybe injuring another though he might have just scared the shit out of him from the way he hit the sand.

The charge up the beach had slowed to a crawl. Most of the bloc forces were now lying on the ground behind hastily dug berms of sand, advancing slowly behind the light armor.

"Bring up those ManPATs!" He ordered, waving.

Teams of men were lugging crates forward from the central part of the Island, running along the trenches as much as possible, or out in the open when not. Liam nodded thanks as one crate was dropped at his feet, kicking the crate open with one boot before kneeling to pull out the Man-Portable Anti-Tank Weapon, in this case a lightweight SRAW (Short Range Antitank Weapon).

Liam flipped it up over his shoulder and took aim down the beach, glancing back to ensure everyone was out of the backblast radius before he flipped the safety off. The closest armored vehicle was a few dozen meters away, heading right for him and his section of the berm.

He drew a bead on the tank, finger curling around the grip and firing stud.

"Watch the back blast," He called before firing the rocket.

The SRAW was a lighter and cheaper version of the old mainstay for killing main battle tanks, the Javelin, but it was nearly as effective for all that. The rocket lanced away from his position, locked onto the tank as its guidance took over and caused the warhead to suddenly climb away from the beach before reaching a peak a couple dozen meters up.

It slammed back down into the top of the armored vehicle, where the armor was thinnest, and punched through easily with the shaped charge ejecting a molten jet of copper through into the interior of the vehicle's battery bank.

The batteries erupted into flames as the vehicle ground to a halt, hatches popping open as men piled out and started scrambling for cover.

Liam tossed the SRAW over to another Marine.

"Grab some rockets and start popping those bad boys, corporal."

"Oorah, Major!"

*****

Hadrian hugged some dirt as a rain of bullets kicked up the sand in his face, rolling over as he tossed an empty mag and grabbed another from the box beside him.

He seated the mag in the Sig assault rifle, letting the bolt slide closed to chamber a round, then flipped back over onto his belly as he looked down the optics across the blood-soaked beach.

The Bloc advance had ground to a halt on the beach, but they were trying to dig in he could see, and having some success. He wasn't sure how many had died already, on either side, but it was clear that the Bloc forces were well-disciplined, because any lesser force would have broken already under the casualties he could see.

It's been a long time since we've fought a true top tier military, Hadrian thought grimly, wondering if the country was ready for what that likely meant.

He'd spent his career peacekeeping and hunting terrorists.

The thing with terrorists, though, was that they were irregular forces by definition. That didn't always mean they were bad fighters, not by any means, but group discipline? That wasn't really a thing in that kind of warfare. Terrorists considered death to be a victory condition, they set things up so that they won whether they killed you, or you killed them.

That made them tough to deal with, but more so on a political level. In the field, terrorists versus regular force soldiers? You could put money on a lot of dead terrorists.

This sort of fighting was another game entirely, however.

Hadrian didn't see either side giving up easily, and that meant that the winner would truly be decided by who was still standing when it was all over.

Standing in an inch deep of blood, no doubt.

He forced those ponderings away, however. They had no place in the current situation.

His Sig bucked as Hadrian started firing with a slow cadence, taking his time to aim, and put his target down before moving on to the next. He could hear the steady chatter of the 50 cals and the bigger 25mm machine guns tearing up the enemy from either side of him and left that kind of shooting to the belt feds.

"Jesus, Gunny! This is nuts!"

"Shut up, Mac," He growled. "And keep shooting!"

"We're *mechanics* damn it!"

"We're Marines, and a Marine is a rifleman first. Besides all that, today? Everyone on this island fights, no one slacks." Hadrian snarled, glancing over. "So get the barrel of that rifle up over the berm before I kick it, and you with it, over myself."

The man swallowed, but nodded quickly.

"Oorah, Gunny."

Damn right. "Oorah, Marine."

"Airstrike!"

Everyone cursed and hugged the ground as the explosions intensified.

*****

EBAN HuangLung

Admiral Chien watched in silence as the aircraft swept in from the east and delivered their ordnance along the beach. A few were too close to the water, catching the landing troops in their blast radius, but that was a risk with this sort of close air support. The explosions did far more along the defensive lines, though it was impossible to determine just how effective it was due to the myriad of trenches they'd somehow managed to dig in since landing.

"The defenders are resisting fiercely, Sir," His Executive Officer noted.

"Unsurprising, if somewhat irritating," Chien grunted.

He really would have preferred to have left the men languishing on the island, perhaps with a small picket to keep any from being snuck off in small boats under cover of night. In a few weeks, they'd have been begging to surrender. He believed that would have been a far better propaganda coups than merely taking the Island, but the Council did have a point that this particular island would hit the Americans where it hurt.

They had been telling themselves the legend of Iwo Jima for so long it had entered their cultural myth. Chien suspected that a great many Americans didn't even know that the Island had been returned to Japan a century ago, or he wouldn't be surprised to learn that at any rate.

Still, taking the island from hundreds, or more… he didn't have an honest count yet, of devoted defenders would be… expensive.

"Admiral! The Changsha was just struck by torpedoes!"

Chien turned, swearing under his breath.

"Someone find those blasted Submarines!" He snarled.

It seriously should not be that difficult to deal with the American submarines. Like most of their gear, the Americans had been stretching out the duty life of their fast attack subs, doing refits rather than building new equipment as the cuts dug deep into all parts of the global economy. The Huanglung had already eliminated several submarines in this fight, yet this one refused to bow to the inevitable.

They were trying to find outdated submersibles with some of the latest in submarine technology from anywhere in the world.

It really should not be this hard.

*****

USS Miami

"Chalk up another destroyer, commander," the SONAR man said, smiling easily as he listened to the sound of the ship breaking up as it went down.

"Good work. Keep an ear out for our little friend, though," Morgan ordered, patting the man on the shoulder lightly before he dropped back to where the captain was observing.

"We've thinned the destroyers out, Sir. Orders?"

"Leave the tin cans for the moment," Burke said. "Focus on their support ships. The less gear they can land on Iwo, the better off our boys will be."

"Aye, aye, skipper."

Fed up with dancing around with the enemy sub, Burke had decided to try and flush them out by making them show themselves to protect the surface ships. So far, it had been less than successful on that part, but the sheer tonnage of Bloc ships sent down to the bottom of the Pacific more than made up for that.

Crew morale was better, despite the sheer devastation to the task group above them. They were getting their licks in, at least, and those that made it to shore were putting up a fight if the radio signals were to judge by.

The Miami was starting to run low on ADCAPS, however, and it would only be a matter of time before the magazines were entirely dry.

Everyone on board knew that they needed to make every shot count before that happened, because there wouldn't be anything to come back to by the time they made Pearl, got rearmed, and turned the boat around.

*****

Iwo Jima

"The fighters are circling, coming around for another pass," Lieutenant Ichiro Sagata said from his position on the hill, not putting down the field glasses he was using.

"Got it," Master Sergeant Jiang said as he entered the information directly into the Combat Controller System, flagging it as a priority for the ground commander.

He had grabbed a few men from the JSDF who knew their shit before all hell came down, and they were now running a makeshift spotting network across the island, trying to make anything work.

"Marines on the north beach and calling for artillery if we've got it."

They had it, that wasn't the question. The question was whether they dared to use it.

Kiran Jiang knew just how precarious the situation was, and he didn't want to waste artillery on what was likely just a probing strike.

"Strongly advise we don't use it," He said. "Tell the Major to keep up the pressure and they'll fold it in. We don't want to show them where our armor is."

"Right."

Technically, Liang was the lowest-ranked person in the hide they'd put up on the volcanic mount, but as he was also the only one with training in the job he was doing, he'd found himself making calls that normally went to the officers. A master sergeant who knew what he was doing outranked lieutenants who didn't know where they were, so to speak.

"Major Gibb concurs, master sergeant. They're putting on the pressure now."

Liang grabbed a pair of field glasses, turning them on the North beach. The fighting was strongest there, where the Bloc had chosen to test their defenses. He could see an intensive increase in fire, including what had to be small rockets hammering into the small tanks that had rolled off the landers first.

He almost held his breath, waiting to see the results.

"They're pulling back to the landers!"

The breath exploded out of his lungs.

Sure enough, the Bloc forces were dragging their wounded and withdrawing to the amphibious landers. As he watched the first of them reverse back into the ocean, the Air Force Master Sergeant slumped in place.

The first wave had been repelled.

*****

Chapter Twenty-Two

Washington DC, Whitehouse Situation Room

Given slumped in his seat as the Bloc landing craft withdrew from the Island, only then noticing just how tense he'd been.

"They did it," He said, shocked.

"No sir, that was just a probing strike," The Brigadier to his left responded. "Neither side really cut loose."

Givens blinked, "There are hundreds dead on that beach."

"Yes Sir, but the Marines didn't use their artillery, and the Bloc forces didn't even try flanking them. It's a small Island sir, but it'll be pretty hard to cover all sides at once." The Marine General said. "This fight is just getting started. Both sides have cards left to play."

"That Major, Liam is it?" The SecDef spoke up, "He's trending."

"He's what?"

"Look at this," The SecDef slid a tablet across the table to the President.

Givens lifted it up, looking at the picture on it, of the man standing in front of an explosion with a Marine Kevlar helmet sitting crookedly on his head and a rifle balanced on one shoulder.

"The memes are basically making themselves at this point."

Givens rolled his eyes, "Oh lord."

"That's the upside. Russia and China, among others, have started counter-memes already. It's having trouble getting traction, thankfully, because no one is bad mouthing those men right now, but it's only a matter of time before they figure out some avenue of attack." The SecDef sighed before looking somewhat hopeful. "But for the moment, he's winning the internet."

Givens groaned, rubbing his head.

He *hated* that part of the job.

It felt so *damned* childish, but he'd also seen the numbers. People actually *believed* the crap that got posted on social media, often more so than they believed actual facts.

"Ok, get our people on it," He ordered. "Try and keep this from blowing up in anyone's face who doesn't have it coming."

He sighed, turning to the Marine General, "I'm going to need the files of the Major on my desk. God, I hope he's not got anything buried in his history for the Bloc to use against him."

"I'll have them pulled and on your desk within the hour."

"Thank you."

Givens could feel a migraine coming on.

*****

Alamogordo New Mexico

"Easy now," Eric said as he balanced himself over the open weapons bay of the F-22, hunched over in the cramped environs. "Lift it up easy."

The device was being raised on a hydraulic lift, inch by inch. They'd done all the measurements, and he was pretty sure it would fit, but Eric needed to be absolutely certain because they were going to have to bolt the damn thing to some of the internal weapons pods in order to be certain it had strong enough mounting points to keep from tearing the airframe apart during maneuvers.

Hopefully.

It would mean fewer weapons, but they could use the external hardpoints for missiles and probably get ten times the ammo for the gun crammed into the rest of the interior spots if his math was right. Stealth would be for shit, but judging from the experiences of the F-35 pilots over Japan and Iwo, he wanted the guns.

They also had an order out for laser pods, but those had suddenly become quite in demand, so it was a toss upon whether or not they'd be able to get any.

We'll make do, one way or the other.

The device rose up under him, and he got out of the way of it as he eyed the positioning carefully.

"Ok, slowly… Bring it back a touch, easy… easy… there!"

Eric reached out, pulling the mounting point as hard as he could to get the holes to match up, before he dropped the bolt in.

"One down, let's get the rest."

Slowly repeating himself until all the mounting bolts were dropped into place, Eric then got an impact drill and tightened them all up before he let the team below drop the hydraulic lift and prayed.

There was a bit of a creak as the airframe took on the weight, but that was all. He slowly squeezed himself out of the bay and dropped down to the ground under the plane.

"Alright, let's get it wired up and get the powerplants installed in this thing," He said, clapping dirt off his hands.

Only a couple people were listening, he found, much to his consternation. The rest were, again, crowded around the big screen.

"Damn it, I swear if you guys don't cut that out, I'm going to put a wrench through that thing," He growled, walking over. "What is it this time?"

"Marines on Iwo repelled the first attack."

Eric looked at the screen with more interest, reading the scroll quickly as he watched the recap.

"Good for them. Now get back to work."

He hit the power button, turning the screen off, and turned back to the fighter.

"The longer we take to get this right, the longer the Bloc own the skies."

*****

Shortly after, Eric found the researchers in his office, reading through the notes he and Bradley had spent the past few years working on.

"What do you think?" He asked hopefully.

Diane looked up at him, "Well the physics PHDs are complaining that it breaks the universe, so I think there's something here. We did manage to plot the stressors from the F-16 frame and there's good news there."

Brian Cooke nodded, "We're pretty sure that the F-22 airframe will take the load… assuming it's at full spec and hasn't been damaged. The F-16 just didn't have the internal stiffness to handle the load from the directions the device was pulling. It was designed for very different thrust vectors."

Eric nodded, "That is good news. We've got new engines being installed, and assuming it all checks out I'm test flying it tomorrow."

Diane looked up, concerned, "There's no way you can get that flight-ready in twenty-four hours."

Eric glanced at his watch, a bit of anachronistic tech he happened to prefer over carrying a phone with him every second of the day. "A little under eighteen actually."

"Eric," She said, almost pleading. "You'll be killed if this doesn't work."

"Well, let's make sure it works then."

He took a breath, holding up his hand to stop her from trying again. "We're out of time. Men are dying on Iwo, around the Philippines, and in Israel right now. We *need* to achieve at least parity with the enemy in the air, or we're going to lose two-thirds of the planet to the Eastern Alliance Bloc... possibly more. I'm sorry, Doctors, but we're not going to have time to do things by the books. You still on board?"

He could see them hesitate.

"No hard feelings if you want to walk out now," Eric said. "I'm not press ganging anyone into this, but this is how it's going to be."

The two looked to one another for a moment, resignation showing in their expressions. Finally, they nodded.

"Good. Then let's do what we can to make sure I don't die tomorrow, deal?"

"Deal." Diane said firmly.

*****

World Media was playing the events from Iwo over every channel. Streaming services had twenty-four hour feeds dedicated to the video coming out of both the Marines' encampment as well as the delayed feeds that were being allowed out of the Bloc.

The difference between the two had resulted in the extensive mocking of the Bloc Security Council when they had censored the loss of life on their side during the fighting, making it look like they'd decisively won a scouting skirmish compared to the unedited feed from the Marines that showed the intensity of the fighting and the lives it took on both sides.

Armchair tacticians and analysts were going over every frame of all the feeds, some even making decently salient, if late, points.

The sinking of a Bloc cruiser in the background of one shot had been highlighted by some of the more popular ones, with various conspiracies being spouted about the ship until someone pointed out that there had been four submarines assigned to the Enterprise task group and nowhere was there any mention of them being sunk.

That, of course, led to an entire group of internet denizens scouring every frame of ocean shown in all the videos, looking for any sign of said submarine to little effect, but it seemed to keep them entertained.

The events at Iwo Jima had changed world events in startling ways, people quickly realizing that this wasn't a war in the way they were used to. There were no precision strikes here, no Special Forces sneaking in to take out a target. The fighting was brutal and close, and there was little doubt that the Marines were going to lose.

Somehow though, that didn't make anyone feel helpless.

It made them angry.

It was a frustrated rage, unable to help, unable to do anything… yet determined to all the same.

It started slowly, a few people in some bars set down their drinks and looked up something on their phones. Then they walked out of the bar, and down the streets, and into the nearest recruiting center.

It was not just in the United States either.

The Canadian Military had to add servers to their recruiting sites, just to keep the load from crashing them. In the UK, Germany, France, and elsewhere, similar phenomenon was recorded.

Overnight, recruited went up over a thousand percent.

And climbing.

*****

Late the next morning, Eric woke with a start to find himself draped over the ratty old couch he and Bradley had kept in the back of the Hangar. He had to move someone else's leg to get up but didn't bother looking to see who it was.

He grabbed a coke from the cooler on his way out to the front of the hangar, blinking the sleep from his eyes as he looked at the fighter they'd been getting ready.

The F-22 was a hell of a beautiful gal, he decided.

With the preservation plastic stripped off and the power plant installed, the fighter looked right again, not like some skeletal remains. Men and women were perched on her, fiddling with last-minute checks, hopefully to keep him alive past the next few hours.

"How's she look?" He asked, taking a long pull from the cold coke, the temperature, sugar, and caffeine acting like a jolt to his system.

"Looking good, Sir." A tech from Lockheed, if he remembered correctly, offered as he climbed down from the cockpit. "I can't vouch for that doodad you got bolted in her belly, but the systems we designed all check out."

"Good," Eric said, "Thanks for coming down."

"Hey, no worries." The man chuckled. "I was looking for work when they called me in. Glad to be working on a fighter again."

"Laid off?" Eric asked, grimacing.

"Most of us were when the YF-31 project fell through."

"That's rough, sorry I didn't get your name, or I forgot sometime in the night," Eric admitted, extending his hand.

"No worries, Doug Wright," The man grinned. "Yes, spelled the way you're thinking. No, no relation as far as I'm aware."

"Get asked that a lot, I assume?"

Doug snorted, "Working in this field? You don't want to know. Anyway, yeah, most of us here were laid off over the last five years. I was lucky, caught the ax only a few months ago, but the writing has been on the wall for a while. I was starting to worry I'd have to take one of the job offers from COMAC. So fucking glad I didn't now, of course."

Eric nodded, understanding that.

COMAC was the Chinese commercial aircraft manufacturer. Working for them, at a time like this, would be little different than working for the Chinese military industrial complex, and that was no way to have a decent life through what was coming.

"A lot of people take them up on it?"

"You have no idea," Wright sighed. "I've got a lot of friends over there right now... haven't been able to get a hold of any of them since Japan."

"Shit."

"Yeah."

That pretty much meant they were, at best, under house arrest within the Bloc. Some might be working willingly, others... not likely to be. Eric had vaguely known of a brain drain running over to China and India since both governments had been ramping up military and infrastructure spending while most of the west was cutting back, but it had only just occurred to him that some of them had likely helped design at least *some* part of the fighters that had torn the ever-living hell out of the American and JSDF fighters over Japan.

"Well," Eric didn't have anything much more to say, "Is she ready to fly?"

Wright snorted, "I don't know what the hell that thing you put in her will do, but yeah, our systems are good to go. We had to load ballast, though, cause we don't have the gun installed yet, and there's no missiles or munitions of course."

"Well, let's pre-flight this old gal," Eric said. "Because I am *itching* to burn up some sky."

*****

Chapter Twenty-Three

USS Miami

Morgan and Burke stood in silence, eyes sweeping around the command deck as they and everyone else barely dared to breathe.

The Miami had been stalking another one of the enemy fleet's supply ships when a torpedo had launched from a few dozen miles off. That would have been bad enough, but it was one of the super-cavitating ones the Bloc seemed to use sparingly.

Noisy as all hell, you couldn't miss the damn thing in the water if you were half-deaf, but impossibly fast.

Screaming death coming at you at speeds in excess of two hundred knots wasn't something you ever wanted to deal with.

Burke had waited until the last damn second, then blew the emergency surface protocols to send the Miami shooting up like a beachball held under the waves. They'd breached the surface as the torpedo blew on past under them, evading that bit of death by the narrowest of margins, then had been forced to do an emergency dive in order to avoid being shelled by the Bloc surface ships.

Morgan was pretty certain that he had been bent, just a little, from the shift in pressure despite the Miami's pressure hull supposedly being able to prevent it. His elbows felt like he'd just put them through some serious torture, and his knees were complaining about standing around.

The dive had brought them back down under the thermocline, the Miami going to silent running as they started to sneak clear of the area.

Ignoring the protests from his joints, Morgan limped over to the SONAR station and leaned in so he could see the screens and get an idea of what was around them.

The waters in the area were deep, some of the deepest in the world in fact. Challenger deep wasn't all that far from them, only a few hundred miles south. Islands like Iwo were the result of tectonic pressures, pushing up volcanic cones until they reached above the depths and kissed the air.

It was perfect for submarine warfare.

Which kind of sucked when you were being hunted by a submarine, frankly.

There wasn't much on the screens that he could see, the expected sounds of the surface ships above them, some biologicals going about their business, and even some murmurs from the rocks that were likely micro tremors or something along those lines.

No sign of the enemy sub, however.

How the hell is that thing so quiet?

He knew it had to be a hybrid. Several countries had built them, mostly diesel hybrids though. Silent as a ghost on their batteries, but noisy little buggers when charging. This one wasn't showing any of that, however, and no one had that many batteries.

Which meant it was a nuke.

Nukes were almost always making some noise, however. Cooling systems were critical in traditional nuke design, after all.

But maybe it's not traditional.

There were reactor cores that had been designed that could be 'shut off'. Pull the rods, and the system just shut down. No more heat generation, no threat of meltdown… no need for cooling. They were usually fairly large, built for power generation on land, but Morgan was thinking that the Bloc had managed to get one down to a size and power capacity suitable for a sub.

Figuring that out was cool and all, but it still left the same damn problem.

How the hell do we find the bastard?

*****

EBAN HuangLung

"Where are the little fatherless scuts?" Chien swore softly, glancing around to see if anyone had heard him, not that they'd say anything of course.

They had blown a *clean* shot at the American submersible, allowing it time to once more escape into the depths.

He wasn't sure if it was just the one submarine or not. The HuangLung had accounted for a couple others early in the fighting, but there were perhaps more out there he did not know. What he did know was that there was at least one left, and it had destroyed *five* supply ships and another two destroyers since the attempted landing on Iwo Jima.

It had to be dealt with, preferably before the other available fleet arrived, in order to properly ensure the victory over the island's defenders.

The American Fast Attack sub was a traditional such platform, which had known weaknesses. Their coolant system could not be shut down, which gave them an audible presence at all times. The issue was that in the current fighting, there was so much environmental noise to reliably get directional vectoring from the sound.

They could hear it out there, just in the background noise… constantly humming away… but thus far it had been elusive to track down.

That likely meant that the enemy submersible was playing games with the thermoclines, moving between temperature gradients, and thus masking its location within the different acoustic properties of ocean levels. This was going to be an irritant, of that there was no doubt.

"Lieutenant," He grumbled.

"Yes, Admiral."

"Inform the Captain that the American submarine is to be the priority for the immediate future. Either kill them or chase them away."

"Yes, Admiral."

*****

USS Miami

Captain Burke silently read the reports from the LSS, unhappily checking the stores' information for ADCAPS.

The Miami had another four torpedoes before they were bone dry, so to speak. Four fish that, unfortunately, would not be enough to have any significant effect on the fight. He'd prefer to save them for the enemy sub, but that boat was proving damned hard to pin down.

So that left him a choice.

He could continue to play hide and seek, hoping for a clean shot at the enemy submarine, or he could pop another couple enemy supply ships and head for Pearl.

Strategically, the enemy submersible was the more high-value target, of that there was no question.

Tactically, for the men on Iwo, however?

Supply ships it is.

It probably wouldn't make much of a difference, but every little bit would mean the world to the men on the beach. Bagging the Miami, a sub kill? Well, that was a little bit of personal pleasure that he would have to forgo this time.

We'll get you next time, Burke promised the phantom sub as he got up and made his way forward to the command deck to break the news to the command crew.

It was going to break Passer's heart, he thought with a hint of a smile.

*****

Morgan took it surprisingly well, Burke thought after delivering the news and getting the Miami moving again.

His XO was a hard charger, which was something that Burke appreciated a great deal as it allowed him to play the role of the voice of wisdom when needed while still having that fire burning for the crew to look to and embrace.

Morgan was also far from reckless, however, and he knew the play here as well as Burke did.

So, Burke stood at the back of the Command Deck as Morgan took the center and set them in motion for their last run.

"All ahead one third," Morgan said softly, "Do not cavitate. One-and-one-half degrees up bubble. Take us through the thermocline."

"Aye, ahead one third," The helmsman said. "Do not cavitate. One and one half up."

The Miami smoothly accelerated forward, tilting her nose up just barely perceptibly. Burke braced himself between the wall and the console with a foot to jam himself into place and said nothing.

He expected Morgan to get a promotion after this mission, assuming there were any slots open. The younger man was overdue for it, and Burke had actually passed on a couple unofficial offers to him already, but without any boat command slots open, accepting them would have resulted in Morgan being beached behind a desk.

That would have been a criminal waste, and was the reason why Burke himself had squashed the offers before they became official, making sure that Morgan could refuse them without it going on his official record.

If this war keeps winding up, there will be slots coming available in the near future, that's for sure.

Not right away. There weren't enough boats in the water, but soon. There were a few in drydock that could be extended if Congress got off their ass and authorized the money… and he knew that there were a few new designs that had been bandied about, using new reactor concepts. Burke just didn't know how long it would take to make those actually *happen*.

Suppose we'll find out, He thought as the Miami pierced the thermocline and the acoustic signals from the surface ships became all the cleaner.

*****

EBAN HuangLung

"Contact and bearing on a submerged contact!"

"Where are they?" Chien demanded, striding forward.

He could see the contact already up on the SONAR screens, triangulating with the systems from the fleet.

"Twenty-three kilometers North by North East, Admiral. Tightening the vector now."

"Get us moving," He ordered. "We'll adjust our course in motion."

"Yes, Admiral!"

They moved a long way from the last spot we'd had them, He noted, working out the numbers in his head.

The American sub was coming up on the other side of the fleet, likely making a run on the supply ships again. He thought to warn them, but they would know soon enough anyway, and right now the ships were providing focus for the enemy. Focus he wanted them to keep, so focused that they didn't see the HuangLung coming.

He walked to the weapons control station, tapping the officer on the shoulder.

"Prepare a full spread of SC loads," He ordered.

"Yes, Admiral."

"Flood the tubes, but keep the doors shut."

"Yes, Admiral."

He didn't want the additional turbulence from the open tubes to give away their position, and they could open those doors and fire within seconds. He just wanted to get close enough that the enemy sub couldn't evade them.

Just... close enough.

*****

USS Miami

Morgan stepped on the pedal to lift the periscope mast, leaning in to look through the optics as the mast extended. It wasn't like the old boats, where the mast was this massive telescoping structure that passed right through the sub and had to do so, just to store it. No, the fiberoptic system was far more efficient and easy to use, but he felt it missed some of the romance of the original design.

Still, that was neither here nor there. The new system was more efficient, slimmer, and by far more effective.

"Target ahead," He said softly, clicking a command as he focused in on one of the transports. "Sending bearing to your system, Weps."

"Got it," The weapons control officer said. "Locked in. You want two on that?"

"You know it. Second target… mark. Give him our last two."

"Yes sir. Targets loaded. Torpedoes assigned."

Morgan leaned back from the periscope, looking back to the Captain. "We still have some missiles left, Skipper."

Burke nodded, "Give them the whole package."

"Yes sir," Morgan said, smiling nastily as he leaned back in. "Weps, let's assign some missiles."

"Aye, aye, Commander."

"Commander…" SONAR spoke up hesitantly, frowning as he tilted his head and looked closer at his screens. "I've got screws in the water, moving hard."

Morgan blinked, quickly scanning the surface ships through the periscope. "I don't see any movement like that up top. Skipper, we might have company coming."

"Understood," Burke replied. "Mission is your call, Commander."

"Aye, aye." Morgan responded, brow furrowed.

"SONAR, stay on that," Burke ordered.

"Aye Skipper."

"Continuing on mission," Morgan said. "Flood the tubes and open the hatches."

"Aye Commander, tubes flooding!"

****

EBAN HuangLung

"They've flooded their tubes, Admiral… and… yes, hatches are opening."

"Good. They haven't detected us yet," Chien said. "Continue on course."

"Yes, Admiral. Should we open our hatches?"

"Not yet."

The surface ships were starting to move now, he could see. They'd finally picked up on the threat that his crew had detected from several kilometers farther away. That was something he would need to talk with their commanders about in the future, but for now it played to his advantage.

The HuangLung had smoothly accelerated to what was their top 'quiet' speed. Any more and they would begin to create more turbulence than the baffling technology could adjust for, but it should be more than fast enough.

"I want a firing solution on that submarine, gentlemen, and I want it *now*."

*****

USS Miami

"Firing one."

Weps hit the button, sending the first of the ADCAPS on its way. With the fish hot in the water, there was little more point in silence.

"Ahead all flank," Morgan called. "Fire two."

The boat surged ahead through the waters of the Pacific, no longer hiding its presence as it closed the range on the surface vessels. Alarms could be heard through the water, conducted through the ship's hulls as they began to power up and try to evade.

Too late by far, Burke thought as he watched the crew work, one eye always on the SONAR station.

"Fire three?" Weps asked.

"Neg," Morgan said. "Switch to missile guidance."

"Yes sir, Missile guidance ready."

Burke nodded to himself, recognizing what Morgan had opted for. He could have fired the torpedoes. Burke wouldn't have faulted him for it, but with the enemy sub coming, Morgan was hoping for a shot at the enemy boat.

"Cruise missiles launching."

The Miami shuddered a bit as the cruise missiles were ejected from their vertical launch tubes, throwing them up through the water to just below the surface where their rocket engines would ignite.

In a few moments all their vertical launch tubes were as empty as their magazines.

Just the torpedoes left…

*****

EBAN HuangLung

"We have a firing solution, Admiral."

"Excellent," Chien smiled.

"There is an issue," The officer said. "We'll be firing through our own convoy."

Chien nodded, "I understand. Fire the torpedoes."

"Yes, Admiral."

Chien watched as the commands were sent and felt the slight shiver through the deck as the supercavitating torpedoes were ejected from the HuangLong. He knew that they would coast out for a few meters before their rocket engines would kick in, part of the exhaust would be filtered out through the skin of the torpedo, surrounding it in hot gasses, reducing contact and thus friction with the water.

They were not weapons of subtlety, but they were incredibly deadly nonetheless.

"Torpedoes away."

*****

USS Miami

"Supercavitation in the water, Commander!"

Morgan swung the periscope, looking through the enemy surface ships in the direction he was pretty sure the enemy sub was coming at them from.

"Got it. New mark for torpedo guidance!" He called, clicking the switch.

"Got it."

"Fire em both."

"Torpedoes away."

Burke stepped off from the wall. "That's it, we're done. Rig for dive!"

"Aye Skipper, Rig for dive!" Morgan called, pushing the periscope up and out of the way as he checked the numbers. "Three degrees down bubble!"

"Three degrees down, Aye!"

The Miami dipped its nose, and they all had to hang on and brace themselves as the boat began its descent.

"Torpedoes hit one hundred knots, Sir. Coming right at us."

"Launch decoys," Burke ordered.

"Aye, Decoys away."

"Hard to port," Burke said, planting a foot on the console in front of him and wedging himself against the wall again.

"Aye skipper. Hard to port."

The sub leaned over as it turned. In addition to the steep dive, leaving everything feeling like it was more than a little out of wack.

"Torpedo contact in three… two… one!"

"Brace for impact!"

The ocean heaved, the ship seemed to twist, and amidst it all they felt their stomachs lurch and their ears suddenly pop as the world dropped out from under them.

*****

EBAN HuangLung

"Torpedoes detonated, Admiral."

"Did we get them?" Chien demanded.

"Uncertain. We're instructing the surface vessels to begin active searches for wreckage."

Chien nodded, irritated, but he knew that was the best he was likely to get just then. Hopefully, that was the end of this particular irritant. But even if it was or wasn't, there would always be another coming along soon enough.

He started to turn away from the screens when the SONAR operator screamed in horror.

"Admiral!"

"What is it?" He demanded, twisting back.

"Torpedoes in the water. They must have been masked by our own…"

"Evade!"

"Too late, they're in terminal guidance!"

The HuangLung heaved suddenly, shaking like it had been punched by a massive fist, and Chien was thrown across the command deck.

Everything went black.

*****

Chapter Twenty-Four

Iwo Jima

Liam looked out to the north as a flash of light caught his gaze, followed a time later by the rolling thunder of one of the Bloc supply ships exploding.

The bubble heads are still kicking, I see.

They had to be hard-pressed, he knew that for a fact. They hadn't had a lot of contact with the subs since the Enterprise went down, they'd gone silent, stalking the stalkers. How well that had worked out, he didn't know.

"Corporal."

"Yes, Major?"

"Hand me the glasses, would you?" He asked, outstretching his hand as the corporal dropped the pair of powerful field glasses into them.

Liam brought them up and swept the sea, noting the sinking transport quickly. *One less load of weapons coming after us, thanks for that boys.*

The destroyers were circling fast, obviously hunting for the sub, but they didn't seem to be getting any shots off.

Shit. Maybe I thought too soon.

He swung to see a plume of water rise up out of the sea, something exploding under the waves and stayed focused as the seas rained back down. There was no wreckage, but something had taken a hit there, no question.

"Major, check to your left."

Liam swung over, quickly spotting another plume in the water a long way from the source of the attack or the other ships.

"What the hell got hit out… oh. Holy shit," He breathed out as the submarine's bow pierced the water.

He wasn't even sure he could call that a submarine. It was bigger than the Makin Island. Hell, it wasn't that much smaller than the Enterprise.

"Jesus, Major, what is that thing?"

"I don't know, but I think we just got to see another of the Bloc's hole cards."

*****

EBAN HuangLung

Admiral Chien held the bandage to his head as he wobbled slightly, walking across the command deck.

"How bad is the damage?"

"A hole amidships, Admiral. Repairable, but it will take some time," His XO said.

"Let us hope we got the enemy submarine then," Chien grumbled, but finally nodded. "Very well. See to the repairs. Are our flight decks serviceable?"

"Yes, Admiral."

"Good. Recall the fighters for refuel and resupply, we will need them when the third fleet arrives."

*****

Iwo Jima

"Well, that explains where the fighters have been basing out of," Gunny Hadrian said from where he was slumped against a berm, a canteen in his hand. "I'd been wondering about that since we haven't seen carriers among the Bloc's line of battle."

"Can you build a boat that big?" Meer asked, somewhat stunned.

"Apparently," Hadrian shrugged. "What are you asking me for? I fix planes, I don't build those suckers."

"You think they're going to attack again?" A private asked nervously.

"Sure, eventually. Not right away though," Hadrian said thoughtfully. "They've taken some hits out there, lost supply ships. They'll wait, get more ships in if they can. Come ashore tonight maybe, or at dawn."

He checked the time and whistled, "I did not realize how late it had gotten. Time flies when you're having fun, Marines."

The looks the men gave him after that almost made the whole last few days worth it.

Hadrian boomed with laughter, his mirth echoing across the beach.

*****

On Mount Suribachi, Kiran was focused on the submersible carrier that was drifting out to the north of the Island, taking note of every detail he could see and putting it down into the files to be sent along to PACCOM.

They'd lost contact with the last submarine from the Task Group, no word since they made that last run. That could mean they were *deep*, but the silence wasn't a good thing. The submariners had done their job, and then some, however, and now Kiran had one more piece to the puzzle that was the current Bloc line of battle.

The fighters, those he could accept that they'd snuck some ultra-secret technical development past everyone. A little luck, a lot of security, build them in some new factory maybe far from any of the normal population centers. Sure, it was possible to keep that secret.

How in the ever-living *hell* did they hide building that *thing* out there, though?

This couldn't be explained by someone dropping the ball and the Bloc getting a little lucky.

They've infiltrated our intelligence division. They have to have.

Sure, to some degree that was normal, but this wasn't 'some degree'. This was treason.

He finished taking high-resolution photographs, sending them up the satellite link, and packed his camera away. There was more work to be done, and the sun was coming down.

It would be a long night, Kiran knew.

*****

The sun was going down when Liam told his men to get some sleep, keeping only a minimum up to keep watch. They'd done all the preparations they could, and that meant that the next move was up to the enemy. He expected them to come ashore after dark next, but it depended on whether they had enough resources on hand to make it work.

If not, then they'd wait for reinforcements.

Either way, he figured there was time for some shut-eye.

He set his rifle down against the berm and took a seat in the sand, ignoring the slight discomfort.

"MRE, Major."

Liam caught the soft pack tossed his way and waved thanks with a two-finger salute off the brim of his helmet. He flipped the Kevlar pot off his hand, let it thud down in the sand and ripped open the MRE package. The chemical heater was soon hissing away happily, warming up the beef stew while he popped a square of chocolate in his mouth and let it melt slowly.

"Coffee?"

"Thank you, no," He said to the JSDF soldier who'd offered. "I'm going to try and catch a wink or two after this. I'll be fine with water."

He hefted his canteen, smiling at the man, who nodded and poured himself a cup.

Another man was by a few minutes later, dropping off magazines and grenades. Liam took his share of each, setting them next to his rifle. He had no doubt they'd see use in what was coming.

Men were running up and down the trenches, delivering kit and meals, water, and computers so they could write letters home. Liam hadn't thought about that last one, but he approved. They had the bandwidth, so he hoped some of the men got a chance to talk to home too.

It's damn strange, the ways the world turns on you.

He'd never have predicted what happened, but then a lot of things in his life had been such that he could never have hoped to predict them. Maybe he just sucked at predicting things, Liam chuckled softly as he spooned the stew into his mouth, chewing mechanically without really tasting any of it.

It filled him up, left a warm weight in his gut. That was all he really needed just then. Liam doubted if he'd have tasted a good T-Bone if it had been in front of him then. Not that he'd have turned one down, mind you, it just would have been a waste with how fast he was eating.

He closed his eyes briefly, resting his head back against the sandy berm, but only for a second.

Liam opened his eyes abruptly and sat up, looking inland then South to the volcanic cone where it was bathed in the setting sun.

He got up, waving a couple men from around him. "You two, with me. Private, Go find me a jeep."

"Yes Major," The Marine nodded, heading off.

The JSDF man looked confused, but Liam just waved him on, and they started walking after the Marine.

"Who's your CO?"

"Captain Ishida, Major."

Liam nodded, "I need to talk to him."

*****

Mount Suribachi

Kiran had packed most of his kit away, having taken all the notes he could think of for the moment and sent all the pictures he could reasonably take back up the line. He was resting and waiting for the next attack when he heard a motor approaching, coming up the curving road that led to the top of the mound.

Getting to his feet he spotted the Marine transport Mule, one of the lighter rigs designed to move men and gear around a battlefield in a hurry, coming up the hill with a full load of men.

"What's this then?" He asked aloud, dusting himself off and slipping out of his hide, brushing the camo netting aside and walking out to the road.

The Mule, what the Marines called a Jeep just because they were Marines and couldn't be bothered to use the official designation, slowed as it approached him, and he waved them down.

"Major," He greeted the man in the passenger seat, recognizing him on sight. "Help you with something?"

"No, Master Sergeant," The Major shook his head. "Just some unfinished business at the memorial before the sun goes down."

"Alright…" Kiran drawled as the Mule crept past him while they were talking, then accelerated off again.

He watched them go, confused, but just shook it off.

"Marines."

The JSDF Lieutenant looked at him oddly for that, but didn't say anything.

*****

The jeep rolled to a stop at the memorial spot that was located near the top of the volcanic mound, the men on board hopping out. Liam had grabbed another couple Marines and JSDF people when he met up with their Captain.

They took a moment to look around, nodding respectfully to the memorial that rested there.

"This island has seen enough blood and death for a thousand its size," Captain Ishida said gravely.

"No doubt," Liam nodded in agreement. "But few are the places that get to choose between life and death."

"True."

Liam nodded to the men with them.

"Gentlemen, raise me a couple flags."

*****

Kiran's rest was once more disturbed, this time by a surprising sound from nearby. He looked over and saw the Lieutenant looking up the hill, pointing.

He once more climbed out of the hide, frowning as he looked up the hill and stopped in surprise as he spotted the American and Japanese flags waving in the wind as they were bathed in the light of the setting sun.

"Major, you sentimental bastard," He said, shaking his head with some amusement, but even then he couldn't help but nod once respectfully to each before he turned back to settle into the hide.

It was a romantic gesture, in the classical sense, but Kiran suspected it would have the intended effect.

*****

From the beach, the flags were only just visible, but those with magnification quickly showed or told the rest.

Marines and JSDF rose from their positions, saluting the flags as they flew in the fading light.

A few from each group began singing their national anthems, which quickly devolved into a horrible mismatch of the two that made no sense to anyone as the two groups tried to out yell one another rather than actually singing in any sense of the word.

No one seemed to give a damn, though, and within minutes the beach felt more like the site of a party than a battle.

The men didn't notice when Liam returned. The Major just slipped back into the trench where he'd been and settled in to catch a nap.

*****

EBAN HuangLung

"Admiral… you may want to see this."

Chien frowned, looking up from his desk, "What is it?"

"It's the island, Sir. It's… hard to explain."

"Just… spit it out."

He was in no mood for word games, not after the day he'd just dealt with.

"The Americans and the Japanese sailors, Sir… they're… partying?"

Chien set his digital pen down and got up, "Perhaps you had best show me."

"Yes sir."

He walked out through the sections of the ship, up the stairs and out into the open air above decks. There were several officers already there, and they wordlessly handed him a magnifier. He put the digital device to his eyes and swept the image across the beach, noting that it did in fact look like a party there.

"Are they drinking?" He asked, not quite believing it.

"Uncertain, Sir, but we don't believe so from what we've seen in the streaming feeds," His XO told him. "Water, juice mix, nothing alcoholic… though, I would suggest that is likely more due to a lack of availability than any sense of discipline."

Chien snorted, "That seems likely, yes."

He swept the island more, pausing on the southern mountain and pushing the zoom in as his lips drew into a single tight line.

The two flags flying there were clearly in defiance.

"How long until the third fleet arrives?"

"Another hour, Admiral."

"Signal our ships, tell them to begin preparations. We attack as soon as we have reinforcements."

"Yes, Admiral."

*****

Chapter Twenty-Five

Alamagordo New Mexico

The roar from inside the hangar caught Stephan by surprise as he stopped admiring the fighter and made his way over to see what was up. Something certainly had the bunch inside in a mood. He could hear them laughing... which was something they'd done a lot of since he'd shown up.

He stepped in, seeing that they were all around the flat screen again and couldn't help but roll his eyes.

Eric is seriously going to put a wrench through that damn thing if they don't cut it out.

Eric wasn't there, though, so he figured he'd find out what was going on. It couldn't be bad, not given the reactions.

"What's going on?" He asked, walking up. "They beat back another attack?"

"Naw, kid," A big guy grabbed him around the shoulder and gave him a hug, which seriously weirded him out. "Check it out."

Stephan looked at the screen, blinking in confusion.

It was just a couple flags.

"What's with the flags?"

"It's not just the flags, kid, it's where they are. The Marines and the JSDF boys put them up on Suribachi there on Iwo. That's what you call two big middle fingers to the Bloc forces."

Stephen's eyes widened as he suddenly understood what they were cheering for.

Damn. That's a ballsy move to do while they're under the gun like that.

He wondered if he'd have had the guts in their place. He liked to think so, but he wasn't sure.

"Whoa."

"Damn right." The man hugging him said as Stephen tried to extricate himself from the grip.

These old dudes are strange.

*****

Washington DC, White House Situation Room

Givens was exhausted, but he refused to sleep though he'd been up all night and the afternoon was well upon them.

Need to check what party that Major favors, cause if he votes for the other team, I need to make sure he never chooses to get into politics, He thought with some amusement.

Putting the flags up was poetic perfection, he had to admit, and was somewhat ashamed that he'd not considered it earlier himself. Of course, it would be a bit more of a kick in the guts when the Bloc eventually tore them down, but that could be turned to their advantage too. It was all about framing each event just right.

"Mr. President... we have an issue."

"Another crisis?" Givens groaned.

"Maybe?" His aide said. "This is filtering up through the Pentagon now. SecDef will bring it to you officially later today, but we have... unprecedented volunteers for military service."

"Ok... what's the issue?"

"Recruiting quotas were exceeded within the first hour of the Iwo streams, Sir." His aide told him. "The services don't know what to do. They don't have the money to take any more people..."

"Oh for…" Givens grimaced. "Alright, get me an executive order drafted to authorize new recruiting mandates, along with the declaration of a state of war with the Eastern Alliance Bloc for reference. Then call the Speaker of the House and the head of the opposition and get them both in here as quickly as you can."

"Yes sir." She said, running off.

"Because of *course* they can't open recruiting without congressional authorization or an executive order," He said to no one. "Jesus, we need to get on the ball here or we'll be conquered before anyone can figure out we're supposed to be at war."

Givens checked the time and sighed deeply.

Three days.

He should have signed that order within the hour of the Japanese invasion, but somehow it had slipped through all the cracks. That was on him.

What a fucking mess.

*****

Alamogordo New Mexico

Eric stepped out of his office, wearing a high Gee flight suit, only mildly surprised that it still fit. He ignored the lollygaggers hanging around the flat screen. There was work to be done, and it was more important than something he couldn't change. He'd get the highlights in the evening.

The F-22 was resting just outside the hangar, the small flight crew composed entirely of former Lockheed Martin employees were waiting for him.

He was met by Wright as he walked up, the man pacing along with him.

"We've checked the software, patched it to the latest we could get our hands on and everything checks out green," Wright assured him. "The avionics are latest generation… we couldn't get a hold of the originals anyway, it was cheaper to pull some top-of-the-line stuff off the shelf. Are you qualified on it?"

Eric nodded, "I flew F-35s until a few years ago, but I've kept my certifications up to date since."

"Ok good. Now I don't know what your doohicky is going to do, so you're on your own there," Wright told him. "Good luck."

Eric paused, grinning as he shook the man's hand, "Thanks."

He got up to the fighter and climbed up the ladder, dropping into the cockpit easily, taking a moment to re-familiarize himself with the controls while the crew chief followed him up and cinched the straps tighter around him. When the chief dropped back down, the ground crew unhooked the ladder and pulled it away.

Most of the kit was pretty standard. Throttle and Stick, no VTOL controls because of course there weren't any.

Note to self, we need to figure out how to rig something for that if this device works as planned.

It would be *so* much easier if they could just design a purpose-built airframe, but beggars and choosers he supposed.

They'd make do with what they had.

"Alright, everyone back up. I'm going light the fires." He called, punching the canopy controls to drop the bubble down around his head.

The whine of the turbines spinning up finally seemed to pull everyone's attention away from the flat screen inside, he noted as people streamed out of the hangar to watch as he nudged the aircraft down onto the runway.

The entire field was privately owned, and generally only used by the owner, a friend who was currently in a different state, so he had the tarmac to himself.

"Project A Dash A One Two, Contacting Holloman Control."

"Go for Holloman AA."

"Signaling intent to take off on a test flight, request clearance over White Sands," Eric said off by rote.

"Clearance granted over White Sands, AA."

"Thank you, Holloman."

Eric looked out to either side, making sure the tarmac was clear. He didn't have a tower crew watching for him here, so he also made sure the flight path was clear before running real power to the engines. With that final check done, he put power to the engines while keeping the brakes on, setting the whole fighter rumbling under him as the sensation of chained power just kept increasing.

Finally, he let off the brakes and pushed the throttle the rest of the way up and was slammed back into the seat as the F-22 airframe screamed down the runway, easily reaching take-off velocity as he pulled back on the stick and felt the tires leave the ground as he was eased down into the seat.

Eric wasn't pushing anything hard just yet. He wanted plenty of altitude under his ass before he did anything that might require a punch out, so he continued to climb easily and then looped around to the West and flew out over the White Sands salt bed, settling in at FL-30.

"Project AA-12 in-flight testing to commence," He called. "Activating test equipment."

"Roger AA-12. We have you on our screens," Holloman Air Force Base told him. "Good luck."

"Thanks, Holloman, might just need it." He smirked, but couldn't quite mask the shiver in his voice as he reached out to flip the switch wired to the Device in the fighter's weapon's bay.

"Equipment powered on. Flight controls... nominal." He said, wiggling the fighter a little. "Increasing power."

There was a spin dial hot glued to his dash controls, the wire leading down to the equipment zip-tied off to keep it out of the way. He grimaced at the ad-hoc nature of things, but needs must he supposed. Eric reached forward and eased the dial around.

Something shuddered and he stopped instantly, sitting back, and taking stock.

Flight computer, check. HUD, check. AirSpeed is Three hundred knots... check. GPS... what the fuck?

He doubled checked the GPS, and before he was finished Holloman control was on the radio.

"Jesus Christ, AA-12, what the hell did you do? You're over the border into Arizona! You weren't cleared to break Mach!"

"Didn't know I did," Eric grumbled back, easing into a turn, and bringing the altitude up a little more, settling at FL-35 as he headed back into New Mexico. "Throttling down a little. Request speed check, my airspeed indicator did not exceed three hundred knots."

"Well, it's busted as fuck, AA-12, we had you at Mach 1.2 crossing the border."

"Well, at least I wasn't flying South, Holloman."

"Don't even joke about that, AA-12. You do *not* want to know what the paperwork on that would be."

"Roger that. Speed check." He reminded the flight control officer.

"We have you at… just under seven hundred knots, AA-12."

Eric frowned, "Damn it, my airspeed indicator says I'm approaching stall speeds."

"You need to chat with your mechanic, AA-12."

The guy who designed this system for Lockheed put it. I don't think it's a simple system error… Eric thought, though he couldn't quite count it out. Mistakes happened, even to professionals, of course. He didn't feel like he'd broken Mach, however. The flight had been too smooth.

"Roger that, Holloman. Am proceeding with testing," He said.

"It's your funeral, buddy."

"Gee thanks, Holloman," Eric said, rolling his eyes.

He snapped his oxygen into place, checking the flow.

"AA-12, doing a speed test. Max power in three… two… one…" He said, before putting the throttle all the way forward.

Instead of the sudden slam of thrust pushing him into the seat, Eric felt a gentle pressure before that same shudder happened. Everything else looked fine, though, so he continued to accelerate.

"AA-12, back it off. You're about to go over a civilian population center!"

"What?" Eric blinked, easing back. "What population center?"

He looked down and was surprised to see a city just ahead, so he turned away and headed back toward the South.

"You hit Mach 2.3 and damn near flew over Albuquerque, AA-12. We're going to spend the next three days answering complaints about the sonic boom!"

Huh. I would say it works, but something's not right, He thought, checking everything and grabbing a notepad and flipping it over to the calculations they'd made. *If our best-case math was right, I should have gone hypersonic or nothing at all. Why did I get Mach 2.3? And why is my airspeed indicator so badly off?*

"Roger that, Holloman. I think we have what we need for today," He said. "Heading for home."

Just figuring what the hell was going on with what they knew now was going to take a couple weeks.

We need to cut that time down… somehow.

*****

Washington DC, White House Situation Room

"The enemy reinforcements just arrived, Sir."

"Huh, wha?" Givens blinked, shaking himself away.

"Sir, maybe you should get some…"

"I'm fine," POTUS grumbled, getting up. "What is it?"

His aide hesitated, but finally gave in, "The third enemy fleet just arrived at Iwo, Sir."

Givens nodded slowly, "Understood. How far out are the bombers?"

"Close, sir. An hour, maybe less."

"Jesus Christ." He said, but nodded resignedly and made his way over to the conference table where people were already arguing while watching the satellite feed.

"Alright, gentlemen," He said as he took a seat, "Let's get back to work."

*****

Chapter Twenty-Six

Iwo Jima

Looking through the night vision magnifier, Liam sighed as he counted off the ships.

Twenty-five more destroyers, half a dozen cruisers, and their accompanying support ships... including a full amphibious assault group from the looks of it.

It was no worse than he'd been expecting, of course, but it was certainly a far sight worse than he'd hoped.

His Marines and the JSDF sailors and soldiers who'd escaped Japan hadn't been entirely slacking off, with more trenches and even tunnels dug into the Island. With the earth moving equipment they had, they might even have managed a fraction of what the original Japanese defenders had a century and a bit earlier.

Unfortunately, he knew what happened to them.

They were putting boats into the water, more landing craft especially, so there wasn't any question as to their intent. Liam debated waking everyone, but elected not to bother. They'd all be up shortly anyway, and if they weren't, the shelling would give em a good shot of adrenaline when it started.

It was going to be a long night.

*****

EBAN HuangLung

"Welcome to Iwo Jima Admiral Hai Ron," Chien said with a forced smile. "I understand you had a successful operation through Guam?"

"Quite successful, thank you, Admiral." The other man tipped his head. "I see you've had some issues here?"

Chien's eyes narrowed, but he kept the smile on his face, "Some yes. After eliminating the *Carrier*, the rest decided to be problematic. Our projections indicated that they would keep running, deciding to make a stand here wasn't in the Council's projection."

"You appear to be missing quite a few vessels."

"Our mission included several American fast attack submersibles," Chien said. "Someone had to take the more… challenging missions."

"Of course." Hai Ron gestured placatingly, ending the little back and forth. "My assault crews stand ready. Will yours be joining the operation?"

"Yes," Chian responded. "The Council wishes this to be finished, decisively."

"We had best do so then."

*****

Iwo Jima

It was just after one fifteen in the AM, local time, that the Bloc naval forces began shelling the island of Iwo Jima again. A hundred and a hundred-and-thirty-millimeter cannons opened fire with air-bursting rounds that exploded over the beach, sending shrapnel down with lethal force. Hundreds of rounds in the first few minutes, then thousands more shortly after.

The men on shore stayed low, hugging the dirt, and just praying that the walls of the trenches would be sufficient to protect them, which they were… for the most part.

Corpsmen still had plenty to do, however, and the calls for help put them at higher risk than nearly anyone else.

Hadrian was covered in dirt as he huddled there in the damp trench, getting showered by sand and metal fragments from the shells. He'd been hit twice in the back with pieces of shrapnel, but his vest took the hits. One other had skimmed off his helmet, ringing his bell good and proper, but he was lucky for all that. No blood of his was soaking into the sand.

"Everyone get ready," The Major's voice somehow carried over the explosions. "Landing craft incoming!"

"You heard him, boys," Hadrian bellowed as he gripped his Sig and got ready to pop up.

All along the line, Marines and JSDF got ready to once more defend the beach.

*****

"Master Sergeant, call the play."

Kiran Jiang nodded, "You got it, Major."

He set down his radio and picked up the coordinate chart, checking off a couple notes before picking the radio back up and changing the channel.

"Guns One, targets entering engagement envelope."

"Roger that. Guns One ready."

"Target is… bullseye plus four hundred. Engage when ready."

"Roger that. Guns one… shot out."

Kiran watched the section of the sea, noting the splash off to the side of the enemy lander.

"Adjust fire," He commanded, "Grid AB 380 490."

"380 490 confirmed."

"Send it."

"Shot out."

The next shot landed right in the center of the enemy lander formation.

"That's it, repeat. All guns, fire for effect."

*****

Dug into various places around the island, the Marine Corps M777D3 artillery pieces roared to life, sending 155mm shells out. Firing M795A high explosive shells, they rained all hell down on the water surrounding the targeted grid square over the run of several minutes. At seven rounds per minute, over seven hundred rounds hammered into the Bloc landing craft, sending many of them to the bottom of the pacific even before they breached the light reef surrounding the island.

Kiran continued to call in adjustments, tracking the fire in for as long as they dared, before finally ordering the guns quiet and *moved*.

The crews immediately broke down their weapons, knowing that if they stayed, they would be begging for an enemy ship to drop some fire on them, and they firmly preferred to be the ones doing the dropping.

On the beach, the remaining landers surged through the surf and up on the sand as the second landing began.

*****

Hadrian knew that the landing had started the moment the enemy shelling eased up a little. It didn't stop, but it clearly shifted inland a bit, lightening the load on the beach so the landers could drop off their lethal cargo.

He popped over the top just as the ramps hit the sand.

SRAW missiles roared from behind him, screaming past as they hammered the Bloc light tanks before they could unload. Half a dozen were burning in the mouth of the landers they rode in on, and he imagined that they were making life miserable for the men behind them.

Couldn't happen to a nicer folk.

That still left more than a dozen others hitting the beach, with men pouring out behind them… and more landing craft coming in behind.

He dropped his Sig over the edge of the berm and pulled the stock into his shoulder, and took a second to get a good cheek weld. He settled in then and waited.

*****

EBAN HuangLung

The overhead imagery from the Bloc's satellite network was better than it had been some time ago, but it still left a great deal to be desired.

Modern satellite constellations tended to be cheap, low orbit birds. It was excellent for communications purposes, but they left a great deal to be desired when it came to optics. There were a great number of things that one could miniaturize with the miracle of modern technology, however, optics were not among them.

In that, he was well aware that the Americans had a significant advantage. They had launched most of their satellites in the early years and specialized in putting up large high orbit equipment. Among all the massive communications satellites it had been easy to hide high-value surveillance gear among all the dross.

The Bloc, however, had a harder time. If they put up anything larger than a few cubic meters, the Americans would know exactly what it was, and shooting down satellites was sadly a rather easy pastime for the Americans in these times.

That meant that the infrared imagery he had available were of little value, at least for tactical uses. He was fairly certain he knew where the American artillery had been positioned, but he was also pretty sure that they'd moved after shelling the landers.

If I recall correctly, the Marine Corps only has a single artillery piece in current service. Old, but effective, and unfortunately highly mobile.

Thankfully, the Island was small, so they would be able to track the pieces down, but it would take time. Likely the invasion force would capture them by chance before that could be done.

Still, he issued the order to start the search. Wasting a few hours of some desk analyst's time wasn't something he was overly concerned with.

That done, he made his way back to the strategic command center.

*****

Fighting across the beaches of Iwo escalated furiously, missiles and shells flying both directions as the Bloc light tanks rumbled up the beach with men doggedly following along behind them using them as rolling barricades against the massed fire from the Marines and JSDF assault rifles.

Despite furious defensive fire, however, there were too many of the landers disgorging far too many of the Bloc's light tanks, to hold the beaches for long.

Liam saw the writing on the wall and issued orders to start pulling back the troops from the first line.

"Lay the claymores," He ordered. "But don't arm those suckers. We'll do that on the way out."

"Yes, Major."

He got the non-combatant specialties moving first, keeping his combat arms holding the line until the last minute.

Every Marine might be a rifleman, but some were better at it than others.

*****

"Move your asses, boys," Hadrian ordered, pulling back from the berm.

He grabbed a few claymores and pushed his men on ahead of him, down through the exit they'd dug.

On the way out he set up the anti-personnel devices, covering both the trenches and the ground above them, but left the safety rigs intact. The major and the last marines out would get the pleasure of setting those in play.

He and his would be busy in a few minutes, setting up the next line of defense for them to retreat to.

"You done?" He asked, looking over to his men.

"Hoorah, Gunny."

"Good, fall back."

Hadrian made sure his baby marines were out of the line of fire before he finished up setting the last claymore and withdrew himself.

The fighting was more than he'd bargained for when he signed up, but he'd always known it wasn't impossible. Usually support crews were pretty safe, but even in the smaller wars he'd been in prior to this, incidents happened.

He had joined the Marines, after all.

Hadrian took one last look around before followed his man through the bolt hole back to the next line of defense, keeping his head low in the dark as dirt and shrapnel continued to rain down around him.

*****

Liam swept the beach from his cover, noting the positions of the advancing tanks. He'd love to call in some more artillery, but everything was moving to new positions at the moment for fear of a counter strike taking them out.

Well, we expected this. Time to fall back.

"Alright, it's time," He told the man next to him. "Pass the word, pull back, arm the claymores as we move. Hoorah?"

"Hoorah, Major."

Liam nodded, taking a knee behind the berm as a tank round tore a chunk out of it a few years west of him, showering him with dirt. He ignored it as best he could, firing a few rounds down the beach, unsure if he hit anything that mattered, then dropped back into the hole and grabbed the spare mags from the dirt before he started heading back up the trench. He paused at the bolt hole exit, nodding to the marine who was waiting for him.

"Pull the pins, let's get out of here."

"Oorah, Major." The marine grinned, doing as he was told.

The pair of them vanished back into the night, leaving the boobytrapped trench well behind them.

*****

EBAN HuangLung

"The American line has fallen, Admiral. Our forces are pushing up and off the beach," A commander announced, causing a little bit of a cheer.

Chien nodded with satisfaction.

"Good," He said. "Drive them into the interior of the island, get all of the rats in one place. Then, if they do not surrender, well… fire has a way of cleansing out pests, does it not?"

"Yes Admiral," The Commander grinned. "It does indeed."

The defense of the island had been furious, but the outcome had hardly been in doubt. With the limited resources at their disposal, there was little question that they would fall, no matter how stubborn the fools might be.

Though, stubborn beyond reason they clearly were.

Chien shifted his attention to watch the screens that were streaming from the cameras mounted on the light tanks as they rumbled slowly up the beach to the berms the Americans had been defending.

*****

The thirty-ton Chinese built Type-19 Light Attack Tank was powered by four independent electric drive motors running off a small turbo-charged diesel electric generator. With the batteries low slung in the chassis the Type-19 was capable of running silent for nearly fifteen minutes, as well as impressive top speeds and a reasonable armament in the hundred-millimeter rifled gun that served as its primary weapon.

The design made for a potent weapon in the Bloc's amphibious assault forces, capable of delivering a decisive punch while remaining light enough to land in relatively small spaces from even smaller landing craft.

For its size, the active armor on the Type-19 was no joke. Getting a shell or even an armor-piercing round through the front, side, or even back armor was a difficult task. Heavier tanks with much bigger guns could pull it off, of course, as could decent ground emplacements. Light missiles were hit or miss when it came to penetration of that level of armor, which is why the Marines' SRAW and Javelin missiles were designed to pop up over the target and bring the hammer down from above.

If you knew where they were going to be rolling through, however, there was one other option.

*****

Rumbling up the defensive berm, the Type-19 teetered for a moment before the weight balance shifted and the front began to come down into the trench beyond.

The moment the tracks came down in the trench, though, the soft sand gave way and the tank bottomed out close enough to set off the magnetic switch in the anti-armor mine buried there. As far as mines went, the US M-21 anti-armor mine was relatively anemic, but sometimes power wasn't the key to effectiveness.

A copper shaped charge blew upward in a jet of molten metal not much thicker than a small pen in diameter. Against a main battle tank, that level of force was less than a joke. Even a small light tank from the second world war wouldn't have been disabled by such a blast.

A hybrid tank, however, that had a *ton* of high-capacity batteries buried in its belly… well that was a story of a very different tale.

Electric vehicles had many great qualities to their name. By the early twenty-first century, they were outperforming gas-powered vehicles in nearly every single metric. Only the cost, consumer momentum, and the infrastructure built around gas kept electric vehicles from entirely replacing the civilian market.

They did have one defect that surprised most people when it was revealed, however.

Batteries with a full charge tended to burn *very* hot when damaged in specific ways.

For consumer vehicles, it wasn't a significant issue. Better plating around the batteries kept the incidents lower than fires in gas cars, and local fire departments learned to keep a couple containers around to fill with water to store damaged electric vehicles for a few days until the charge had fully drained.

Few electric cars were targeted by shaped charges blowing up directly under them, after all.

Tanks, however, they ran into that issue somewhat more often.

The stream of superheated copper blew through the light steel armor under the tank, carving a hole through the batteries and up into the tank above. The blast was small enough that the crew didn't even notice the charge go off as they landed in the trench and began to crawl up the other side.

Smoke filling the compartment a few seconds later was their first notification, then the jet of flames and rapidly rising heat as the tank turned into an oven served to fill in the rest. The Type-19 ground to a halt bridging the trench as the crews were forced to bail out as the heat inside the tank exceeded what they could stand.

Dropping into the trench, the crew fled the burning tank in a rush of coughing and wheezing.

They didn't even see the little wire along the ground, or the sandy-colored plastic box decorated with the words 'front toward enemy'.

*****

Chapter Twenty-Seven

EBAN HuangLung

Chien ground his teeth as the reports began to filter back.

They'd lost several more tanks to anti-armor mines, something he hadn't even realized that the Americans were still fielding. Of course, they'd not actually fought many enemies who used tanks in quite some time, so he supposed he might be forgiven for that lapse of knowledge.

The claymores were somewhat less of a surprise, though barely any less aggravating.

The Americans had mined their path of retreat, as was merely good tactics, so he could not truly be angered over that no matter how frustrating it was to have it occur. It was simply part of the cost of capturing this worthless chunk of rock.

No. No anger issues at all.

"Instruct them to press forward," Chien ordered dispassionately.

"Yes, Admiral."

*****

Iwo Jima

Liam skidded into the second line of trenches, sliding in some muck as a rain of fire pattered down around him.

"They're pushing through, Major," The Gunny told him. "Determined little bastards."

"I figured," Liam said as he rolled over and crawled back up to the edge of the second berm to peak over.

There were a lot more tanks stalled out and smoking than there had been a moment earlier, but more of them were coming right along.

Too bad we didn't have time to make that field properly dense, He thought grimly.

A pop from another claymore going off made him smile briefly, but it was time to get back on the job.

"How are we on rockets for the SRAW?" He asked.

"Still decent," Gunny Hadrian answered. "Don't have an exact count if that's what you need, but we're not quite in the yellow yet."

"Good enough. We haven't cracked open the Javelin cases yet, have we?"

"No sir, Major."

"Good," Liam said. "I hate to waste them on light tanks like these, but…"

"Needs must, Major."

"You can say that again, Gunny."

*****

Spirit Flight, FL 65 Over the Pacific

Captain Richard Bligh adjusted the engine output of the B-2A Spirit Bomber, then checked the GPS. They were a few hundred miles from the target still, but the days of a bomber needing to be *over* the target were a long way behind them. He opened a channel, "Iwo Combat Control, Spirit Flight."

"Go for Iwo, Spirit," The voice of Air Force Master Sergeant Kiran Jiang came back quickly.

"We're in range. Can you laze the targets?"

The Master Sergeant laughed, "Captain, we can laze half the pacific."

"Roger that, Iwo. If there's anything you want to go away, paint it now."

"I hope you have enough munitions to make that happen, Captain. Targets lazing."

"If you have a hole, Sergeant, climb in and pull it shut behind you."

*****

Iwo Jima

"Major, got news for you," Kiran said over the radio. "Check Secure."

"Secure confirmed," The Major replied. "What's the good news?"

"We have air support... well, we have an airstrike. Request from Spirit Flight for you to laze anything you'd like to go boom."

The Major paused. Kiran expected that he'd switched channels to start issuing orders. While he was waiting, Kiran finished initializing his laser designator and grabbed a pair of high magnification NVDs.

"Roger on the laze," The Major came back. "Thanks for the heads up. Tell the flyboys I owe them a drink."

"You and me both, Major."

The major signed off, leaving Kiran to heft the laser onto a solid tripod. He didn't think he'd be able to hold it steady at the range he wanted to use it.

"Now, where are you?" He murmured, sweeping the sea with the NVDs until he found the Bloc submersible carrier. Getting the laser to hold steady on the target at more than a couple of miles took a steady mount. Actually, even that wasn't enough, but thankfully the designator had a built-in stabilizer to help with that.

He got the sub lit up with the laser, just above the waterline, the invisible beam showing up nicely on his NVDs. With that done, he clicked off on the system and left it running while he swept over the island with his imagers.

Reflected laser beams were lighting up all over the beach, making him smile slightly.

They have no idea what's about to come down on them.

*****

EBAN HuangLung

"Admiral! Problem!"

Chien scowled, looking over, "What is it?"

"RADAR contacts, just over five hundred kilometers out, from the east."

Chien walked over, "Identify them."

The RADAR man snorted, "They're not running transponders and the signal is *very* faint."

"American bombers then."

"That would be my guess, Admiral, yes."

Chien sighed.

He really should have expected this. It was an inevitable response, he supposed. The Americans couldn't entirely abandon their men out here, particularly not with the entire event being streamed for global audiences by both sides.

"Scramble the ready response squadron, and ensure that our anti-missile defenses are at full alert." He ordered.

"Yes, Admiral."

It was time to deliver another lesson to the unruly students.

*****

Raptor Flight

Tony Dawkins frowned as his flight computer beeped at him, leaning closer to look at the readout.

"Spirit Flight, Raptor Actual," He called.

"Go for Spirit, Raptor."

"I've got a blip on the forward RADAR sweep. Can you confirm?"

"One moment..."

Dawkins waited, tapping his screen. The system seemed to think *something* was out there.

"We've got a ghost, could be stealthed aircraft," Spirit Lead came back a moment later.

"Roger that, Spirit. Hold tight, we'll check it out."

"Watch your butts, Raptor Lead," Spirit responded. "This airspace is going to be rocking."

"Just do your thing, Spirit, we'll watch our backs," Dawson said before flipping his channel over. "Raptors, let's go investigate."

He pushed the throttle forward, engines roaring as he was pushed back into the ACES ejection seat while he tinkered with the RADAR instrumentation, trying to get a better signal. The ghost signal was fading in and out, but he was pretty sure it wasn't a signal interference issue.

"Spread formation, stay with your wingman," He instructed. "Watch for any sign of trouble. These bad boys are fast and maneuverable. If you get in a furball, get close and stick them deep. You all ready for this?"

"You done talking, Tony? Let's do this."

Dawkins chuckled, "Alright. Let's."

The Raptors accelerated away from the bomber flight, vanishing into the night sky as they went hunting.

*****

Iwo Jima

"Targets painted, Major." Gunny Hadrian said, dropping into the trench beside Liam.

"Good work."

"What now?" The Gunny asked, risking a glance over the berm.

"Keep our heads down and pray," Liam said under his voice. "The gods of close air support are notoriously nearsighted."

Hadrian snorted, "I'm usually on the other side of this equation… *Way* on the other side."

"Join the club," Liam said wryly. "No choice though, so pass the word, Gunny."

"You got it Major."

*****

Raptor Flight FL-50 over the Pacific

Dawson tapped the screen in front of him, noting that the signal was firming up. It was definitely a Bloc contact, given how fast it was moving.

"Raptor Lead, Sky Eyes Three."

"Go for Raptor Lead." He said, responding to the AWACS that was pacing the bomber flight.

"We've got your targets, inbound hot on your location. Handshake on twelve."

"Roger," Dawson said, reaching out to twist his system over to channel twelve, then running the secure authentication protocols to link into the AWACS advanced system. "Raptor flight, go secure, channel twelve for AWACS patch."

The AWACS system linked into his own gave him a much better view of the battlespace that was forming up, including distinct vectors for the enemy fighters. They were ignoring his Raptors from what he could tell, vectoring right for the bombers.

Not on my watch. Dawson grumbled, keying in a few commands to split the targets up among his squadron. "Raptors, you have your targets. Go hunting."

He saw the lights on either side of him peel off quickly, leaving him and his wingman ready to take on their target.

Here birdy, birdy, birdy…

*****

AWACS 137 Fl-35

Major Jerricho Sanders crawled back over the gear that his team had pulled out together from the ranks of computer equipment that lined both sides of the Boeing 767 AWACS. He didn't say anything about the mess, but only because some of it was his.

"Coffee, Major?"

"No." He said curtly. "What do we have?"

"Multiple contacts, moving fast. They're coming for the bombers."

"Roger that." He sighed, picking up the radio. "Spirit Flight, Sky Eyes Three."

"Go for Spirit, Sky Eyes."

Sanders looked over the systems, "I'm sure you know we have company coming. Bad news, they're looking to bag *big* game from the looks of it."

"Yeah. That doesn't surprise me. What's the play, Major?"

"Just a suggestion, but you might want to lighten the load, Captain. I hear there's an island not too far away that could take some of that weight off your hands."

"Roger that. Good advice, Major."

Sanders signed off, looking back over the rest of his crew.

"If they're half as fast as the records out of Japan says, we're on the chopping block too. Make sure we have a live feed, sending *everything* we get back to PACAF. They can use it, even if we can't."

"Yes sir."

No more needed to be said. He made his way forward again, to take the stick.

*****

Raptor Flight FL-50

"Raptor Two, follow me in." Dawson ordered. "Back my play."

"You know it, Lead. I'm with you."

"Never a doubt. Raptor Lead out."

Dawson checked the signal, ran the numbers in his head one more time on the intercept vector. The computers were, of course, faster, and more precise than any human could be. But for a fighter pilot being able to be *leaning* in the right direction before the computer confirmed it, that could save entire seconds when fractions of a second were the difference between life and death.

He was really good at leaning in the right direction before the real numbers came down.

Dawson waggled the wings slightly to give notice to his wingman, then peeled out hard, confident that Raptor Two would be tight on his six as he began to blood altitude and boost speed. The Raptor's afterburner roared to life, shaking the fighter around him as he approached the speed of sound, then smoothed out suddenly as he blew through it.

The F-22 maxed out at Mach 2.25 and he was able to edge another couple hundred MPH in the dive. Might even have broken a record, Dawson didn't know, didn't care.

He armed the missiles, and the laser, then made sure that the Vulcan cannon was spinning up. It would save him a half-second or so if he needed to pull the trigger, rotary cannons liked to be moving before they started pumping rounds downrange.

And Dawson expected he was going to need to pull the trigger.

Fly the friendly skies.

*****

Spirit Flight FL-65

"Alright, let's take the Major's advice," Captain Bligh said. "Arm the weapons."

"Which ones?" His co-pilot asked.

"All of them," Bligh responded. "If those fighters get past the Raptors, we only get one shot at this. Start arming procedures now, we're firing *everything*."

"Yes sir."

*****

Chapter Twenty-Eight

Alamagardo New Mexico

Eric dropped to the ground, not bothering to wait for the ladder. The F-22 was hissing slightly as coolant cooked off the still hot engines, men rushing around him to do a post-flight check.

"Pull it into the hangar as soon as it's cooled down," He ordered. "I want to pull the device and spot check the entire airframe for stress."

"You got it, Sir."

"Call me Eric," He said over his shoulder. "I'm not *in* anymore."

"You sure about that?"

Eric sighed, turning back to face forward.

"Brigadier General Kelsey." He said with mixed feelings. "Been a while."

"It has. Major General now, Captain."

"Former Captain," Eric said, "and you always were a Major something."

"Don't get cute with me, Captain," The General grumbled. "You made some serious waves with that test flight."

"There's no way you got called down here because of that," Eric jerked a thumb over his shoulder. "I just landed the damn thing."

"No, the project was interesting enough that it crossed my desk yesterday," Kelsey admitted. "Your name on it didn't hurt. My contact list started burning up my computer fifteen minutes ago, though. Had to mute them all finally."

The General sighed, "I'm probably going to pay for that later."

"How many pissed off calls about the sonic boom?" Eric asked, mostly just curious.

"None. No one recorded a boom, Captain."

"Huh."

That was interesting.

"Well, now that your little toy there has proven out, we've got some teams that want to talk implementation," Kelsey told him.

"Hey, whoa. I get it, seconds count and all that, but there is *no damn way* we're ready for that," Eric said with a hard chop of his right hand. "We're going to be pulling the test platform apart tonight, looking for stress on the airframe. It practically turned a Falcon into a taco, with me as the meaty center."

"There's a pleasant image," Kelsey said dryly. "How long?"

"Ask me tomorrow, I might have some kind of idea," Eric said, before giving in a little. "But if the airframe held up… maybe we can have a squadron outfitted in a couple weeks? Mass manufacture of the device… that's not my specialty. You'll need to talk to the Lockheed boys about that, maybe."

Kelsey nodded, "That's more than I expected, to be honest. Tomorrow then?"

"At least," Eric stressed, irritated. "Look, are you here for Corps, the Pentagon, what?"

"DARPA."

Eric looked at the General flatly, "Who in the *hell* assigned you as a DARPA liaison? Kelsey, I've never known anyone as technologically ignorant as you."

"Har har, Captain."

"Do I really need to remind you of that time in Pakistan?"

"Just stop being a wise-ass, Captain, and keep me apprised."

Eric pinched his brow, "Jesus. Could you people please figure out who's in the loop on this and get all your info from one source? I do not have enough hours in the day to update every last jackass from my past who has the pull to get themselves looped into this damn thing."

"Be very *careful*, Captain. You're toeing a line here."

Eric locked eyes with the General, stepping into his space, "Listen, Eugene. It's Mr. Weston. I'm out."

"That could be… changed, Mr. Weston."

Eric sighed.

The General wasn't wrong, he knew that. His contract with the military had a re-up clause, and he still had a few years to go before it was voided. Honestly, he expected the Government to call it in sooner or later given the current situation.

Given his project, however, he was pretty confident that they'd rather have him as a contractor than one more jarhead with his hand on a stick and throttle.

The General knew that too.

"Don't try the hard sell on me, Eugene," Eric said, stepping around him and walking into the hangar, making the Marine follow. "You want me in an F-35 cockpit, go ahead and call in the re-up clause."

He turned around, facing the General again.

"I'm already pushing as hard as I can. You don't need to ride herd on me, General. You know this," He said. "Why are you really here?"

Kelsey glared before sighing himself.

"You've attracted high level attention… Eric," He said pointedly. "Some very powerful people are watching you closely, and they're calling up everyone you've ever worked with and asking questions. A lot of them."

"If they're asking you for my references, I'm half surprised I haven't been shot."

"You're an asshole, Weston, but you're a good soldier and a patriot."

"Don't call me that."

Kelsey snorted, "And one of the few soldiers I've ever known who considers being called a patriot an insult."

"It's not being called a patriot that's the problem," Eric said. "It's what most people *mean* when they say patriot, General."

"You always did think too damn much too. What I ever did to deserve a philosopher when all I wanted was a Marine, I'll never know." Kelsey sighed.

Eric just shrugged; there wasn't much he could say honestly. The General wasn't wrong. He always did think too much. It was something of an issue when he'd been a young officer, becoming less of an issue as he gained rank.

It had held him back while in the service, and was one reason he did well with the work he'd done since.

"No doubt you deserved it," He said dryly. "Probably something you did in a past life."

"I *hope* I wasn't that much of an asshole in a past life."

Eric laughed, shaking his head as he turned away. "Call me tomorrow. I'll let you know what I know."

"Alright, Mr. Weston. Tomorrow."

*****

Washington DC, White House Situation Room

Givens shook himself, waking up as much as he could when he heard someone shout something.

"What is it?" He asked, blearily, wiping his face.

"The fighters have engaged, Sir. Spirit Flight is launching their weapons, and the Island is under siege again."

"What? When...?"

"An hour ago, you were asleep. Nothing you could do, Sir, we let you sleep."

Givens grumbled, "If I wanted you to let me sleep, I'd be in my bed next to my wife."

"Sorry, sir."

"Never mind. What's the current situation?"

"Marines have been forced to retreat from their first lines, back to the second rank of defense." The Marine General said. "They still hold the majority of the island, and have lazed the targets for the bombers."

The President nodded, "Good, good."

"Unfortunately, we think the Bloc spotted Spirit Flight. The AWACS confirmed contacts on an intercept course. The Raptor flight has moved to engage."

Givens slumped, "Great."

"We knew it was likely, Sir."

"Yeah, but I could hope."

"Well, it's in the hands of the men on site now."

*****

Chapter Twenty Nine

Raptor Flight FL40

The F-22s of the Air Force escort squadron dove hard in on the enemy fighters as they slashed in from the West, leading with missiles from twenty miles out, a range that would normally be almost unthinkably close for them to hold their fire until. Given the enemy fighters' speed, however, giving them less time to react seemed like a strategy worth following.

Captain Dawson scanned the skies through the Augmented Heads-Up Display, looking for the enemy contacts, but they were *fast*. Not just speed either, but their maneuverability was insane. His F-22 could approach Hypersonic speeds, but if he tried to maneuver the way he'd see the enemy do, he'd be pulverized right in his seat… assuming the fighter didn't tear itself apart around him in the process.

"Contact, bearing 139 point 5," He said as he spotted the enemy fighter. "Laser heating up."

No matter how fast, or nimble, they were they couldn't dodge *light*.

Dawson led his wingman through the night sky, lighting off their targeting RADAR as they got in range, getting active locks on the enemy fighters as the two sides converged at insane speeds.

"Ok, here they come, Boomer," He called to his wingman, sending targeting data across the network. "You go high, I'll go low."

"Slice them down the middle, boss man," Charles 'Boomer' Kenderson responded. "Let's do it."

Dawson lined up, quickly getting tone on the approaching contact. "Raptor Lead… Special Munitions Laun… Oh fuck it, Pew, Pew, Pew."

He fired the laser, laughing as he did.

His eyes spotted a flare up in the distance, which he figured signified a hit. A flaming trail began to arc downward. He kept a tag on the target but decided that it was a kill, so he signaled Boomer to take the lead.

"Your turn, buddy."

"On it," Raptor Two responded, moving forward, "I have tone… Raptor Two… Pew, Pew, Pew."

Dawson grimaced.

I am never going to live that one down. He thought, sighing. *Oh, fuck em if they can't take a joke.*

*****

AWACS 137 FL-35

Major Sanders reached out to adjust the trims slightly, compensating for minor turbulence, while keeping one eye on the screens. His crew were keeping Spirit and the Raptors apprized of the changes, but the enemy was stealthier than he'd expected them to be.

Well, that's not exactly right…

It wasn't that they were stealthy, to be honest. His systems could pick up a B-2 in flight. What he was having trouble with was picking them up *fast enough* given how quickly the enemy fighters could close the distance.

Normally he could count on a few hundred miles of buffer, minimum, even when facing off against a fairly well stealthed opponent. Now that was plenty if you were dealing with a normal supersonic bomber or fighter, but a hypersonic foe was another thing entirely. They could cross that space faster than a bullet and be in your face before you could blink.

So, he was stretching his gear, getting everything he could out of it, to try and extend that warning gap to something he and the others could work with.

"Spirit Flight, Sky Eyes Three."

"Go for Spirit."

"Give the Raptors some room," Sanders instructed. "The enemy can close the range too fast for us to react if we don't."

"Roger that, Sky Eyes, Spirit easing off the throttle," The leads B2 responded.

Sanders checked his scope and nodded, "Thank you Spirit. As you were."

"Never stopped, Sky Eyes."

Indeed, they hadn't. The Spirit flight was in the process of putting missiles in the air, long-range cruise weapons with multiple payloads. In a few more minutes, it wouldn't matter if the Raptors couldn't hold them back.

*****

Raptor Lead

"Raptor Five, watch your six! He's coming around!"

"He just passed me! How the…"

Dawson flinched as Raptor Five's radio signal broke up and he could see a blaze of flame erupt in the night sky where he knew the other fighter had been flying.

Damn it. We've lost three fighters already, and they're barely even paying attention to us!

The enemy fighters were living up to every report made about them, and worse by far was that the enemy pilots were adapting. Every trick that had worked on them before was becoming harder and far more troublesome to implement as they learned how to leverage the speed and maneuverability of their platforms.

Certainly, both sides were learning at the same time, but that process was entirely weighted to the Bloc with their far superior equipment.

No matter how good you were, skill and pluck could only even the board just so much.

*****

AWACS 137 FL-35

Sanders grimaced as he watched another Raptor vanish from his screens, their IFF going silent as the fighter plummeted through ten thousand feet. Those pilots were getting torn up out there, trying to keep the enemy away from the bombers. So far, they were holding the line, but he didn't like the way things were leaning.

"Spirit Flight, Sky Eyes Three."

"Go for Spirit."

"I don't think the Raptors can hold much longer. Get the job done and get out of here." Sanders ordered.

"We're unloading as fast as the system will run, Sky Eyes."

"Understood."

And he did, really. The bomb bays on the B-2 had to cycle each of the missiles they were launching, and that took real-time. Gravity bombs were faster, as they were smaller and less complicated, but the JASSM cruise missiles took more time to move into place for deployment.

It was the most frustrating part of his job. He could see *everything* coming, but sometimes that didn't mean he could do anything about it.

All he could was keep feeding the intel to the fighters, keeping them from getting caught with their pants around their ankles.

"Sir, we've got movement from the South."

"What?" Sanders twisted around, eyes widening.

All the action was happening to the West.

"Localize it, NO-"

Before he could finish his sentence, he saw his RADAR operator pale and start to shout a warning. Sanders was still turning back when the missile took them mid-fuselage, tearing the Boeing right in two and jerking the few surviving AWACS crew around as they began to spiral into the dark sky and darker sea below.

*****

Spirit Flight

"Shit!"

Bligh was swearing over an open com, no longer giving the slightest fuck for transmission protocols. They'd lost the AWACS feed, and from the last transmission he didn't have to take two guesses at just why that was.

"Sir, what do we…"

"Just keep firing those missiles!" Bligh ordered his co-pilot. "That ordnance needs to get where it's going. Our stealth should keep them off us."

"Yes sir."

His co-pilot didn't sound convinced, which was fair since neither was he.

It didn't matter, though. They had a mission to finish, the men and women on Iwo Jima were depending on them to deliver on what they'd promised.

Bligh checked the load numbers for his own B2 Spirit, then did the same across the squadron.

Just over thirty percent launched. We need more time.

Without the AWACS feeding them data, however, he had no idea how far away the enemy might be, and that was a big problem. With his co-pilot continuing to enter targeting information and firing missile after missile, Bligh focused on the instrumentation as he tried to locate the enemy fighters before they located Spirit flight.

They didn't have many options, no matter what, unfortunately.

It all came down to two choices.

If they ceased operations and closed the bomb bay doors, the formidable stealth capability of the B-2s *might* save them. It wasn't a certainty, unfortunately, since the Bloc used RADAR of Russian and Chinese make, which was not remotely as accurate as their Western counterparts but had the advantage of being more sensitive against the radar absorbing materials used to help the B-2 hide.

Or, Blight thought, *we can stay on mission and put as many missiles into the air before they get us as we can.*

Bligh glanced over at his co-pilot for a moment, catching the man's eye. He and Joseph Banks had worked together for several years, and knew each other like brothers. He didn't need to say anything for Joe to know what he was asking.

Joseph just nodded once, then went back to firing missiles.

Decision made.

*****

Raptor Lead FL-20

Dawson worked the pedals as he put the F-22 into a flat turn, bringing the nose around to meet the fast-approaching contact from the North.

He didn't know where they'd all come from, but shortly after the AWACS feed had gone down, everything went to hell. Contacts came out of nowhere from every compass point it seemed, and he wasn't sure if any of his squadron were still flying aside from him.

He was running full ECM, jamming the enemy's missile lock as best he could, and making them come to him. Unfortunately, they weren't making the same mistakes they had over Japan and with the laser pods installed on the enemy fighters they could engage from well outside his cannon range.

He'd fired his own laser pod dry already, and was now down to guns.

His Vulcan was a six-shooter, six barreled air-cooled rotary cannon, with only five shots loaded. Of which, he'd expended three already to no avail.

That left him with roughly a hundred and eighty to two hundred rounds loaded in the cannon, his missiles gone, laser fully expended, and too many enemy to count coming at him from every damn way but down.

He had no idea if the mission had been completed or not, and there was nothing he could do about it at this point if it hadn't.

With that firmly in mind, he focused on bleeding the enemy dry so much as he could.

A flicker of motion to his left caused him to stomp on the pedals, putting his fighter into a fast spin that jerked him about and sent a wail of straining metal straight through him. The nose of the F-22 snapped onto target just as a flash caused him to glance back and he spotted smoke curling from a ling along his wing, the speed of his turn had kept the enemy laser from burning a hole through him.

He snapped his head back, spotting the enemy fighter through the HUD in his helmet, and automatically banked over and spun the fighter into position. The enemy fighters had taken their shot from over fifty miles out, but at hypersonic speeds the over-eager Bloc pilot had closed that range in literally a *second*.

Clearly, he'd not expected to miss, and had overextended as a result, slipping into the F-22 Vulcan range.

"Raptor Lead. Guns, Guns, Guns."

The fourth shot of roughly a hundred rounds snarled out from his fighter, crossing the space between him and the enemy at thousands of feet per second as the enemy slammed into it at several times that rate, turning the enemy fighter to shrapnel mid-air, blazing briefly in the dark sky before the flames winked out and the wreckage vanished from sight.

One shot left... Dawson thought as he started looking around for a place to put his last burst.

A flicker of motion across his HUD caused him to turn back the way he'd come, but it was too late as a flare of light erupted from his right wing, warning alarms screaming to life as he felt his stick response basically turn to mud.

"Shit."

That was about the only word he could put to his lips as he worked automatically trying to maintain control of the F-22 as it began to die around him. The *metal* of the fighter behind him appeared to be burning, and he could feel the fighter dipping to the right and dropping fast.

"This is Raptor Lead, I am declaring an emergency. Mayday, Mayday, Mayday. Going down. Coordinates to follow..." He said, quickly checking his gear before rattling off his location in the open over the radio and then sending on the information via the combat network as well.

"This is going to *suck*," He grumbled, looking down at the hints of whitecaps in the Pacific below him, then reached for the handle between his legs.

Dawson hesitated briefly, but then just grimaced and pulled hard.

Explosives in the cockpit around him blew the canopy off as the rockets in the seat roared and threw him up and out of the fighter into the dark night beyond.

*****

Spirit Flight

"How many left?" Bligh demanded.

"A little over half to go," his co-pilot said.

"Shit."

The cockpit was screaming around them. Alarms from every warning system they had seemed to be going off. The airspace around them was filled with hostile RADAR, and while about the *only* thing they didn't have for sure was a confirmed lock on, the computer didn't much seem to know for sure either way on that.

The lock on warning ended that minute reprieve as he tightened his grip on the stick, "Keep firing."

"You got it, boss."

A flare of fire in the sky to his left caused Bligh to half turn and swear as one of the black wings of a fellow B-2 erupted in flames, silhouetted against the night sky. The flight crew called a mayday as they started going down.

Another to the right cause both he and his co-pilot to jump.

They were sitting ducks without a fighter screen or AWACS support, and both of them knew it.

Even so, they kept firing weapons as long as they could, until a brilliant flash turned the night sky to pure white before it all went dark and the B-2 began dropping from the sky.

*****

Chapter Thirty

Iwo Jima

A hail of fire from the beach tore up the dirt around them, causing the Marines and JSDF to flinch back.

"Hold the line! Keep those lasers steady," Gunny Hadrian called at the top of his lungs as he leveled his sig over the berm and opened fire.

The 6.4mm assault rifle roared, bucking into his shoulder, high velocity rounds tearing into a Bloc soldier who'd exposed himself at just the wrong time. Hadrian fell back a moment later when a furious riposte tore into the spot he'd been, spattering dirt and sand all over them as he rolled out of the way.

"God damn it, Gunny," Charleson swore, brushing sand from his face. "You want to stop taunting the bastards?"

Hadrian just looked at him for a moment, his expression more clearly communicating 'are you stupid?' than words ever could.

Charleson just sighed, rolling over to get his own Sig under him as he edged up to the berm and took a peek over.

The tanks were advancing on their position despite heavy resistance from SRAWs, Javelins, and anti-armor mines. The Bloc just had more tanks than the defenders had weapons to take them out, or at least more tanks than they could move munitions around.

Marines and JSDF had been trampled under the second line as the tanks rolled over the berms before they could withdraw entirely, the light armor moving faster than anyone expected due to the power in the electric engines that gave them shockingly quick scoot capability.

They were left just barely holding on then, holding the line as they waited for the promised support.

*****

Liam patted the helmet of the Marine with the laser designator, taking a knee beside the berm there as he scouted the advancing enemy line. The Bloc was determined to make this a fast battle, but there was no way Liam would let that happen.

If he had to, he'd go out and drag the fuckers back into the sea one by one, carrying them on his back.

Liam really hoped he didn't have to, though.

He was mentally counting down the seconds, waiting on the airstrike that they'd been promised, and hoped it would be enough, but at this point he was happy to take *anything* he could get.

He brought his Sig up, firing a couple quick bursts downrange, making the enemy take cover more than hitting anything when a flash of motion from the sky followed by a flash of light caused him to hit the ground hard.

The hissing sound of the missiles coming in was almost entirely eclipsed by the rolling booms from the sound barrier being shattered and the thunderous cracks of the payloads going off. Cruise missiles hammered into tanks on the Island and ships offshore, while JASSM weapons deployed guided and unguided sub-munitions high over the island and let them rain down from above.

Iwo Jima vanished in a blaze of fire for a brief moment, the beaches in particular turning into a charnel house of flame and shrapnel.

All too quickly, however, it was over.

Liam hesitated, not wanting to poke his head up in time for a second strike to take it clean off, but finally he looked around.

That wasn't a full strike...

"Combat Control, Major Gibb," He said.

"Go for Combat Control, Major."

"What happened? I know that wasn't a full strike…"

"Major, I don't have contact with the air wing any longer," The air force combat controller said seriously. "I'm not sure, but I think that might be all we're going to get."

"Fuck."

Liam was cursing more for the apparent loss of the wing than the lack of further strikes, but he *really* wished they had more incoming munitions.

No use whining about it, He thought, grounding himself grimly.

Girding his thoughts, Liam rose to his feet and lifted his rifle high.

"Push them into the Ocean!" He called at the top of his lungs, going over the top as he did.

For a few brief seconds, Major Gibb was charging the entire Bloc landing team on his own, his Sig roaring as he started forward before a roar from Marines and JSDF soldiers rose up behind him and hundreds more came over the top and joined the charge.

*****

EBAN HuangLung

Chien swore as he held on, the deck heaving underfoot as the missile struck the HuangLung amidships. They'd just gotten finished patching the previous hole, and now an American missile went and opened another.

"Damage report!" He snarled, struggling forward.

"Teams moving now. We'll know shortly."

"Sooner than that!" Chien ordered, turning then to the flight control officer. "Word from the fighters?"

"The American bombers were destroyed, Admiral. However, as we found out, they managed to fire off many of their weapons first."

Chien nodded tightly, irritated, but there was no one nearby to take it out on.

The American weapons were fire and forget, so it mattered little whether the bombers were eliminated once they were in the air. Still, losing a flight of bombers should make the Americans think twice about sending another any time soon.

He turned his focus back to the combat control officer, "The situation on the Island?"

"Most of the missiles landed there," The man confirmed his fears. "The American and Japanese forces have used the distraction to their advantage and have pressed an offensive, retaking land we had captured from them."

"Show me."

The officer nodded quickly, gesturing to the large screen where he sent several streaming signals.

"Some of those are ours," He said by way of explanation. "Others are from the Americans side of things, taken from public streaming."

"How long of a delay are they putting on it?" Chien demanded.

"As near as we can tell, they are not," The control officer answered. "American news services have done so. Their government is touchy of what they broadcast, but the online streaming services are very nearly in real-time, with only the satellite and server delays accounting for any discrepancies."

Chien closed his eyes.

Americans. Their government is insane to allow the military units on the island to do this… How they managed to get permission, I will never know. Normally not even American Generals are quite this insane.

"The forces on the Island have drive ours back to the beaches, Admiral. Once we lost cohesion due to the airstrike, they took the advantage and have not given it up."

Chien glowered at the screen, hands gripping a rail under him until his knuckles were bone white.

"Signal the withdrawal," He ordered.

"Admiral?"

"Pull them off that worthless hunk of *rock* before we lose everything we've committed," He snarled.

"Yes, Admiral!"

This will take a different tack, Chien decided angrily.

*****

Iwo Jima, Mount Suribachi

Jiang clenched a fist as he spotted the first of the Bloc landing craft loading men and powering up. Sure enough, as he watched, the amphibious craft began to draw back into the ocean as it retreated under the onslaught of the Marines and JSDF troops charging the beach.

"The Bloc forces are withdrawing, Major." He advised. "Best get your men undercover."

"Roger Controller, got it." Liam responded.

A few moments later the island's defenders were running back up the beach and diving for the cover of the trench they'd sheltered in previously. It wasn't a moment too soon, either, as the Bloc ships renewed their shelling of the Island in full force.

Master Sergeant Jiang himself crawled back into the hole they'd half dug, and half found, lest any of the ships spot his location and decide they didn't want him around any longer.

Rumbling thunder took over the island, followed by a steel rain.

Bad weather to be out and about today, Jiang thought with some humor.

*****

Gunnery Sergeant Hadrian sheltered under the smoking wreck of a Bloc light tank, where it had bridged over the trench just after a mine put a hole through its battery pack it had provided a decent enough armored shelter, as long as they took care to avoid the jet of flame still blasting out of the hole like a blowtorch.

It did warm the bones a little, though, as they dried out their mud-caked gear and listened to the steel rain tear down about them.

"Well, round two to us, boys," Hadrian told his baby Marines and the others who'd been fighting shoulder to shoulder with them.

They cheered, the Marines chanting their Oorahs, while the rest just laughed.

They'd lost a lot of people on that second wave, but for the moment the morale was staying high. Hadrian didn't know how long that would last, but he would take it while he could get it.

"What do we do now, Gunny?" Meer asked from where he was pressing against the side of the trench.

Hadrian leaned back, resting his head against the dirt, "Not much to do. Ease in, boys, relax. Let the soft gentle sounds of the shrapnel on the tank armor ease you off to sleep."

A few of them couldn't settle down, but Hadrian ignored them and relaxed under the shadow of the Bloc tank, tipping his pot forward over his eyes and just left them to it. There really wasn't anything else to do for the moment. Steel rain wasn't something you walked out around in with an umbrella, after all.

The sound of men moving and murmuring sharply caused him to sit up and push his helmet back quickly, though, in time to see the Major slip in under the tank treads and look them over.

"You boys ok?" Liam asked.

Hadrian nodded. "My boys are good, and the rest of the lads here did themselves proud."

"That they did," Liam smiled at them all, "Looks like we're going to have some time before the next attack, I think they're going to want to soften us up before they try their luck again. You boys get some sleep, if you can, I've got men fetching rations, coffee, and I think there might be a few bottles of something stronger kicking around, so I'll see if we can't get one up here for you lot."

The men cheered a little, relaxing visibly.

"Hey Gunny, have a word?" Liam asked, nodding out in one direction.

"Yes, Major." Hadrian pushed himself up, brushing off as much sand as he could as he walked over.

They slipped out a little from under the tank but stayed under the cover of the trench and berm of piled up dirt as the ordnance continued exploding overhead and around them.

The Major looked over his shoulder as Hadrian dropped to a crouch beside him, obviously checking the position of the men before he spoke.

"Not going to lie to you, Gunny," Liam said, tone shifting. "It's going to get bad."

Hadrian nodded softly, "Figured, Sir. The airstrike felt a little light?"

Liam nodded, his voice lowering, "Bloc took out the squadron in flight. Don't know how much they got off, but couldn't have been much more than half of what they were packing."

Hadrian grimaced.

That was bad news, more for the loss of the Air Force squadron than the ordnance, but the loss of the ordnance was going to be felt in the coming hours or days.

He risked rising up a bit, glancing out over the Pacific Ocean to the North.

"How long before they try again, you think?" Hadrian asked.

"Couple days, I'll bet. They're going to try and wear us down now," Liam answered. "It's a siege."

"No chance of support?"

"Out here? Even if they moved everything out of Pearl right now, you know how long it would take to get here?" Liam said, shaking his head.

Ten days, couple weeks, maybe more depending on what they sent, Hadrian knew that too well. He nodded wearily, tilting his head to look back at his men out of the corner of his eye.

"Don't know how long we can keep the spirits up, boss," He admitted.

"I know, just do what you can," Liam said, rising to his feet.

"Yes Sir."

Liam smiled and clapped him on the shoulder, pulling something from his pocket as he walked them both back under the tank. He put his hand up to his mouth, then leaned in close to the torch of flame shooting from the tank's batteries, puffing as he lit the pair of cigars in his hand, then passed one off to Hadrian.

"Keep up the good work, Gunny," The Major said in a cheerful and boisterous tone, looking around to the others, "I'll have that bottle I promised sent down soon as I can. Get some rest, you all earned it, and then some."

"Oorah, Major!"

Hadrian took a puff of the cigar, tasting the smoke but not inhaling it as he'd never smoked in his life and figured that coughing up his lungs in front of his Marines and the Major wouldn't be a great start. He lifted the cigar in a salute as the Major waved back and headed off.

"Oorah and Semper Fi, Major," He said to the man's departing shadow.

"Well, you heard him," Hadrian said a moment later. "Get some rest. I'll let you know when the hooch arrives."

"Oorah Gunny."

Hadrian watched over the group. They were all his men now, and with what he knew was coming… well, he could think of worse people to have at his side.

"Oorah, Marines," He said softly, including the JSDF and the Navy squids in that statement.

*****

Chapter Thirty-One

Eric wiped the sweat from his face as he stumbled out of the hangar and collapsed on a bench that overlooked the tarmac that was just starting to heat up in the light of the late morning sun. He'd been up all night and all morning, working on tearing down the F-22 and checking the data he'd gathered on the test flight.

In between, he spent spare moments catching up on what was happening on Iwo, but since the airstrike and the defenders pushing the Bloc off the island for the second time, it was clear that the Bloc forces had a new strategy of wearing down the island before they tried another invasion.

They'd been shelling the island for almost a full day since.

It made for lousy watching, but the streams were still the only thing running on any news station, and the most popular thing on the web as best he could tell. He didn't really know what to make of that, whether it was morbid curiosity on people's part or something… more.

Eric supposed that he would find out in time.

"You look like shit warmed over."

He didn't bother looking up, "Fuck you too, Max."

"What's the low down on the project?" Max asked, walking over, and taking a seat beside him.

Eric sighed, "Who's asking this time?"

"Scuse me?"

"I thought you were with DARPA. So how come Eugene Kelsey comes by and starts asking questions you should already have fed them the answers to?"

"I never said I was with Darpa, Eric, Sue is. I'm with Homeland these days."

Eric groaned, "Fine. Why didn't she fill them in?"

"Too busy working?" Max shrugged. "So, the General came by. Can't say it shocks me. Have any good news for him?"

Eric rolled his eyes, but leaned back against the wall of the hangar, "The F-22 airframe held up well. We've found some signs of stress fractures, but they're in places we can reinforce."

"So, we're good to go?" Max asked intently.

Eric looked at him, "Why are you pushing so damn hard?"

"Eric… we lost a Raptor squadron last night, as well as an AWACS and a flight of B-2s," Max admitted quietly. "We are up against it. We need this. The country needs this. There's a lot of pressure coming down, your project here has reached the highest levels. We need to know, are we go?"

Eric leaned out and looked around, back into the hangar where the stripped-down skeleton of an F-22 was resting, the device in its belly.

"The device is good to go, we can put a squadron together in a couple weeks… maybe a little faster," He said. "But we need weapons, we can't just go in there with a knock off version of what the Bloc have already perfected and expect it to end well."

Max nodded, "Already ahead of you. I've been calling in projects here, and abroad."

"Abroad?"

That surprised Eric actually. Classified projects tended to be tough to recruit for, even within the country.

"Team from Toronto have been working on some meta-materials I think will come in handy," Max said. "The interface team from Stanford will be here later today to talk with you, and we have three teams of high energy laser specialists from MIT, Oxford, and Berlin flying in."

Max stood up, looking down at Eric.

"It's all hands on deck, buddy. You might want to get some sleep, cause it's going to get busy here soon."

Eric snorted, picking up an empty can and chucking it at Max as the other man walked away.

"Soon? What do you think we've been doing here for the last couple days you lazy ass?"

"Watching the net streams best I can tell," Max called back over his shoulder, ignoring the can as it bounced off his leg.

Eric rolled his eyes and got to his feet, shaking his head.

I should go home and get some sleep, He thought, considering it briefly before he just shambled back into the hangar and headed for his office, grabbing a pillow off the couch on his way by.

The floor was calling out to him.

*****

Stephen grunted as he lugged a big battery capacitance system across the hangar to where one of the doctors had needed it. He barely understood one word in five coming out of their mouths, though he thought he was improving since it had been more like one in ten when he started, but he could still help even if it was as a gopher.

He was worn out, but everyone here seemed so certain that what they were doing was important that it was infectious in its own way. He couldn't just leave and not help, so he was doing whatever he could. It freed up some of the smarter people to do whatever it was that they did best anyway.

He paused near the airframe where a couple of people were working on the device and frowned as he saw what they were doing.

"Hey, you got those connections wrong," He offered.

"Says who, kid?"

Steph rolled his eyes, "Says the kid who's been watching Eric and Bradley build, teardown, and rebuild that thing for almost three years."

"Oh yeah," One of them gestured. "So educate us."

"Hey, I don't know if this is a good…" The other started, but he was cut off.

"It'll be fine," The first said, turning back to Steph. "You going to put up, kid?"

Steph clambered up the ladder and carefully checked his footing as he stepped out onto the airframe. He'd learned the hard way that you looked for instructions on where to step when it came to planes, especially the expensive ones.

"See these wires are tricky," He said. "They used to color-code them, but Eric burned them out so often that they gave up on the prototype. He probably already has a note about it, but I think I'll remind him to make sure they order enough wire to color code any new models. You have the hand tester?"

"Here kid," The first man said, his tone softened a bit and now more curious than challenging.

Steph took the computer and plugged it in, running a diagnostic before showing it to the man. "See?"

"I'll be damned."

"We'd have caught it when we run the tests," The other man said.

"Sure, but by then we'd have had to pull the cowling back off, saved us some time kid. Thanks."

"It's ok," Steph shrugged self-consciously as he handed back the tester and pulled the wires, plugging them back in quickly without checking. "There, have a look."

"Sure," The challenger said, plugging the computer back and running the tests. "Looks good. What's your name, kid?"

"Stephen Michaels," Steph said, accepting the hand offered.

"Woodrow," The man said, "Paul Woodrow. That's Jason Graves over there."

"Hey," the other man waved from the other side of the fighter.

"So, you've been hanging around for the last three years?" Woodrow asked.

"Whenever I could," Steph confirmed. "Eric taught me to fly. Got my license this year. Was going to get jet certification next, but not sure Eric is going to have time."

Woodrow chuckled, "Probably not. Still, lot of us around here have our permits and wouldn't mind an excuse to get our hands on a stick. You got a bird?"

"Eric's," Steph grinned, "He's got an old Tutor that we were starting on, and half a handful of others that he's used for different reasons the past couple years. Even had a F-16 for a while…"

Steph shook his head, looking disturbed, "It's a crime what happened to that."

"Crash?"

"Is it a crash if you didn't get it off the ground?" Steph asked, honestly curious.

"Technically… no."

"Then no."

"Sounds like there's a story there."

"Not one Eric likes to tell," Steph grinned.

"My boy," Woodrow dropped an arm around his shoulders. "That's exactly the reason such stories need to be told by others. No need bothering him with the effort of telling it, after all."

"Right, it would be a favor to him?"

"Exactly."

Steph smirked, "I suppose I could take some time… if someone made it worth my while."

"Let's talk."

*****

Washington DC, White House

President Givens sighed deeply as he washed his face and looked at himself in the mirror.

He'd finally gotten some sleep, fitful though it had been. He couldn't remember actually going to bed, but his wife had told him he'd been helped in by one of the White House aides.

Probably owe her a bonus this Christmas, he thought with some humor while reaching for a towel to dry off.

He'd already checked the morning's alerts, finding that the situation in the Pacific hadn't changed from the last he remembered. The shelling continued on Iwo Jima, while the Bloc forces had secured their occupation of Japan and Taiwan, while North Korea had moved solidly into South Korea with the support of Chinese forces.

The Middle East was on fire, with Israel the lone holdout from Bloc occupation.

Normally that might be a sign of them severely overreaching themselves, but the Bloc was an alliance of at least twenty-odd nations, the last he'd checked. With each of them making moves in their regions relatively independently, but under overall coordination, it would be a massively big problem even without the new technology being fielded.

With the new technology, Givens wasn't sure they could be beaten at all.

He tossed the towel in a hamper on the way out, grabbing his tie and looping it around his neck as he left the bedroom.

*****

Oval Office

"Morning, Mr. President."

"Good Morning, Jeff," Givens greeted his secretary. "I don't suppose anyone has any good news?"

Jeffery McAllister shrugged as he got up and followed the President into the office, "Good news is in short supply, I'm afraid. Some interesting notes have filtered up."

"Oh? From where?"

"DARPA reports on the Bloc's fighter tech," Jeff said, tapping a folder on the table.

"Really?" Givens picked up the folder, flipping it open.

He only managed to read a few lines before he felt his blood pressure spiking.

"Are they *fucking* kidding me!?" He blew up, slapping the folder down. "We've had someone in the country working on a prototype for three years, and it's *workable*? Why the hell have they been working without funding for three years?"

"Page three, Sir."

Givens shot a glare at Jeff, but flipped over to the third page and started reading. After a few moments he just groaned, slumping in the chair.

"I'm going to assume there's a full briefing on this project?" Givens asked.

"It's your one o'clock, Sir."

"Thank you, Jeffery."

"I live to serve, Mr. President."

Givens snorted, "You may go now, Jeffery."

"Yes Sir."

I swear, if that man wasn't so good at his job…

Givens sighed, smiled with some exasperation, and got to work.

*****

Holloman AFB, Alamogordo New Mexico

Maximillian Murphy groaned as he wiped some of the sweat from his face and reached for a spray can of sunblock.

Why did Eric have to set up in New Mexico, damn it?

He was watching the Air Force Globemaster as it unloaded, bringing with it more equipment and personnel for the project. He was rapidly reaching the limits of his discretionary budget, so he was hoping someone higher up got a hold of the file in a hurry.

This was only the second of several deliveries over the next couple days, but one of the more important ones.

A woman was shepherding a container as he watched, growling at the Air Force cargo handlers who were, as far as he could tell, doing their level best to ignore her while they got the equipment unloaded.

Max decided to take pity on them, well that and he needed to talk to her anyway. Might as well distract her from the poor people just doing their jobs.

"Doctor Brooke?" He asked, approaching.

"What? Yes," She said, turning away. "Who are you?"

"Max Murphy," He told her.

"Oh, you're the one who got me yanked from my rather comfortable lab and told to bring my life's work down into the middle of the desert."

That could have gone better, He supposed, only smiling in response. "That would be me, yes."

"I hope you don't plan on stiffing the University on the funding you promised," She grumbled. "We've put a lot into this, and OIT needs it."

"I assure you, the funding I promised is secure," He said. "Hopefully, within a short time, even more will be available. Is this the material?"

She followed his gaze to the container, nodding.

"Yes, it's our meta-material. I'm really not sure what the military wants with it, we already proposed it as a camouflage option, but were shot down." She said sourly.

"Oh? Why is that?" He asked though he knew the reasons for the most part.

"They said it was too expensive, and most combat was conducted miles away through non-visual means anyway," She sighed. "Static camouflage was considered to be far more cost-effective."

"Ah," He nodded sympathetically. "Well we're not too concerned with camouflage, though that may be a bonus in the application we're thinking about. I'm actually more interested in your Laser experiments."

"Those?" She asked, her nose crinkling as she thought about it. "What possible use could they have for you? The material certainly can be modified to reflect or absorb radiated light, but there are far more common materials that would do a better job."

"Come," He gestured. "I've arranged a truck to pick up your material, and a transport to bring us to the project site. We have a great deal to talk about."

At the transport he opened the back door for her, helping her in.

"Doctor Brooke, this is Doctor Fields," He smiled. "She's from Stanford. Doctor Fields, Brooke here is from the Ontario Institute of Technology."

"A pleasure," The blond greeted Brooke with a smile and an extended hand.

"Likewise, I'm sure. Do you specialize in metamaterials as well?" Brooke asked curiously.

"No, prosthetics research, mind/machine interface," Fields answered, before asking curiously, "Metamaterials?"

"You two have fun," Max said. "I have to arrange a few more details."

He closed the door as the pair started talking shop, only too happy to be getting clear of that mess before he got dragged in somehow.

Academics.

*****

Chapter Thirty-Two

Iwo Jima

Liam jerked awake, blinking as the glare of the sun caught his eyes. He looked around, squinting as he tried to work out what it had been that woke him up. Something had, he knew that, but he couldn't quite place it.

Finally, he realized what it was.

The quiet.

They've stopped the shelling.

He rolled over onto his belly and crawled up the berm, grabbing his magnifiers as he did, setting them to sweep the ocean quickly while he keyed his radio on.

"Master Sergeant, report." He said curtly.

The Air Force Combat Controller was quickly back to him, apparently having been expecting the call.

"Looks like they're just sitting there, Major," Jiang told him. "No signs of movement. Reloading perhaps?"

"Maybe."

Liam didn't know one way or another, but that didn't feel quite right to him. He could be getting paranoid, though. Being shelled for several days did that to a man.

It was...

He had to stop and count back, the hours and days had already started to blend into one another.

Damn, has it been nearly a week?

The Bloc fleet hadn't moved yet, shelling the island off and on, usually at the worst possible hours of the night and morning, all by the book thus far. They'd tried a couple more probing runs on the

Island, landing troops at different beaches, sometimes two or three at once, clearly gauging response times and what equipment the defenders could move around and make available.

To confuse things, and to bolster their supplies, Liam had ordered men to scrounge whatever they could from the fallen enemy. Chinese Type 90 automatic rifles were now almost as plentiful as Sigs on the Island, and a few of the men were happily using those in the place of their issue weapons.

He let them, there was no reason not to, after all.

Discipline hadn't degraded so much as morphed into something more fitting the situation. He certainly didn't expect his men to be turned out like they were ready for inspection, and in turn they didn't let any of their gear go the same path. As long as they kept their kit in fighting order, Liam was happy to ignore pretty much anything else.

Almost.

He'd had to step in to put a stop to the small squad that fought off one particular Bloc incursion in the nude.

Not even the enemy deserved that.

Not at noon hour in full sun, at least. Marines.

"Roger that," He replied to the Air Force man. "Keep me apprised if they move."

"You've got it, Major. One thing, though, looks like they've got the big one patched up," Jiang said idly. "Not sure if it can handle pressure, given it's a field repair, but figured I'd let you know."

Liam nodded, "Thanks. I'll keep it in mind."

He settled back into the trench, thinking about things for a bit before he came to a decision.

"Lieutenant," He called, waving a young officer over.

"Yes sir?"

A few weeks earlier, the man in front of him had been one of the freshest faced officers Liam had ever seen. He specifically remembered thinking that officers were getting younger and dumber every year when he saw the kid trying to keep his squad in line, much to the amusement of both Liam and the Gunny who'd been watching until they took pity on him and Liam sent the Gunny in to straighten things out.

Now, the kid looked like a twenty-year veteran, and Liam damn near trusted him like one.

Lieutenant Hood had come through the crucible, and somehow not shattered yet.

"Grab a squad," He ordered the kid. "I want a patrol of the Island, stay to the trenches as much as you can, but get eyes on as much as you can too. Head south."

"Yes sir."

The Major nodded, waving him on. "Send any other officers you spot awake my way."

"Oorah, Major."

Liam waved him on, grabbing at a tablet and a digital pen. Power for their gear they had aplenty, thanks to solar and wind generators. The Island was basically ideal for both, so they'd not had to use up the fuel supplies all that much yet. That would change if they started using the vehicles on hand heavily, but that was unlikely to happen while the Bloc ships controlled the waters.

An armored transport would be a nice fat target for them, so Liam figured he'd rather walk.

The low-slung MULES were running, mostly just with cargo. They were hard to spot, built to be low and slow, but they run on batteries themselves and were efficient enough not to be a big drain.

Washington might not be able to afford us much backup, but at least they've given me full access to satellite surveillance.

That was a luxury in his experience, even with the modern satellite constellations running only around three hundred and fifty miles up, good surveillance came from bigger birds a hell of a lot higher and more expensive.

He zoomed in on the Island in real-time, slowly examining a given zone before moving on to the next. While he was working a half dozen more young officers found their way over to him and he gave them similar orders, sending them off to different sections of the island with whoever they could scrounge up.

He didn't know if the Bloc were up to anything, but if not… well, the worst thing was that he gave him men something to do. That was worth it alone.

*****

Mount Suribachi

Kiran Jiang knelt along the ridge his little hidey-hole was located in, eyes on the loose formation of the Bloc naval ships.

The big one was showing motion on the deck, men milling around and getting something in the water. He didn't know what exactly, but Jiang called it down to the Major anyway while he kept watch.

The shelling hadn't done much to his location, but the island laid out below him looked like it had been through a war, which was fitting of course. The runway was completely trashed. He doubted anything could land there as it was not, even VTOL rigs wouldn't fare well in now uneven terrain that was completely filled with FOD.

Not many had been killed outright in the shelling, however. The widespread nature of the entrenchments made it difficult to deliver a real solid killing blow. Overhead drones could have done it, but it seemed like the Bloc forces were still holding to the Miami Treaty of 2042 that forbade deploying, or even constructing, armed drones.

All the major powers still had them, of course, but no one wanted to put them into service publicly since the terror incident in South Florida killed over thirteen thousand people using surplus drones from India, China, and the US.

Overnight, public perception of the weapons had gone from vaguely positive to regarding them as barely any different than a WMD.

He doubted that would stop the Bloc from deploying them if it needed to, but as they held the upper hand, they seemed happy to maintain some air of moral superiority.

Movement from the ship caught his attention and broke Jiang from his thoughts, and he quickly put his glasses back to his eyes.

"Major," He called immediately.

"What is it, Sergeant?"

"Gig from the Bloc submersible incoming. Seems to be coming in alone."

"Roger that. Thanks."

"No problem, Major."

*****

Trenches

Liam made his way up to check the report from the Master Sergeant, eyes scanning the waters through the magnification system.

Sure enough, there it was. An admiral's gig, unless he missed his guess.

Well, don't that beat all.

He dropped back into the trench and set the glasses down, picking up his sig and making his way east through the trench.

"Major," The Gunny said as he approached. "News?"

"Enemy boat incoming," Liam said. "Looks like an Admiral's gig."

Hadrian looked surprised, then thoughtful in short order.

"Surrender?" He asked.

"Them or us?" Liam asked with a chuckle. "But yeah, most likely."

"Should we burn the colors, Major?" Hadrian asked, a little uncertainly.

"Nuts to that," Liam responded with a grin. "But I'll talk to them."

Hadrian looked sharply worried at that, "Major, no. I'll go."

"Thank you, Gunny, but they're going to want to speak to the man in charge."

Hadrian looked uneasily between them, "We're close to the same size, Major."

Liam smiled, "They've seen me on the stream."

"How much you want to make a bet that we all look alike when we're covered in mud and blood, Sir?"

"I'm going, Gunny," Liam said firmly.

Hadrian sighed, "Fine. I'll walk with you."

Liam looked ready to say something to that, but finally only nodded.

Hadrian looked back on his baby Marines, suppressing a smile as he did. They'd come a long way in a short time.

"Hold the line," He said, "Oorah."

"Oorah, Gunny!"

*****

Liam made another stop, checking with Captain Ishida to get his thoughts on the situation. IT didn't take long as the Captain too decided to… tag along, despite Liam's objections this time.

"We need to ensure there's a strong chain of command, Captain," Liam said. "Better if you stay back."

"Better, I should think," Ishida corrected. "That *you* stay back. You command the largest contingent of ground combat forces on the Island. My men are willing, but they are sailors for the most part, not soldiers."

"Yeah well, that ain't happening."

"No, but this is," Ishida said calmly, falling into step beside him. "We will project a united front."

Liam nodded, "As you say."

They paused at the outer line of defense, watching the small boat as it approached the shore. It was flying a white flag along with the Bloc colors, which told him that his initial thoughts were likely true.

They were coming to demand a surrender.

The trio, among many others spread through the trench, watched as the boat was pushed up the beach and some men jumped out and started forward. One in what looked like a Bloc Naval Captain's uniform was holding the white flag as he approached.

"Alright," Liam said, setting his rifle down. "Let's meet them halfway."

The other two nodded, putting their own rifles down as well, and the three jumped up, climbing over the berm, and dropping down onto the beach beyond.

Slowly the three made their way down the beach, as the Bloc representatives paused halfway up and waited.

*****

Captain Duei Lei watched as the three dirty men approached, looking like mud-covered urchins from the streets of Beijing more than soldiers in a modern army, but even he could admit that they had most certainly earned the right to wear the dirt they carried.

"Captain…" His second shifted nervously.

"Silence," Duei said firmly, waving him back. "Listen, do not talk."

Duei nodded respectfully as the trio came to a rest in front of him, just a handful of meters away. He recognized the Major easily enough, the man had featured prominently on both the public streams as well as the Bloc Intelligence briefings compiled from them.

The Japanese man was a Captain, presumably from one of the ships they'd sunk earlier, though Duei knew it was entirely possible that he was also a refugee of sorts from the fall of the island nation and hadn't been assigned to any of the ships in question.

Either way, it was irrelevant. The JSDF were much like the nation itself, no longer a concern.

The third man wasn't an officer, so Duei ignored him.

"You came to talk," The Major said bluntly, nodding to the flag. "So talk."

Duei nodded, "Very well. The forces of the Eastern Alliance Bloc wish to offer you the option of surrender. We assure you of fair treatment for your men and yourselves. Food, water, medical attention, and an option to contact your government to negotiate for your return."

The Major looked him over carefully, a piercing gaze that made even Duei suppress a shiver as it passed.

"Well, I can't speak for our Japanese friends," He said, nodding to the Captain of the JSDF beside him.

"I would sooner commit seppuku."

The Major chuckled, "Well, that seems rather definite."

"The… Captain and his men have no remaining government to speak for them," Duei said simply. "You are the only authority here with any semblance of such, Major Gibb."

Liam nodded, eyes sweeping Duei and the man with him, then skimming over the boat behind them.

"Your answer, please."

"Captain, in all our history, the Marine Corps has surrendered exactly three times," Liam said. "Each of those times, the order to lay down arms came from a non-Marine in the chain of command."

Liam looked to his left, then to his right, and finally back at Duei.

"I don't see any politicians here for you to appeal to."

Duei stared, not quite believing what he'd heard.

"Perhaps you do not entirely understand your situation," He insisted. "This Island will be under the control of the Eastern Alliance. You cannot hold it. It will be ours."

"Yeah," Liam nodded, "I know. But to quote a more *laconically* eloquent man than I, if you want this Island, my friends... *Molon Labe*."

Duei just stared in confusion, "What does that mean?"

"It means, come and take it." The Major said with deadly serious intent.

Duei took half a step back, eyes wide as his hand flicked in a pre-arranged sign. "You are all insane."

The man he'd ignored suddenly moved, startling all of them, lunging to the side and slamming into Major Gibb with all his strength. The Major was thrown to the side bodily, tangling with Ishida as the pair struggled to stay on their feet.

Two sounds filled the air in that moment.

The Gunnery Sergeant yelling one word, "Sniper!"

And a single shot rolling up the beach.

*****

Liam paused, half turning back as he regained his balance in a half-crouch, eyes falling on Gunny Hadrian. The man was standing still there where Liam had been a moment earlier, as though frozen in place. Time stretched out as everyone on the beach held their breaths, a single second of the clock that felt like an eternity.

Hadrian crumpled to the ground as time sped up again.

The Major lunged forward to the fallen gunny, turning him to his back and looking down at the wet stain that was spreading across the man's chest. He didn't need to look closer, and there was no point in calling for the corpsman.

A scuff of sand caught his attention and Liam turned to see the Bloc officers retreating as a red rage enveloping him. He straightened up, drawing his personal Colt 1911 without any conscious thought.

The Bloc captain was trying to run backward, hands up and screaming something, but frankly, he didn't care to hear it.

The forty-five roared as he pulled the trigger, steadily advancing at a walking pace. The two 'negotiators' went down quickly under the close-range fusillade, but Liam didn't even break pace as he continued to fire into the boat beyond as it fired up its engine. He changed magazines twice as he advanced, feet in the water when he finally came to a stop and lowered his weapon as the Bloc boat began to turn a hundred yards out and point its nose back to the sea.

"Major! Are you alright!?"

Liam turned, eyes sweeping the figures rushing down the beach until he found what he was looking for.

"Marine," He pointed. "Front and center!"

"Major, Sir!" The Marine carrying the SRAW obeyed instantly.

"Your weapon, Marine."

"Sir."

Liam accepted the rocket launcher, flipping the sights up and handle down as he turned back around and put the weapon to his shoulder. Men dodged wildly away from behind him as he lined up on the departing boat.

"Watch the backblast," He called as the targeting system locked onto the boat.

Liam fired the rocket, casually turning and tossing the now empty weapon back to the Marine.

"Someone get the Gunny's body," He ordered, walking up the beach as the rolling thunder of the explosion behind him tore through the air. "And get back under cover before those bastards open fire again."

"Oorah Major!"

*****

Chapter Thirty-Three

EBAN HuangLung

Chien glared at the smoking ruin of his personal boat, rather irritated by the entire farce.

It had been obvious from the start that the Americans would not surrender, not while they had an intact chain of command at the very least. The idea of assassinating the major in charge had been floated by the Council and gained enough momentum that it had been strongly suggested that he do so.

He had told them that if they wanted to do that it would be best to simply use guided munitions from an overhead drone. However, despite the... enthusiasm of the North Korean forces during the initial strikes, the Council was still of the opinion that such weapons were not to be used quite so publicly.

Which led to this fiasco, of course.

Now the Americans will be all the more stubbornly foolish, Chien thought with more than a little exasperation. *As though this operation were not already problem enough.*

He didn't even want to know how the public would react.

The Bloc feeds had enough of a delay to hide and cut out the sniper's shot from the boat, of course. The official records would likely show the Major firing first, while the brave men who offered to find a 'peaceful' solution merely defended themselves before being slaughtered.

Unfortunately, even within the Bloc, it would be impossible to entirely stop the American's feeds from being streamed. Long gone were days when the 'Great Firewall' could halt any signal the government chose, or that they pretended they could at any rate. It had never been entirely as solid as the propaganda suggested.

Now the Americans could broadcast internet connections in the open from low earth satellites?

The Great Firewall was an old joke, sadder than funny, unfortunately.

Still, that was something for the Council to deal with. His problems were much closer at hand and of a more… tangible sort.

"Signal the ships to continue the bombardment," He ordered.

"Yes, Admiral."

*****

Iwo Jima

Major Gibb swore as he slid undercover, the first shells screaming in and exploding in the air overhead.

"Stupid, stupid, stupid," He snarled, mostly to himself.

He'd *known* that the odds of betrayal were extreme, but he'd figured the risk was almost entirely on him. *Goddamn Gunny.*

"Are you alright, Major?" Captain Ishida asked in the man's quiet way of speaking.

"I'm fine. Just royally pissed off," Liam told him.

"That is understandable," Ishida told him. "However, we all three knew the chances were good of violence when we walked out."

Liam nodded grimly.

That was true. He'd opted to do it for a number of reasons, some good, some bad, few worth the price of life. However, if he hadn't, the hit to public perception would have been noticeable, and while he might not be able to defend Iwo or save the lives of those under his command, he damn well could make the Bloc pay for what they were taking.

And there are more ways to make someone pay than to bleed them physically.

Wars were fought and won first at home, in the public eye. Lose the support of the average citizen, and you *would* lose the war. It didn't matter how righteous you believed your cause to be if the perception at home swung against you… it was all over. That was a truth of war, especially in the modern-day, that few truly understood deep in their souls.

It was a truth, however.

With the world watching, every action… every *inaction*… would shape that perception. So, he chose to walk out there, knowing what was likely facing him… because a bullet between his eyes would have made for one *hell* of a motivator to many of those watching.

Instead, the Gunny took one in the heart. Goddamn it, Gunny.

"Major…"

"What?" He asked gruffly, looking over.

"Lieutenant Hood just called in."

Liam frowned, but grabbed his radio and fit the bud back in his ear.

"Lieutenant Hood, Major Gibb."

"Major, good to hear from you. Have an issue."

"Report."

"My squad is pinned down here, looks like the Bloc snuck a strike team onto the island."

Liam blinked. That would make sense, in some ways, he supposed. The talks would have provided a nice distraction, and an explanation for why they stopped the shelling. However, what would a team be looking for? There were many real high value targets on the island, aside from the supplies off loaded from the ships… but those were spread out, a single team couldn't do much there.

Other than that…

"Shit!" Liam swore, snapping to his feet and getting on the move while he spoke. "Location, Lieutenant."

"Just West of Mount Suribachi, Sir."

They're after the combat controller.

"Master Sergeant," He called after changing channels. "You've got trouble coming!"

*****

Mount Suribachi

"No shit," Kiran swore as he heard the radio warning but didn't have time to answer as he was leaning heavily into his Sig, firing short bursts down from his entrenched area.

The Bloc had dispatched a small strike team, clearly members of their naval special operations unit. He wasn't sure which one, but given the area of operations, Kiran assumed it was the Sea Dragons rather than the Marine Commandoes or one of the other units attached to Alliance Nations.

They were good. Perhaps not on par with their Western counterparts, but he was also aware that could easily be a little bit of western chauvinism rearing its head and befuddling his ability to properly evaluate such things. It hardly mattered anyway, since either way they were better than what he had on hand to hold out against.

Three men were dead at his side already, a pair of JSDF sailors and the Flight Control Officer from the Enterprise.

They didn't have much security in close since more men just meant being more visible, and staying hidden was a hell of a lot better defense against naval artillery than a security detail. Good protection against ships several nautical miles away turned out to not be so great against a special forces team knocking down your door.

Who knew?

His Sig beat back into his shoulder as he continued firing, keeping the team pinned down. Those he could see of them, at least. Jiang was well aware that if you couldn't *see* a special operations soldier, he was probably moving into position to put a bullet in your head, but there wasn't a lot he could do about that being the only person left defending the location.

Should have moved my position a few times, He sighed, hindsight being twenty-twenty. Unfortunately, there just weren't many places on the island that could afford him all that much cover while giving him decent observational space.

A spattering of whizzing 8mm rounds tore through the berm he was hiding behind, ricocheting off stones and whatever else, driving him to the ground in a roll as he evaded the fire and wound up on his back staring at the sky with wide eyes.

Too close!

Jiang palmed an M69 canister grenade from his tactical harness, gripping it in both hands so he could snap the safety off with a twist before he thumbed the firing actuator and then tossed the cylindrical explosive over the berm in the direction the fire had come from.

Without waiting for the explosion, he flipped over on his belly and started crawling for the tunnel.

Over a century earlier, when the Japanese prepared to defend against the American invasion of the island, tunnels had riddled the area, used as entrenchments, storage, command, and control, and basically every other function that could be conceived.

They were not the most comfortable of places, with many of the original workers being exposed to sulfur fumes as they worked, often in situations so bad that the work crews had to be relieved within minutes by the next team.

Over a century later they weren't much better, though thankfully the ventilation was somewhat better.

The entrance near his position was one of the crawl spaces, so Jiang squeezed in and started working his way deeper into the island, pausing only to rig the explosives as he passed to ensure that anyone pursuing him were properly welcomed.

A few hundred feet in he dropped into a larger section, just as a deep thud went through the ground and a cloud of dust puffed out of the hole he'd exited. Jiang only spared a moment to glance back, then he was moving again as he headed for the next concealed exit from the system.

Glad some of these tunnels survived the years, He thought as he moved.

*****

Liam crunched low as a series of shells detonated overhead, black smoke filling the sky and shrapnel raining down.

He could see Mount Suribachi from where he was. Not like that was a hard thing on the island really, but still he was close enough to *taste* the frustration as the shelling pinned him down.

With all the losses they'd suffered, both in terms of people and equipment, they couldn't lose the Air Combat Controller too. It wasn't just the equipment: much of what the Master Sergeant had deployed could be replaced with various more commonplace satellite uplink gear, it was the skill set that Jiang represented.

One might think that, without fighters to coordinate on their side, the Master Sergeant's skills were crippled, but that wasn't even remotely close to the truth.

Being able to control the battlespace was all about intelligence, and an Air Combat Controller was an expert in decoding real time intelligence, turning even the smallest hints of detail into useable tactical data.

The importance of the Master Sergeant to the defense of Iwo Jima was second only to the importance of the intelligence he was able to feed back to home.

Liam looked around as a lull in the shelling moved in.

"Let's move!" He called, breaking from cover and making a run for the next trench, which would take them to where the closest M.U.L.E.S were waiting.

*****

These guys are not giving up easily, are they?

Jiang found himself playing a rather deadly game of hide and seek with the Bloc special operations squad, and it quickly became clear that the Bloc had equipped their team with advanced tracking. He didn't know if it was heat, or something else, but it was clear that they weren't milling about blindly as they were already heading in his direction when he popped his head out of the ground.

This is bad.

He took a knee behind a wall of sandbags, resting his Sig across them as he drew a bead through the floating red dot optic.

Three 6.8mm rounds tore through the lead man's torso, dropping him in place as the team scattered behind him. Jiang twisted, firing into those he could see or what cover looked like it might be masking the position of another.

He was going to have to fight and move, hopefully keep them from catching up to him and maybe buy just enough time for some help to arrive from elsewhere on the Island. Unfortunately, most of the defenses were arrayed outward, focusing on the beaches, and with the current shelling Jiang knew that could take a while.

After getting off another few quick bursts, driving the attacking men to the ground, Jiang backed away from the sandbags and started to head back into the tunnel.

He froze when a blur of motion flew past him, plummeting right into the tunnel opening. Instinct drove him to one side as he heard a hiss-crump sound and suddenly the air around him went up twenty degrees in an instant as flame shot out of the tunnel before he felt the ground move as it collapsed.

Thermobaric shell, damn it.

They'd come ready to storm caves and tunnels, he realized, and that left him in a bad spot as he rolled back over to the sandbags and checked his supplies.

Two more magazines after his current one was empty, three grenades, his knife, and enough curse words to choke a pissed off elephant.

Fuck.

And there he went, wasting one of his curse words.

Jiang hit the ejector on his Sig, dropping the partial mag to the ground at his knees before he seated a full one in its place. He made sure the partial was within easy reach before he popped up, rifling seeking targets as the top of the volcanic mountain erupted into automatic weapons fire.

*****

It took Liam and his men almost twenty minutes to get up to the top of Mount Suribachi, even after grabbing a Mule and basically gunning it as fast as they dared run the electric vehicle.

As the Mule slowed, they hopped out, running along side as they slowed down, with their weapons out and seeking.

Everything was quiet, which didn't bode well in Liam's opinion.

"Check the observation position," He ordered, waving two men off.

They nodded and quickly jogged over in that direction.

"Got two men over here, Sir."

Liam made his way over, checking the bodies. They were Chinese nationals, he'd bet, and clearly special operations. That meant the two bodies belonged to the Sea Dragons, the Chinese response to the SEALs.

"Grab their weapons, ammo, whatever they have of use," He ordered. Supplies weren't low, yet, but they would be.

"Yes Sir."

"Major!" The pair he'd sent over to the observation post were waving.

"What is it," He called, walking in their direction.

"No sign of the Master Sergeant, Sir, but Lieutenant Erwin and the JSDF Ensign are there," One said, shaking his head. "They went down hard, Sir."

"Fuck. Ok, fan out, find the Master Sergeant."

*****

They found him lying against a sandbag wall, hand clutching a wound that was seeping dark blood.

One body was laying across the Master Sergeant, an SP5 survival blade stuck deep in his chest. Three more were splayed out some distance away, riddled with shrapnel from a grenade burst.

Liam didn't mind checking any other bodies, he went straight to the Master Sergeant, "Get a corpsman out here! Now!"

The Air Force man rolled his head slightly, pale and sickly looking as he smiled wanly.

"This sucks," He told Liam, licking at his lips.

"Yeah, here, drink this," Liam popped the cap on his canteen and put it to the man's lips as a Corpsman jumped the sandbags and immediately unrolled his medical kit, grabbing a pair of shears as he started going to town on the Master Sergeant's uniform. "You'll be fine."

Jiang laughed painfully, "None of us will be fine, Major. We're on a death trap, but that's good by me."

He turned his head, looking out to where some of the enemy bodies were.

"I think they sent twelve special ops guys to take out three of us... even if they got off of us, it's not a bad trade."

"No, Master Sergeant, it's a damned bad trade. You're worth more than a hundred of them," Liam said. "Corpsman?"

The Navy man shrugged, "He'll live, for a while anyway. Needs surgery... I don't know if we can do it under these conditions, Sir."

"Fuck that," Jiang said. "Just patch it and prop me up at the observation point."

"Don't go all macho on me, Master Sergeant," Liam snapped.

"I'm not. Job needs to be done," Jiang said. "We probably only have another couple of days before they overrun us anyway. You know I'm right."

Liam grimaced, hesitating a moment, before he nodded. "Patch him up."

"Major!"

"Do it. If you can get someone up here to work on him in position, fine, but he's right. We need him, now more than ever. Patch him up."

*****

Chapter Thirty-Four

Washington DC, White House Situation Room

Givens stepped into the room, eyes immediately moving to the large screen that had been dubbed the 'scoreboard'. It held the estimated numbers for the men remaining in defense of Iwo Jima, along with the best-known data for how much in the way of supplies were remaining on the island.

The numbers looked bleaker than the day before, of course. That was nothing new. He'd been watching those get grimmer and grimmer for nearly the past two weeks.

That was almost two weeks longer than anyone had predicted they could possibly have held out, however, and that fact put a rather positive spin on the numbers.

The people in the US, and every US ally even, had been buoyed up by the defiance of Iwo Jima even against every other loss that had been suffered. The Bloc had taken Taiwan and Japan, secured the Philippines, and made incursions into Australia before withdrawing under intense fire, both in the real world and in terms of public perception.

In the middle East, Israel had fallen after the first week. Not even the presence of an American carrier in the med had been enough to secure their skies against the superiority of the Bloc aircraft, and fighting under a hostile sky was a deadly difficult thing to manage.

Loss after loss had staggered the Western Democracies, leaving their people stunned and reeling. When the Russian Federation moved into Eastern Europe, it had actually been received with less than an eyeblink by comparison.

People were that numbed to events after just three weeks.

Iwo Jima, however, had been the one defiant blaze in the darkness. The light that just would *not* go out, despite every prediction to the contrary.

Talking heads had predicted the fall of the island right from the first day, casually changing their predictions each day over the first week until it seemed to occur to them that something different was happening out there. After that, they became... cautiously optimistic, even ebullient about the fortunes of those fighting, bleeding, and dying on that worthless rock.

The problem was that it couldn't last.

That had been known from the start, Givens knew, but the people had started to forget that. They had latched onto the hope those men and women offered, and started to talk about how long before the Bloc *gave up*.

That would not happen, Givens knew.

Satellites had already spotted another fleet being redirected in their direction, though it would be days yet at best before it arrived. The Bloc would not allow themselves to lose face over a single little hunk of rock, not when the entire world was watching.

The Major and his men had managed to slow the Bloc advance in the Pacific, however, effectively pinning down *three* entire fleets for almost two weeks so far.

The public loved them for it, but that only made what would inevitably become even grimmer. Givens didn't know if the public could take the blow to morale that would be dealt when Iwo fell.

He read the daily brief, then quickly signed off on a couple directives before he could move on to what was on his mind that morning.

"Where are we on the Double-A project?" He asked, signing the last document with a flourish.

"Project head Weston reports that he should have a squadron ready within the week," The Brigadier confirmed.

"And these new platforms, they're based on the F-22?" He asked.

"Yes sir."

"But they're VSTOL?"

"VTOL, actually," The Marine answered. "They've added a new thruster system. Used up a lot of space in the weapons bay, but they're going back to external hardpoints anyway."

"VTOL..." The President said, nodding. "Alright, I need to speak with Vice-Admiral Gracen this morning... and this Mr. Weston. Make it happen."

"Yes sir."

*****

USS Doris Miller, Pearl Harbor

Vice Admiral Amanda Gracen walked smartly across the deck, heading for her office. The call from Washington had taken her by surprise, but she had been expecting *some type* of call at nearly any time.

The Dory had been ready to put to sea for weeks now, her refit rushed to get her back in fighting trim, only for the orders to come down that all ships were to limit themselves to American territorial waters and ports until further orders.

She understood the reason, of course, even if she didn't agree with it.

They didn't want to lose any more carriers, and didn't have a solid countermeasure, so the solution the brass had come up with was simply to not risk the queens of the fleet. The losses thus far in the Pacific had been horrendous, one of the only bright points was the fact that the Miami had managed to limp into port a few days earlier, damn near crippled but with most hands accounted for. Those losses were putting the fear of elections into the politicians, however, making them stupidly cautious at a time when some level of balls were in demand, even from the REMFs.

That frustrated her, because while the danger was unquestionably real, sitting in port and dying of old age was no way for a lady like the Dory to go out.

She closed the door and took a seat behind her desk, pausing to check that her hair was properly set, then opened the video call.

Her eyes opened only marginally wider in surprise as she recognized the face on the other side, but her back stiffened as she automatically saluted.

"Mr. President."

"As you were," He said with a wave of his hand, "Admiral, I have a job for you."

"I am listening, Sir."

*****

Alamogordo New Mexico

"Eric!"

Stephen practically screamed across the hangar, causing everyone to turn and look at him as he ran out of the office, looking like something was chasing him.

"ERIC!"

A muffled thump and a similarly muffled curse were followed by Eric slipping out of one of the four F-22 airframes currently resting in the hangar, and glaring out at the screaming teenager who was running his way.

"What!?" Eric snarled.

"You've got a call," Stephen said, skidding to a stop.

Eric grumbled, rubbing his head, "And that's a reason for you to scream at me so loud I crown myself?"

"Sorry?"

Eric shook his head, "Just tell them I'll get back to them. I have work to do."

Stephen swallowed, "I... I don't think that's a good idea, Eric. I really think you should take this one."

"Why, who is it?" Eric asked.

"I'm not sure, but I've never seen that many ribbons and medals on one uniform before," Stephen blurted.

"Oh great," Eric wanted to scream in frustration. "Do they think I'm just lounging around here, soaking up the sun or something?"

One of the former Lockheed techs laughed from where he was still inside the fighter airframe, "No they think you're a normal project manager, you know? *Managing* the project? Your own damn fault you want to be hands-on."

Eric flipped him off, getting nothing but a laugh in response as he dropped from the airframe and waved to Steph, "Alright I'll get it. Thanks kid."

Steph nodded as he walked by.

Eric closed the door to his office, blocking out most of the sounds from the hangar, and slumped in the seat behind the desk, clicking the button to open up the video call.

"Yeah, what is it?" He asked.

"Mr. Weston?"

"Yeah, that's me," Eric said, frowning as he looked at the man on the screen. "I know you from somewhere?"

The man smiled, eyes lighting up as he seemed to be honestly amused and even trying not to laugh openly. "I expect you do, Captain."

"Former Captain," Eric said immediately, not even thinking about it while he looked closer.

The man on the screen looked *really* familiar, but also incredibly worn down. Like he'd just been through the sort of week that Eric had experienced, only he wasn't nearly young enough to deal with the sort of shit…

Eric froze, eyes widening as he recognized the man.

He stiffened instantly, hand flashing up to pull off a cover he wasn't wearing, a move which quickly turned into a rough and fast attempt at smoothing out his grease-streaked hair.

"Mr. President, Sir."

"I'd say at ease, but as you pointed out, it's *former* Captain Weston," Benjamin Givens said easily, "Please, relax before you hurt us both."

Eric took a breath and made himself relax, nodding, "Yes Sir. What can I do for you?"

Givens looked pained, "I have a big favor I need from you. The word I have on your project is that you can have a squadron ready in a week, is that accurate?"

"Flight ready? Yes Sir, that should be accurate."

"What about combat ready, Mr. Weston?"

Eric leaned back, blowing out a breath as he considered that.

There was really only one reason he could think that the President would want to push things that fast.

"Iwo, Sir?" He asked tentatively.

Givens nodded silently.

Eric leaned in, covering his face with his hands, and running them through his hair as he rested his elbows on the desk, thinking about it.

Technically, the fighters might be ready on that schedule, but he knew that there *would* be bugs to hammer out. He'd have to start running flight tests immediately on the first versions, and hammer out any problems down the line, hoping to get them right the first time.

That *might* be possible… but it left another problem.

"Sir… we don't have a flight manual for this, and we're integrating multiple prototype technologies… they will have issues," He said earnestly. "The control interface alone…"

"I know about the neural network and its requirements," Givens said. "I'm prepared to have pilots sent to you, Mr. Weston. The very best."

"It's not just good pilots, Sir," Eric said. "We need pilots who can be *test* pilots as well as combat pilots. In many ways those are two very different skill sets. I…"

He thought about it, "We'll need to test people here."

Eric sighed. "Send your men, I'll submit some names myself…"

Givens nodded, "I will expedite their files."

"Thank you, Sir."

"So, can you be ready in a week?"

"In a word, Mr. President?" Eric laughed, "Not a chance in hell."

Givens looked down, his face dropping.

Eric stopped laughing, his own expression dead serious a moment later.

"We'll do it anyway."

*****

Pearl Harbor

A little more than a day after a certain call from Washington, the USS Doris Miller put to sea under cover of a rather dark and cloudy night. The task force, along with extra fueling and supply vessels similarly vanished, while work crews on the docks spent the entire night moving old hulks into their places and throwing up camouflage netting unlike anything largely seen since the second world war.

Security around the naval base tripled, pushing people as far back as they could, water patrols locked down the harbor, and other ships were moved into position to prevent anyone from getting close up pictures of the docks for as long as possible.

Everyone knew that it wouldn't keep, of course, but every man and woman on those docks were determined to buy every second of time they could for the Dory Task Group.

Many did wonder about the squadron of F-35s they unloaded from the carrier just before it left, but no questions were asked, no lies were told.

They just felt better that the Navy was once more at sea and moving.

*****

Alamogordo New Mexico

Kimberly Fields looked up from her work, the sound of an argument filtering through her focus. She'd arrived to work on her project this morning and, instead of actually getting to install more of the equipment as she'd been looking forward to, she found herself instead being instructed to run compatibility tests on a whole host of new people, pilot candidates she was told, with dozens more supposed to arrive over the next few days.

It was both frustrating and invigorating.

Her work was about to get a *major* field test, but it was also terrifying for exactly that same reason.

I wish they weren't rushing this into the field quite so quickly...

She had specialized in Neural Induction Sensors as a means of improving prosthetics for people with missing limbs, spinal injuries, and other medical issues. Her system built on the work of dozens of others over the last few decades, but had the potential of being far more sensitive and precise than any of the previous projects because she had elected to go to the source, so to speak. That was what had brought her to the attention of DARPA just over half a decade earlier.

The potential military applications for neural induction scanning were essentially limitless.

Using prehensile surgical needles as the base, it was possible to slip a very thin induction sensor right up against specific nerve clusters and read impulses along the nerves with micro-precision.

After that it was all in the software, which frankly was by far the hardest part.

The ongoing argument down the line distracted her again and she looked up from the testing she was doing, exasperated.

It was the boy, the teenager she supposed, in an argument with Mr. Weston it seemed. Weston was attempting to pull the boy out of line, looking exasperated himself, while the teen was resisting quite effective, if loudly.

Everyone else was looking rather amused.

She wasn't in the mood, however.

"Kid, you're too young and not trained anywhere near the level one of these babies needs," Weston was saying. "And you're not in the military either."

"Neither are you," Stephen snorted. "Or most of these guys."

"We all *were* military," Weston grumbled. "And we're better equipped to figure this gear out on the fly."

"Says you," Steph told him derisively. "I say the old farts should step aside and let the young blood in the game."

"Listen here you little," Weston growled amid a mixture of laughter and vociferous objections from the other pilots in line.

"Ahem," Kimberly cut in loudly. "Would the pair of you cut the sideshow out, you're distracting me and the work I'm doing is slightly on the delicate side."

Weston held up his hands, "Sorry Doc, my bad. Steph, this isn't the place. Come on."

Kim could see the teenager getting puffed up for another round and cut in, "Leave him. I'll give him the test."

"Doc…"

She cut Weston off, "Another candidate is a good thing, you can worry about flight qualification once we know if he's even compatible."

With that she turned on her heel and went back to work, leaving Stephen smirking smugly at a somewhat gobsmacked Eric Weston staring after her and several pilots ribbing him in amusement. She didn't worry about it. The kid wasn't likely to be a compatible candidate anyway so it was easier to just give him the test to keep him quiet as far as she was concerned.

*****

Chapter Thirty-Five

Iwo Jima

Major Gibb poured water over his head, roughly working it into his hair, noting that his scalp was shaggier than he'd normally ever let it get. He didn't have a brush cut. Being an officer had some perks, and over the last few weeks he'd *definitely* missed an appointment with the barber.

He was kneeling in the mud and sand while rinsing out his hair, more to wake himself up than to wash anything since he didn't have any soap to speak of any longer. They were running low on everything by this point, even food wouldn't last much longer. The Makin Island had been equipped to land and supply a Marine landing force for several weeks, but they had a lot more than that currently in residence.

Thankfully, he supposed, they had weapons and ammo aplenty.

There wasn't much to shoot at unless the Bloc was trying a landing, but for the past several days they'd been content to do airstrikes and shelling from a distance. That left no real use for the munitions they'd unloaded from the Island, nor for that they'd captured from the previous Bloc attempts.

No, weapons were not what they were running out of.

Water, thankfully, was available on the island and they'd managed to keep the location of the wells from being too obvious, so they hadn't lost them to enemy shelling thus far. Food, toiletries, and such were the issue. He'd put his men on a rationing system almost immediately, but even so things were tight.

They'd attempted to keep the public streams from revealing that, but he suspected that more than enough had gotten out to tell the Bloc forces what the situation was.

It would explain why they had opted to hold off, possibly hoping to starve his people out.

Or perhaps they just want to get that other fleet in to make a big show of it for the world.

Probably both, if he were being honest with himself.

He stooped low, not sticking his head up since that was a good way to invite a grid square fuck you from the enemy, and made his way back from the edge of the island, heading inland. It was time to check in on someone.

******

Mount Suribachi

Kiran heard the soft hum of the MULE as it approached but didn't get up to see. He hadn't popped any painkillers for a while and didn't feel like incurring the literal gut-wrenching pain he would if he moved.

He lifted up the imagers, scanning the ships out past his blind as the sound of boots crunching on gravel got closer.

"How you doing, Master Sergeant?"

"M'fine Major," Kiran said, slurring his words just slightly. "Not ship shape, but good enough."

Liam nodded silently as he dropped into a crunch beside the wounded man, eyes drifting to the white patch over his exposed belly.

"You taking your pills?" He asked conversationally.

"I'm taking the antibiotics, don't worry." Kiran confirmed.

Liam nodded again, not commenting on what they meant concerning the pain killers. They'd gone round and round on that subject a hundred times already in the past week, and nothing he had to say was going to change things. The bullet had torn the Air Force man up inside, and while the corpsmen and docs had done their best, the island was not a particularly good place for a recovery from such an injury.

When he was awake, Kiran insisted that he couldn't be fuzzy from painkillers, so he only took them before he was planning on sleeping, which was mostly during the afternoon.

"Just another day in paradise."

Kiran smiled tightly, "Got that right."

The Air Force Master Sergeant waved out to the ships, "They're shifting formation."

Liam nodded, "Expecting the new fleet."

Kiran looked over at him, "They'll have a proper landing complement with that one."

"Yeah."

That was the crux of things, Liam was well aware. The initial fleets they'd been dealing with had been configured for taking on other ships at sea. That was why they'd been sent after the Enterprise task group. They didn't have a lot in terms of landing power, a few amphibious boats, a few tanks, not much else.

The inbound fleet would be different. They knew what they needed out here now, and the Bloc, for all their faults, weren't fool enough to not bring the right tools to the job now that they knew what those would be.

"Anything more from PACCOM?" Liam asked, knowing that the Air Force Master Sergeant was actually better plugged into the military network than he was, rank be damned.

"They're up to something," Kiran confirmed. "But they're being damn sneaky about it. Nothing is coming over the active networks, I think they believe that we might be infiltrated."

"Shit." Liam swore, frowning in confusion, "Us as in the Island? Or the network?"

"Either, both? Probably the latter, though, I don't see how the Bloc could be tapping into a secure satellite uplink," Kiran said. "They're feeding us tactical info, same as always, but something has caused them to get really cagey about strategic movements."

"Well, I'm not surprised about that," Liam said. "That was inevitable. With the loss of air superiority, cagey is good. Cagey is needed."

"True… Kiran said, eyebrows furrowing slightly as he looked out to sea and involuntarily started to lean forward.

A gasp of pain caused him to settle back and lift his imagers, taking deep breaths.

"Well. Fleet's here."

"Shit."

*****

EBAN ChiangLung

*Three **insufferably** weeks of this insanity!*

Chien felt like pulling out every strand of hair from his own head over the mess he was trying to deal with. The Americans had held the worthless piece of *rock* for three weeks! They'd forced him to pull in proper landing forces to deal with them, and all because they'd made a stupid *infantile* challenge to the Bloc Council that those damned *fools* had taken seriously.

Not that he dared to say that, of course. Letting that sort of criticism out in front of the wrong people would end his career more surely than failing to take this *stupid* island would.

Prior to this, his star within the ruling party had been in ascendance, but he doubted that would hold true now no matter what happened going forward. With luck he would be permitted to keep his rank, though that was not even certain.

Chien sighed.

At least it was almost over. The arriving fleet had proper landing equipment and forces, enough that no manner of stubborn foolishness would ever manage to turn back.

He took a breath and made his way up to the surface deck. It was time to greet his counterparts and prepare to *end this*.

*****

USS Doris Miller, Pacific Ocean

Vice Admiral Gracen looked over the deck and the eight strange birds currently resting on it. Watching those things land on her flight deck had been one of the most existentially *terrifying* moments of her career.

Usually flight operations were fairly routine, if gut clenching tension could be considered routine. Any mistakes could easily cost lives on a flight deck, even before you added in the heaving of the sea, shifting winds, tight spaces, and every other factor at play.

Watching eight experimental fighters come in for a landing however, when she knew five of the pilots didn't even have carrier qualification, had damn near given her an ulcer all on its own. Add in that the fighters were *not* in any way carrier qualified themselves, well that just made things worse.

They'd landed at night, another terror box ticked off, one by one coming into a slow hover over the flight deck before settling in gently to touch down.

Patently impossible, since the aircraft in question were all F-22 Raptor airframes, which didn't *have* VTOL capability.

Her people had handled it well, however, moving as swiftly to secure the aircraft as they would a flight of Marine F-35s.

The pilots were just as unconventional as their craft, something she would have been able to see even if she hadn't read their jackets.

Gracen's fingers tapped the files in front of her idly as she looked out over the deck where preparations were ongoing. She thought someone in the chain had lost their damned mind, putting that many experimental technologies into one platform and then actually throwing it at the enemy, but that wasn't her call.

The leader, Weston, was perhaps the most normal of the bunch, which spoke volumes for how bad the rest were. Only two were current active-duty service pilots, and one was a *fucking* teenager with no combat time under his belt. The President *had* to be desperate as hell for this to be the play he opted for, but she'd seen the streams out of Iwo too.

Those poor bastards didn't have any more time.

Never in my life did I expect to see us pushed so hard we had to resort to this. There had been moments in history, of course, where such things had been the keys to holding the line or victory, but they had been a long time ago. Over a century, sometimes a lot over.

Everything old is new again, she supposed. *The wheel turns, and grinds us all into the dirt.*

Gracen stilled her fingers and got up.

It was almost time.

*****

Eric Stanton Weston looked over the pilots that had managed to pass the Doc's test, and swore mentally once more. If he'd known just how few people were qualified for the neural induction systems, he would *never* have allowed them to be installed on the fighters, not even knowing how effective they could be.

After all the testing, only seven pilots had qualified.

Seven.

Plus one irritating little *brat*.

He could have left behind a plane, of course, but he needed every set of wings, and Steph was actually a damn good flyer with the new system. One of the best in the squadron, and it was composed of people with thousands of hours more experience than he.

It likely helped that Steph was being introduced to the new system entail, while everyone else was having to unlearn some things to make it work.

Dumb kid just turned eighteen a short while ago, and he was volunteering for this shit.

Reminded Eric of himself.

Too much of himself.

"Alright, you've seen the mission brief," He said. "We're to provide air interdiction for friendly forces. If it flies, and it isn't flying the red, white, and blue… make it *swim*. Clear?"

Everyone nodded, most of them looking too eager by half, but that was something he'd gotten used to over the years. The best pilots, the best men, always wanted to be at the point of the spear. Chewed them up to damn much, but that didn't matter to the next ones in line. It was part of what made them the best.

Aside from Steph, everyone else was a qualified fighter pilot. One other Marine, four Navy boys, and two Air Force. Best men and women all.

"Kid," Eric looked over to Steph. "You're with me, for my sins I'm babysitting."

Steph glared at him, but everyone else laughed, which was the point. Tension needed to be broken.

"You're all familiar with the enemy birds," He said, tapping the screen behind him, where a picture of the Bloc fighter was taking up the full size of the monitor. "Intel has given them the Code Designation 'Mantis'. Hypersonic capable, probably with better versions of the device in their belly than we have, and certainly with a lot more time behind the stick. Missiles are only partially effective, assuming you can trick them into coming head on into your fire. Same with guns. They can literally outrun bullets, don't waste the ammo if you're chasing them."

They all nodded, so he went on.

"We've instead mounted two laser modules with fiberoptic gimbals," Eric said. "The enemy fighters are fast, but they can't outrun *light*. Unfortunately, neither can we, and they learned from the F-35s over Japan and the Pacific Theatre that they don't want to tangle too close, so they have mounted laser modules of their own. That's where our first trump card comes in…"

Eric nodded to the Doctor who was standing on the edge of the group, and the woman walked in.

"Thank you, Captain," She said, nodding to Eric.

"Former Captain," He mouthed silently to her as he passed by, but the smirk on his face took any heat from the comment.

Doctor Brooke looked over the men before she started, "We've reskinned your aircraft with an experimental nano-polymer metamaterial invented by my team. It is an adaptive material that can, in layman's terms, change color according to however you program it. In addition, we've placed high sensitivity photopolymer material as a base structure. If the enemy targets you with a laser, the photopolymer will communicate the precise frequency of the beam to your computers, which will then adjust the metamaterial to adjust to nearly perfectly *reflect* that beam."

"Are you saying we can tank lasers intended to take out aircraft, Ma'am?" The Air Force Captain, Tracy Parrow, asked slowly.

"If the frequency can be adjusted quickly enough, yes," Brooke said. "But there is a catch. The frequency change takes several seconds from detection to adjustment."

"Those beams will burn a plane out of the sky in barely a second, Doc," Tracy said firmly.

"They do, yes."

"Well pardon me for asking," Jason Noll, one of the Marines spoke up. "But what possible good does that do us?"

"Two things," Eric cut in, saving the flustered Doctor from having to answer. "First, if you can evade the worst effects of the first beam, the second won't be much of a threat…"

"And second?" Null asked, sounding as though he wasn't sure he wanted to know.

"The combat network will feed updates to everyone else."

"Jesus," Null swore, "So if we spike it, everyone else gets to benefit from our crash and burn?"

"That's about the size of it," Eric confirmed.

Null glared at him for a moment before cracking a grin, "Better deal than we've ever had before."

The others nodded, smiling suddenly.

"Yes it is, as long as they're using beams," Eric said. "If they switch to guns somehow, just remember the best defense is not getting hit, ok? That info won't do the rest of us any good if you crash and burn."

The pilots chuckled, nodding in agreement.

Brooke cleared her throat, "We've consulted with Intelligence Assets and have pre-programmed the meta-material to what we believe is the frequency range of the Bloc laser pods, so you should have a little longer than the second it normally takes."

"Don't trust that," Eric stepped in. "Military Intel is an oxymoron for a reason."

The pilots chuckled, making Brooke look more flustered.

"Yes well, it's the best I was able to find, but…"

"Relax Doc," Eric held up his hand. "That's not a patch on you or your work. We just know this tune and I don't want them forgetting that Intel is ninety percent rumor and nine percent lies."

"Nine percent?" A Navy Pilot by the name of Jake Sully laughed, "You had better experience than I."

Eric just shrugged, not answering that he'd spent some time in the intel field after getting out, even if it was as an asset rather than an agent or handler. He'd done his best to make sure everything he brought back was good, but even he couldn't filter out all the rumor and lies that were fed to him.

"Captain Weston."

Eric half-turned, eyes locking onto the uniform in the corner of his eye and before he even finished his pivot he was straightening to attention on reflex.

"Admiral, Ma'am."

Admiral Gracen, nodded in a clipped manner, "We're commencing operations."

"Aye Ma'am." Eric said, looking back at everyone. "You ready?"

"Ready or not, I don't think the Chicoms care," Sully said with a crooked grin.

Weston didn't bother correcting him, he just nodded, "Then saddle up. We have a mission to run."

*****

Chapter Thirty-Six

Iwo Jima, Mount Suribachi

"Major, Jiang here."

"Go."

"They've put landers in the water, Sir."

"How many?"

"I'm thinking… all of them."

"Shit. Alright, thanks."

"No problem, I'll keep watching for anything new," Kiran Jiang said before signing off and picking up his imagers again.

The Bloc Navy wasn't as smooth at this as the US Marines were, he noted with some satisfaction, but it was a fleeting thought. They didn't need to be smooth, not with the advantage they held, and they would undoubtedly get better over time if given the chance.

He counted off the number of landers he could see, punching that into his tablet and making sure the Major was in the loop when he sent the estimate. With Landers already on the move it didn't look like the Bloc were wasting any time, they wanted to end this and end it now.

On a hunch he checked the streams and saw that the Bloc were broadcasting it from multiple channels, and after a few moments checking he didn't think that they had much of a delay on it either.

It didn't surprise him… much. They had to know what Iwo had defending it by this point, and what they were bringing to bear was certainly going to steamroll right over them. They were pulling out all the stops, going for a spectacular curb stomp to end what had to be a growing debacle within the Bloc's borders.

So be it.

Kiran checked the streams from the Island, making sure they were going out too. Everyone deserved to see what was going down. He reached over and pulled the camera near him around to focus on his face.

"This is Master Sergeant Kiran Jiang, US Air Force, currently serving on Iwo Jima," He said with a grimace of pain, carefully holding an arm over his wounded belly. "The Bloc forces have put landers into the water, and it looks like they're getting ready to call an end to our little beach party here."

He looked out over the Island for a moment before turning back to look straight into the camera again.

"It's been fun," He said, forcing a smile through the pain. "They thought they'd roll us over in a day. It's been three weeks. Fuck the Bloc, and remember Iwo. Enjoy the show."

He turned the camera back, so it looked over the island, then gestured to one of the JSDF sailors to give him a hand.

"Sir?" The sailor approached, hesitant. "You're injured. Are you sure...?"

"Don't sir me, Shiro, I work for a living," He made the joke so old it, smiling through the pain. "Call me Kiran. And yes, I'm sure. I've bled a little in this dirt, time to do it some more."

"Very well, Kiran." The sailor smiled, helping him up. "Let us bleed together."

*****

EBAN ChiangLung

On the foredeck of the ChiangLung, Admiral Chien looked over the men as they worked to clear the pressure hull from where it covered the flight deck, exposing the ChiangLung's flight deck to open air. They could launch and recover their 198s without retracting the pressure hull, of course, but the tactical and transport helicopters were not quite so flexible, unfortunately.

The crews were preparing the choppers for flight, even as the landing craft were already underway. It would take a half-hour to move all the landers into position, and by then the sky would be filled with aircraft.

It was time to bring an end to this farce.

*****

Iwo Jima

Liam looked out over the rolling blue of the Pacific, to the ships that were sitting out there off the shores of the island. He could just make out the motion around the fleets, but not any of the details. Jiang said that they'd put their landers in the water, though, so that was enough for him.

"Get moving, Marines," He called. "They're on their way."

The Marines, Sailors, and JSDF all jumped into action at his order. It might be sacrilege to many, but he agreed with Gunny Hadrian on this. Every man and woman on this Island was a Marine in his eyes, and he'd fight anyone who challenged differently.

He grabbed the closest Lieutenant, pulling the young woman close, "Get everyone ready for increased shelling. They're going to let us have everything they've got, right ahead of the landing."

"Yes sir." She nodded as he let her go, running off to deliver the message.

Like automatic fire from assault rifles, wide-area artillery bombardment wasn't particularly good at killing the enemy, but it sure as hell made them keep their heads down.

If the Bloc had properly trained, he knew that they would run their landers right up to the very edge of the bombardment, not cutting the artillery off until the last second. That was how his men would do it if the situation was reversed.

The question was, were they that well trained?

Liam didn't think they were, they hadn't the years of experience and practice needed to properly refine that sort of technique. It was impossible to do that sort of training in the real world without it being spotted by satellites, spies, drones, or something, and there had been no significant reports of the Bloc forces doing such.

That meant that they would either stop the shelling early, rather than risk hitting their own men and equipment, or they were likely to keep up the artillery barrage to the last moment and quite likely catch their own front line in the splash.

Figuring out which would be a hell of an advantage, but frankly he didn't have any way of knowing, so Liam started sending more orders down the line to cover both eventualities.

*****

Brian Meer steadied his nerves as he braced against the trench wall, his Sig in his hands. He was an aircraft mechanic, but like the Gunny said, he was a Marine and Marines were all riflemen first and foremost.

The Gunny had seen them all through some tough times, most of which had been in just the past month. He didn't deserve to go out like that, shot down in cold blood. It wasn't even a fight.

Going out taking a bullet for the Major isn't the worst way to go, but those assassin pricks still need their teeth put down the back of their throats.

For the first time, Meer found himself regretting his choice of Occupational Specialty. He liked fixing things, especially gear like the F-35s, but right now he would honestly prefer something with a little more reach out and touch someone.

If I survive, maybe I'll put in for a different MOS...

He smiled grimly to himself.

He knew he wasn't going to survive.

"Fuck it," Meer said aloud, turning to the others from the small group they'd kept together since Japan. "Come on boys, let's show em what the Gunny taught us about being Marines."

"Oorah!"

*****

The Bloc landing craft maneuvered into position a couple kilometers off the shores of the island as the attack and transport helicopters began to form up overhead. Once everything was in position, the order was given with a single short transmission and the gathered forces began to move toward the island in formation.

Behind them, the ships opened fire once more, and the island of Iwo Jima became a firestorm of destruction.

*****

Liam ducked down lower as the first of the Bloc's shells exploded overhead, peppering the beach with shrapnel. He waved to the closest troops, ordering them down as well, not that they really needed the urging.

They all knew what was coming, and everyone just dug in to ride it out.

The ship's guns were light, especially by the old measures, but the newcomers had replenished the available missiles, and those were a hell of a lot heavier. Still, even the best air to ground munitions were more of a 'to whom it may concern' sort of assault, particularly to a well dug in adversary.

The shockwaves from the explosions were, in many ways, more of a problem than the shrapnel for the most part, constantly hammering down around them. One of those explosions, close enough, didn't need to hit them with shrapnel. The pressure change alone would end anyone within its sphere, which was why they'd dug trenches and put corners and overhangs and piled up sandbags all around.

The barriers would block shrapnel effectively, certainly, but hell a lot of things would manage that. Making pressure waves propagate around corners, bounce off walls, and generally expend their energy in any way possible was just as vital as stopping the shrapnel.

Liam was familiar with the tactic the Bloc were currently using, it was one that was in a lot of waves perfected by the Marine Corps. Technically it was known as Establishing Military Dominance… more commonly people just called it Shock and Awe.

Just hammer the enemy until they can't see straight, ideally, and then drop an attack force in their faces while they were still trying to recover.

It was a good tactic.

It played a lot better, however, if your enemy didn't know it was coming…

And a hell of a lot better if your enemy isn't an expert in its usage themselves.

He waved the others in his line of sight down, letting them pass on the order down the line, waiting for the moment the fire stopped.

*****

EBAN ChiangLung

"The landing craft are nearly to the beach, Admiral."

Chien nodded, "I see it."

The men and women in the ship's command center exchanged nervous looks but said nothing for the moment as the first wave of landers hit the sands of Iwo Jima as the guns of the ship continued to fire.

"Admiral..."

Chien held up a hand, silencing his second in command.

He watched the streams from the landing craft as they opened up and the men at the front were forced to charge out onto the beach lest they be run over by the light tanks behind them.

"Ceasefire," He said finally, eyes never wavering as the command team rushed to issue that order.

He saw the last few rounds from the shelling land, shrapnel cutting into the Bloc forces, probably more than they did the defenders, but that was the price of getting them close to the defenders' lines without being cut down.

*****

Iwo Jima

The moment the shelling let up, Liam was on the move. He didn't bother to issue orders. He trusted his men to know their job and do as he'd instructed. He dropped his Sig-Saur Rifle down on the sandbag berm, looking down the optics with his right eye while surveying the beach with the unobstructed left.

The Bloc had run the shelling close, he saw. Too close. They'd taken out some of their own men in the last round of explosions, leaving bodies broken and bleeding on the beach while the rest of the Bloc soldiers hit the sand and pushed forward.

He swept the beach as the guns opened fire, getting a rough count of the threat, and knew that the jig was up.

They're coming in full force this time, using everything they got with the reinforcements they just got.

Bloc helicopters roared by overhead, bypassing the lines, and bringing troops into the interior of the island, while combat helos hovered angrily over the landers like pissed off insects looking for someone to sting.

Missiles hissed up from the surface, blowing some of the enemy birds out of the sky, but were quickly answered with the rapid-fire of rockets tearing into the locations they'd fired from. He could hear explosions tearing the air asunder from behind him, and knew that the Bloc were clearing landing zones and probably hammering any artillery units they spotted.

Iwo Jima just didn't have sufficient cover to properly disguise such things, so he doubted he'd have any artillery at all in short order.

"Hold the line!" He called, leveling his rifle and firing into the charging Bloc formation. "Make them earn every grain of sand they claim!"

The beach descended into the chaos of battle.

*****

Mount Suribachi

Master Sergeant Jiang looked out grimly as he spotted the Helos headed his way.

"Aichi," He called.

"Yes Sir?" The JSDF sailor asked.

"Get the others," Jiang ordered. "We're going to be busy here shortly."

The JSDF sailor glanced nervously out at the choppers filling the sky, but nodded quickly and headed out. Jiang clutched as his bandaged injury, the dull pain waking up with every motion he made. He hesitated briefly, then grabbed a couple of the pills from the supply he'd been given by the Doc and swallowed them dry.

He figured that his time doing vector and ballistic calculations in his head was just about out.

Time to put down the laptop and pick up the rifle.

*****

As the shelling from the ships died off, the fighting blazed across Iwo Jima as Bloc landing vehicles unloaded their tanks and troops right into the face of massed defensive fire.

The initial balance of casualties fell heavily against the invaders as they rushed defensive emplacements, but with air cover and superior numbers and equipment on their side, the tide did not take long before it began to shift. Within ten minutes of the landing, the beaches were swarming with Bloc forces and they were pushing higher up into the island proper, even against everything the Marines and JSDF could bring to bear.

Helicopters buzzed overhead, angry insects with lethal stingers raining down hell on the defenders, tearing up the Marines' lines far more effectively than the longer ranged shelling and missiles strikes had managed simply due to the pilots' ability to pick out targets and be more careful with their aim.

The first line of the island's defense fell in just under thirty minutes, Bloc tanks and troops swarming over the trench even as the defenders fell back in a retreat under fire.

The attackers barely paused as they rolled over the booby traps left behind this time, some tanks being left behind as they burned out from the inside, but most just continuing forward implacably.

*****

"Sir, we're going to lose the second line of trenches!"

Liam swore, but he had plans in place for that.

"Pull the safeties on the heavier explosives, then pull back," He ordered. "We need to bleed them out as much as we can."

"Yes sir, Major!"

Liam looked out over the berm, a calm falling over him.

So, this is the end, He thought.

He looked out over the water beyond the landers, completely unable to count the number of ships the Bloc had amassed to deal with one utterly worthless hunk of rock in the middle of the ocean, far from any strategic value on either side.

Mission accomplished.

Liam grabbed a pair of spare magazines and stuffed them in his jacket as he started moving through the trench, heading toward the beach as his men withdrew back in the other direction.

*****

EBAN ChiangLung

"Admiral!"

"What is it?" Chien demanded, turning from his observation of the invasion.

"Contacts on the long-range RADAR, looks like American F-35s inbound at Mach Two."

"Scramble everything we have left," He growled. "Reassign all of our new fighters to air interdiction. I want those fighters shot down before they can get into range of the island!"

"Yes, Admiral!"

Chien fumed, unable to quite believe that the Americans were going to waste *another* flight of aircraft for a worthless piece of rock.

"Any sign of their bombers?" He asked after a moment's thought.

"No Sir."

"That doesn't make sense. A flight of F-35s don't have the firepower to affect this battle," He said. "The Americans would know that."

He looked up sharply, "Have we detected any refueling aircraft?"

"No Sir."

"There's a Carrier out there, Find it!"

*****

Chapter Thirty-Seven

USS Doris Miller

The last of the F-35s had cleared the decks a few minutes earlier, along with all of the Dory's transport and attack helicopters, leaving the flight deck almost eerily empty as Eric walked to his fighter and gently patted the nose as he walked back to the ladder.

The former F-22 hardly looked much like its forbear at this point, with the streamlined laser modules slung under each wing, linked to wingtip gimble mounted emitters via thick fiber cables. They'd put a couple AMRAAMs on the spare hardpoints, mostly on the theory that having them and not needing them would be preferable to the opposite. No one much expected missiles to play a role in the coming fight, given the nature of the Double A birds and the enemy fighters.

Over the last week of tuning, they'd learned a *lot* about the device.

It wasn't anti-gravity, as Eric had originally believed, but something... subtly different. More of an anti-mass device, though that wasn't exactly correct either.

Counter-Mass perhaps? Eric thought as he eyeballed the equipment and made sure all the linkages were good.

Anti-gravity or mass implied that the device should be able to create negative gravity or mass, but as best they could tell that was not what the device did at all. Instead, it somehow managed to 'mask' the mass within its bubble of effect from the rest of the universe. The physicists were all very excited about it, but it was above his understanding by a considerable degree, so Eric was just happy it worked.

It was that bubble of effect that had given them some of the biggest problems, though, and why his first test flight hadn't quite matched up to the calculations they'd made. If the bubble extended too far past the back of the fighter, the jets were affected by it and had less mass as they exited the ear of the fighter, which meant they had far less effective *push*.

That little tidbit had necessitated rebalancing the device more forward, and calibrating its power output to keep the geometry of the field ideally located.

He thought they had it close to optimized, but he supposed time would tell.

"Are you ready?"

Eric half turned, surprised to see the Captain of the Dory, Admiral Gracen, approaching.

"Ma'am," He saluted quickly. "We're good to go."

She nodded coolly, walking past him as she examined the fighter.

"Doesn't look like much difference from a conventional fighter," She said after a moment.

"Most of the changes are internal," Eric confirmed. "We haven't had time to develop an entirely new airframe that is properly optimized to the lift system."

"I see." She turned to look at him evenly. "I want it straight, Captain. Can you do this?"

Eric snorted, "Admiral… I don't know."

Gracen stared for a moment, then nodded, "I'm surprised you admitted it."

"There's a time and place for bullshit, Ma'am… this ain't it." Eric said simply. "We're going up against a foe that has a more refined version of the system we're using, and a lot more experience using it… but we have some advantages of our own."

"I read the brief on the interface…"

"Yeah, that," Eric said. "But more realistically, we're going to get a first strike. They have *no idea* what's coming down on them. That's going to hurt them more than anything else we've got, I'd wager."

A chime beeped and Eric checked his wristwatch.

"Time to go, Admiral."

"Good luck, Captain."

Eric nodded and turned around to wave to the others, sweeping his hand around in the air over his head.

"Saddle up!"

*****

Stephen dropped into the cockpit, his guts dancing in his belly. He had less than a hundred hours in the fighter he was sitting in, considerably less actually, and was about to take the damn thing into a fight.

I'm out of my mind.

All the more so because he'd not only volunteered for the job, but he'd twisted Eric's arm in order to convince him to allow it.

Part of him was honestly flabbergasted that Eric had folded, but considering how much pressure was on the man, Steph was half convinced that he could have gotten a particularly well-trained dog into the cockpit of one of the fighters if he tried hard enough.

"Double-A Squadron, D-A Lead," Eric's voice came over the radio.

The squad responded, with Steph himself inserting his own response nervously before adding, "We need a better name. This double A shit sounds stupid and takes too long to say."

Laughter filled the channel briefly before Eric cut it off.

"Can the chatter," Eric grumbled. "A little professionalism, D-A Eight."

"Cut the kid a break, Weston," Sully said, chuckling. "He's not wrong. Besides, we're the definition of irregulars, you know that as well as I do."

Eric sighed audibly, "Yes I know that. I'd still like not to sound like idiots when someone inevitably plays this back later. The world is listening, or they will be."

That was a point, Steph thought. One he'd not considered, if he were honest. Of course, that made the name even more important, in his opinion.

"Doesn't that make it more important?" He asked tentatively, running through the pre-flight checklist and powering up his systems. "Or do we want people calling us 'Double-A'?"

"Are we really doing this now?" Eric asked, exasperated.

"Kid has a point, boss man," another pilot, Captain Parrow laughed. "Double-A Five, pre-flight clears. Good to go."

"How about Angel Flight?" Steph offered, smiling a bit. "We're going to the rescue and all."

"Not a chance, kid," Sully cut him off. "Angel flight is… something else. Probably be one of those after this is over, but it won't be us. Double-A Three, pre-flight clears. Good to go, Boss."

"He's right," Eric said. "Besides, we're no angels."

The men and women on the channel laughed, occasionally announcing that their fighter had cleared the flight check.

"Hey," Parrow cut in. "What about Archangel? We're looking to kick a little ass, and it uses two A's, so we're still project double-A."

"Archangel," Steph said, "I like it."

Eric again sighed audibly, "If I say yes, can we focus on the mission please?"

"Sure," Steph grinned.

"Works for me," Parrow laughed.

The others all chimed in their acceptance.

"Fine. Archangel Lead, Pre-Flight checks. Clear to go." Eric said firmly. "Archangel Squadron is green. Dory Control, Archangel Flight request clearance for lift off."

"Roger that… Archangel Squadron," The voice from the Dory's 'Island' was barely able to keep his laughter suppressed as he responded, "You are clear for takeoff."

"Let's do this. Eight, you're with me," Eric said.

"Roger that, Lead," Steph replied by rote.

He pushed the throttle forward, putting power to the device as he directed thrust down and out of the vents under the fighter. The tension in his gut was gone as Steph felt the fighter wobble a little on takeoff, but corrected easily and threw more power to the thrust.

Eight advanced fighters lifted straight off the deck of the Carrier, hovering briefly over the big ship before they shifted power to their main reactors and accelerated smoothly away to the West.

*****

Eric checked the information he was getting over their satellite link, noting that the enemy had apparently noticed the F-35s that had gone on ahead of them.

Making barely Mach 2, the F-35s were still several minutes out from the Island, the Dory's helicopters another fifteen minutes behind them, while the newly christened Archangel Squadron was capable of hitting high hypersonic speeds to easily overtake both.

"Archangels," He said. "Full power on my mark... three... two... one... Mark."

He pushed the throttle all the way forward, igniting the afterburners as he did, and felt only a gentle push as the fighter roared ahead. The device had an odd effect on everything within its influence, one that wasn't compensation for inertial forces exactly but had a similar overall outcome. The impact of acceleration was nearly as nothing to him even as he hit hypersonic in seconds.

Eric looked out to either side, making sure that his squad mates were still with him. The acceleration and speeds involved were such that even a slight mismatch in timing could result in being dozens or hundreds of miles ahead or behind your wingman.

He was pleased to see that they were all close by as the miles fled past below them.

"Archangels, engage the interface and make your weapons hot."

There was griping on the channel, and Eric didn't blame them. He hesitated to press the button to activate the interface himself, so much did the very *idea* of it make his skin crawl, but in the end he did it because he'd seen how much more control it would give him.

The two prehensile needles barely made a pinching sensation as they slid into his neck, curling carefully around the nerve cluster at the base of his skull. A crawling sensation rippled down his back as the system integrated the fighter and his body, making them almost a single entity.

Eric glanced down, seeing the telemetry data from the others shift over to green as they too activated their systems.

It's time to go to war.

*****

Timing was, in battle as in many things, one of the most pivotal elements one could bring to the table. Sometimes you wanted to be first to the board, sometimes you wanted to be last, but you always wanted to control the *exact* moment you revealed your tactics and strategy down to the very *second* if it were possible.

Often, it simply wasn't.

Maneuvering large numbers of ships or military forces tended to be rather noticeable, and tended to give away your plan to a well trained eye. There were ways around that, of course. Decoy forces to distract the enemy were an old favorite, and simply trying extra hard to sneak your forces into position under cover of night or weather or whatever you could manage to use had been proven to work.

Speed, however, was one of the most reliable of these methods. Proven time and time again, from the earliest days of recorded history, through the writings of Sun Tzu, to the Blitzkrieg of the second world war.

Eric learned it as a subset of the military doctrine of *establishing military dominance*, but he just called it **shock and awe**.

On his display he could see the Bloc fighters advancing to intercept the Dory's squadrons of F-35s, two hundred nautical miles from intercept and closing *fast*. He and the newly christened Archangels dropped to the deck, skimming the waves at Mach *Six*, and blew past the F-35s even as they used their RADAR link with them to get positive tone on the approaching Mantis fighters.

As low as they were, Eric knew that the enemy RADAR would take a few moments longer to differentiate between them and the sea, and the more powerful RADAR on the Bloc ships were still just over the horizon.

It all came down to timing.

With only seconds to react, the Bloc pilots never saw it coming.

The Archangels went vertical on the intercept, locking onto the Bloc Mantis fighters from below, leaving clouds of steam erupting from boiling patches in the ocean below them as they climbed.

"Archangel Lead, I have tone." Eric said calmly. "Beams Beam Beams."

*****

The pilots of the Bloc fighters, focused on their strike intercept of the F-35s, almost entirely missed the high speed, low profile F-22 airframes that tore in below the more obvious line of American fighters and suddenly went vertical.

That left the bellies of the Bloc fighters open to the beams from below.

Megawatt class lasers lanced out and up at the speed of light from eight sources, burning so hot that the metal skin of the Mantis class erupted in flames in an instant.

Panicking pilots fought their suddenly unresponsive controls, most completely unable to determine what happened as fires burst into existence around them. As they began losing altitude, the front wave of the Bloc fighters reluctantly punched out at forty thousand feet over the Pacific.

Even as they were doing so, however, flashing blurs of motion tore past them, still climbing at impossible speeds into the upper atmosphere.

*****

At FL-70, Eric eased his fighter over into a smooth inverted roll, time seeming to pause briefly as he looked out at the curve of the earth in all directions around him through the bubble canopy and in that moment a revelation struck him.

The Bloc developed this thing, and it could have taken them… us… all to the planets, and what did they use it for? War?

It was such a criminal waste.

The moment passed, however, as the nose of his fighter dipped back down, and he felt any hint of weight lose its grip on him. In freefall, the Archangels began their descent back to the Pacific and the Island so far below.

Eric opened up the squadron's channel, "Everyone, stay alert. We got our first strike and caught them with their pants down. Don't count on that staying the case. This battle just barely got started."

The team responded quickly, aside from Steph who took a moment longer. Eric frowned, hearing something he wasn't sure about in the younger man's voice. He switched over to a private channel.

"Steph, kid? You ok?"

"I… I'm fine," Steph said, unconvincingly. "Just… not what I was expecting."

"It's not the movies kid." Eric said, taking a guess at the issue. The kid was untrained, no matter how great a pilot he was, there was more to it than just skill behind the stick. "When this is over, if you decide it's not for you, I'll back you on anything you want to do… but right now, here and now, I… *We…* need your head in the game. Copy?"

Steph took a moment as they were plummeting through the atmosphere, but finally he responded.

"I copy, Eric. I'm in. All the way."

"Never doubted it, kid. Let's finish this."

The squadron of experimental fighters lit their afterburners, going from weightless to negative gees in an instant as they arrowed straight for the small rock in the ocean below.

*****

Chapter Thirty-Eight

EBAN ChiangLung

"What happened!? What Happened!!?" Chien demanded, slamming his hands down on the console in front of him.

No one seemed to have an answer. All they knew was that they'd lost one of their forward squadrons in the blink of an eye, while they were still well out of the range of the American forces.

"A moment... a moment," The officer standing the RADAR watch said, looking intently between a pair of displays.

"We do not have moments," Chien growled. "What do you see?"

"New contacts," The officer said. "Moving Hypersonic, climbing past fifteen thousand meters, Admiral... slowing now..."

"Missiles?" Chien demanded.

"I do not believe so, Sir. Aircraft from the way they're maneuvering. They've topped just above twenty thousand meters and are coming back now."

Chien nodded curtly, grabbing a headset from the communications officer, and pulling them roughly over his own head.

"Fighter wings, this is Admiral Chien. We have hypersonic aircraft in the field, descending from twenty thousand meters. They should be on your screens... destroy them."

He took the headset off, casually handing them back off to the communications officer.

So, the Americans have managed to close the air superiority gap far quicker than expected. But why send F-35s then?

He frowned, considering it only briefly before the answer hit him.

They only have a limited number, perhaps even just what we see. They have not had time to launch into full manufacturing. We have a window, but it is closing. Damnation.

"Give me a secure line to the Alliance Council," He snapped at the communications officer. "I will be in my office."

*****

Mount Suribachi, Iwo Jima

Master Sergeant Kiran Jiang leaned heavily on the berm he was sheltering behind, keeping his weight off his injury as best he could while aiming through the holographic sights on his Sig rifle. The Bloc helicopters had made it through the last-ditch barrage of anti-air missiles launched by the defenders as they flew over, for the most part at least, and now they were landing troops on the hill.

Whether they were aiming for him personally, again, or looking to simply take the symbolic victory of bringing down the flags, the Major had put up he didn't know, and frankly didn't much care.

The entire island was now in the full-blown blazing fires of battle, so it made sense that Mount Suribachi would be no exception. He could hear the explosions in the distance as he readied himself to make the final stand alongside the US and JSDF sailors who'd taken up duties alongside him.

There was something rather poetic in it, Jiang thought.

A Chinese American Air Force Sergeant, shoulder to shoulder with US Marines, Sailors, and Japanese Self Defense Force personnel, along with a smattering of other allied nations ranging from Canadians to even a couple Brits if he remembered the count correctly… all defending the island of Iwo Jima against an invasion force.

It was like the major said, they were fighting on holy ground.

He refocused through the rifle's optics, about to open fire, when his radio crackled to life.

"Master Sergeant Jiang, this is Lancer Lead. Standby for close air support, copy."

Jiang's eyes widened as he stared for a brief instant before lunging for the radio.

"Copy Lancer Lead, it's damn good to hear a friendly voice, however, be advised the enemy has advanced air assets in the theatre."

"We copy advanced air assets, Master Sergeant. The Archangels are keeping them busy for us. Can you laze?"

You're goddamn right I can, He thought, before speaking, "Roger Lancer. Will laze targets as best we can. Be advised, we are under attack, and the enemy is danger close to friendly positions."

"Copy danger close. Keep your heads down."

"Roger that."

Jiang dropped the channel and swapped over to the island command network.

"All points, all points, be advised of friendly air support inbound. Laze priority targets if you can," He ordered. "If you are dangerously close to enemy targets, get low and intimate with the ground boys ad girls. The Cavalry is coming and they're bringing the heat with them."

He closed that channel and tossed the radio aside, looking over to the closest man, "Get me a laser designator!"

*****

Liam paused as he heard the call go out from the Combat Controller, blinking in surprise. He'd not expected any more help, not after the last attempt by the Air Force and the losses that entailed, and honestly, he wasn't sure he *wanted* help. Not if the outcome was the same as the last time.

Too many people had died already with no change to the eventual outcome.

It wasn't worth losing more.

That wasn't his call to make, however, so he shrugged off the thoughts and continued making his way through the trenches to the next position alongside a few Marines who'd stuck near to him. The enemy tanks were a real pain in the ass, and that was *before* they had to try dealing with the Bloc attack choppers buzzing over the island like locusts.

"Do we have any anti-armor left?" He asked, not expecting anything.

"Sorry Sir, blew the last of our SRAWs on that pair of light attack tanks about ten minutes back," Corporal Meer told him apologetically.

"Well, nothing to be done. What about laser designators?"

"Those we have."

Liam nodded, "Alright, let's find a place to hunker down and start painting this island red."

"Hoorah Major!"

*****

The defenders fell back according to their battle plans, being pushed into retreat by the strength of the landing force and their air support.

Losses were high, an inevitable result of a fighting retreat against a well supported and equipped foe, but not entirely one sided. The beaches of Iwo were littered with smoking armored wrecks and the bodies of Bloc marine landing troops who'd paid in blood for the ground they'd taken from the defenders' clawing grips.

Fighting ranged from the beaches to the interior of the island, with tanks rolling up to the airfield and liberally shelling the buildings they passed just on the off chance that anyone was sheltering within them.

The armored units didn't have their own way entirely, however, faced with fierce resistance in the form of the island's defenders' remaining portable anti-armor weapons, mines, and even some hastily repurposed artillery pieces. However, those resources were in short supply on the defenders' side and by the time the first units of tanks crawled into the airfield, effective resistance was all but finished.

Behind them came the ground troops, clearing the places the tanks couldn't see into properly, making sure that there were no stragglers waiting with a rocket or some other nasty surprise, while above them the Bloc's ground attack choppers hovered angrily, waiting to end anyone who stuck their head up.

No one did.

The fighting seemed to fall into a lull as they took the airport. Stray explosions still rocked the air in the distance, but infrequently and with less regularity.

The Bloc forces slowed, not stopping but clearly slowing as they tried to determine what to do next. Requests for orders were sent out, and directives to search out any remaining defenders were issued, and then they began to once more roll on as they started spreading out from the central location in search of the enemy.

None of them noticed the invisible smattering of infra-red light that had appeared on many of the tanks.

There was nothing they could have done about it if they had.

*****

The airstrike led by the Lancers' F-35s came down on the island like the wrath of an angry god.

The Navy pilots had been sitting on the Dory back in Pearl, watching their comrades die in battle after battle starting in Japan, Taiwan, Korea… all across the region, and all coming to focus on a little island in the middle of the ocean where someone finally drew a line in the sand.

Now they were ready to deal themselves in, and they did just that with all the fury they could mount on their fighters' hardpoints.

Thousands of pounds of ordnance slammed into the Bloc forces, just seconds ahead of the screaming jets roaring by overhead, and the whole balance of the fight shifted in an instant as the skies went from friendly, or hostile depending on your side, to neutral in the blink of an eye.

Defenders and invaders both paused for a perceptible moment, many of them shocked to their core by the sudden shift.

When the moment passed, fighting resumed across the island with a true vengeance.

*****

USS Chicago SSN-898

"Screws are chewing the waters up there, skipper."

Captain Jarin Pascale nodded, largely unsurprised by that bit of news. The fighting had just taken a turn, and he was certain that the enemy were scrambling to adapt to the new situation. That didn't mean that things were going well for the good guys, but the cakewalk for the Bloc was *over*.

His job now was to make sure that they knew exactly how true that was.

"Give me firing solutions for the lead elements of the task group," He demanded.

"We have solutions for the destroyer screen ready, sir. We can't get in range of the big boy, however," His weapons control officer informed him.

Another non-surprise as far as Jarin was concerned, the Bloc had learned from American doctrine and they were protecting their carrier with concentric and overlapping lines of defense. To get through to the big ship, they'd have to punch a hole through those defenses.

"Understood. Share targets across the pack," He ordered. "let's get to work."

"Aye, aye, skipper. Targets shared. The pack is waiting for the order to engage."

"Well then, let's not keep them waiting. Fire."

*****

The fast attack wolf pack, stealing the nickname from their world war two counterparts, had moved into position ahead of the carrier group. Armed with a full load of ordnance and the hard-won data gathered from the Miami in her earlier engagements with the new Bloc ship types, the US Navy had set out to put as much of a crimp in Bloc shipping as was imaginably possible.

They were limited by the, frankly anemic state of the submarine fleet at the end of the 2070s, but that still left them with options.

The Chicago and their compatriots were one of the first moves to manage that, stealing the idea of the Submarine Wolfpack from the Germans in World war two, their mission was first to aid in the current operation but then they were to move on to harass shipping all through the South China Sea and generally do what they could to grind the Bloc offensive to a halt on the open sea.

The five-boat squadron shared firing solutions and target selection across their ELF transceivers, and coordinated their attack down to the second.

Ten ADCAPS hit the water in the first salvo, followed shortly by another ten before the squadron broke off and vanished back into the depths while the Bloc forces were panicking over the torpedoes they could see.

No one even thought to fire back before they faded back into the dark depths, explosions shaking the ocean in their wake.

*****

EBAN HuangLung

"Hohot and Zibo have been struck! Zanhou is foundering! Second salvo of torpedoes in the water, Admiral! We're under assault!"

Chien rolled his eyes at the statement of the obvious, but said nothing about it.

They'd spent *far* too long wasting their damned time with this rock, in more than just the ways he'd thought of before. Having the Bloc fleets pinned down in one known location as they had been had given the Americans time to plan a counteroffensive that had the potential to be *entirely* out of proportion to the level of power they were able to bring, both in terms of propaganda value and in terms of actual military effect.

Damn it.

He could blame the council, he supposed, or any number of others… but Chien felt the failure weighing on his soul as he saw the ramifications unroll before him.

If the Americans managed a win here it would be utterly insignificant compared to the losses they'd incurred in the early days of the war, but it would not be perceived that way. They'd allowed the enemy to make this damned island appear to be something of value, even *played into* that idea, and now it was going to cost them.

"Find the submarines," He ordered the tactical officer. "I want our submarine warfare units moving."

"Yes, Admiral!"

Chien shifted, looking over to his dive officer. "Prepare the HuangLung for submersion."

"Yes, Admiral… Admiral…"

"I am aware that our hull is not capable of deep dives," Chien said. "we will remain shallow."

"Understood."

Chien moved back to the strategic display, looking at the known locations of the various units engaged in the battle for the worthless chunk of rock out there beyond the hull of the HuangLung. The distraction provided by the American hypersonic fighters had allowed the air strike team to get close enough to deliver their payload, which had once more *completely* reversed the course of the battle in an instant.

Where resistance had been falling off, now it had redoubled in every corner of the island with no signs of flagging.

The defenders now had hope.

Hope was the greatest fuel for warriors ever found. If you didn't have it, you were lost. If you did… the universe could not stop you. Kill you, perhaps, but stop you? Never.

Now he had to take that hope away, or simply kill every last one of them.

Either would work.

"All decks report. Secure for submersion!"

"Very good," Chien said with a sharp nod. "Submerge."

*****

USS Chicago

"Sir, the big boy is diving."

"Damn." Jarin swore lightly. He'd been hoping that the previous damage the big submersible had taken would have been sufficient to keep its pressure hull from taking the stresses of a dive.

Apparently, he'd been wrong.

"Track them," He ordered, hoping it would be that easy.

"Aye skipper. They're turning North, away from the Island."

"Who's up there?"

"The Portland, Sir."

"Let them know they have company coming."

"Aye, aye."

*****

USS Portland SSN-968

"Confirm receipt of the warning," Captain Joe Piper nodded. "And track that contact, don't lose them."

"Aye, aye, Sir. They're staying shallow, twenty meters down, moving without cavitation."

"Very good," Piper said. "I want a firing solution on them as soon as they clear the destroyer screen."

"Yes sir."

Piper stood calmly at the center of the command deck, eyes moving regularly between the contacts display and the communications readout. Organizing operations between subs was a non-trivial task at the best of times, doing it in the rapidly changing environment of an all-out warzone at sea? That was a challenge and a half.

The wolfpack had their orders, though, and he'd see them through in one way or another.

*****

Chapter Thirty-Nine

Archangel Lead, FL-60

Eric's feet worked the pedals, turning his nosedive into a spiral as he got sight of the island so far below. The enemy fighters had withdrawn from the theater of battle, clearly regrouping so they could work out a plan to deal with the Archangels, but even so it worked out well as it allowed the Dory's force to deliver their airstrike while everyone was still blinking.

The Super Cobra gunships and aging Seahawk helicopters were coming in right on the heels of the airstrike, preparing to make Iwo Jima into a warzone the enemy would dearly regret stepping into.

All according to the plan, thus far.

The Dory's AWACS aircraft were hanging well back, but high enough to keep track of the aircraft in the zone and send that information on to his systems, so Eric could see that the enemy fighters had only pulled back a few hundred nautical miles and were almost finished regrouping. They'd turn their focus back in short order, he knew, and at hypersonic speeds a few hundred miles could be crossed in seconds.

That left him and the Archangels a decision to make.

They could give pursuit, push the battle farther out over the ocean, away from the island below, or they could keep the fighting centered. Both had advantages and disadvantages to consider. Primarily, it was a decision of whether or not the ability to trade support with Dory's forces were worth more than the benefits of keeping the air to air fighting well clear of the island.

The decision was easy, really. It wasn't a populated city they were fighting over, and the mission wasn't specifically to hunt down the enemy fighters. The mission was the secure the lives of the men and women on Iwo Jima.

"Second team, secure overwatch," He ordered, "First team, on me."

They acknowledged the order, and half the squadron broke off and took the CAP position as they passed FL-50, while the other half continued to follow him through the dive toward the island below.

"As long as the enemy fighters are giving us breathing room, let's clear some of the same for the men on the ground," He said. "Attack choppers, close air support, anything that's flying over the island and isn't one of ours... doesn't keep flying over the island. Clear?"

"Clear!"

He smiled thinly, noting the near perfect unison response. *Eager lot.*

They were good pilots, all of them, but not the ones he'd have picked if he had a choice in the matter. The Neural interface was too problematic, he was going to recommend against installing it in any further fighters, it being too hard to man a single squadron as it was. Maybe that would change in time, but for now, no.

Eric changed the channel to speak directly to Archangel Eight, Stephen, the kid who shouldn't even be along with them.

"You ok?"

"I'm fine." Stephen responded, his tone tense, voice not quick cracking.

It was as good as he could expect. Eric wanted to think that kids weren't sent into battle for a reason, but he knew better. He'd been barely older than Steph himself the first time he'd been in a fight for his life. It sucked. Glory was for fictional stories, told over one too many drinks or in books and movies.

In reality? It just sucked.

"Stay close, pick off any strays I miss," Eric said. "Every Bloc chopper we knock out of the sky will kill a few less of our guys on the island below. You with me?"

"I've got your back, Eric. Always."

That was not quite the response Eric expected from a kid with no experience. He wondered if Steph knew what he was saying, if he meant it as deep as he sounded.

Well, I suppose we'll find out.

"Save your lasers for the fighters," He ordered, switching over to the forward cannon and winding the multi-barreled weapon up to speed. "This is a knife fight."

The screaming fighters of the Archangel Squadron hit the deck at four hundred feet over the ocean and pulled out of the dive so sharply that they had barely lost another hundred feet before they were level and barreling in on Iwo Jima at Mach four.

*****

Iwo Jima

Liam crouched low as he cursed the lack of anti-air ordnance in their possession at the moment. They'd used most of what they had in the early minutes of the fight, most of which was rendered worthless by countermeasures launched by the Bloc forces of course. They'd taken a few of the choppers out, though, bleeding that much more from the enemy's toolbox.

The airstrike from the Dory, as he found out from chatter on the radio after the fact, had been a godsend but it was the sudden releasing of pressure in the air that really changed the feeling on the ground.

They weren't fighting under a hostile sky any longer, and he wasn't sure how exactly it had happened.

It wasn't a *friendly* sky, mind you. The Bloc helicopters were still buzzing around angrily dispensing munitions over all of creation, but they weren't having things entirely their way any longer, and the Dory's F35s were hammering the enemy positions at least as hard as the choppers were hammering his Marines.

Liam didn't bother to wonder exactly when he'd started thinking about every man and woman on the island as his Marines, regardless of service or nationality. It just happened, sometime after the Gunny died. When didn't really matter beyond that, just the fact that they were exactly that.

A call over the radio from a position under assault got his attention. It was near the beach and from where he was. He could see three Bloc attack birds buzzing angrily over the area.

"Hold tight," He ordered. "I'm coming to you."

He grabbed a China Lake Version Four from the crate at his feet, carefully dropping HE grenades into the tube of the pump-action launcher, then flipped a belt loaded with more over his shoulder as he started running down the trenches in the direction of the pinned down Marines.

****

Corporal Meer ducked as the buzzsaw rent the air asunder overhead, the ground shaking from the impact of the heavy bullets from the helicopter-mounted cannon. His mouth was filled with sand from where he dove into the dirt in response to the attack.

"Does *anyone* have any anti-air left? Please!?" He called out.

No one responded.

Of course.

Shit.

He crawled through the dirt, pulling himself up the wall of the trench and risked a quick look over the top before he instantly dropped right back as the big guns buzzed again and sand filled the air.

"Jesus!" He swore, covering his head with his arms as sand rained down around him. "This shit is so fucked up!"

"Stay down!"

Meer didn't bother to look up to see who said that. He didn't need to be told to stay down when someone was firing a twenty-millimeter cannon at him. His mama may have raised a fool, but not *that much* of a fool.

"Hold position, stay undercover," The Major's voice called over his tactical set. "Grenade out."

Grenade? What the hell is a...

The dull thump was a sound he recognized, and Meer twisted so he could see where it came from.

The Major was standing up in the *goddamn open*, a Marine issue China Lake grenade launcher in his mitts, already pumping a new forty-millimeter round into the tube and firing again. Meer heard a third thump from the monster ass shotgun before the sound of the first HE round going off rolled back over him.

Holy shit.

He risked a look. Couldn't help it.

Sure enough, the Major was taking on an *attack helicopter* with a pump-action grenade launcher.

And the Major was winning.

The Bloc whirlybird had taken some serious damage, smoke curling from its fuselage and being blown out by the rotors as it twisted in the air, moving away from the crazy man with the big gun. While Meer watched, another round struck home and a cascade of flames splashed over the chopper, tearing up the lightweight armor and sending the bird into a flat spin as part of the shrapnel must have damaged the rear rotor.

Meer heard cheering and actually looked around briefly before he realized that it was coming from him.

"Hoorah Major!"

Unfortunately, the Bloc attack bird wasn't alone.

Called, presumably, by the stricken chopper, a pair of attack birds whirled on the Major's position a few seconds later, even before the first chopper had hit the ground. Meer saw the first dip its nose as it began moving in for the kill and waved at the Major, trying to warn him off.

"Major! Incoming!"

*****

Liam heard the warning and twisted, eyes scanning the sky for the threat. It wasn't hard to spot, a helicopter on an attack run was a riveting sight to begin with, when it's focused on *you*, well the sight was downright bowel loosening.

He angled the China Lake a little higher, firing off a round then pumping the action and dropped the muzzle a bit to fire again, and then repeated the action a third time to empty the weapon. Unfortunately, the grenade launcher wasn't a pinpoint weapon, and while he was experienced with it hitting a nimble attack bird in flight was hard enough when it was holding still.

The grenades fell behind the chopper as Liam threw himself to one side, diving for the trench as the buzzsaw of the Bloc twenty-five millimeter rent the air asunder.

Still scrambling for cover, Liam suddenly felt himself almost lifted from the ground by a pressure wave passing over the trench, his fingers clawing at the sand as for a moment he thought he was going to be lifted into the sky like a twig in a tornado.

Then it passed and the crashing roar of an explosion shattered the air and the returning atmospheric pressure slammed back into the ground with force enough to empty his lungs.

Gasping and rolling onto his back, Liam managed to rasp out a question.

"Wh… what the hell… was… *that*!?"

Someone heard him. He no idea who or how, but an answer came.

"I don't know Major, but it went that way!"

Liam painfully propped himself up and looked in the direction pointed out, eyes barely able to pick out a dot in the distance.

What. The. Fuck?

*****

Steph looked over his shoulder, back to the fire they'd left in their wake after a low pass over the island, unable to quite wrap his head around the blazing seconds of violence that had just happened.

The pass had taken perhaps two seconds across the entire island, and he'd followed Eric through the maneuver, firing the gun in only a single burst. Honestly, he didn't even know if he'd hit anything, it had gone by so quickly.

In their wake, however, fires were blazing as Bloc helicopters were still falling from the sky, so fast they'd gone through.

"Unbelievable." He murmured to himself.

"What's that, kid?"

"Sorry, Eric, just mumbling," Steph quickly said.

"Understandable, but try and keep radio discipline just the same," Eric chided lightly. "Our playmates are heading back in."

Steph glanced at the screens and nodded. The Bloc fighters were indeed on their way back.

"Got it. Plan?"

"Let's play a game of chicken."

"Bad plan, Eric! That's a *bad plan*." Steph retorted instantly without even thinking about it.

He felt his blood chill as Eric chuckled slowly over the channel.

*This is going to **suck**.*

Nevertheless, he matched Eric's maneuver as they came around and centered back on the Island, with the enemy fighters approaching on their screens from the other side.

*****

Eric focused on the fighters in the distance, despite them being so far away that they could not yet be seen even as a dot against the pale blue of the sky. He trusted the data being fed to him from the Dory's AWACS.

They were accelerating on an intercept course, coming in from the West, while he and Steph were turning to match from the East.

"Archangels," He called to the others. "We're going to play a little game. Cover the maneuver, be ready to pick off the enemy when they break."

"You sure they're going to be the ones who break, boss?" Sully asked, his tone amused.

"You want to bet they won't?" Eric challenged.

"No Boss, not going to take that bet."

"Didn't think so. Go."

Eric pushed the throttle forward, again lighting off the afterburners and rocketing forward. He felt pride as he noted Steph right on his wing, not missing a step. The kid was one of the best natural pilots he'd ever known, let alone trained, and he took to this mess like a duck to water. He felt bad about getting him into this situation, it was hard enough for someone with full training, but sometimes you just did what you had to do.

He barely noted the slight tremor as his fighter broke Mach, climbing fast into the hypersonic, the enemy contacts matching his move. The island was looming large in front of them, growing at insane rates, and then it was flashing past underneath as proximity warnings screaming at him from all sides.

A hint of smoke flashing off his fuselage told him that the enemy had fired, but Eric ignored it, putting the armor material to the test as he bore down on the fighter while the lock on screamed in his ears.

The Bloc pilot was tougher than he expected, Eric had to admit, but at the last moment he flinched, suddenly going vertical at hypersonic up ahead. Eric grinned and yanked his own fighter into a matching climb a second later, putting himself right on the enemy's tail.

They twisted around one another as they climbed, the Bloc pilot trying to shake him, but the advantages that served them so well in the early fighting were now evened out. Eric matched the maneuvers easily, getting tone back as they climbed past FL-40.

"Archangel One... Beams, Beams, Beams."

He fired both lasers as they climbed, the megawatt beams cooking off the rear of the enemy fighter as it tried to evade but the stabilizing gimble on the emitters kept the weapon on target for the precious slices of a second needed, causing the Mantis fighter to erupt into flames.

"Splash one," He called, breaking off the climb as the fighter broke up, peeling hard away from any flaming debris he might have to deal with as he checked his computer. "And I think I have a read on their laser frequency. Copy new data."

"Roger Archangel One," Archangel Three said. "We copy, armor frequency adjusted. Let's go get em."

*****

The Archangel Fighters began a rampage across the skies, tearing into the enemy fighters with speed and maneuverability that matched what their enemy brought to the table, but double the firepower, an increase in precision and reaction times, and finally a secret defense that eliminated the threat of the enemy's only real weapon against them.

In a few moments easily half the advanced fighters in the war space had been destroyed, and the rest had fled back outside the AO where they milled about, seemingly waiting for orders.

On the island below, now fighting under a friendly sky, the Marines and JSDF threw themselves into the fighting with a vengeance, throwing their foes back on their heels as the previous march to victory turned suddenly into a death march.

Streaming feeds from the Bloc were abruptly cut off.

*****

EBAN HuangLung

"Yes, Councilor. I understand. Are you certain this is the… Yes. Very well. As I am commanded."

Admiral Chien stared at the blank screen after the Council Member had cut off the communication, seconds ticking by as he considered his orders.

This is folly.

It was, however, his orders.

Chien stood up and walked from his office, back to the command deck of the submersible carrier.

"Admiral?" His XO asked questioningly as he saw Chien's face.

"Prepare the special weapons."

"Sir?"

"Orders. Prepare them."

"Yes Sir."

*****

Chapter Forty

USS Portland

An alarm sounded that nearly sent Piper through the overhead deck, his eyes going wide as he snapped around.

"Confirm that," He snapped intently.

"Neutron runaway confirmed, Captain. We have a live nuke in the field."

"Bring us shallow," He ordered. "I need satellite access."

"Aye Skipper," His XO confirmed, turning to the front. "Ahead one third, do not cavitate. Make your depth thirty meters, two degrees up bubble!"

The boat tilted noticeably, moving forward and up through the dark seas of the Pacific. As soon as they got close enough for the satellite mast to get a signal, Piper got connected to PACCOM's satellite tracking system and started looking for the nuke they'd been able to find.

A live nuclear weapon was normally held shielded for multiple reasons, for them to have picked up a runaway neutron signal meant that the weapon had to be exposed, likely prepared for launch.

Piper put the warning out in case no one else had detected it, then grabbed the satellite data of the region as he looked for the hotspot that would give him a location.

"Got them," He said tersely. "Make your course Two Nine Five Mark Three One, ahead two thirds. Do *not* cavitate."

"Aye skipper!"

"Open the doors," He said. "I wanted primed torpedoes in the water the *second* we have a firing solution."

"Aye, aye, skipper!"

*****

EBAN CHiangLung

"Enemy submarine closing on our position, Admiral!"

"Inform the screen," Chien said as he entered the firing codes. "They will have to cover us for a few more moments."

"Yes, Admiral."

Chien glanced over at his XO, who had also just finished entering authorization codes for the two hundred kiloton tactical weapon. His XO nodded back and they both inserted their digital keys into the system.

"Weapon is armed."

Chien nodded absently, entering the coordinates for Iwo Jima into the system.

"Targeting data accepted." His XO said. "Final check. Are you authorizing weapon release, Admiral?"

"I am."

"Accepted. Missile firing to your control."

Chien nodded, then flipped over a protective safety plate. He considered it for a moment, then pressed down.

*****

USS Portland

Piper swore as he saw the Destroyers move into their path, their active sonar on definitive search and destroy, torpedoes churning up the sea. The enemy knew what they were up to and were *not* happy about it.

"Launch countermeasures," He ordered. "Ignore those destroyers. I want that…"

"Skipper! We have a missile launch!"

Piper paled clammy *white*, but didn't swear. He had no time to waste on that luxury.

"All stations, all stations," He called over the battlefield network. "We have a confirmed nuclear launch. Likely target is Iwo Jima. I say again…"

*****

Iwo Jima

Liam heard the call over the command network, the warning overriding everything else, and just stopped where he was.

He didn't know exactly where the missile was coming from, but he knew there wasn't a single blessed thing he could do about it. Briefly he thought about sending the word down through the lower clearance channels, but frankly there wasn't anything *anyone* in his command could do about it.

All this… well, I knew I was going to die out here. Least we're going out with a big goddamn **bang**.

Belatedly he noticed that a lot of the fighting was dying out around him. While he might not see much point in informing his people, since they were stuck on the rock they were on, the enemy had apparently decided to inform at least some of theirs.

The helicopters were already gone, those who'd survived that far at least. Fighting had stalled out as Bloc forces withdrew back to the beaches, in too much of a hurry to keep shooting.

Liam could hear the cheers starting up, in ragged fashion.

They think we've won… let them.

They'd go out in victory, if nothing else. A nuke couldn't wipe that out. They'd held off the Bloc navy for *weeks*, pinning down not three but *four* enemy fleets in the end.

Marines, one and all.

"Hoorah and Semper Fi, you magnificent bastards."

*****

Archangel Lead

"Find me that nuke." Eric snapped tensely as he put his fighter into a powered dive, reaching forward to flip a few switches.

"What are you planning?" Steph asked, following him into the dive automatically. "Cause I'm pretty sure these babies can't take a nuke at damn near any range, boss."

"Our laser pods were adapted from anti-missile systems," Eric said. "I'm going to shoot that sucker down, or die trying. Get back with the rest of the squad."

Steph laughed at him, "Get fucked. If you're that crazy, you need company in Hell."

Eric didn't have time to fight with the kid, so he focused on the dive and again growled over the command channel. "Does *anyone* have coordinates on that damn nuke!?"

"Hold one, Archangel Lead."

"Damn it, we don't have one to hold," He answered the AWACS commander. "I need a target!"

"Roger that. Cruise Missile on your screen."

Eric checked, tapping a blinking icon.

"Got it. Is it still boosting?"

"Roger. At four hundred feet and beginning to level out," the AWACS commander said. "Expect acceleration to low hypersonic over the next forty seconds. ETA to Iwo is… thirty-five seconds."

"Target locked… Archangel Lead on intercept course," Eric said, flipping a switch. "Lasers are hot."

He pulled level with the ocean surface, only a couple hundred feet off the deck. An explosion in the distance threw water high into the air, and Eric distantly noted that a Bloc destroyer was on fire.

Subs are pissed, it seems.

He ignored it, eyes searching for the missile, but it was such a small target that there was really nothing more he could do than trust his computer for the most part.

"I have it on my screens… intercept in two seconds," He reported as his targeting system found the target and started locking it in. "I have tone… Archangel Lead… Beams, Beams, Beams."

It was slightly unnerving, Eric decided, just how quiet the firing of the lasers was. There was no rush of a missile flying loose, no rattling of the cannon firing, and even the distinctive snap click of the capacitors discharging was lost to the sound of the fighter's own thrust.

Just the computer telling him that he'd fired as his eyes sought out any sign of flames erupting in the sky.

Nothing.

"Negative contact! Negative contact!" He called. "Screens still read positive! What's going on!?"

*****

AWACS Flight 498

Commander Watson cursed as he checked the system, trying to figure out what was going on.

"Fuck, they're spoofing the signal!"

Watson looked over sharply at his second, "You sure?"

"Too damn sure. We have ghosts all over the place!"

"Break the spoof!"

"We don't have time!"

Watson closed his eyes, grimacing, then opened the channel.

"Enemy is spoofing the signal, Archangel Lead. Get out of there, you can't do anything."

*****

Archangel Lead

"Fuck that I can't," Eric snarled, throttling up briefly before putting his fighter into a flat spin.

"What the hell are you doing, Eric!?" Steph swore as he blew past Eric's position, belatedly trying to come around without matching the insane maneuver Eric had just pulled.

With the device, the Counter Mass system, running now at full power, Eric let his fighter scream *sideways* through the air in a way the airframe had never been designed to even dream of while he scanned the skies with his eyeball mark one.

"Find that missile," He snapped. "Digital spoofing only affects computer systems. Find it! Find it now!"

He was looking for the trail it would leave. This low to the surface even moving as fast as it would soon be, contrails wouldn't be visible, but that didn't mean the missile's passage would be as well.

Something... anything. I'll take an exhaust trail, heat shimmer, something... come on...

"Eric, got something. Glint of sunlight to your eleven o'clock," Steph said, snapping him back to the moment.

Eric twisted, eyes scanning to his left, but there was no hint of any gleam of light. He almost gave up, ready to look elsewhere, then he saw it. The heat shimmer from the exhaust made a ship on the other side flicker slightly, and Eric automatically slammed the throttle all the way forward.

"On it," He called, hand coming off the throttle to start punching in numbers on his targeting system. "Missile is passing Mach One Point Five, less than one hundred nautical miles to the island. Manual targeting."

"You'll never hit something like small without your computer, boss," Sully called a warning.

"Not even going to try," He said. "Just need to be leaning in the right direction when the computer kicks back the numbers…"

The Missile broke Mach Two as Eric and Steph both hit hypersonic, making up ground on the weapon as it closed on Iwo Jima. Eric was running the numbers on the intercept in his head, calculating where he'd need to have his weapons and putting his fighter and laser as close as he could. He couldn't hope to match the precision of the computer in such an effort, but he *could* be leaning in the right direction when the computer finally caught up.

"Archangel One… I have tone," He said a second later when just that happened. "Beams. Beams. Beams."

He fired again, megawatt level beams lancing out through the atmosphere, seeking their target, but again there was no answering burst of flames.

"Shit! Recalculating!"

"Get out of there, Boss! You're flying right into a nuclear detonation! Get clear!" Sully was screaming.

"Archangel Four, I have tone," Steph said suddenly, his voice deadly calm as he pulled just ahead of Eric's position. "Beams, Beams, Beams."

Eric held his breath, his throat dry as the moment drew out into eternity.

Then everything snapped back as a burst of flame erupted ahead of them and he watched the missile break up and crash into the sea below as the two Archangels screamed past, splitting as they passed over Iwo Jima, peeling away to either side of Mount Suribachi where two flags still flew.

******

EBAN HuangLung

"Admiral…"

Chien ignored the urgent word, staring out at the island through their observation mast.

"Admiral, we must leave."

How was it possible? He wondered, honestly bemused by the situation.

Korea, Taiwan, *Japan*.

They all fell.

Iwo Jima.

How could they be undone here, at a worthless rock in the middle of the Pacific, after succeeding everywhere else?

"Unbelievable."

"Admiral!"

"What?" Chien snarled, turning on his XO.

"Sir, the American subs are closing. We've lost much of our destroyer screen. It is time."

Chien sighed, but waved his agreement.

"Withdraw. Let them have the worthless rock."

"Yes, Admiral."

*****

Iwo Jima

Liam found himself on his knees, but didn't remember falling to them.

The expected death in nuclear fire averted, all he could do was turn his gaze to the south. He couldn't see the flags from where he was, of course, but he knew they were still there and that was enough.

He bowed his head as the breath left him, arms limply hanging to his side, then he reached down and grabbed a big handful of dirt, closing his fist around it.

Holy ground.

Twice sanctified in the blood of defenders and invaders alike, there was no more question in his mind.

He was resting on Holy Ground, and those poor Bloc bastards had no idea what they'd been getting into.

The war was just starting, of course. One battle won for their side would only make the Bloc double down if he was right, but for the moment he was just going to appreciate it. Tomorrow… tomorrow, he would be ready to fight again.

He ignored the cheering that was starting to gain steam around him, the sound of helicopters from the Dory arriving to retrieve them, the roar of jets overhead. He ignored it all.

Holy Ground.

●●

Made in the USA
Middletown, DE
09 February 2021